The Outside Lands

Hannah Kohler grew up on the south coast of England. After studying English and American Literature at Cambridge University, Hannah completed the City University MA in Creative Writing. She has worked in television for several years, lives in London and is the recipient of the 2017 Eccles British Library Writer's Award. *The Outside Lands* is her first novel.

HANNAH KOHLER

The Outside Lands

PICADOR

First published 2016 by Picador

First published in paperback 2017 by Picador
an imprint of Pan Macmillan
20 New Wharf Road, London N1 9RR
Associated companies throughout the world
www.panmacmillan.com

ISBN 978-1-5098-0212-8

1 3 5 7 9 8 6 4 2

A CIP catalogue record for this book is available from the British Library.

Printed and bound by CPI Group (UK) Ltd, Croydon, CR0 4YY

For Phil

Out of the Sunset

Jeannie / 1963

Every year, after Kip had blown the flames from his cake, their mom told the story of how he'd nearly killed her.

"Nurse said she'd never seen so much bleeding, and for such a scrap of a boy," she said, tipping back an old-fashioned.

"Mom," said Kip, spraying dark crumbs; they scuttered over the tablecloth.

"Mom," said Jeannie.

Their mom licked her lips and fingered the maraschino cherry from her glass. "Your daddy said he could hear the screaming all the way out in the parking lot."

"Nearly turned my wagon around and went straight home."

"They fogged me with all those medications, but the nurse said I was clear-mouthed as a preacher, said I called out to the Lord to take me."

"The Lord didn't want her," their dad said, smiling. Each time their mom told the story it got bloodier, and their dad would rock on his Weejuns and push her words away with a smile, before winding it up with a joke. Then their mom, muss-haired and glitter-eyed, would squeeze the nape of Kip's neck and fall into the easy chair. Their dad would set an Edith Piaf record on the turntable and a song would play that would make their mom cry.

"There's the Texan coming out," their dad said. "All that humidity growing up, and now she's all heat and water."

Their mom was raised in the Texas Panhandle, on a small-holding with a pick-your-own pecan orchard and six beehives. As a girl, she cracked nuts for three cents a pound until her nails bled; and she'd had nothing to do with pecans since, not even on Thanksgiving. Their dad came from Eureka, California, where the weather was clean and cool, and his mother grew citrus trees in the garden.

"You grow up with lemons, you end up sour," said their mom.

"Lemonade from lemons," said Jeannie.

"That's my girl," said their dad.

Her mom had always been superstitious about Kip's birthday. So when Jeannie was called into Mrs. Harris's office that November afternoon to take her dad's telephone call, it felt like a prank. It was dark out; typing drill was nearly through. Jeannie stood at the ink-spoiled desk, looking out at the rain, the receiver tacky on her cheek.

"Jeannie, you got to come home." Her dad's voice was swollen and strange.

"What's the matter, Daddy?" A fly landed on the orange on Mrs. Harris's desk and picked at the rind.

"Uncle Paulie's on his way to get you."

Jeannie hadn't seen Uncle Paulie since her dad kicked him out of their house for fooling around with his ceremonial sword.

"What's going on?" Jeannie heard the warm sound of men talking. "Who are you with?"

"I can't get into it, honey. Just come home."

"Is everything all right?"

"Please, Jeannie. I'll explain." Her dad's voice rose.

"We're not done with our typing exercises," said Jeannie. Her face grew hot. "I'm not coming till you tell me what's going on."

She watched the fly climb over the curve of the orange and wondered if they'd been disconnected.

"There's been an accident."

Jeannie's heart flickered. "Is Kip all right?"

A blow of breath down the line. The fly twitched.

"He's all right, Jeannie."

Something in his emphasis made Jeannie wince.

"It's your mother."

"What happened?" Jeannie's hands were wet.

"The cops are here."

Jeannie swallowed. "Is Mom all right?"

"They said—"

Jeannie heard the stickiness of her dad's mouth. "Daddy?"

"She was in an accident, and Mom—your mother . . ."

Jeannie's breath stopped rough and solid in her throat. The receiver slipped against her cheek and she said something, but it lost its shape in her mouth.

"Uncle Paulie will be outside. Come now, honey." Her dad's voice caught, and the dial tone pushed into her ear. The news disappeared down the telephone line, back through the cables and into the earth. Outside on Dolores, two women with shiny-wet overcoats ran arm in arm under the rain, their dark lips stretched in laughter. If she stayed right where she was, if she didn't move a fiber, the news might not come back for her; it might sink between the rocks that moved beneath the city, back into the slime below.

"Operator. May I help you?" The voice was far-off, from Oregon or the nineteen forties.

Jeannie opened her eyes and set down the receiver. She sat in Mrs. Harris's chair and caught her head in her hands. The thing that had been climbing up from her stomach since she'd been pulled from class (perhaps it had always been there) broke free from her lips in a wheeze of noise and spit. The fly lifted away.

Uncle Paulie stood on the sidewalk, his face white as milk.

"Sweetheart," he said, and collected her in his arms.

Jeannie pressed her head against him, his smell of dirt and soap. She couldn't blink to cut the tears from her eyes. Her chest ached.

Uncle Paulie let go. "Here," he said, opening the door of his car. He drove and they stared at the rain bleeding on the windshield, listening to the rub of the wipers. He kept his right hand clamped on her knee. They were passing Sunset before Jeannie could ask—

"What happened?"

He turned his head to look at her; his face was striped with shadows.

"You got to talk to your father, Jeannie," he said.

At home, Jeannie found Kip and her dad staring at *Temple Houston* on the television, drinking root beer. It could have been any Thursday; she half expected her mom to be in the kitchen, fixing cheese biscuits. Then Kip turned to look at her, and his expression reminded her of when he was four and he lost his toy jeep at the beach.

"What happened?" she said.

Her dad stood to switch off the television. Kip watched the empty screen, his hands moving in his lap like birds.

"Honey," said her dad, taking her in his arms and squeezing her too tight. Jeannie felt the spaces between his ribs as he breathed large. She struggled free, knocking him in the chest with her elbow.

"Tell me what the hell happened."

Kip's shoulders jumped.

"I'll go," murmured Uncle Paulie. He clicked the door behind him.

Her dad sat back in his chair and rubbed his cheeks. His eyes were small and red. "She wouldn't have felt anything, honey," he said. Kip got up, left the room, and slapped his bedroom door shut.

Her mom had taken Kip to Sears Fine Food for his annual birthday treat. Kip was fourteen now, a baby man, hair burrowing out of his smooth cheeks and pimples budding on his chin. He wasn't a kid anymore, he'd told Jeannie that morning when she'd caught him slipping a cigarette from their dad's overcoat. Even so, Kip had allowed his mother to scoop him up from school and take him into the city. It had been a tradition since he'd turned eight: every year, Kip would order the stack of eighteen pancakes with syrup, whipped butter, and links; and every year, he would eat and talk and jiggle until his legs stilled, his jaw stopped, and a thin sheen of perspiration formed across his face. "The kid was sweating sugar!" her mom would say when they returned home, and her dad would swipe Kip's legs with his *Chronicle.*

It had rained all day. The two Cadillacs sat outside the restaurant, creamy pink like strawberry malts, blowing hot air and music onto the line of waiting diners. Jeannie decided that must have been it—the Cadillacs must have hidden the approach of the cable car, muffled its thunder. She imagined her mom stepping out, her eyes digging in her purse for a Tums, her white heel jamming in the track. Or perhaps something had drawn her gaze the other way—perhaps she was distracted by the tramp outside the Sir Francis Drake, who wore dirt for gloves and cursed at pretty women, or by a toddler screaming after a lost balloon. But Jeannie didn't know exactly how it happened. Kip was full of tales, but this one he wouldn't tell.

—

The day after the accident, things started to accumulate in the house: roses stuck into baby's breath; a jellied meatloaf; cigarette smoke; and the liquory hit of Aunt Ruth's perfume. Jeannie's dad stood at the telephone, murmuring and smoking; Kip had the television dialed loud. Jeannie sat in the backyard alone, the wind pinching her skin.

"Come on, now, honey, get inside," called Aunt Ruth, standing at the back door, her ankles sliding over her laced shoes like dough. "That cold'll burn you up."

"I'm all right."

"Mrs. Luciano brought some nice fat meatballs. You want me to warm them for you?"

"I'm not hungry."

"You got to eat, Jeannie. You're thin as a whip already."

Jeannie was slim, but like Jimmy Collins once told her, she had plenty of squeeze on her. "I'll stay here," she said.

"I better come to you, then." Aunt Ruth levered herself through the back door and pulled up a deck chair. The fabric gulped under her. "Here," she said, "take one of these." She shuffled two Luckies from her pack, cradled them at her mouth, and handed one over.

They sucked on the cigarettes in silence, Aunt Ruth's eyes trained on the side of Jeannie's face. The older woman was shaking out another smoke when Kip came to the door, his face ripped of color.

"You got to see this."

Inside, Jeannie's dad stood close to the TV set, his cigarette burning down to a wand of ash. Walter Cronkite was on the screen, looking toward a voice off-camera.

"Well, that's a repeat of something that you heard reported to you directly a moment ago from KRLD television in Dallas—"

"What is this?" asked Jeannie. Her dad raised his hand; the ash broke to the floor.

"The rumor that has reached them at the hotel, that the president is dead—"

"Shit," said Kip. Her dad whistled.

"Totally unconfirmed, apparently, as yet. However, let's go back to KRLD in Dallas." Cronkite blinked twice, bent his head, and slid his black frames over his face.

"Sweet Jesus to hell." Aunt Ruth crossed herself.

"No one's going to give a shit about Mom anymore," said Kip.

"Shut up, Kip," said Jeannie.

Kip was right. The president's killing punched the breath out of Forty-Sixth Avenue. Drapes were drawn and housewives sobbed as they swept their front yards.

"Never seen a thing like it, not even with old King Franklin," said Aunt Ruth.

"They're all acting like his dying belongs to them," said Kip.

"It does belong to them," said Jeannie.

"Doesn't belong to nobody."

The flowers and dinners stopped as fast as they had started. Her dad had trouble organizing the funeral—Shirley's Flowers and The Sunset Florist closed out of respect for the president. Over the coming days, as Jeannie watched the wet, blotched film roll over the television screen, it was like her own news was broadcasting on CBS: the cops hanging around; the unfolding burial arrangements; the girl and boy gazing at the casket. Even years later, the sight of that newsreel made Jeannie feel she was watching her loss exploded onto a network screen; and it bothered her that other eyes were gobbling it up.

———

Her mom's funeral went fast-slow, the smell of shoe polish and carnations and cologne. All the while it felt like they were rehearsing a show, until the small casket sailed down the aisle.

"A real dainty lady."

"And always so well put together."

"How's Frank doing?"

"That man's seen such a lot of death."

"Death and taxes, you don't get used to them—"

The funeral director, Mr. O'Sullivan, had recommended a closed casket—"Let's remember her for the lively woman she was." When it was her turn to pay her respects, Jeannie knelt and pressed the casket with her palms, like a prisoner feeling for a loved one through the wire mesh of his cell. There she was, right there; Jeannie imagined climbing in next to her, like she used to scrabble into her parents' bed after a bad dream. A grip on her shoulder: her dad, telling her to stand.

The Lord is my shepherd; therefore can I lack nothing.

At the wake, old women pressed her with dry hands and slicked her with kisses.

"You're the woman of the house now," said Mrs. Davis, nipping mouthfuls of sherry, her eyes scurrying around the room.

"How's your little brother doing, honey?" Mrs. Fleish adjusted the bulge of her breasts beneath her woolen dress.

"He's doing all right," said Jeannie. Kip had been locking himself in his bedroom for hours at a time, silent save for the odd bounce of noise—the throw of a Wiffle ball, a gasp, the cork of a Daisy gun.

"As well as can be expected," said Mrs. Davis, holding up her glass for a passing Uncle Paulie to fill. "You've got to take care of those men of yours."

They watched Jeannie's dad moving around the room, never saying more than a word or two to any guest, clearing mess as soon as it was made. His cheeks were shaved raw and his suit pants bagged at his waist. He looked like a stranger: a lost, unlucky cousin of the soft-bellied father of her childhood. Jeannie slipped away from the women and pushed through the room to find Kip. Her dad's friends from the Corps stood outside drinking bourbon, making jokes. They seemed far away, like people standing inside a television screen. In the kitchen, Aunt Ruth was buttering bread, pausing to lick her cracked fingers.

"Where's Kip?" asked Jeannie.

"I don't know, honey. Here." She handed Jeannie an overstuffed garbage bag. "Help me out, will you?"

Jeannie was hauling the bag out front when she saw Kip sitting against the trash can, flipping the pages of a Spider-Man comic. His khakis were smeared with dirt and his face looked sore.

"What are you doing?" said Jeannie.

"I had to get out."

"Scoot," said Jeannie. Kip hauled himself out the way, flinching at the reek of spoiled food.

"Everybody's so fucking excited in there," he said.

Jeannie thought of all those wine-blushed faces, the old bodies shedding heat and noise, Uncle Paulie pressing through the party with his bottles of liquor.

"Assholes," said Kip.

"I got stuck with Mrs. Davis," said Jeannie, wiping her hands together.

"Mom hated her."

"She did?" Her mom and Kip always knew each other's secrets. Kip's bike was lying on their mom's sage plant; he went to grab it. "Kip," said Jeannie. "You got to help me out in there."

"Can't do it." He swung himself onto the saddle and raced away, standing on the pedals to glide down the street, through the stop sign, toward the ocean.

It was ten o'clock before the last guests left. Jeannie found Kip asleep in his bedroom, fully clothed, his bedspread kicked to the floor. Her dad tidied, stepping and bending like Kip's old windup robot. Uncle Paulie picked over the sweaty hors d'oeuvres; Aunt Ruth rubbed her corns. Jeannie sat in her loose black dress, feeling the spell beginning to break.

Life came knocking. Her dad returned to work at Muni, where they moved him from the planning desk and onto clerical duties for a little while; Kip returned to school. Every morning, as soon as they'd left the house, Jeannie would stop getting dressed and go to her mom's room, unfolding scarves and sweaters to release the last drifts of her mom's scent, the smell that held warmth and memory and was always nearly vanishing. She brushed her mom's face powder onto her wrist, pressing the dusty smell to her nose, and reread the last dog-eared page of the novel her mom had left on the nightstand. Those bright, blustery days of winter, the house was alive with her mom's ghosts; they would catch Jeannie like spiders' webs as she walked the rooms. But the smell faded from her mom's clothes, and the chicken potpie her mom had left in the refrigerator was thrown out, and one day, after Uncle Paulie had driven her dad home late—the slam of the front door, shouts, the sound of glass breaking—Aunt Ruth came to pack up her mom's possessions.

"Your father can't be looking at your mother's things everywhere he turns," she insisted, ignoring Jeannie's protests; and Jeannie felt a balloon swell inside her. She waited until her aunt was outside fussing at the trunk of Uncle Paulie's car, then grabbed the nearest carton—marked *Nightstand*—and shoved it into Kip's room. When her aunt had left, Jeannie slipped into Kip's room and opened the carton, digging through the haul—the tissue-pocketed housecoat, the hairbrush spindled with hair, the coral vanity case—before carrying it to her bedroom and pushing it inside her closet.

Christmas came and went—maple ham and long silences at Aunt Ruth and Uncle Paulie's place—and a new year. Jeannie cut class at secretarial school until, come February, Mrs. Harris suggested she take a break from the program. She quit volunteering at St. Mary's, and lived out the rest of the winter perching at the soda fountain with Nancy, or lying for long dull hours on the living room floor, browsing through her mom's back issues of *McCall's*. She spent her days waiting: waiting for the hands on the clock to move and for her dad and Kip to come home, when they would heat three dinners and watch TV until *The Tonight Show* started and their dad switched off the set.

"Your father doesn't mind you lazing around all day long?" asked Nancy one day on Ocean Beach. It was Washington's Birthday, and sunny out; mothers had come to run their children on the beach. Nancy knelt behind Jeannie, tying a scarf around her head.

"Hasn't said a lot about it," said Jeannie, pushing her bare feet into the sand.

Nancy touched the top of Jeannie's head—*Head up*. "My daddy would kick me out if I wasted my days that way," she said.

“Your mom would beat him to it.”

Nancy made the noise of a smile. “There.” She patted Jeannie’s shoulders.

Jeannie turned; Nancy’s face glared in the sun, like a coin catching the light. Jeannie shuffled to sit next to her.

“What were you going to tell me?” she asked.

“I don’t know if I should,” said Nancy, unpicking a carton of her mother’s Newports and pulling out a cigarette.

Jeannie nudged her friend. “Tell me.”

Nancy placed the cigarette between her lips, lit it with her father’s Zippo, and slid her brown legs to her chest. She blew smoke. “He told me not to.” She squinted at the sailboats swinging on the ocean and took another pull.

“Who?” said Jeannie. “Tommy?”

Nancy leaned in to whisper, the wind flicking her hair into Jeannie’s face. “Mickey Riley,” she said, her breath warm on Jeannie’s ear.

“Mickey Riley?” Mickey had graduated high school as their homecoming king and was now working as a meat wrapper off Twentieth Avenue. He was also married, having knocked up the homecoming queen, Sandra Simmons, (so the rumor went) on prom night.

“Hush,” said Nancy, checking for listeners. Just a heavy-diapered toddler, squashing sand into a tin can.

“What happened?” said Jeannie.

“We did it.” Nancy smiled, her canine teeth showing over her bottom lip.

“What? When?”

“Last night. Over there, by the rocks.”

When Kip was six, he was climbing those rocks when he slipped and fell into the water and—had it not been for a nearby man plunging in to help him—was almost swept away.

When they got home and told their mom, she slapped Jeannie so hard her cheek was still red the next morning.

"I got sand everywhere," said Nancy, voice rising. The toddler's mother gave Nancy a sharp look. "All the way up—"

"Keep it down," hissed Jeannie. "Jesus, Nancy."

"You're such a prude." Nancy smiled.

"You weren't afraid somebody would see you?"

"I think we might have shocked a couple of seals." Nancy laughed and buried her cigarette butt in the sand.

Jeannie shook her head. "You got to be careful you don't get in trouble."

"I'll be fine." Nancy caught her pale hair in the crook of her arm and swept it behind her shoulders. "You got to watch you don't miss out on trouble altogether."

They stayed on the beach all afternoon, until the sunset dragged the warmth from the sand and it was cold and dark under their feet. At home, the sound of men filled the living room; it was her dad's turn to host his Corps friends for poker night. Jeannie felt their presence like static, all noise and heat and roughness, stuffing the house, pushing itself into every space; and the absence of her mom ambushed her with such violence her breath caught. She stopped in the hallway, waiting until her breath eased. The sound of yelling and whistling boiled over from the living room—an unexpected hand revealed, a foolish bet placed. Jeannie pushed her hair from her face and stepped into the kitchen. Her dad was scrubbing the countertop, muscles taut like rubber in his thin brown arms; and something in the smallness of his labor, in the brightness of the room and the smell of Ajax, returned the house to itself, and her mom's shadow folded itself away in the corner of the room.

"Daddy, it's clean," said Jeannie. "Go be with your friends."

Her dad grabbed a tuft of steel wool and worked it over an imperceptible stain. "What did you do today?" he asked. Bernie Garubbo walked in, his belly pressing against his shirt, his eyes scanning the kitchen for snacks.

"I went to the beach with Nancy."

"Who's Nancy?" said Bernie, shaking a pack of peanuts into a bowl.

"A girlfriend," said Jeannie.

"You spend too much time with that girl," said her dad.

"That's what she said too."

Her dad straightened to look at her. "What about Mrs. Harris? Want me to give her a call?"

Bernie leaned against the counter, cracking nuts with his fingers. Jeannie wished him away.

"She won't have me, Daddy. She didn't mean for me to come back."

"So, someplace else."

"I don't know if I want to be a secretary anymore."

Her dad and Bernie swapped a look.

"You got to do something," said her dad. "All this lying around'll make you soft."

"I got Aunt Ruth fretting I'm too skinny and you saying I'm getting heavy." Her dad didn't smile.

"Your father's right, Jeannie." Bernie splashed shells onto the floor.

"Jesus, Bernie, we're not in a goddamn bar," said her dad, scooping up the mess with his hands.

"You're a nineteen-year-old woman," Bernie continued, spitting nut fragments. "You got better things to do than jaw with your girlfriends all day long."

"It's not like that—"

"I talked to your father." Bernie brushed his hands together. "There's a spot for you at my place."

Jeannie slid a pleading look to her dad; he frowned down at his dish towel.

Kip slunk in. "Jeannie's going to flip burgers?"

"A waitress job," said Bernie.

"Thanks, Mr. Garubbo, but I'll pass."

"Not so fast," said her dad, opening a Pabst and handing it to Bernie. "You got another way to pay rent around here?"

"Kip doesn't pay rent."

"Kip isn't grown," said Bernie. He sucked greedily on his beer.

Kip made a face; Jeannie glared back.

"It's a nice gig, Jeannie." Bernie wiped his lips on his knuckles. "A buck and a half an hour; you keep the tips."

"Honestly, Mr. Garubbo—"

"It's no problem. Come tomorrow at eleven. I'll show you the ropes." Jeannie's dad nodded; Kip grinned.

"Jackson, your hand isn't going to play itself!" came a yell.

"Let's go." Bernie put his hand on her dad's shoulder and steered him back to the game.

"Sucker," said Kip.

"What the hell am I supposed to do?"

Kip cracked a shell and caught a peanut in his mouth. His eyes shone. "You're going to boot camp, sis. Bernie's gonna bust your ass."

"Screw you," said Jeannie. She went to her bedroom and shut the door.

Bernie's Hamburgers was a dive with oily windows and sticky leather booths. But the hamburgers were generous and the French fries had just the right salt and bite, and in any case, it was the only place to eat within a block of UCSF. Everybody who came in seemed to be waiting: for a relative to get better, or worse; for a shift to start; for the next procedure. One thing they didn't want was to hang around for their food.

"The patient ones are in the hospital," joked Anita, Bernie's longest-serving—and favorite—waitress. She was forty going on twenty-five, with a spare inch of makeup and, as Bernie put it, two spare handfuls of patootie. Jeannie wondered if she'd heard about the accident, because from her first shift Anita had maneuvered Jeannie around the diner with the quiet care of a school crossing guard. The rest of them, for the most part, ignored her: Esteban and Gaël, the chefs, who talked only to each other, in Spanish; Patty and Linda, who saved their smiles for the doctors; and Bernie himself, whose attention was rare but unwelcome. The work was enough to trick her out of her grief, sometimes for hours at a time. At the end of each shift, Jeannie returned home with tender feet, stinking of fried meat. "Hey, Jean-Burger!" Kip would call, and Jeannie would give him the finger before collapsing into bed, too stuffed with the smell of food to think of eating.

Whole months worked themselves away that way. Jeannie found the rhythm of her labor and rolled through the days. As summer came and gave way to fall, the temperature outside rose, making the windows sweat and leaving moisture on her upper lip. Every night she counted her dollar bills and tucked them inside her mom's vanity case, which she kept hidden beneath her bed. At the end of each month she pushed twenty-five bucks under her dad's bedroom door for rent, and the next day she found the bills returned in a neat pile on her dresser. When Linda quit to marry her high school sweetheart and move to South San Francisco (she never did hook a doctor, sniped Anita), Jeannie picked up the extra shifts. Now that

Nancy was spending all her spare time with Mickey, there wasn't much else to do. Fall deepened to winter. Jeannie got to feeling like there was never a time when she wasn't pacing over the days, sliding plates on and off tables before sliding into bed. She could go long spells without thinking about her mom's death, but three, maybe four times a day it would skewer her like a knife. It was like riding the Limbo at Playland—long stretches of dark riding, and then, when you least expected it, a horror lunging from the shadows.

On Halloween, Nancy came over, her plaid skirt rolled high, her hair ratted into a lump on the top of her head.

"It's me," she said in a flat voice as she pushed into the house. Her eyes were thickly and unevenly lined. Kip was at the kitchen table studying a Sgt. Fury comic; he started out of his chair.

"Kip, honey, how are you doing?" Nancy folded Kip against her chest. He angled himself away, snatched up his comic, and left the room.

"What's he in now, seventh grade?"

"Ninth."

"Cute little guy!"

Jeannie heard Kip's door click shut. "You okay?"

"You got anything to drink?"

"I think we have seltzer."

"I mean something to *drink*."

Her dad was out bowling. Jeannie hesitated, then pulled a bottle of Old Crow from the cabinet.

Nancy's nose wrinkled. "Your mom didn't keep any vodka?" Something catty touched Nancy's face, then vanished; Jeannie saw an apologetic heat spread at the root of her friend's neck, and decided to ignore it. She cleared her throat.

"This is it," she said. "Take it or leave it."

Nancy shrugged and sat at the table.

Jeannie took two coffee cups from the kitchen closet and poured. "Something happened at Bernie's today," she said. Jeannie turned and saw Nancy picking up a letter addressed to Jeannie's dad; Nancy let it go and it drifted to the floor. Her face was pale and spiteful. "What's the matter?" asked Jeannie, sliding over a cup holding an inch of bourbon. Nancy looked at her head-on for the first time since she'd arrived; she had a tightness about her eyes, as though she'd been crying.

"I'm late."

It took a moment for Jeannie to understand what Nancy was talking about. "How late?"

"A week." Nancy took a gulp from her cup and gave Jeannie a strange smirk.

"A week's not so long," said Jeannie.

Nancy sent her a dead look. "I'm never late."

It was true: Nancy prided herself on being regular.

"You were careful?"

"Mickey doesn't like to be careful."

You'd think Mickey would have learned. "You been to the doctor?"

Nancy shook her head.

"Does Mickey know?"

"Of course not."

"Shit, Nancy."

Nancy scratched at the table with a pink frosted nail. The sound of the Beach Boys bled through Kip's door.

"What are you going to do?" asked Jeannie.

"I'm not going to end up like that stupid bitch, that's for sure." Jeannie thought of Sandy Riley, with her thin face and her furious baby. It would be worse for Nancy—not even Mr. Cooper could shotgun an already hitched guy to the church.

Nancy must have seen something in Jeannie's face, because all of a sudden she looked scared. "I don't have a choice," she said.

"What do you mean?"

Nancy stood and went to the cabinet. She tipped three glugs of bourbon into her cup.

"CeeCee's cousin knows somebody who can take care of it," she said. Jeannie heard the shade of challenge in Nancy's voice.

"You told CeeCee?" Jeannie checked herself. Nancy sat, her face smoothed with something like satisfaction.

"She knows about stuff like this," said Nancy. CeeCee Adams had lived in a Manhattan skyscraper until she was eleven, and she still acted like she'd learned everything about the world staring down at the dirty streets and the little yellow cabs.

"She wants you to think she knows," said Jeannie, a rash prickling her chest.

"Don't be jealous," said Nancy, a smile pulling at the corners of her mouth.

Jeannie adjusted her voice. "I'm not jealous," she said. "But you can't just go get rid—"

"You're getting religious on me? The Virgin fucking Jeannie?"

The rash had crawled up Jeannie's neck and over her face. "You could get hurt."

"I knew I shouldn't have told you."

"Come on, Nancy."

"You know what Mickey and his friends called you in high school? Icebox. Because you're so damn frigid." Nancy was standing, hard-voiced, with that odd smile still touching her mouth. Suddenly she looked how she might look in ten years, like the former pageant girls in the grocery store whose beauty didn't last—plump faces that dragged to fat and cute-nipped features that sharpened with age. You'll be just like them, Jeannie thought; and the cruelty of the thought had a kind of power, stopping her tears.

"Maybe it's okay. Maybe you're not gone," she offered.

"Maybe you're fucking clueless," said Nancy.

The scratch of a key at the front door. Jeannie and Nancy downed their bourbon, Nancy gagging on the last swallow.

"Hello, girls," said Jeannie's dad, setting down his bowling bag and removing his shoes. His shirt collar was loose, and the skin around his neck looked plucked and raw, like a turkey's.

"Mr. Jackson," said Nancy, coughing to recover herself. "I was just going."

"Don't leave on my account."

"My mother's expecting me." Nancy brushed out her skirt and nodded. "Goodnight, Mr. Jackson."

"Goodnight, Nancy." Jeannie's dad turned on the kitchen faucet and squeezed Lux into the sink.

"Nice girl," he said when Nancy had closed the door behind her.

That night, Jeannie couldn't sleep; she kept replaying Nancy's words—jealous, frigid, clueless—and letting them hurt her all over again. She sat up in bed, looking out the window at the browned-out front yard, headlights blaring over her every few minutes, then every hour. A scratch against the wall behind her head—Kip was awake too. The sound of the back door sliding open. A long sag of time, the chink of glass bottles on the doorstep; then, nothing.

The next day, Jeannie was hiding behind the counter at the diner, sweeping up broken glass. Bernie had reamed her out in front of everybody after she fumbled a tray and sent a half-dozen new water tumblers crashing to the floor.

"Guess who showed up!" Anita's face appeared, pressed powder breaking into excited cracks across her forehead.

Jeannie gazed up at her. "Who?" She wondered if it was Nancy, who never stayed mad for long.

"The doctor who's always making eyes at you—the one with the specs and those red cheeks."

Jeannie sat back on her heels and pushed her wrists to her eyes.

"Honey!" Anita threw her a paper napkin. "You'll spoil your face."

"Table Five," barked Bernie.

"You go, honey."

"I've got to finish up—"

"Here." Anita rounded the counter and took the dustpan and broom. "He's yours."

He was bowed over a newspaper, his glasses pushed into his hair. He was becoming a regular. The previous day, he'd been in with a couple of bigmouthed doctor friends, and she'd felt their amused eyes on her from across the diner, heard their loud-voiced banter, caught his look of hope and horror as she approached to take their order. Jeannie wanted to creep back under the counter; but Anita popped up and mouthed, *Go.*

Jeannie's approach jerked him from the *Chronicle;* his

knuckles caught the saltshaker and spilled a mouthful of salt onto the table.

"What can I get you?"

He swept the crystals with his palm; they scuttled across the newsprint.

"Sorry." He set his glasses on his nose. "I was in here yesterday." A bashful smile. "I'm here a lot." He half stood and nodded his head. "I'm Billy."

"Hello, Billy."

A pause; he lowered himself to his seat. His eyes darted to the button fastened at her chest. "You're Jeannie," he said. His cheeks purpled.

"What can I get you, Billy?" Jeannie felt Anita's eyes on her neck.

"Sorry about my friends yesterday. They were pretty loud."

"It's always loud here."

"I'd like to take you on a date." Billy clamped his jaw shut and blinked in surprise, like a fish had just leaped out of his mouth.

"Oh. Well—"

"*A New Kind of Love* is showing at the drive-in by the Cow Palace. Have you seen it?"

"I haven't." Jeannie remembered the billboard. Paul Newman and Joanne Woodward locked in a romantic somersault, Woodward's frothy green dress spilling to reveal a bite of petticoat.

"Tomorrow night?"

A date. About time, Nancy would say. And with a doctor. Billy's face was working in a twitch; his own nervousness eased Jeannie's shyness. "Sure," she said, in a steady voice.

Billy nodded and beamed. He gathered up his newspaper and grabbed his coat from the seat.

"You're not eating?" asked Jeannie.

"Jeez—" Billy pulled back his sleeve to look at his wrist. "I can't. I've got to run." He wasn't wearing a watch.

He left the diner, and Jeannie watched him jog across the street, then run back and push his head through the door.

"Pick you up?" he asked.

"Here," replied Jeannie. "Shift finishes at six."

"Well, there you go," said Anita, sidling up to give Jeannie a pinch on the hip. "Who said breaking glass was unlucky?"

Billy picked her up in what Kip would have called a clunker.

"You live in the city?" he asked, thumping the stick shift with the heel of his hand. "Darn thing."

"The Sunset," said Jeannie, her body stiff against the leather seat. "What about you?"

"Born and raised in the city. On Spruce."

"It's fancy up there."

Billy shrugged. "I live near the hospital now, up from Parnassus."

"You a doctor?"

He looked at her and winked. "Almost."

They listened to the gripe of the engine.

"Sounds fatal," said Billy, and Jeannie laughed, and her shoulders loosened.

As the car squashed over the gravel, Billy seemed embarrassed to discover it was buck night.

"I didn't know," he apologized, handing over the dollar bill. "I'm not being cheap, I swear."

"You're nuts," said Jeannie, and gave him a smile.

He smiled briefly back. "Now, where shall we go?" he said, and, seeing a spot, drove all the way to the front of the pit.

I guess I'm safe, then, thought Jeannie.

As the movie started, Billy pushed out his knee so it touched hers, and she didn't move away. But after a few minutes, her leg cramped, and as she shook it out, Billy shifted in his seat and pivoted away from her. When Paul Newman called Samantha "a semi-virgin at the ripe old age of twenty-five," Jeannie felt exposed, like someone had thrown a hot white spotlight on her. It didn't look like she was going to get laid any time soon.

After the movie, they shared a malt at the soda fountain on Geneva.

"Thanks for taking me," said Jeannie.

"You liked the movie?" asked Billy.

Jeannie considered the question. "It was a little lame," she said.

"I thought it was fun."

They lapsed into silence. Jeannie stirred her malt; she wondered what Nancy would say next. "He only fell in love with her when he thought she was a hooker," she said.

Billy swallowed. Jeannie felt a crackle of power.

"He's cute, though. Paul Newman." Jeannie watched Billy; he leaned in on his straw, a blush rising at his jaw. Maybe men weren't all that complicated after all. "What about Joanne Woodward?" she asked.

Billy scratched his head, his face crinkling. "I'm more of an Elizabeth Taylor kind of a guy."

"She's beautiful." He preferred brunettes. Jeannie dared herself to hold eye contact; two beats, and he looked away, jerking his head to give a shy smile to the pretty waitress who wiped the counter in front of him.

"So." He drummed his fingers on the countertop. Jeannie

feared she'd been too obvious; embarrassment scuttled over her skin. "Tomorrow," he said.

"Tomorrow?"

"You voting?"

"Oh." Jeannie shook her head. "No. I can't."

"You're not twenty-one?" He leaned close, as though examining her for a time stamp.

"Still a baby," she said, sensing his eyes on her as she lowered her lashes and pulled a sip of malt.

"Well," he said, swiveling on his stool. "It's been keeping me busy. Been to so many fund-raisers I'd be happy never to see a stuffed egg or pickled shrimp again." He let the remark rest like he'd made it a half-dozen times before; Jeannie guessed it went down well with the kind of ladies he mixed with.

"You're interested in politics?" asked Jeannie.

"My mother," he said, pouring a slurry of chocolate into his glass and taking a gulp. A slop of malt washed onto his top lip. "Had me campaigning every spare minute. Had to tell her I was working tonight, otherwise she'd have me walking the streets with a clipboard."

"My father says he's got it sewn up," offered Jeannie, eyeing the mess on Billy's mouth.

Billy laughed. "You're talking about LBJ. No, we're gunning for Goldwater—In Your Heart You Know He's Right!" He placed his hand over his chest and grinned.

Jeannie didn't have much more to offer on the subject; she searched for something to say. "My father says never trust an Army man."

"And your mother? She a Democrat too?"

"From Texas," said Jeannie. She nearly added *was,* but the word stuck.

Billy clicked his tongue. "So that's a yes." He turned to her with a pink, open face; his eyes shone. "My mother would disapprove of you," he said. Jeannie shifted on her stool, feeling the awkwardness of her hips and legs. Billy pushed his hand into his pocket and threw down a fistful of coins. A *Goldwater in '64* button scurried over the counter.

"Here," he said. He plucked up the button and fastened it to her sweater. His fingers trembled. Jeannie turned her head to stop herself breathing on him. "There's still time to change your father's mind," he said. He sat back to look at her, nodding in satisfaction.

Jeannie thumbed the edge of the button. "What about your mother's mind?" she ventured.

Billy was looking at the headline of a newspaper that somebody had left folded on the stool beside him. VIET CONG ATTACK SAIGON AIRPORT. "My mother never changes her mind." He picked up the paper and stuck it under his arm. "Come on." He pulled a thick, final smile, the kind her dad did when he wanted to go to bed. "I'll drive you home."

At her front door, Billy rattled the keys in his pocket and cleared his throat. He leaned in; she rocked back on her heels, then held herself still. And he kissed her, a wet mash of tongue and teeth, spit and chocolate.

The next afternoon Nancy called by, her lilac skirt bouncing under her raincoat, a paper bag squashed in her hand. Jeannie noted the easy look on her friend's face and felt relieved.

"It came," said Nancy, bending her knees in a small skip for joy.

"It did?" said Jeannie, a smile spreading over her face.

"That was so scary," said Nancy. Jeannie beckoned her friend inside. "I was ready to throw myself under a streetcar." Jeannie felt a sharp sting, like she'd been touched by the edge of a whip. "Because you know that if my mother had found out, she'd have pushed me in front of one." She stopped and took Jeannie by the wrists. "Oh, Lord, I'm so sorry, Jeannie."

"It's all right," said Jeannie. "I'm glad you're okay." She slipped her hands into Nancy's and squeezed.

Nancy pulled Jeannie to her bedroom. "It came this morning and it ruined my best capri pants, but honest to God, I've never been happier to see Rosie Red." Nancy smiled at her own junior high turn of phrase, sat at the mirror, and shook a can of Aqua Net from the paper bag. "You're not ready?" she asked, flicking her eyes over Jeannie through the mirror. (A week ago, Mrs. Cooper had asked them to chaperone at the middle school sock hop; Jeannie had assumed, after her fight with Nancy, that she was no longer needed.)

Jeannie opened her dresser to find her gold pullover.

"You okay?" asked Nancy, bringing a comb down on a white-blond ribbon of hair.

"I went on a date," blurted Jeannie.

Nancy's comb stopped, her eyebrows drawn high. "With who?"

"Someone from Bernie's."

"Gaël?" Nancy shredded the hair to a tangle, then picked another strand. "I told you he was hot for you."

Jeannie smiled and pushed her feet into her saddle shoes. "A customer."

Nancy put down the comb and scooted around to face her. "Is he older?"

Jeannie nodded. "A doctor." She threw the word like a pebble into a still pond, and watched the ripple.

"A real doctor?" Nancy leaned forward, as if to hear better. "Is he cute?"

Jeannie thought of Billy's flat nose, his thick-knit eyebrows, the hairline creeping from his forehead. "He looks a little like Paul Newman."

"Tell me everything. What happened? Where did you go?" The tips of Nancy's ears were growing pink.

"He kissed me," said Jeannie.

They clicked down Noriega, the sunset tearing bloody strips out of the sky, the wind whipping dust from an empty lot. Nancy slid her arm around Jeannie's waist; she smelled of soap and lemons.

"You're so lucky dating a doctor," she said. "Mickey just got fired for stealing a ham."

"It was just one date." Out across the highway, the ocean waited; it had been waiting and sighing that way since Jeannie was a child.

"He got a friend for me?"

"I'll ask," said Jeannie, snugging her own arm around Nancy's middle and feeling a flush of contentment. They held each other tight as the wind charged them, slapping their raincoats against their legs and lifting their hair.

In the morning, her dad told her that President Johnson had taken the election. "This country still has some goddamn sense, thank God." Jeannie dressed carefully for her shift and wondered if Billy would stop by.

"It's not going to pop itself," said Nancy, untangling Christmas lights from a dusty carton Jeannie had found under her parents' bed.

"What are you talking about?" asked Jeannie, crawling back under the bed for the other carton.

"Your cherry."

"Jesus, Nancy." Jeannie wriggled her head from under the

bed. "Keep it down!" Kip and her dad were in the living room, putting up a Douglas fir. They'd picked it up by the roadside on Sloat; it had cost three whole dollars.

"You're twenty years old," said Nancy, blowing on the lights and bouncing dust bunnies into the air. "You're going to close up."

"You're full of it," said Jeannie, lifting the lid of the carton and unwrapping a Shiny-Brite from its wax paper.

"I'm serious. It happened to my aunt Sylvia."

"You're kidding," said Jeannie as she unpacked another ornament. "Your aunt Sylvia never had a loolie."

Nancy laughed. "You're going to do it with him, right?"

Jeannie and Billy had been dating for six weeks. They had been to the movies, the creamery, the bowling alley, and the railcar diner on Pine. Always just the two of them; she had never met his doctor friends again, or even seen where he lived. Whenever he drove her home, he stopped by the beach and sat for a while—maybe being a gentleman, maybe finding his pluck—before leaning to kiss her, his fingers testing a button on her blouse, his hand sidling up her thigh. She let him hold her breast through her bra, keeping his hand in place with her own; once or twice he sneaked his fingers underneath the fabric and rolled her nipple like it was a bean. That week, after watching a Sophia Loren movie, he didn't wait to kiss her; he slid his hand up her skirt, thumbed aside her panties, and pushed his finger inside her. She could feel her warmth against his cold hand, his knuckles pressing at her. The whole thing felt separate from her, like she was observing a scientific experiment. He took her hand and urged it against the hardness in his pants; Jeannie wasn't sure what to do, so she let her hand rest there for a while, before pulling away and smiling. She never should have told Nancy.

"First time you do it, it'll hurt," said Nancy. "Get him to spit on his fingers first." She took a sip from her bottle of Dr Pepper. "The main thing is, he's got to pull out. You don't want to get knocked up."

"I don't know, Nancy," she said.

"He's going to want to do it, Jeannie," said Nancy. She threw the bottle at the wastepaper basket; it missed and rolled across the carpet, dribbling soda. "If there's one thing I know about guys—put out or get out."

Jeannie took a long bath before Billy picked her up that night. She washed her body using her treasured sliver of Yardley and dabbed her mom's Unforgettable on the backs of her knees and wrists. She rolled and set her hair the way her mom had shown her, and painted her face. By the time she'd brushed out her curls and applied Nancy's peach lipstick, it was seven o'clock. She walked into the kitchen to collect her purse; and Kip, who was setting the table for dinner, looked at her like he was watching a ghost.

"Where are you going?" he asked. Anxiety and need mixed in his face; it was the look he used to get when he was little and their mom left them with the babysitter, and it made Jeannie want to run.

"Meeting a girlfriend," said Jeannie.

"Liar."

They drove to Winterland, where they scratched over the ice, hand in sweaty hand, and sipped scalding cocoa from tall glasses. On the way home, Billy pulled off Lincoln and parked by the wasteland. Jeannie saw the old windmill, its vanes stuck still among the scrubgrass. When she was twelve, she saw a story in her dad's newspaper about a pair of lovers who parked out here to be alone. A man smashed their window and dragged the girl from the car and into the park, where he stripped, beat, and raped her; he hacked all of the girl's hair off. Jeannie felt a quick stride of fear climb her body. Billy sat in his seat, a dull light edging off his spectacles. Outside, it was pitch-dark, the only noise the sigh of the ocean. Then fingers tapping on the window. Jeannie's throat tightened.

It was only rain, the kind that scuttled over everything and stopped as suddenly as it started. Billy turned on the radio, and "She Loves You" played out happily; he turned to her, and Jeannie could see from the movement of his face that he was smiling. She unbuckled herself and climbed into the backseat. *Come on,* she said. A beat, and Billy clambered back, his neck stooped, his body crouched. He pulled her pedal pushers and panties down over her white thighs; undid his zipper, fumbled, and pushed himself inside her. Jeannie held still. Nancy was right—it didn't take a minute—all of a sudden, Billy stopped as if someone had put a gun to his head, then shivered once, twice, and sighed. Then he put a blurry kiss on her mouth and they hurried home, Jeannie facing out the window, her thighs growing damp. At home, she wrapped herself in her mom's housecoat and lay on her bed, staring at the ceiling until the seagulls started yelling and sleep came.

A new year arrived, and Jeannie realized she was in trouble. She waited for her period with a superstitious vigilance, and when it didn't come, she realized she'd known it wouldn't, maybe even that night in the car. The first thing Billy did was tell his mother, Dorothy, and by March, Jeannie was on the steps of St. Dominic's wearing an ivory taffeta empire-waist gown with off-the-shoulder cap sleeves that Aunt Ruth had sewn from a dollar pattern. The dress was stiff and shone metallic in the sunlight, and Dorothy's expression—as if the dress itself had said something unforgivable to her—could, as Aunt Ruth put it, have "outstunk a skunk."

It was cold that day, but Jeannie felt her own heat, felt sweat crawling between her skin and her dress, a smell like lunch meat rising from her armpits. There was something furtive in the quietness and brevity of the service; Jeannie had the strange sensation that they were conducting the whole affair behind her mom's back and that at any moment, her mom might sweep into the church wearing her wide-brimmed hat and ruched dress gloves and order the priest to start over. Jeannie's dad and Kip wore the suits they'd worn at the funeral over a year back—her dad's too large, Kip's too small, like a double act who'd switched clothes—and afterward, at the luncheon in the mansion on Spruce, Kip wouldn't leave her side, to the point where Billy's uncle Jesse joked that he couldn't figure out which one—Kip or Billy—was the groom. Nancy had run up her own short, flare-skirted dress in candy pink, and she drew eyes like bugs to a lantern.

"That little girl's going to get herself into a mess," said Aunt Ruth, watching Nancy take a walk in the garden with Billy's boss.

"Messes have their perks," said Uncle Paulie, flicking a wink at Jeannie as he threw back the last of his champagne.

Jeannie played her part—as best she could—and waited. If she could get through the day and into their new place down on Noe, she might feel safe again.

The house on Noe was a Victorian the color of egg yolk, with steps running up to a door set with stained glass. They had the rooms on the first floor; the upstairs rooms were kept by two quiet older men—brothers, Jeannie assumed. Billy's father, Dr. Richard Harper—a large man whose taut belly and sprouting ear hair gave him the appearance of being overstuffed —handed them the keys shortly after their engagement: "All lovebirds need a nest," he said, taking the couple in his arms and letting his fingers wander over Jeannie's ass. Where the Sunset was caught in the whip of a westerly wind, Noe Valley was still and noiseless: standing on Twenty-Fourth gave the sensation of standing inside one of her mom's snowglobes. Except that no one was shaking this particular globe: Jeannie was surprised each morning to find sunshine waiting quietly at the windows.

"I didn't know there was sun in the summertime till I was old enough to drive out of the Sunset," said Uncle Paulie as he stood at the bay window, rubbing his back.

"You could live a whole life here," said Aunt Ruth, taking in all the corners of the room, as though she were picturing all the babies and heartaches and sicknesses that would breathe their hours there. "That's it—you're going to die here," agreed Nancy when she visited a week after the wedding, trailing her fingers over the furniture like a customer who, in the end, wasn't minded to buy.

"Can I feel it?" she asked, pushing her palms against Jeannie's belly, her eyes saucering like a little girl's, and Jeannie loosened herself from her friend's hands and asked about Mickey and Sandy and the tramp at the soda fountain who still refused to serve Nancy because of some scandal way back in high school.

"It's all the same," said Nancy, clicking her heel against her ankle. *There's no place like home.* She paused, then sighed. "I got to go," she said, and Jeannie watched through the window as Nancy walked down the hill, her shadow stretching along the sidewalk.

Those months Billy worked days and nights at SF General, and Jeannie got fat with her baby, accepting visits from her next-door neighbor Cynthia, who had an overbite, an explosive toddler, and nine yards of advice. Every couple of days Jeannie would get on the streetcar and ride it all the way to the Sunset, where the wind blew and life happened, and after a soda with Nancy or Kip she'd ride home, fold herself in her mom's old quilt at the bay window, and wait.

Kip / 1966

Here's a true story. Me and Bobby were fishing on Torpedo Wharf. It was hot as hell—this mean sun had fried off all the fog. Bobby was cranked about catching a bunch of sand dabs. Ugly fucking fish, all grease and teeth, don't even taste good. So Bobby's setting the lines and I'm hand-scrabbling for a cigarette. Like Uncle Paulie says, "God created fishing so a man can smoke in peace." The guy has wisdom crammed into him like shit in a sewer.

So there I was, smoking a cigarette, and I saw it—this man falling away from the Golden Gate Bridge. There he was, crawling down the sky like a spider; the bay took him and his body fucking exploded in the water. Then it was done and the ocean closed over and the bridge just stood there and the sun was still furious. I turned to Bobby, but he was digging in his bag, asscrack creeping out of his pants, whistling the Supremes. It was like I imagined the whole damn thing. True story.

That was the summer the rats came. They ate up the carpet, dropped shit in the kitchen, and smeared fur on the walls. One bought it in Mrs. Fleish's pond. It was brown and soft, like a rotten pear. We fished it out and Bobby tried to get Blackie to chow it, but she just sniffed and turned away, flicking her tail to show her asshole. "I hate that fucking cat," said Bobby. He flipped the rat over the fence into Mr. Kowalski's yard: "I hope he steps on it." Bobby didn't like Mr. Kowalski ever since he called the cops on him way back for exploding a cherry bomb under his Oldsmobile. "Fucking Polack," said Bobby, which was funny because Bobby was a fucking Polack too.

A couple dollars a week to do Mr. Fleish's work—cut the

lawn, weed the grass, paint over the rot. At the end of the afternoon, Mrs. Fleish would slip us the money like she was doing us a favor. The bills were damp and wrinkled and smelled like old-lady skin, like she kept them stuffed down her shirt. One afternoon I saw her tits, saw her washing in the bathroom when I was window-cleaning—they were long and white, with nipples big as baseballs. I reckon she wanted me to see her, wanted me to climb in through that window and nail her right there on that purple bath rug. Didn't do it, though—not my bag. Bobby didn't believe me, said it was bullshit and truth be told he had a nasty streak, but he had a Rambler sedan and a dead mom too, so we found ways to get along.

That summer was so damn boring it made your balls ache. The days came in clean and wide and we fogged them with being broke and lazy. But we had too much sun in our blood to bother with anything steady, and the dollars bought us movie tickets and the odd make-out with one of the Byrne girls, so we made do. But all those days rolling over us and I couldn't shake this sense that there was something waiting for us, something naked and ugly, like that rotten rat waiting to be stepped on in Mr. Kowalski's yard. We didn't talk about it, but the way Bobby drove his car like the Devil was chasing him made me sure he felt it too.

The summer turned sour by the time the moving truck pulled up across the street. The skirts had gotten long and the beach had gotten sad, and I couldn't walk in the house without my dad talking about getting serious for senior year. Two delivery guys with heavy asses chewing up their shorts piled beds and bikes in Dead Daisy's front yard. That house was cursed—three owners in three years, all dead, one by one: pop, pop, pop. Some Indian chief was skinned and knifed there, I reckoned, bones bleeding pissed-to-hell evil into the soil. They found old Daisy with a broken neck at the bottom of the stairs. Tripped and fell, they said, but we knew the truth, knew the ghost had taken her by her bald head and hurled her down, just like he'd stuck that wiener in Mr. Ritchie's throat and kicked that music teacher off the roof. And now these guys moving in, thinking they'd got themselves a deal at eleven thousand dollars.

"Assholes," said Bobby.

"I give it nine months," I said, and wondered which one would go.

It was a family this time, a full set: mom, dad, three sons. The oldest kid was our age, then maybe a sophomore and a who-gave-a-crap little one. The mom was muddy with freckles and the dad looked like Ed Sullivan, all teeth and lips and eyes that wouldn't blink. The oldest kid seemed like he'd taken a few face knocks on the football field.

"My guess is it'll be the jock gets it," I told Bobby.

"Shut up with your bullshit," he said.

All the girls got pretty fired up about Pete Marshall. He even caught Nancy's eye, which was hard to take. She didn't come by too often since Jeannie got hitched, but there she was, sitting in our kitchen, brown thighs squashing against the wicker chair, and you could see it pressing its patterns into her. Jeannie had given her Charlie to hold and as she bounced him her breasts rolled like water balloons. Two trails of lime snot ran down to Charlie's lip, but nobody cared to fix it.

"Who's that?" said Nancy, watching Pete Marshall wipe his face with his shirt on the slowdown from his run.

"They the new neighbors, Kip?" asked Jeannie.

"The Marshalls," I said.

"He's cute," said Nancy, tickling Charlie under his armpit and making him screech. "Nice and strong-looking. Think he needs breaking in?"

"Nancy! Not in front of the boys!" said Jeannie, and Nancy laughed, but she was looking at me and she had a question in her face.

"Screw you, Jeannie. I'm not a kid," I said, and gave her the finger as I turned away. I went to my room and locked the door and lay down and just as it was happening I heard Nancy burst out laughing in the next room like she knew.

It turns out Mr. Marshall was a Bible-thumper, while Pete Marshall was a natural-born troublemaker, smashing up those commandments one at a time, drinking and stealing and coveting and no honoring at all. He had to hide it, though, or get the shit beaten out of him by his dad. "The guy can beat the music out of your soul," Pete said, and if anybody else had said that kind of thing, Bobby would have smashed their nose, but Pete Marshall was different—he could say things the rest of us couldn't.

By the time school started up again in the fall, the three of us were pretty tight. We left school at recess and hid out in Bobby's garage, drinking my dad's Buds and smoking grass Pete had bought from some guy on roller skates at the Beach House. Pete always brought something special with him, shook it out of his bag with real ceremony like one of those showgirls with a prize on *Let's Make a Deal*—*Playboys*, Marlboros, Premium saltines, and melted Borden's Golden Vanilla ice cream that we drank straight from the carton. Whole days bled away that way. They say when you bleed to death you feel cold and light and sick, and that's just how it felt when night folded around us and Pete's mom called him for dinner.

Sometimes Pete would disappear for a couple days and next time we saw him he'd be beat purple and he'd say he was going to murder his dad. What we didn't get was that Pete was bigger than his dad, could have taken him any day, but just let it go ahead.

"You know what's going to happen," I said one day when Pete's bedroom drapes had been closed for three days straight.

"What?" said Bobby.

"One day Pete's going to get mad and he's going to take his dad's rifle and he's going to shoot him in the back."

"You and your bullshit," said Bobby.

"I was wrong," I said. "It's not going to be Pete that goes, not right away. It'll be his old dad bleeding his Jesus blood all over Dead Daisy's lawn, and then they'll take Pete away and gas him at San Quentin."

"Pete wouldn't shoot anyone in the back," said Bobby.

Bobby never got to see what happened because one of those nights, after Pete had been called to his beef Stroganoff and the CBS Friday Night Movie had already started—it was *The Alamo*—Bobby got into his Rambler stuffed with smoke and graham crackers and drove straight into the eucalyptus tree on Noriega. The car smashed so hard it made the tree bleed, and they only knew it was Bobby from the plates.

Those days after what happened with Bobby, Pete stopped getting hit so much by his dad and Jeannie came by more. If I held Charlie she would make her special casserole and we all sat together, Charlie sucking the sauce off the chicken and trying to slap the wet meat into my mouth.

"I'm happy he's doing that to you, and not me," said my dad.

"It's a compliment," said Jeannie. "He's telling you he loves you."

"Your mom is lame," I said to Charlie. "But not as lame as your dad."

"Kip—" said my dad.

"Where is Billy, anyway?" I asked. "Saving lives?"

"One at a time," said Jeannie.

"He never comes here," I said.

"He works late, Kip. You know that." Jeannie leaned to spoon a heap of potato into Charlie's mouth.

"It doesn't matter anyway," I said.

Bobby had been knocking his heels in his custom wood casket nearly two weeks by the time second semester came around. The fact of his death felt far-off and magic, as if it didn't belong to us, like when we were juniors and Chad Burton disappeared hitchhiking on Highway One. They found him tied to a sycamore tree, bare-ass naked, and dead. We didn't know him, but we felt the electricity of his death, felt it crackling up and down the hallways of Liberty High. Now it was Bobby's turn. Except he was "Robert Nowak" now, and his name smudged the local paper and rose like smoke from the lips of cheerleaders. None of it seemed to have much to do with the pimple-pasted Bobby we knew.

"Who the fuck is Robert Nowak?" said Pete one morning recess, and this cracked me up.

"You're disgusting," said Linda Green.

"You're fucking disgusting," said Pete. If anybody else had cussed out Donnie Rawl's girl, he would have gotten slugged; but nobody took up with Pete—all the fear had already been beaten out of him, and it showed in his small gray eyes.

—

Death was no stranger to us. He'd visited our neighborhood a few times, making his big entrance and then hanging around, stinking up the place and wearing everybody down.

"Whole business is like make-believe, isn't it?" Uncle Paulie had said as he watched the Nowaks step into the black sedan bound for St. Anne of the Sunset. "But trust me. Soon the truth of this is going to kick you in the balls and it's going to hurt like a bitch."

For all Uncle Paulie's world-spun wisdom, on this he was wrong. Bobby didn't get dead to us all of a sudden, he got dead by degrees. Little facts flapped in the air and stuck to us like bugs till it was hard to think for the itching of them. The leaf-scuzzed square where he parked his Rambler, the spare glove at ball practice, the look on Mr. Nowak's face Monday mornings.

"I miss the goon," I said one afternoon as we sat smoking Pete's Marlboros, watching Mr. Nowak rake the leaves all slow and solemn.

"Yeah. Gotta say, though, he was kind of an asshole," said Pete.

"He was a mean motherfucker."

"He really fucked up that tree." Like I said, Pete was funny.

When I was a kid, my mom was into silver linings, and one cold clean dawn I saw the silver lining of this particular sky-bruiser. That shit-breath Devil that had been chasing us all summer, giving us the evil eye through Mrs. Fleish's hairy big roots—it was Bobby he wanted, and boy did he get him, ran him silly down those wet streets all the way till he smashed into that tree.

"You know what this means," I told Pete.

"You're going to tell me."

“That asshole ghost that’s been hiding under your house . . .”
“Big Chief Howling Wolf?”
“I’m serious. We thought you’d be next.”
“You did? Fuck you, man.”
“He got Bobby instead.” I clicked my tongue. “Maybe he thought it was you.”
Pete whistled.
“But we’re safe,” I said. “Bobby’s our lucky charm.”

By March, everybody had gotten to forgetting about Bobby; my dad took off drinking with his buddies, and Pete’s dad started cracking his belt again. Spring came scratching, pulling green snubs from the dirt and sending the songbirds into a fury, and Pete got restless. He was stealing again, pulling scrawny miracles from his bag—the Fran Gerard *Playboy*, a box of Dutch Masters, cheese packed in red wax. But bigger things were coming—I could see it in his face.

And one day he said it. “Let’s boost Ted’s.”

Ted’s was the liquor store on the corner of Thirty-Fifth and Rivera. It was a soul-rattling dump, with bottles of scotch pressing at the window like they wanted to escape. Old Ted was a cowboy without a horse, full of shout and powder but nowhere to take his fight. He stood on the sidewalk yelling at the kids, and they yelled right back, and this just made him madder. Ted packed a twenty-two behind the counter, told everybody all about it, swore he was going to blast the next asshole that looked at him the wrong way. All this wasn’t too good for business, and most days the store was shut-up dark, with the old rascal dumb drunk upstairs. Pete had cased the place and said it had potential.

“Problem is,” I said, “he’ll blow our asses off as soon as we set foot inside.”

“Old bastard’s so bombed he couldn’t find the trigger,” said Pete.

“You want to find out?”

“You a pussy now?”

“Fuck you, man.”

Pete lit his cigarette. “Come on—Old Ted’s long gone. Everybody knows he owes money. He got the hell out. Skipped town.”

It was true that we hadn’t seen Old Ted in months.

“He didn’t shut the store?”

“No time. Those loan sharks are nasty sons of bitches.”

“Right.”

“Old Ted’s as good as dead.” Pete grinned.

“I don’t know, man.”

“Remember Bobby,” added Pete. “We’re safe. Bobby’s got us protected.”

I thought about Bobby and knew that the last thing he wanted to do was protect anybody from anything.

“’Course,” continued Pete, “you don’t want to help, I’ll find somebody else.” He twisted his cigarette into the wall. “You know who’s got balls? Rosales.”

Carlos Rosales was the sort of kid who had to do everything first—whether it was grow a mustache or touch Tammy Smith’s tits—and I’d be damned if he’d be first to this too.

“If Old Ted’s gone, we can do it,” I said.

Pete grinned at me; his eyes were cold as dimes. “Tomorrow’s Sunday,” he said. “We’ll do it then. It’s simple.”

But nothing was simple with Pete.

The next day, while Pete’s dad was shouting up to God in church, Pete was in his kitchen preaching all he knew about the Five Finger Discount.

"Faith is everything," he said. "You've got to believe you can do it. Faith can move mountains. You let in doubt, it'll eat the ground from under you and swallow you whole. Three years I've been stealing," he said, and he looked at me with those gray eyes, "and I've never been caught."

If Bobby were here, he would have called Pete on his bullshit. Six months back, Pete got caught stealing Donnie Rawl's new football cleats from his locker; Mr. Marshall beat Pete so hard his face bruised all the colors of the rainbow.

"There are three rules to steal by," continued Pete. "Know what you want. Don't get greedy. And get the hell out."

"You're talking like I don't know all this already."

That afternoon we weeded the dirt in Mrs. Fleish's backyard and listened to the Giants game on the radio. It was a strange day: the sky was blank and the birds were quiet. There we were, working the earth, and it was honest and sound and silent. We were hauling redroot into Mrs. Fleish's garbage can when Donnie Rawl wheeled past on his bike, his jacket flapping.

"Afternoon, faggots," he cried.

"Climb it, Tarzan," said Pete, giving him the finger.

"Get a fucking car," I said.

Rawl turned and ran his bike straight at me, squeezing the brakes to bring his wheel to the edge of my boots.

"You better watch it, shrimp," he said.

I watched him speed up the street, his jacket lifting like a parachute behind him. One day, I decided, he was going to know about me, know what kind of man I was.

We waited till night was set, after Pete had eaten his chicken à la king and me and my dad had cleared out the refrigerator.

The houses were folded away in their drapes and nobody saw us walk across the street, heads bowed like a couple new-in-town cowboys, heels ringing on the deserted street. Nobody saw us crawl off in Mr. Marshall's Chevy, headlights dark, radio down low.

"Look under your seat," said Pete, and I felt beneath me to find a brick wrapped in a towel.

"Use it to break the window, then unhook the latch and go in."

"Why the towel?" I asked.

Pete ignored the question. "Go for the Maker's Mark. That's the good shit," he said. "And the Smirnoff. Chicks dig it."

I nodded and slipped a cigarette from my pocket, this being the sort of moment a man might take a smoke.

"If Old Ted shows up, we cut out. I'll gun the engine."

"You're not coming in?"

"Like you said, you've done this shit before," said Pete, and I thought on this. Pete grinned, like he knew that I knew he was calling bullshit on me; he enjoyed being an asshole. We drove in silence, and I smoked and squinted at the dark streets. As we turned onto Thirty-Fifth, I thumbed the dead cigarette out the window.

"Here we are," said Pete, shutting off the engine. The street was empty, save for an old lady rolling heave-ho drunk along the sidewalk. We looked over to Old Ted's, the sign hanging like a broken finger, bottles watching through the window.

Pete whistled. "This place is fucking creepy."

Fear scurried up my back; I peered at Old Ted's and saw something move behind the glass.

"He's in there, man," I said.

"Bullshit." Pete leaned across me; I felt his dead weight in my lap, his hair at my mouth.

I pushed him away. "Get the fuck off me." He settled back into his seat, a shit-eating smile pulling across his face.

"Nobody there," he said.

I watched the glass, but behind the bottles everything was dark, and the window above the shop had its blinds pulled shut. The drunk disappeared down Rivera.

"Do it," said Pete.

I hesitated, glanced at Pete; saw the steel in his eyes. It was going to happen. I opened the door all slow and casual, leaned to spit on the ground, then stood, letting the moment rest clean and heavy on me. I squeezed the brick.

"Get moving!" said Pete, and as I walked across the street, I heard him fire the engine.

I peered through the glass for a sign of Old Ted, a boot or a hat or a whisker. But it was just shadow and dust—the store had been empty awhile. I stood back and lifted the brick, catching my reflection in the glass, and it came to me all of a sudden that something nasty was going to happen. But the brick was flying and the glass was splashing and time started racing. I scratched my arm through the door and unhooked the latch, and was scrabbling at the bottles when I heard a bang and a shout:

"You're fucking dead, shitbird!"

Of course I got the hell out, the door hit me on the ass and I ran blind across the street. Pete was already driving like the getaway cat he was and I was wondering what kind of horse-jumping cowboy move I was going to have to pull to get myself into that car. Behind me Old Ted fired his gun and it put ten kinds of fear in me, made my legs run so hard they nearly came loose. But Pete was too fast and the getaway car was getting away and there was another bang and my heart was knocking and I was sure I was getting lined up to meet Bobby again. The sound of that siren was a relief.

They say you're not a man till you test yourself against the Law. Here I was throwing spitballs in jail, cuffed and crowded up with the smashed and the colored and the lawless, waiting for my dad to bail me out. He was so mad he couldn't speak; that ride home put more dread in me than Ted's Remington. He was silent for days after, all gray-skinned and dry-lipped like an alligator lizard, like any minute a tongue would fly out and sting me dead. Two weeks later, I was getting ready to go to the courthouse; he knocked on my door and handed me his baggy old funeral suit and the golden eagle necktie Aunt Ruth gave him for Christmas.

"Speak when you're spoken to. Let your top lip meet your bottom one for a change."

"Yes, sir."

"You be polite, you say you're sorry, you eat crow."

"Sir."

"Give me your shoes."

He took my oxfords and buffed them wet. Then he took the leather case that stood on the john, drew out his straight razor, and ran it along the leather band till it was sharp as a snake tooth. "Come here," he said. "Hold up your hand." He took hold of my thumb as gently as if it were a baby's and touched the blade against it. He eased it against the skin, and a bubble of blood cried up.

"Shit, Dad—" I took my hand back to suck the blood.

"It's sharp, so you got to go slow and smooth." He turned

to the sink and whipped the froth in his shaving bowl. "You think you're a big man, you go and shave like a man."

Mr. Harry Huffacker met us on the steps of the courthouse, pink head and brown suit shining in the sun, gripping his briefcase like it held a secret. "Okay, kid," he said, his eyes drifting over the top of my head. "We tell him about your background, we got a chance of getting off lightly."

"And the burglary charge?" asked my dad.

"Dropped if we plead guilty to vandalism."

My dad looked at his watch and tapped his foot.

"It's time," said Huffacker.

"Well, your sister's too late now," clacked my dad. He shook his head all long and sad, then turned to me and squeezed his arm around my shoulder. "It'll be all right," he said. "Just do what you're told."

The courtroom was brown and airless, like we'd stepped inside Huffacker's brain. Justice Choate sat, gray-cheeked and yawning, and below him, lifting and placing papers, a blimp-lady whose peepers blazed in the light so you couldn't see her eyes. Old men slow-talking and honking snot in their handkerchiefs—if it hadn't been for my dad's black eyes cramming into me, I might have been invisible. Sleep was buzzing on me when Justice Choate looked up all Droopy Dog and said, "You've had a hard time, son, but you've got to get your life straight." A thread of white slime pulled and sagged between his upper and lower lips as he spoke, like some rotten puppet master was hiding behind his teeth and working his mouth with string. "The order of this court is you finish high school or you join the military." The slime snapped; Choate licked his lips. "I need a decision by the end of the month." He hit his little hammer, my dad blew breath, and Huffacker bounced his head. As I shuffled out, razor-bitten and zoot-trou'd, Justice Choate frowned and picked something nasty from his earhole.

Outside, my dad clapped Huffacker's back and almost ran to his Chevrolet. He drove one-handed, the other hand hanging from the window holding a Marlboro, the wind digging up his hair. "You graduate, you can still get to college," he said, pulling hard on his cigarette. "You got lucky, Kip. No more bullshit."

I hadn't spoken to Pete since that night at Old Ted's, but I'll tell you what happened to him: his dad got wind of the whole business and smacked all the trouble and inspiration out of him. Pete kept his dad's belt tender for a week; I knew it because that whole time, all the drapes were drawn in Pete's house and nobody went in or out but Mr. Marshall, with a face full of release and shame, like he'd just shit his pants but it sure felt good. By the time another Monday pulled around with no sight of Pete at school, I started feeling sorry for the asshole.

The night after the trial, I found Pete at the playground on Forty-First and Ortega, lying on his belly at the top of the bleachers, crushing a cigarette into the stands. I stood over him and the wind tried to push me around and he looked up at me, and even in the dark I could see his face was fat with a beating.

"You bring anything with you?" he said, and his voice was squashed and faraway.

"I went to the courthouse today," I said. "Thanks to you."

"And wouldn't you know, you're still here." Pete sat up and scratch-shook his hair like it was full of bugs.

"You're an asshole," I told him.

"Yeah, fuck you too," said Pete; but he said it all beaten-down and limp, and as he shifted to push his hand in his pocket, his face ooh-aah flinched. This time, his dad had hit his left eye shut—the lid was red and crusted, like a Cherry Slice—and his lip was split from top to bottom.

"You okay, man?"

"Yeah." He pulled a pack of cigarettes from his pocket.

I took a seat beside him. "Judge was a freako," I said. Pete handed me a cigarette. "Kept looking at me like he was hungry, and licking his lips. I told him I wasn't sorry, told him he could stick his courthouse and his big words and his fucking little hammer."

"So how come he didn't throw your ass in jail?" He rattled the carton of matches.

"'Cause I got a dead mom." I struck a match; the wind sucked the flame right off. "How the fuck do you light this?"

"So that's it, you got off?" He took the cigarette, tunneled his hands on it, and passed it back, the tip glowing like an eye.

I sucked the smoke and all the noise inside me went still. "Judge said graduate high school or join up."

"The Army?"

"I guess."

Pete laughed. "Private fucking Jackson! Those Japs would shoot holes in you and use you for pussy."

"Fuck you, man. And it's the Vietnamese."

"Same thing." Pete danced his feet on the stand. "That's hilarious!"

I threw my cigarette into the wind. "Your dad got you good this time."

This settled him down. "Thinks I been hanging out with you too much," he said. "Won't believe I had nothing to do with Old Ted's."

"You're lucky you got away, you son of a bitch."

Pete pulled a big slack grin. "That's what getaway drivers do, brother."

The next day Jeannie came by holding Charlie and a banana cream pie.

"I'm so tired, I thought we could just eat this," she said.

"He doesn't look all that delicious," said my dad, creeping his fingers under Charlie's chin. Charlie laugh-cried and dived into Jeannie's shoulder.

"How are you doing, Kip?" asked Jeannie, setting Charlie down; he squeezeboxed to the ground and screamed.

"We expected you there yesterday," said my dad, looking at her with his slow reptile eyes.

"I had to see the doctor," said Jeannie, and padded into the kitchen. I could tell this was bullshit, and my dad could too. He smacked his tongue in his mouth and sneaked a taffy from his pocket. "Here," he whispered. Charlie cut the yelling, gave a crafty look, and let my dad peel him off the floor. I went after Jeannie. "Anybody ever think about shopping for groceries?" she wondered aloud, pulling her head from the refrigerator. She saw me watching her and put her hand on my shoulder. "I'm glad it worked out, Kip," she said.

After the pie, my dad set about scrubbing the place and Charlie got wild, throwing everything he could get his claws on.

"He's getting stir-crazy all cooped up in here," said Jeannie, catching him in her arms. He wrestled like a caught skunk.

"So take him out," said my dad. He had that look about him, that all-of-a-sudden saggy look, like someone had snuck up and unzipped him at the back. Next thing it would be the

Frankie Laine records and the long, bone-shaking sighs that rolled all the way up from his feet and blew all the daylight out of the room.

"I'll come with you," I said.

We took Charlie to the playground near the beach, the one where Bobby broke his leg playing kickball and Debra Davis once hawked Frenchies for a nickel. The place had shrunk, and all those snot-nosed kids that came after us had stamped all the grass out of the ground. A couple middle schoolers looped their Schwinns like they owned the place. Jeannie dragged Charlie out of his stroller and he staggered toward the slide like a drunk to a bar.

"Here we are." Jeannie plunked Charlie at the top of the slide and down he came. "Again," he cried. A dozen slides in and I started to think that we might just be stuck there till the world stopped turning.

"Damn, this is boring."

Jeannie slid me a look. "You doing all right, Kip?"

"I guess."

Charlie headed for the tire swing.

"How's Daddy doing?"

"Still mad as hell."

"He's just worried about you. You better stay out of trouble and graduate."

There it was again, the story that I would settle down all nice and good and do my homework and get my diploma; that I would sit down every night for the next four hundred nights to a TV dinner in our dark-funk living room, just me and my sad old dad, watching happy families on TV, hoping-please-God that one day somebody would throw me a job loading boats in Oakland, so I could scratch some dollars and buy an apartment and fill it with some sick-hearted bullshit of my own.

"Judge said I could join the military instead," I said.

"Mmmm?" Jeannie balanced Charlie on the swing; he heel-drummed the rubber.

I wanted to make her look my way, make her fucking see me. "I was thinking I might join up."

This got her. "You don't want to finish high school?" She moved her green eyes over me, and I thought on it, thought on the Spam stink of the homeroom and the sophomores whispering at their lockers, the sticky hallways and the fucking cafeteria. "The country needs men like me," I told her.

Jeannie turned her head to cough and when she looked back, she had that smile-squashing face that used to get her in trouble with Mom. An all-grown, rich-living doctor's wife now, but she could still be a real bitch sometimes, still treated me like I was some thirteen-year-old shrimp with a cracked voice and a pathetic comic-book habit.

"You can be real fucking stuck-up, you know that?" I told her.

She frowned. "You're serious? About joining up?"

I shrugged.

"Fast!" yelled Charlie.

Jeannie gripped Charlie's waist as she swung him; he pinched at her hands. "What does Daddy say?"

"Haven't talked to him about it."

Jeannie screwed up her eyes like I was standing all the way at the back of California; like she was really seeing me. Then she blinked, and the connection was lost. "I don't know," she said. She sighed. "Charlie, stop wriggling."

I wanted her back. "You heard about that kid from Lincoln High?" I said. "Got blown to pieces. They just sent his foot back in a casket."

But she was watching Charlie, who was bitching and squirming in her hands. "I've got to hold on to you, Charlie." Something flew across her face—frustration or weariness or who-the-hell-knows—and then vanished, her expression smooth as a stone again. When I was a kid, I was real good at seeing those wisps that rose up from that great big fire inside her. I used to call them her smoke signals. "It's a big decision," she said, all flat and quiet.

"Let go!" yelled Charlie, and Jeannie paused and moved her hands away. But the dumb kid was still kicking and raging and managed to boot himself right off the tire, headfirst into the grit. His face spilled into a scream that wouldn't come. "Shit," said Jeannie.

And then it came, yanking a dozen heads our way. Jeannie took him and shushed and bounced. Spots of blood steamed through the back of his shirt and his hair was flicked with stones.

I lifted his shirt. A graze skimmed the white meat of his back. "He's all right," I told her.

Jeannie stroked his hair till he was quiet again, then blew a raspberry into his neck to force a smile. She lowered Charlie back into his stroller, letting her hair fall over her face like she was ashamed. She slipped a piece of candy into his mouth and frowned. "You're grown now, Kip," she said, all uptight. "I can't do everything for you anymore."

This pissed me off, and I took off to the beach, hoping and unhoping I'd find Pete there, watching girls. But it was just more stupid moms and kids, and seagulls creeping over the sand. When I got back home, the place felt empty—Jeannie and Charlie had gone. I went to my room and lay down, listening to the ocean breathing its spit, and the crickets rubbing their legs, and my dad's radio crackling news. I must have dropped dead asleep because next thing I knew I was drool-soaked and rotten-breathed and the sun had gone.

And there it was again—a scuff and a scratch and something that sure as hell sounded like crying.

When I was a kid, Uncle Paulie would come by every Sunday night and get happy on his rotgut hooch and do my dad's confessing for him. Dark salty yarns about my dad's wartime days: how a sneeze dodged his head from a mortar shell; platoons disappearing in smoke-bursts; dead blanketed Marines covering the ground like pinecones. A place that stank of farts, where the ash got into your skin-creases and made you look a thousand years old. My dad would sit in the easy chair, belly slopping over his pants like he'd swallowed up all his secrets and it had made him fat. He wouldn't say a word, just sat and drank and let that slow straight-line smile run across his face all the way till it spilled into a scowl and he told Uncle Paulie it was time for him to leave.

But that was before everything that happened.

The back door was open; I tipped my head out, but there was nobody. I was sliding the door closed when I saw a trail of smoke. There was my dad, sneaked up against the wall, holding on to himself like if he let go he might clean unravel. His grungy old bathrobe swamped off him and his hair was all frazzled up like he was wearing a question mark on his head. I ducked my head, but it was too late.

"Kip," he said, and his voice was all dusty.

"I'm going to bed," I told him.

But he was moving closer, arms wide like Jesus at the feast.

"Kip." I thought about sliding that door shut and leaving him there to preach at his own reflection. "Come outside." His eyes bulged red.

I stepped out and then he was trying to fucking hug me, dragging me into his stink of skin and breath, and all I could think of was the last time he did this, which was when they put my mom into the ground.

"I'm glad you're all right," he said, clamping my shoulders. He still had some kind of Devil-strength in his fingers.

"I'm okay, Dad. Just tired."

"You got your whole life waiting for you."

"Right."

"I always wanted to go to college."

"So why didn't you?"

He tightened his grip on my shoulders, then released me. "I came home from the war, and I had a family to take care of." He dropped his head like something had run over his foot; a frog-croak leaped out of his mouth, and I saw that he was crying. He looked into my face, snot and spit webbing his mouth. "Mommy always wanted you to get a college education."

Mommy? I was waiting for him to hear it himself, but he just made that strange froggy noise again and his shoulders jumped. Whatever was holding me to the ground came loose and I felt myself fly up like a balloon.

"Your mommy was so proud of you." The voice was somewhere else, like a TV movie with the sound turned low. But that word again, I couldn't help it—I couldn't tame the smile that roared over my face.

"Come here," my dad said, bringing his arms around me, and I stepped back, and something naked peeked out of him, then disappeared.

"Something funny?" he said. He smudged his words and I realized he was snockered.

"You're pathetic," I told him. I saw the words lift out of my mouth in a speech bubble like I was Charlie fucking Brown.

The old man blinked.

"What did you say?"

"You're pathetic," I repeated, nice and loud.

My dad came close; I could see the hairs wriggling from his nose. "Say that one more time," he said.

"You heard it," I told him, and stepped back inside the house.

"Get the hell out of here," he said, standing all blaze-eyed with his legs wide, like Tuco in *The Good, the Bad, and the Ugly*. "Before I beat you sorry." His hands went to his waist but stopped at his flannel belt.

I felt a laugh snort up from my throat; next thing I knew my dad was inside with me, his hand on my neck.

"You're going to hurt me now?" I said, but his hand was shrinking the words. "Been taking tips from Mr. Marshall?"

He squeezed, spit leaking from his teeth. "You get out, you hear me?" He let go.

I pushed him away. He staggered and danced to find his balance. "Don't worry," I told him. "I'm gone."

A kitchen chair blocked me; I took it and threw it. A leg cracked on the wall and I looked for my dad's face. He was slow-watching me, his eyes all dark and doomy, his fingers twitching like he was going to draw.

"Fuck you. Fuck high school and college and fuck this place." Energy was shooting through me like a firework; I kicked the kitchen counter, but it didn't leave a nick, just struck my foot dead.

"Stupid kid," my dad said in his bourbon-blasted, slow-fast way. I turned and his expression was loose and open and I saw all the way into him and it came to me how I was going to win this one.

"I'm gonna enlist tomorrow. And I'm gonna get the fuck out of here."

There they were, those words popping out of me, and it was decided, there was no unsaying it; and I'll tell you something, it slapped the old guy sober. I slammed the door behind me, and the fog wet my face; and I felt it again—that nasty, damp-eyed Devil, watching me from the bushes.

When I came home it was past midnight, and the air was stuffed with swelter. The door was unlatched and the drapes and windows were open, like the house was trying to breathe. No sound; but if you were sharp, you could catch the white noise roar of the Pacific Ocean. I was sneaking a look to see if that pie was waiting for me when I saw him perched like a bat on the kitchen counter. Nearly scared the shit out of me.

"You're back," he said.

"Looks like it." I pulled the pie from the refrigerator and found a spoon.

"You don't want a plate?"

I scooped straight at the pie, letting chunks of cream splat the floor. A car drove past the windows, and its headlights lit us up.

"I'm sorry, son."

"It doesn't matter." I dropped the pie-scabbed container in the trash.

"You're not going to do anything crazy."

"I'm going to bed."

"Wait." He took my wrist in his skinny-strong hand. The smell of stale liquor floated from his mouth. "You sign up, they'll send you to war."

"I'm not stupid."

"You don't know what it means, Kip." He was gripping a rolled-up newspaper in his other hand; he shook it out with a crack. "The Marines just took one hundred fifty casualties on some rinky-dink hill in Vietnam. One hundred and fifty dead boys, kids just like you and Pete and Bobby coming home in caskets."

"Bobby's already in a casket."

My dad flinched like he'd been bit by a no-see-um. "This is a nasty war, Kip, and we're fighting for I-don't-know-what and we ain't winning. I'm not giving you up for that."

"You old-timers don't want any other heroes kicking up your parade."

He smiled all hard and heavy. "I was eighteen when I shipped out, and out of the entire company, you know how many came back? How many weren't killed or crippled?"

That gray old roar again hurling in from the ocean.

"Forty-two. Out of one hundred and ten Marines." His hands were on my shoulders now, still as spiders. "I wasn't a hero. I was just darn lucky."

"I never thought you were a fucking hero," I said.

We watched each other. I waited for him to say something. He screwed up his eyes like he was trying to bring me into focus, the way Jeannie did in the park—as though, somehow, I'd gotten all of a sudden smudged and blurred. He sighed and slid from the counter, the newspaper hanging limp in his hand.

"All right, Kip," he said. "Have it your way."

———

The next morning I went to the kitchen, dressed in my good shirt and clean-ish jeans. My dad sat at the table holding his Snoopy coffee cup, looking flimsy and uneven, veins exploding red in the whites of his eyes.

"I'm going to the recruitment center," I said.

He didn't say anything, just shook his head and grim-smiled, snuffing a noise like I'd told a bad-tasting joke. I grabbed my jacket and left the house, leaving the front door wide open behind me, letting the wind blow sand over his swept floors.

I walked twelve blocks to the recruitment center, a big blank building squatting on an intersection, flags stuck on the roof giving the air big noisy licks. The waiting room was rattling with a few whacked-up loons and goons jiggling their legs and chewing gum—I might have been straight back in that jail cell. The guy at the desk wore a green uniform and a pissed-off face, and between scratching his paperwork and hollering names, he fired bad looks at the black kid sitting by the door. I left my name and waited.

"Kipling Jackson."

The recruiter was eight feet tall, with a head like a football and a handshake that could bend steel. "Welcome to the Corps!" he shouted, smacking me on the back. "Take a seat, son."

He asked me every kind of question, how old I was, where I was at school, how tall, was I sick or crippled, was I a citizen, was I a faggot, a felon, or a commie. He got deep into the Old Ted business, turned it over to eye all sides of it, then smiled and shook his head, "Dumb kid." He sent me to stand on the scale and ran his finger over the chart. He frowned a moment before slapping his hands together. "All right, son," he cried, showing his tombstone teeth. "Hand me your paperwork."

"I don't have any."

"Birth certificate, court papers. And you'll need a parent to sign here." He flicked over some papers and penned a sloppy *X*. "Come back tomorrow." He leaned over and breathed coffee-breath over my face. "We'll get you processed—a physical and so forth—and you'll be on your way."

That night my dad came home from work, set down his briefcase, took off his brogues, and sloshed himself an Old Crow on ice. He sat at the kitchen table, twitching his brown-socked feet and hovering his pen over his newspaper crossword puzzle. Thursdays were always hard on him, but a half hour passed and that pen didn't make one stroke. I took my papers and slid them slow and deliberate across the table. My dad laid down his pen and stared at me long and steady, like he was about to tell me the Great Awful Truth of Things. Then he took up the papers and read each line ever-so-slow, his head moving along each one like the caboose on a typewriter. He rolled his pen in his fingers, then lifted it and pressed the ink to the paper. He signed in three loop-and-scrawls and handed back the papers, looking me clean in the eye.

"Thanks," I said, but my throat had gone tight.

In the window, something dark moved, and it had the dank eyes of that hide-and-seek Devil.

"Son," said my dad, and the word came out all scratched and spoiled.

As I left the room, I turned to see him holding his tumbler, staring at the table. I heard that glass-skitter sound and thought it was another baby earthquake starting up; but it was just the sound of the ice in my old dad's drink, rattling.

In Country

Jeannie / 1967

"Gone."

Charlie's eyes were wide, his fat fingers making a starfish.

"Gone, Mama."

"Just a dream, sweetheart," said Jeannie, lifting him from his crib, feeling the weight and the warmth of him. His hair was stuck damp with sleep, his cheeks flushed. Sunlight had slunk in beneath the drapes and lay waiting. Dawn again, falling on them all of a sudden, and with it all those hours to work and fool away. She set Charlie on a towel in the bathroom, kissed his belly and unfastened his diaper. His head turned at the creak of feet on wood.

"Daddy," he said.

"Daddy's at the hospital." It was Eddie upstairs, or maybe Lloyd, fixing coffee or setting the table for breakfast.

Jeannie knew the tricks time played on mothers: the enchanted hours that wouldn't pass, each solid minute needing picking up, dealing with, and putting away, one by one, until you were sore with the labor; then whole weeks falling away, like a ladder pulled from your heels. Jeannie had rationed a clutch of errands for the day, and with dropping Billy's shirts at the dry cleaner's, picking up soup and Pop-Tarts from Safeway, and looking at the donuts in the window of the bakery on Church, soon enough it would be naptime and they could close their eyes, and then it would be three o'clock and they'd have to think about getting uptown for Dorothy's fund-raiser.

Dorothy was president of the San Francisco Republican Women's Committee (Federated), the leader of a company of women who wore their hair like armor and dispensed smiles like bullets. She was raising money to elect somebody called

Rafferty to the Senate, and she'd made it clear that attendance at her fund-raiser was mandatory.

"Where's William?" she asked when Jeannie and Charlie arrived at the mansion on Spruce on the nose of six.

"Caught up at the hospital," said Jeannie, watching their cab disappear down the street. "He'll be here as soon as he can."

Dorothy opened her mouth and chewed it shut. "Well," she said. Charlie was at Dorothy's legs, his hands bunching her silk dress, his head tipped up, face split in a grin. Dorothy pushed her hand through his hair, palmed his chin, and bent—a slight catch in the movement the only tell of her age—to meet him face-to-face. "Let's go find something in the kitchen for you," she said.

The house was full of traffic: Mexican women floating trays of zucchini and glazed ribs to the white tent pinned to the lawn outside; a sweat-glossed colored man carrying a crate of oranges into the kitchen; two girls Jeannie's age dressed like matrons and whispering over clipboards. Jeannie could tell that her mother-in-law was excited—all the touches and squeezes Dorothy usually saved for her son and grandson spilled over to her: the trail of fingers on her shoulder, the press of a palm on her back.

"We're expecting somebody special tonight," Dorothy whispered, and something thrilling moved across her face—something like youth.

Jeannie settled Charlie to sleep in one of the guest rooms and took her time fixing her hair. It was a warm fall evening, and the guests were crowding on the lawn, the Pacific breeze lifting the clink of glassware out to the ocean. Across the dark stretch of the Presidio, the Golden Gate Bridge reached across to the headlands in strings of lights. Jeannie wandered the edges of the party looking for Billy, but he was nowhere. Accepting a cocktail from a passing tray, she found a bench under an oak tree, sat, and watched.

"So you're the slut."

The voice came from above; Jeannie looked up at the windows of the house, but they were fastened dark.

"A slut or a gold digger, they can't decide."

A shake-and-flop noise, like a book falling to the floor, was followed by a confetti of leaves. A girl was standing in the crook of a thick branch, legs apart, one bare foot steadying against the point where the branch thinned and bent like a bow.

"Are you talking to me?" said Jeannie.

The girl brought her feet together, curving the branch almost to a crack, and jumped to the ground. She looked Jeannie's age, maybe a little younger: stalky-limbed, with damp, dark hair that lay on her shoulders in waves. She wore an unfashionable rosebud-print dress; the fit was bad and it slipped off her shoulder, showing skin tanned the color of root beer.

"I was expecting more of a Lana Turner type," said the girl, pulling a pair of stilettos from the base of the tree and pushing them onto her feet. "But you seem pretty normal." She sat on the bench. "I'm Lee." She turned to Jeannie, her face surprisingly close. She was smiling, the kind of free smile seen in photographs of children: wide-cheeked, beautiful-ugly.

Jeannie shifted away. "I'm Jeannie."

"You got a cigarette, Jeannie?"

Jeannie nipped open her clutch, handed the girl her cigarettes and pocket lighter, and waited.

Lee slipped out a cigarette and held it, unlit, in her hand.

"Look at that," she said, nodding toward Jeannie's father-in-law, whose hand was sliding over the buttocks of a heavyset young woman he was guiding to greet his wife. "Richard hasn't even finished his cocktail and his dirty old fingers are already itching."

Jeannie smiled in spite of herself.

"You too, huh?" said Lee, lighting her cigarette and blowing smoke up into the browning leaves. "Why do you think I was hiding up in that tree?" She laughed, and the sound crackled across the lawn. Dorothy's head jerked in their direction, and she stared. Lee saw the look in Jeannie's face and passed her the cigarettes and lighter; Jeannie snapped them back in her purse and stood; and Dorothy turned back to her guests.

"I better find my husband," said Jeannie.

"There's a snake in the garden," called Lee, smoke in her voice. "Watch out."

Dark fell over the party like mud. A sting in the air sent the guests back inside, pulling their stoles close and setting their glasses on the furniture. In what Dorothy called the drawing room (the only one Jeannie had ever seen—really a large living room), a four-piece band played an old Bing Crosby song. Jeannie had drunk her third sloe gin fizz and had managed to avoid speaking to anybody beyond the odd "Excuse me." Billy was still missing. Jeannie watched as Richard Nixon arrived to shake the candidate's hand, before ducking back into his black Cadillac and slipping into the night. His arrival and departure loosened and lulled the party; and Jeannie crept away, liquor-legged, up the stairs to check on Charlie. As she stepped along the hallway, she heard the squashed sound of Charlie's voice, the murmur of an adult.

"More story," she heard Charlie say.

"I don't have any more," said the low voice. "I'll have to go out into the world and bring some back for you."

On the bed, legs crossed, holding a cigarette over an empty glass, sat Lee. Charlie was sitting up, his eyes wide in the half darkness. There was something guilty in the slow way they turned their heads to look at Jeannie.

"What are you doing?" said Jeannie.

"Mama."

"Kid had a bad dream," said Lee, tapping her cigarette against the glass. "Found him wandering around, all torn up."

"Mama, come in bed," said Charlie. His face was soft with sleep.

"He looks all right to me," said Jeannie. She sat on the bed, and delight flashed across Charlie's face. She shucked him onto her lap. "You had a nightmare, honey?"

"Story," he said, nudging his head against her.

"No more stories," said Jeannie, leveling a look at Lee, who was grinding her cigarette into the glass, a smile curling up her face.

"Find your husband?" Lee's eyes glittered.

Jeannie heard the reproach in the girl's question. "You can go," she said. "I'm just going to settle Charlie."

"I'll stay," said Lee. The same challenge in her voice, but the girl's face was gentle in the dusk, and Jeannie, easy from liquor and weary from avoiding everybody else, had no desire to argue.

"What are you doing here?" she asked. "You're a little out of place."

"People always tell me that." Lee blinked lazily, and Jeannie wondered if she was drunk too. "Dorothy's my godmother," she said. She folded her legs underneath her, her dress catching on her foot, showing a long bare thigh. "I'll tell you a secret," she whispered.

Charlie sighed.

"What?" said Jeannie.

"Dorothy used to be—" Lee put her mouth to Jeannie's ear. Jeannie heard Lee's breath, close and secluded, like the sound of the ocean in a seashell. Then the whisper, hot on Jeannie's skin. "A swinger."

Jeannie snorted with laughter; Charlie moaned and shifted in her lap.

"You're full of it," whispered Jeannie.

"It's true." Lee's eyebrows drew high on her forehead. "How else do you think she bagged Raunchy Rich?"

Charlie's lips smacked against his tongue and his head sagged.

"She was also beautiful," conceded Lee.

Jeannie smiled, and felt the weight of Charlie's body in her arms. She lowered him onto the bed. He was asleep, and they should get back to the party, where, maybe, Billy was looking for her. In the shadow of the bedroom, on the give of the bed, the liquor felt warm in her blood, and she closed her eyes for a moment to still herself. She felt a lock of her hair fall against her forehead, then quiet fingers on her face, lifting it away.

"Let me take care of that for you." There was Lee, leaning into her, her eyes firm on Jeannie's, her own hair swinging in dark waves, a smile rounding her face. Charlie lay calm, his body rising with slow breaths. Something hot and shivery, like a fever, prickled the back of Jeannie's neck. Lee moved closer, and her fingers went to Jeannie's face again, but there was no stray hair to fix. Jeannie's breath roughened; the feather of a question.

Lee's hand trailed over Jeannie's cheek and dropped down over Jeannie's breast, resting at her waist.

A shiver of needles, a rush of heat, and Lee leaned in and pressed her lips against Jeannie's mouth, her tongue opening Jeannie's lips, her heart scooping beats in her chest, the warm wetness of her kiss, her hand on the nape of her neck, hair like lace in her fingertips. A shudder of breath, maybe from Jeannie or Lee or the child sleeping beside them; and a feeling—a feeling of falling.

Jeannie woke before light touched the windows—dry-mouthed, a sticky fear crawling over her. It took a moment to locate herself: in her bed, Billy breathing beside her, a stillness down the hallway in Charlie's room. And then it flickered together in a noisy rush of pictures, like the riffle of a cut deck of cards. The long kiss (a greasy bubble of shame in her stomach); Lee's eyes opening at the crack of floorboards; Jeannie standing in time to see Billy checking the guest rooms along the hallway; Lee strolling out of the bedroom moments later, smiling and saying hello; and then they were back in the party, Jeannie trying to steady the totter in her heart as Billy shook hands and pecked cheeks, asked after sick mothers and grown children, until finally it was over, and Billy lifted Charlie from his bed and placed him on the backseat of the car for the woozy drive home. Long giddy hours watching the window for dawn, the groove of Lee's fingers still on her skin, until the night thinned, and sleep fell like an ax.

Jeannie turned from Billy, the dumb weight of a headache sliding from one side of her head to the other. Guilt picked at her, like it might unpeel her.

"What happened?" Billy sat and threw off the bedspread; it dragged her nightgown up over her waist.

“What?” Jeannie clutched her gown and sat.

Billy snatched up the alarm clock.

“Damn thing’s broken,” he said. “I’m late.” He pushed a sweaty kiss on her forehead. “Got to go.”

The next few days brought rain and resentment. Charlie kicked and screamed his boredom away before falling into a sulk that not even a visit from the bread man could shift. Jeannie trained her mind on her labors to tune out the memory of Lee. But eventually the work of the day stopped—Charlie put to bed, the laundry and the pans and the trash put away—and Jeannie was defenseless. Lying empty on the couch, she let the memory play, with all its charm and horror; and at the drop of Lee’s fingers, she closed her eyes and felt her face fill with shame, her heart welter with something excruciating, like hope. Each time she returned to the memory it was a little more worn with use—a loss of sharpness in the image, a blurring of the sequence—until after a while it had the muddiness of a dream, and Jeannie found it hard to connect to the electric charge, the disgrace of the fact that the girl in the picture was her. She wondered about Lee, wondered if she lived in Lee’s thoughts the way Lee lived in hers; and it almost felt possible that if she imagined Lee enough, she might witch her into the flesh—a chance meeting on the street, a strange knock at the door. But weeks passed, and the rain cleared and the fog lifted off the hills, and if desire was like waiting, Jeannie had given up that anything was coming.

One Friday evening more than a month after Dorothy’s fundraiser, Billy and Jeannie were sitting down to a dinner of veal casserole with lima beans when the telephone rang. Billy looked up from his newspaper, wiped his mouth on his wrist, and went to answer it, pausing to push his sleeves up his arms.

"Dr. Harper speaking." He stood, legs wide, his knees slightly bent, ready to drop the receiver and sprint to the hospital.

A pause, and Billy straightened.

"Who is this?" He eyed Jeannie.

What? she mouthed.

"All right," said Billy, a note of disappointment in his voice. Jeannie's anxiety slowed to curiosity. "Who?" she said, but Billy just shrugged, handed her the receiver, and returned to his dinner.

"Hello?"

"Is that Jeannie?"

"Who is this?" Jeannie watched Billy push his face close to his *Chronicle* and shovel beans into his mouth like he hadn't eaten in days.

"It's Lee," said the voice. "Lee. From the party."

Jeannie's heart swallowed a beat. She turned her back to Billy.

"Hello?" said Lee.

The dip-and-drum of Jeannie's heart grew unsteadier. "What is it?" she said, tightening her voice to stop it from giving her away.

There was a pause at the other end of the line. Jeannie wondered if she'd lost her. "Hello?"

"I'm in trouble," said Lee.

"What do you mean?"

Jeannie heard a tapping noise in the background, the murmur of talking.

"I'm at a police station in Oakland—"

"What?"

"—And I need you to come get me."

"What?"

Lee cleared her throat. "I'll explain when you get here."

Jeannie heard the flapping sound of Billy closing his newspaper and lowered her voice. "I can't just—"

"Please." Lee's voice was small with fear. "I can't call anybody else."

Jeannie tried to tug her thoughts together, but they floated away like balloons in the wind.

"It's bad." Lee breathed into the receiver; and it was as though she were right there, her mouth on Jeannie's ear. Jeannie hesitated.

"You're coming?" said Lee.

Jeannie glanced at Billy, who was looking at her with questions stamped over his face, gravy flecking his collar.

"What happened?" asked Jeannie; and she heard the stiffness in her voice, but her mind was making itself up.

"I can't talk right now." The hum of talk in the background rose to yelling. "If you won't do it, I got to go—"

"Don't hang up," said Jeannie. "Where exactly are you?"

"It's just off the freeway, near Jack London Square," said Lee.

"Okay," said Jeannie. Anticipation balled in her stomach. "Okay. I'll do it."

"One more thing."

"What is it?" asked Jeannie.

"I told them you're my cousin."

Jeannie heard the dial tone but kept the receiver to her ear as she assembled a face, and a lie, for Billy.

"I'll see you there. Good-bye," she said, hearing her voice outside the telephone and in the room. She set down the receiver.

"What was that about?" said Billy, sweeping the last slicks of gravy with his forefinger.

"It was Nancy." Billy assumed the doomy expression he always did at Nancy's name; her affair with the head of his department was the talk of the hospital.

"Why didn't she tell me it was her?" Billy frowned. "What's the problem?"

"She thinks she might be pregnant."

Billy looked like he'd been smacked on the nose. He stood and dropped his cutlery onto his empty plate. "This is all I need," he said, his ears glowing red. "As if she hasn't caused enough gossip already."

"She's upset," said Jeannie, talking fast to deliver the lie and see if it was strong enough to stand. "Professor Fairchild threw her out and she can't get home."

"Has she thought about a cab?" said Billy, with uncharacteristic sarcasm.

"Please," said Jeannie. "She needs a friend." She reached for his shoulders and stroked the length of his arms, weaving her fingers into his, feeling a pinch of guilt at the surprise and pleasure that showed in his face. She tiptoed to kiss him on the mouth. "Let me help her out," she said. "She's like a sister."

"Some sister," said Billy, squeezing her hands and letting go. "She only shows up when she needs something. Doesn't stop to think about how you're doing."

Jeannie thought of Kip, and felt uneasy.

"I'll go," said Billy, his shoulders hunching like he'd hauled a load onto his back. He took his keys from the counter. "It's late."

"You want your boss to see you picking up his pregnant girlfriend?" said Jeannie.

Billy paused.

"I'll take a cab," she said, easing the keys from his hand. "I might be late. If you need to go in, Cynthia can watch Charlie."

Before he could answer, Jeannie hurried to their bedroom to retrieve her sweater and purse, stopping to pull her mom's vanity case from the top of her dresser and remove four five-dollar bills.

"'Bye," she called as she opened the front door, not turning to look at Billy's face.

The night was fresh with rain. As she stepped down to the sidewalk, Jeannie felt a loose, empty feeling, and wondered if it was freedom.

"You're just in time to miss all the trouble," said the cabdriver as they crossed over the Bay Bridge, mist smudging the lights of Treasure Island.

"What trouble?" asked Jeannie.

He flicked a hard look at the mirror. "You been living under a rock?" He shook his head. Jeannie had never been to Oakland before; and the looks the driver was giving her through the rearview mirror confirmed it wasn't the smartest place for her to visit. She looked out the window at the lights of the ships bulking the water, the vacant lots fronting the highway, and let her mind fall blank. Then there was a thickening of buildings, a clot of traffic, and they pulled up with a jerk outside the police station.

"Can you wait?" said Jeannie.

The driver tipped his chin in both a "Yes" and a "Fuck you."

Jeannie pushed through the door. The waiting area was crowded and noisy, with what Jeannie assumed to be students sitting among placards and banners. Three cops with loose-strapped white helmets leaned against the wall, watching them. In the corner, a guy Billy's age (whose stringy arms and facial hair were reminiscent of an ape's) thumped his fingers against a typewriter balanced clumsily on his lap. Billy had talked about Berkeley students making trouble; and now Jeannie had the pieces of the puzzle: Lee had gotten caught up in a protest with her classmates, and needed a ride home. But why Lee had called *her*—Jeannie returned to this question with anticipation and discomfort, like pushing her tongue against a loose tooth. She walked to the desk, steadying her breathing, and waited for the officer to get off the telephone.

"I'm here to get Lee—" Jeannie realized she didn't know Lee's last name.

"You're the cousin, right?" The officer reared up, thrusting his belly and rubbing his lower back.

"Right." Jeannie spoke quietly, to make the lie small.

"It's always the same. Kid gets in trouble, parents are no place to be found. Where the hell are they?"

The truth came at Jeannie slowly and surely, like a train making its way along a track. Jeannie tasted blood in her mouth and swallowed. Lee was a kid. Lee—in the half dark, smooth-limbed and soft-mouthed—a child. Lee was a kid who needed an adult to fetch her out of trouble; and who, scared of a scolding from her mother, had picked the nearest grown person she had something on and called Jeannie.

"Lost your tongue on the way over? Jesus." The officer shook his head like he was already trying to forget their conversation. "Wait here a minute."

Jeannie craned her head; the cab was still outside, its windows steamed. She thought of leaving; imagined the smell of stewed meat in the kitchen and Billy's questions, and hesitated. And it was too late—a familiar murmur, and there she was, slighter than Jeannie remembered, wearing a white scarf and an outsized black jacket, bare-legged, as though she might be naked underneath. Her knees were scabbed and her ankle boots gaped at her calves; she looked as small and clumsy as a middle schooler. She saw Jeannie and her face snapped into the smart smile Jeannie recognized from the party; only this time her cheeks were unrounded.

"You didn't bring Charlie?"

"Of course not." Jeannie looked around; the man with the typewriter had paused over the keys to stare at them from across the room. "What the hell is going on?"

"I've got a story for him." Lee hooked her arm into Jeannie's; Jeannie slipped her arm away.

"Hey, kid." The desk officer banged the table and waved them over. "You're not done." He knocked a finger against an open ledger. "Sign here, lady."

Jeannie bent to make an unreadable scrawl. The officer looked it over; and all Jeannie could hear was blood hammering in her ears. Finally, leisurely, he signed next to her name and closed the ledger. He leaned on his forearms, his face crunched in a frown, his eyes shining, like he was going to enjoy this.

"You're not in San Francisco anymore," he told Lee.

Jeannie stared at the floor and counted till she could get out of there. *One thousand, two thousand, three thousand . . .*

"You're in Oakland now; and you bring your bullshit here, you're going to get hurt. You're damn lucky I didn't throw you in jail for the night." His voice rose, and Jeannie suspected that Lee wasn't looking sorry enough. She glanced up; the officer was firing eye-bullets (Kip's phrase) into Lee. "I got enough shit to deal with," said the officer, throwing his head toward the sound of the typewriter knocking in the corner, "without spoiled kids like you running out here to get your kicks."

"Yes, sir."

"And you." He bucked his head at Jeannie. "Tell those folks of hers to do their damn job. Next time she'll get a rap sheet."

The telephone rang. "All right, out of here," he muttered. He sat back in his chair and picked up the receiver, watching them as they turned to leave. As Jeannie pushed open the door, one of the cops leaning against the wall lurched at them and growled like a dog. Jeannie quick-stepped outside, the door closing on laughter behind them. She slid into the cab, Lee behind her.

"Back to the city," Jeannie called, ignoring the driver's look of naked hostility.

They sat quietly for a minute before Lee placed a warm hand on Jeannie's wrist. "You're mad at me," she said.

Jeannie removed her arm and looked out of the window. The headlights of passing cars blurred in the tears that were, babyishly, skinning her eyes. The freedom she'd felt leaving her home earlier that night had turned into something cold, exposing. Jeannie waited until they were on the bridge and her eyes had dried before turning to Lee in accusation; but instead of looking sorry, Lee was watching the approach of the city, her face calm and curious.

"How old are you?" asked Jeannie.

Lee looked surprised. "Does it matter?"

"Of course it does."

"I'll be a senior next year."

"So you're seventeen?"

"Almost."

Jeannie raked her hand through her hair.

"You and that hair," said Lee. "I like it when you look a little tangled." She edged closer to Jeannie. "Are you going to tell on me?" As they crossed the bridge, bars of light flew across

Lee's face, giving her skin a celluloid glow that made her look unreal. One day you'll be dead, thought Jeannie.

"You got to lighten up," said Lee, not unkindly. The driver banged his horn. "Our friend in front here too."

Sitting on the cab's tired upholstery—warmed and worn by a thousand butts—Lee tapping her fingers to the radio, the city stepping before them, bright with hope and money, it was easier for Jeannie to ignore the bud of disquiet that had formed inside her at the police station just a half hour ago. Maybe they could forget about that night, let time bury it. It already had the feel of a lie about it—the kind of dirty tale Kip would tell his buddies.

"Something Stupid" rolled out of the radio up front. Lee called out to the driver. "You like this song, mister?"

He ignored her; she blew him a kiss.

"What were you doing?" asked Jeannie.

"What do you mean?" said Lee, leaning to catch the view from Jeannie's window.

"Out in Oakland."

"Stopping the draft," said Lee, her face in shadow.

"How?"

"We barricaded the induction center." Lee sat back against the seat. "Guys were burning their papers. It was beautiful." She had been inching closer, and now they were touching—thighs, shoulders, arms. She had a familiar, too-near scent, like dirt baking in sunlight. Jeannie shifted away.

"They arrested you?"

"Wrong place, wrong time. Got myself next to some dumbass throwing bottles."

"Did they hurt you?" said Jeannie.

"The cops?" Lee shook her head. She closed the space

Jeannie had made and put her head on Jeannie's shoulder. Her hair tickled Jeannie's neck. "No batons this time." She yawned.

"You have to take care of yourself," said Jeannie.

"We have to take care of our brothers," said Lee, tilting her face so her mouth was close to Jeannie's. "We've got to keep them alive." Her breath had something sour in it, like hunger.

Jeannie's mouth was dry; she wet her lips with her tongue.

"Want to tell me where the hell we're heading?" yelled the driver.

"Twentieth, Potrero Hill," called Lee, then murmured, "You have a brother, right?"

Sensing Jeannie's surprise, Lee lifted her head to give her a frank, mischievous look. She rested her fingers on Jeannie's thigh, and Jeannie didn't move away.

"How did you know where to find me?" said Jeannie.

Lee ignored this. "My brother disappeared," she said. She said it casually, but she straightened to look Jeannie full in the face, her fingers dragging from Jeannie's leg. "They sent him in a big bird over the jungle." Lee peered into Jeannie's face, as though it were she who was listening to Jeannie's story, and not the other way around. "The communists shot it down."

"I'm sorry," said Jeannie; but Lee was staring past her, out the window. "Did he—"

"They took him prisoner," said Lee. Her eyes were wide and black—the way Kip's were when he was high—and they dragged back and forth, playing catch-up with the buildings that skimmed past. "What do you think they're doing to him right now?" Jeannie frowned with concern; but a crack of electric light across Lee's face revealed an expression that was almost dreamy. "I heard they took your brother too," she said, dragging her eyes back to Jeannie's face.

Alarm rushed Jeannie as she scrabbled to remember the last time she'd heard from Kip. "He's flying out next week," she said.

Lee sighed. "Then it's not too late," she said. She pushed her hand into her coat pocket and pulled out a notebook. "You got a pen?"

Jeannie scooped through her purse. "No."

"Give me your lipstick." Lee opened the notebook and wrote on the paper with the lipstick; she tore out the page, slipped the notebook back in her pocket, and folded the paper into a small, thick square. "Here," she said, taking Jeannie's purse and tucking the paper and lipstick inside.

"What is it?"

"For when you're ready."

"Where do I drop you?" called the driver.

"End of the block—McKinley Square," Lee called. "This is me." She placed her hand on Jeannie's knee and paused, before running it under Jeannie's skirt, slowly, up the length of her stocking. Jeannie's breath caught; she moved in her seat.

"Wait—"

"It doesn't matter," said Lee, moving her fingers higher until they reached the naked skin at the top of Jeannie's thigh. Jeannie's breath tightened and she held still, watching the rearview mirror to check that the driver's eyes were on the road. The cab slowed. Lee leaned as though she were going to kiss her; she hooked one finger under the fabric of Jeannie's panties and pushed it inside her. Jeannie heard herself inhale. "We have to take what we want," Lee said in Jeannie's ear. The cab pulled to a halt.

"We're here," said the driver quietly, his eyes leveled on them through the mirror. Lee drew her hand out from under Jeannie's skirt and let herself out of the car.

“How many more?” she yelled as she closed the door, then turned and walked away, disappearing into the trees.

The driver’s eyes rested on Jeannie. “Back to Noe,” she called; and she stared out the window all the way home, her heart slow-clapping in her chest; through the Mission, with its boarded-up buildings, dark-skinned boys, and liquor stores, her heart beating faster; past Mrs. Harris’s academy on Dolores; along Twenty-First with its sleeping intersections and peaceful families; down Noe, over Alvarado; and they were finally there, pulling up outside the house. She pushed three damp five-dollar bills at the driver and ran up the steps as fast as she could, her blood pounding as she closed the door behind her, shutting out the world and all its danger and promise. The clock in the kitchen told her it was past midnight, and a saying of her mom’s flashed through her head—“Ain’t nothing open past midnight but the hospital and legs.” Jeannie undressed in the bathroom so as not to wake Billy, and she crept into the bedroom; but the old floorboards gave her away, and he rolled under the bedspread and groaned. She slipped into bed, the sheets fresh on her bare skin, her heart slowing its punch enough for her to feel the ache that was hollowing her between her legs.

“Nancy okay?” murmured Billy, sliding his palm over her belly, his eyes opening at the feel of skin. She took his hand, paused, and moved it downward. She felt his body tense, his fingers snag her hair before sliding inside her. It wasn’t enough, and she spread her legs wide. Billy grunted and climbed on top of her; she felt his hardness against her stomach and wriggled to let him inside her, closing her eyes to keep the image of Lee steady in her mind as he drove hard and harder: Lee looking down at her, her tongue parting her lips, the go and the thrust and she was reaching for her and kissing her neck and taking her by the waist, fingers pressing into her skin and deep, deeper and she was nearly there, almost there when the rhythm faltered and Billy's weight was on her, his body dense and damp.

"I love you," he said, and rested for a moment before rising onto his elbows and collapsing on the bed.

"I love you too," said Jeannie. In that moment—her body still warm from her husband's, Lee out there waiting in the dark, Charlie coughing in the next room—she meant it.

The next morning, Jeannie sat blearily on the can, the memory of Lee unreal in the frank light of day. She was herself again. She watched Charlie push open the bathroom door and totter toward her, and was struck by how separate those hours with Lee felt from her real life; she wondered if that was how Uncle Paulie had managed his affairs over the years. Then Charlie rested his chin on Jeannie's knee, raised his fist and opened it like a flower—and there was Lee's note.

Jeannie wouldn't have visited the address lipsticked on the paper—wouldn't have walked to the streetcar on Church with Charlie two days later—but her dad had telephoned about Kip leaving for Japan and, after a half hour of silences and silver-ish linings, she needed to escape. Even then, as she looked up at the shabby Victorian, she had no mind to lift her hand to the door—she merely had another blank afternoon to fill, and had been curious to see the address. But the drift of colored men across the street were staring; and Charlie needed to go potty; and the windows were bright against the cold; and there were pots of camellias—her mom's favorite—on the stoop.

Before she could knock, a tall old woman with crimped

white cheeks and hair dyed the color of molasses opened the door and scowled.

"What do you want?"

Her voice was deep and scratchy, bearing the marks of what Jeannie guessed were decades of smoking and hard-drinking. With her loud makeup and slack figure, she reminded Jeannie of Aunt Ruth, the kind of life-gnawed old broad that had never frightened her. Charlie, however, buried his face in her leg.

"I'm here to see Lee?"

"Don't know who you're talking about."

"This is Nineteen-Eleven Haight?"

"It is."

Jeannie would have left it at that, except that the old woman was staring at them; and Jeannie heard one of the colored men holler from across the street; and Charlie was dancing beside her, his body squirming with his need to go. And so she said, "Young? Long, dark, curly hair?"

The old woman nodded. "She crashes here now and again. But she don't call herself Lee."

"She told me to come."

"This is a political meeting. This isn't a fucking kindergarten."

"Hey," said Jeannie, drawing Charlie toward her. "Watch your tongue."

"Man yelling," said Charlie, bringing the itch of a smile to Jeannie's face.

Jeannie stepped back down the stoop. "We'll go," she said.

"It's okay." A man appeared at the door; he had a handsome, empty face and pale hair that reached his shoulders. "Everybody's welcome."

"I made a mistake," said Jeannie.

"Lyla sent you?" he asked.

"Lyla?" Jeannie frowned. "It doesn't matter." She turned to go; but Charlie froze, and she watched as a dark circle spread over his pants. He started to cry. "Oh, Charlie."

"Goddamn," murmured the old lady, turning and disappearing into the house.

"Come inside," said the man; and he was beside her now, his hand on her back. "Come get warm, get the kid cleaned up."

"Jeannie?" Lee was at the door. She was barefoot, wearing a long, translucent skirt; her hair fell loose, a cloth band tied around her head. "I didn't think you'd come." She picked up Charlie, his wet pants soaking her blouse ("Oh, sweetheart, let's get you all dry"), and Jeannie reluctantly followed her into the house.

The house was dark; and the smell implied that either someone had been hard-boiling eggs or Charlie's accident was more serious than Jeannie first thought. Lee led Jeannie and Charlie to the bathroom at the far end of the house. The walls were a queasy peach color and sporadically furred with black mold, the bathtub and sink stained brown.

"What is this place?" said Jeannie, crouching on the tiled floor to ease off Charlie's pants and wipe his legs with bath tissue.

"It's where we make plans," said Lee.

"Plans for what?" asked Jeannie, freeing Charlie's arms from his shirt.

"Stopping the draft. Saving our boys and brothers." Lee squatted in front of Charlie and tickled his naked belly; he giggled and arched himself at her fingers.

Jeannie wondered what Dorothy would make of her daughter-in-law visiting a protest meeting, and smiled. She would get Charlie straightened out, and she wouldn't stay, and no harm would be done.

"It's the old lady's place?" she asked, opening her purse and pulling out a spare jumpsuit for Charlie. She wrapped his soiled clothes in the dry-ish shirt, tucked them into her purse, and, kneeling, pulled Charlie onto her lap to dress him.

Lee nodded. "Mrs. Moon."

"She's out of her tree," said Jeannie, catching Charlie as he wriggled away.

"She has reason to be."

"She didn't know your name."

"She likes to forget things."

"The man had a different name for you too."

"The Reverend?"

"He's a priest?"

Lee shrugged. "Maybe." She stood, touched the damp blot on her blouse, and, in one sweep, pulled the blouse up and over her head. She was naked underneath, her breasts plump, her nipples dark as wine. Jeannie looked away and focused on her own hands fastening Charlie's dry jumpsuit, her fingers slipping on the buttons. Lee tiptoed in front of Jeannie and Charlie, reached up—the stretch of her stomach, the swing of her breasts—and took a man's shirt that was hanging on the back of the bathroom door. She slipped it over her shoulders.

Jeannie finished dressing Charlie and stood, noise in her blood.

"Charlie's here," she said, her voice catching.

Lee's fingers went to a button on the shirt and fastened it. Then the next, and the next, leaving a deep V of bare skin at her chest.

"I didn't mean to come," said Jeannie. "I should go."

Lee smiled. She stepped forward and took Jeannie's face in

her hands. Jeannie thought of Charlie, the unlocked door, the strangers down the hallway, and closed her eyes. A light kiss pushed against her lips, and blood flushed her body; then the kiss was gone, leaving its ghost on her mouth. Jeannie opened her eyes; Charlie was gazing curiously up at her.

"It's only a meeting," said Lee, her face still close to Jeannie's. "You don't need to come again. Please." She waited for Jeannie to nod, then reached past her to open the door. Jeannie lifted Charlie, and Lee led her through the hallway to a living room at the front of the house.

Where the hallway had been dim, the living room was lit by a low sun glaring through the bay window. The room was large and dusty, the walls shedding their parrot-print wallpaper like skin, and it had layers of smell—cat, mold, smoke, a chemical smear of Glade. Sitting in a leather armchair across the room sat a bearded man, smoking a pipe. He was bare-chested but for a waistcoat, his chest and shoulders crawling with hair, his arms bald and welted with what looked like burns. His face was familiar, and it took a moment for Jeannie to place him—the guy with the typewriter at the police station in Oakland. She was about to ask Lee about him when, as though sensing her thought, he caught her eye, and she swallowed her question in a cough. Mrs. Moon was bent over the coffee table, her raw fingers working over a plate of egg-salad sandwiches, arranging them into unsteady piles. Under the bay window, on a couch cratered with newspaper-stuffed holes, an Asian girl lay sleeping. And on a large shag rug by the fireplace sat three girls of indeterminate age—one tear-stained, one crop-haired, one unhappily freckled. They were dressed in acidic colors, smoking rolled cigarettes and murmuring; on seeing Charlie, the freckled girl whistled and waved, and Lee pulled Jeannie across the room.

"Hello, little man," said the freckled girl, too eager; Charlie watched, unsmiling.

"Serious, huh?"

Lee made introductions. The girls each had names like lakes—Crystal, June, Silver—and Jeannie had a hard time keeping them straight. While the girls talked about the march on the Pentagon, Charlie's hands went to the family of china dogs that crowded at the fireplace. There were voices in the hallway, and more people came—maybe a dozen altogether, mostly girls, bare-legged and earnest, in groups of twos and threes, looking for a space to sit on the floor. Jeannie was starting to make her excuses to leave when the freckled girl whistled at Charlie and threw him a carton of playing cards.

"Thanks," said Jeannie. "Although we really need to—"

"We're starting," said Lee, watching the door.

"I've got to get him home," said Jeannie, tugging the carton from Charlie's fingers. He started to cry.

"Wait," said Lee.

Footsteps brought the Reverend into the room. With his cropped pants, hiking boots, and camel shirt, he looked more like a summer camp leader than a priest. He stood by the bay window, spilling a long shadow over the floor, the sleeping girl at his back. Jeannie let go of the cards, and Charlie sat in quiet victory. The Reverend clapped his hands and shouted over the hush.

"All right, everybody, let's start."

The girl on the couch didn't move. Lee squeezed Jeannie's hand.

"Welcome to all our new members," said the Reverend, giving Jeannie a slow, significant look that sent heat to her face. Out of the corner of her eye she glimpsed the bearded man's eyes drifting over her body—still a little soft from carrying Charlie—and moving away.

"We're here because we all have brothers, sons, lovers," the Reverend continued (the teary girl murmured to herself), "who have been sent to destroy a country eight thousand miles away and die in the name of a war that is against God, and against our nation."

"Mama, look."

"Vietnam is burning. Jungles, forests, croplands are burning. Mothers, grandmothers, burning in their homes. Children, babies—little boys like this one." He waved his hand toward Charlie; Jeannie brought her arm around Charlie's waist. "Boys like Charlie, burned alive by napalm."

"Water boils at two hundred and twelve degrees Fahrenheit," said the bearded man, leaning forward in his chair, his eyes on the floor. "Napalm generates temperatures of up to two thousand two hundred degrees." He sat back, steepling his fingers. "It's the most painful way to die."

"The land of the free, the home of the brave, vomiting bombs on our Vietnamese brothers and sisters, slaying more than one million humans. That's more people than live in this entire city."

"I got cards, Mama."

"Most of them children. And for every murdered child, a dozen others made homeless, orphaned, naked, doing anything for food, begging, screwing, selling their sisters."

"Look, Mama."

"Shush." Jeannie snugged Charlie closer and glanced around the room. All eyes were on the Reverend. The freckled girl was nodding, her face misty.

"And what about our men, our boys? Sent back rotting in

caskets like Denny and Tony Moon." Mrs. Moon watched the Reverend, stone-faced, a tremor in her hand as she lifted her coffee to her lips. "Vanished. Crippled, amputated, scalded, blood on their hands, shame in their hearts. For many it's too late." The Reverend was gazing at Jeannie. Jeannie looked away, her eyes searching Lee's, but Lee's eyes were closed. The tap of boots on wood as the Reverend approached and knelt before Jeannie.

"It's too late for me," he said, placing his hands on Jeannie's shoulders. Sweat prickled her skin. The Reverend watched her face as though he was trying to discover something; then, bobbing his head as if he had found it, he stood and walked away. Jeannie's eyes cooled and her breath loosened—but the sweat was still sticky on her skin. She looked again to Lee, wanted to leave, but the girl was still shut-eyed, cross-legged and dirty-soled like a monk.

"I've been there. I've seen it. I've seen a wounded GI tied to a tree, rats crawling from his stomach. I've seen a four-year-old girl running toward us in the jungle, strapped with explosives. I've seen an RPG exploding a plane full of friends, headed for home. I've seen a man literally—literally—disappear in a puff of smoke."

"Oh, no." The cards had fallen from Charlie's hands and scattered across the rug. Jeannie gathered them up, the cards sliding in her fingers.

"I can show you what I've seen," continued the Reverend. He took an album that rested on top of the yellow-toothed piano in the far corner of the room and handed it to the short-haired girl—June, or maybe Silver. The album was red with white polka dots; it looked like the one Aunt Ruth kept for family photographs. The girl let the album fall open in her hands and leafed through the pages like she'd seen them before, then stopped and stared at a single page. Curiosity got the better of Jeannie, and she leaned to take a look.

A child, maybe seven or eight years old, lying facedown on the earth, his black shorts bunched around his buttocks like a diaper, his fatty legs awkwardly arranged. His fists were held tight at his ears, and his head was turned to the earth, like an infant huddling at its mother. On the ground, a large, red stain —and something darker, thicker, spilling at his hair. Next to the photograph, a scrawled note.

"Me see it," said Charlie.

"You took this?" said Jeannie, taking Charlie and holding him against her chest, so that he couldn't see the photograph. She looked up at the Reverend and caught the bearded man smiling.

"One moment," said the Reverend, "for one American soldier. This year there have been—" The Reverend glanced at the bearded man.

"Five hundred thousand."

"Half a million American soldiers deployed in Vietnam. Doing—seeing—things like this."

Jeannie felt Charlie fidget against her, felt the warmth of his body, his unmuscled softness. Lee's eyes were open now, and she was turned toward Jeannie, her palms on Jeannie's leg.

"The Reverend wants us to be practical," she said. "Words and protests are a starting point, but what we really need to do—"

"We need to make it harder for the government to do this to its people." The Reverend spoke as slowly as Lee had talked fast. "We need to save our brothers, one by one, from this war."

Mrs. Moon stood and left the room. The sleeping girl lay still on the couch. Jeannie clutched Charlie, fished up her purse, and stood to leave. She looked up to see everybody else—Lee, Crystal, June, Silver, the other girls and boys, the Reverend, the bearded man—staring at her.

Jeannie's tongue was dry in her mouth. "I have to go," she said.

Lee stood and gripped her by the wrist; she was surprisingly strong. "You're not leaving," she said.

Kip / May 1968

You ever made out with a fat chick and she won't get off you, you know what the heat's like in Vietnam. It lies all over you, sweats on your skin, squeezes the air out of you. You can't shake it. In the bare-naked hour of dawn you wake and it's writhing on you, rubbing its flesh-folds on your body and dry-tonguing your mouth. It's that Devil's work. He's here, no mistaking it. Nighttime, he comes squirming in the dirt, shitting bugs and lice, hanging dead animals on the perimeter wire for us to look at over our morning cup of coffee. And come dawn he's snuck back down into the forest, farting rounds and rockets, waiting for dusk so he can crawl up the garbage chute with the rats and roll grenades from the bushes.

This morning, there was a dead girl on the wire.

Skid got the detail to peel her off. Captain Vance caught him beating off to some tit-shot last night, told him this way he could get some girl action for real.

"Only chance I get to relax is when you assholes are sleeping," Skid told us.

Problem is, Vance doesn't sleep—doesn't even blink, with those hard-boiled peepers of his—just wanders the firebase all night, eyeballing and sniffing for booze and dope. Skid should've known this, but Skid's so dumb, he doesn't know his ass from a hole in the ground.

So here I am, cleaning my rifle while Skid curses, the dust licking my weapon dirty just as soon as I've rubbed it clean. You have to breathe real shallow here, keep your lips shut, no Minnesotan heavy mouth-breathing or the dust just walks straight in, and not even a canteen of water will flush it out.

"You missed some," calls Hutch, splashing his razor in his helmet. Skid's got the body down, but there's hair in the wire.

"Fuck you, Hutch," yells Skid.

Hutch is ducking his head to check his face in the mirror of the jeep that's idling by the lookout bunker. He's the vainest motherfucker I ever met. "Looking real pretty," I say, but the words barely step out of me when my eyes bounce in their sockets and the ground jerks and there's an old-woman scream, and the dust is puffing and the scream's still running like the record's jammed, and there's Skid, wriggling like a squashed bug in the dirt with one leg where there used to be two.

"Holy shit." Hutch is frozen by the jeep, blood striping his face. I grip my rifle, but it's broken up for cleaning; and now Lieutenant Roper has bellied down by the perimeter trench and is pitching bullets toward the scrub beyond the wire. He empties his magazine and curses. "Fucking booby trap." The scream has stopped and Skid is just plain yelling, the same word, over and over.

"Corpsman," Roper hollers, and people are hell-for-leathering past me, and I guess that's what Skid is shouting for. And the place is getting real quiet and real methodical, the way it does right after the shit's flown—even Skid is hushing down—and I guess my dad was right when he told me folks never hear you when you yell, because Skid only has a whisper in him by now, and even through the noise of the Dustoff and the radio and the stay-calm yammering, I can hear him asking for his mom.

The Dustoff sets down, blowing red grit, and a couple grunts help load Skid inside. Hutch struggles through the heat, cheek sliced from where his razor slipped. He's holding something that looks like roadkill raccoon, all chewed-up, black-pink meat—but the light blinks and I see it's laced and booted, and there's no telling my stomach it's time to clench up and take it, it just wheels over and washes puke all the way up my throat. I swallow it down.

Hutch yells something, a word or a scream or who-the-hell-knows, and heaves the leg into the chopper after Skid, who's given up asking for his mom and is lying still as a rock, the corpsman leaning over him and trying to talk him out of going over the Big Ridge. The chopper winches itself into the sky, its gut sagging over the mountains as it drags away, and the firebase gets quiet. Hutch stares at us too long, like he's gathering for something, and I see his hand shake. He opens his mouth like there's something stuck in his throat—like Buck-Buck the stammerer in high school—until finally it comes: "Son of a bitch'll have to sit for his sucky-sucky for a while." And I swallow, swallow, till my stomach stills and I can shout out a laugh, and when I do, Hutch looks relieved. But I can't help thinking he's wrong—that Skid has had his last blow job, if the poor bastard ever got one at all.

Roper clocks my face as we walk away. "Don't think about it, Jackson," he says. "You'll still be dragging your ass in this shithole while he's drinking scotch and watching *Bonanza* back home." But there's water in his eyes and his face is drab and I feel the weakness in his hand when he claps my shoulder.

"Always had him for a screamer," says Hutch; and he's shivering, even though it's ninety degrees out.

"Uh-huh," I say, spitting the vomit that's washing around my mouth. Hutch grips my arm with his Skid-bloodied fingers and walks away. I sit down to finish cleaning my weapon, my fingers dancing like I caught those damn trembles from Hutch; and all I can think about is that fresh piece of Skid on me, and how someday soon, sweet old Momma Skid is going to get the rest of him sewn up and boxed and spangled, mailed with kind regards and solemn regret, courtesy of the United States Marine Corps.

That makes one leg, one foot, and a hand so far, plus one body bag—two if you count Skid, which I'm minded to. Charlie's getting closer. We got probed last week—a half-dozen dead VC inside the perimeter, Roper told us most likely a dozen more dragged back down the hill. One played dead, but old peeled-eye Vance saw his nostrils flare and yanked him to his feet, and I swear that slack-legged, piss-soaked little guy was the same water-buffalo-whipping kid I threw a stick of gum to on our MEDCAP last week. Our first real live prisoner, but just as the higher-ups were figuring out what to do with him, Lieutenant Dinh started yelling all dinky dau and shoved the kid to his knees and shot the back of his head off, blasted all the brains and red fever right out of him; and before his pajamas had a chance to dry in the sun, he was lined up to be buried with his buddies.

All this is enough to wear you down, and eleven hours after Skid went skyward—eleven hours of hole-digging, sandbag-filling, bunker-building, home-dreaming, ammo-humping, field-stripping, bore-cleaning, Skid-wondering, barrel-brushing, wire-mending, fuse-fixing, shit-burning, ration-chowing—I'm ready for a release. Esposito is the man with the plan around here, buys smoke from the raisin-eyed mamasan that does our laundry. Esposito's a Jersey kid all the way to the soles of his feet, greasy even with a crew cut, with ugly eating habits and a sawed-off temper. He's built like a meatball and knows everything about fighting, learned it from the movies. We're squatting in his hooch and he's got his fat tongue out, sealing up the joint and tendering down the edges; he's putting his lighter to burn it when Roper appears.

"Briefing with the captain," he says, his chest rising like he's been running laps.

"What's the matter, Lieutenant?" says Esposito, pocketing his lighter and swallowing the joint in his fist. "You're breathless as a cheerleader riding a quarterback."

I throw Esposito a broad smile and squash it before Roper sees it. Smoke dribbles from Esposito's fingers and the smell of dope spikes the hooch. Roper says nothing, just stares at Esposito; and Esposito watches him straight back with his South Jersey, neck-clenching grin, just daring the lieutenant to order him to open his hand. Roper's strict and straight as a bayonet—he doesn't take shit from anybody, not even from the brothers—but he's standing there and I can see his eyes boring into Esposito's knuckles. I'm betting he's going to call Esposito on it; but he steps back out of the hooch, fading a trail of words—"FDC at eighteen hundred hours."

Esposito curses and shakes the joint from his fist. "Looks like Vance rode Miss Butterbar a little too hard today," he says, sucking down a mouthful of smoke.

"Something's about to go down," I say.

When Captain Vance gets us all together, it's most often the appetizer for a red-letter-day shit-feast. Last time we had a party like this, the next thing I knew I was on a search patrol on the wrong side of the perimeter. Didn't search out a goddamn thing—but on the way back to the firebase, Buchanan's boot found a toe-popper that blew his left foot clean off.

Esposito has sucked the joint all the way down to the roach. "Want some?"

"Sure." I take the roach and put it to my mouth, but I don't inhale—just pinch my lips around it, then blow and squash the butt under my boot. If the captain's looking for more volunteers, I've got to be clearheaded, ready to make sure he doesn't choose me.

Captain Vance is one long, tall motherfucker, with a deep-cut frown like he's been thinking too hard. Everybody's crouching in the dirt, facing forward. Vance is nodding at Roper; and when we hump down at the back of the group, Roper turns to us with black eyes and smiles.

"All right, let's go," he calls.

Vance starts to pace, his face shining cherry red. He keeps telling us this is his second tour in country, but that milquetoast skin of his won't agree, just fries right up as soon as he steps out of a C-130.

"Listen up," he says, and I can hear the tennis lessons and the smooth-skinned girls and the college education in his voice. We all hear it—you can feel it in the clench and shift of the group.

"You're on Firebase Deadwood." Vance pauses like this is news. "This is my firebase, and each and every one of you belongs to me." He slow-pans us, head dipping up and down like he's counting the number of bodies he has at his disposal. A snackle of laughter comes from the far side of the group, and it's one of the brothers, the too-tough, hand-jiving power brother who slugged Pederson at chowtime last week and called him a fucking rabbit. A murmur rolls, and men move. Vance raises his voice. "It is my responsibility to keep you alive. We lost a man today; I don't want to lose any more."

So, Skid bought it.

This settles everybody down; even the brothers stop laughing. The puke I gulped back this morning wriggles in my stomach, and I hold steady and stare straight ahead, counting one-two-three as I wrestle it still.

Vance surveys his men, his feet wide, his hand on his holster, ready for a speech. And I'm wondering what he's going to say about Skid, how he's going to hero-dress a kid we all know was ugly and dumb as they come. "Here it is," he says. "When PFC Cobb's hooch was cleared out, a quantity of what I'm told"—Vance slides a heavy look at Roper, who folds his face in a frown—"is marijuana was found." Vance leaves a long, This-Is-What-Happens-When-You-Smoke-Drugs pause. "Now listen up," he says. "There will be no drugs on this firebase. No pot, no grass, no dope. Whatever you call it, I won't have it on my hill. You want to survive this war, you got to stay sharp."

Skid's still warm in his bag and this asshole can't even say a good word about him, just uses his corpse as a pulpit to preach from, as though the real evil here isn't the crotchrot or the booby traps or the RPGs snouting through the bushes, it's the fucking dope, the ten-minute toke at the end of a day of skin-searing, brain-murdering, run-for-your-life boredom.

Vance paces, then stops to stare into our faces, rocking his crotch back and forth, like he's trying to air-fuck us. "So," he says. "You tell me now if you have anything to hand over. I'll give you five minutes. After that, if I find anything, I'll court-martial you, and you'll spend the rest of the war staring at the walls of the Portsmouth brig." Esposito elbows me and makes an oh-so-scared expression; but there's something held-back in his face and I can tell—two weeks short of flying home, he doesn't want any trouble.

"Five minutes. Give it all up, and we'll move on. Lieutenant"—Vance turns to Roper, who's crouching like a toad in the dust—"set your watch."

The silence gets thick; I can almost hear the tick-tick of Roper's wristwatch, and Skid and all his squirming and shouting sneak back into my brain, so I train my mind on the last time this kind of thing happened, way back in elementary school. Me and Bobby had poured red paint over Mrs. Mahoney's chair while she was out of the room talking with Principal Studebaker; the old lady was pissed, made us all stay through lunch until somebody fessed up to ruining her pantsuit. After five minutes, Kenny Cox cracked and told—fatass just couldn't wait to strap on his feed bag in the cafeteria. (Later in the schoolyard, Bobby busted his mouth so bad the kid had teeth for dessert.) But, man, at nine years old, those five minutes were the longest of my life. In country, you learn how to handle it when time lays itself on you. The trick is to stare down each minute, right till you see the back of it, and don't think about all those others lining up behind it, or you'll go crazy. And I must be getting good, because already Roper is standing and gripping his wristwatch.

"Time, Lieutenant?" says Vance.

"Two minutes, sir."

Vance looks around the group. "Nobody, huh?" He turns to Roper. "Lieutenant, you reported an incident just before eighteen hundred hours, is that correct?"

A nasty smirk burns across Roper's face.

"Private First Class Esposito and Private First Class Jackson, sir."

"Shit," says Esposito. All heads turn to us.

"Esposito and Jackson, up here."

Son of a bitch. We stand, and Hutch wolf whistles.

"Shut up," I tell him.

I pick my way forward, but I've not gone three steps when Esposito slams against my back, grabbing my ass to steady himself.

"What the—"

"Fucking New Guy," says Esposito to the fat kid with the

clean cammies that's sitting at his feet, confusion slapped all over his face. "Get out of the fucking way."

"But I didn't—" says the kid, cheeks wobbling.

"Shut it, blimp," says Esposito. He gives the kid a kick before continuing on his way.

"Move it," says Roper.

We push to the front and stand like a pair of clowns.

"Gentlemen. Anything you need to give me?" says Vance.

"No, sir," we say.

"Turn out your pockets," he says, and I'm hoping Esposito left his stash in his hooch.

Even the lizards are listening as we unbutton the flaps on our jackets and turn out Zippos, dong, photographs, cigarettes, and rubbers into Roper's cracked hands.

"All right," says Vance to Esposito, who's already taking his shit back from Roper while I'm working the buttons on my trousers. "As you were."

So, Esposito was smart. Roper's going to be pissed.

"And your back pockets, Jackson," says Vance.

I scoop one pocket out, handing over a pack of Chiclets and a book of matches, and then the other, and I'm closing my fingers around some piece of cloth or I-don't-know-what, and I pull it out and it opens up in my hand, and there it is, the most beautiful dope I've ever seen, lime green and lush and springy. This is confusing to me, and there's a moment before my brain pieces it together and I realize that I've been screwed, and I know who did the screwing.

"It's not mine, sir," I say, and I hear Hutch and Pederson snickering. I turn to look at Esposito, but he's got his eyes to the ground, innocent as a fucking egg.

Vance leans in close. "I don't want to goddamn hear it," he says, and I see it in his naked face, that bone-cold, live-and-let-die ferocity that makes a man sign up straight out of college for a lifetime of shooting and killing. He watches me for a moment, and I see it all moving through his eyes—disgust, pity, spite, disappointment—like slides in a Kodak Carousel, and I've seen this show before—my dad has it down pat. Vance turns to Roper.

"Where are we at, Lieutenant?"

"Five minutes, eleven seconds, sir," says Roper, his eyes all over Esposito.

Vance smiles, and I swear to God I can't remember the last time somebody smiling meant anything good was going to happen. He turns to the men sitting in front of us.

"Private First Class Kipling Jackson's father"—I listen for the snuck of laughter at my first name, and see the shoulders of the brothers shaking—"was a decorated hero who fought in the Battle of Iwo Jima. Proudest battle in Marine Corps history." Vance glances at me, smug with his information, and I'm guessing Roper's been telling tales. "I wonder what he'd think if he saw his son now." My brain goes to my dad, sitting in his jammies, ever-so-frowning over a long letter before reaching the end of it and spitting out his bourbon. Even here, on Deadman Mountain, up to my pucker in deep serious, my dad's disapproval still finds me, a tracer hightailing through the dark. I catch Hutch's eye. He looks uneasy. Vance steps toward me, and I get the real size of the man, the steak-and-milk-fed heft of him, all big head and broad shoulders, the kind of boy who tears up his mother pushing himself out into the world.

"PFC Jackson," says Vance. "Under Article Fifteen of the Uniform Code of Military Justice, I'm imposing nonjudicial punishment for possession of marijuana." Esposito stands hunched next to me, trying to disappear. He's watching me from the corner of his eye.

"Sir—" I say.

"I'm talking. I'm reducing your rank to private, and you'll forfeit seven days of base pay." This hits me like a punch—all force and stun and I know it's going to hurt like hell later. A slick-sleeve again, and twenty-five bucks the poorer. It's one thing to be sitting up here dust-chewing and cornhole-clenching night and day, but you have to be a damn idiot to do it for free. Somebody in the crowd whistles, and a smile tickles Vance's face. I didn't smoke a puff of that fucking joint and now I'm getting hauled up for it. Roper slides me a look I can't read, and Vance continues. "I'm also restricting you for fourteen days: no MEDCAPs, no R&R, nothing." That smile has run all the way into a grin. "You have the right to refuse this punishment," he says. "But then I'll have to court-martial you. Which I'm guessing isn't too appealing."

I hear them, these words he's speaking—they roll to me one by one, like balls sliding over a pinball table, dropping into my brain with the clunk-clunk of straight losses.

"But, sir—"

"We're done here," says Vance. "Come back at zero six hundred hours tomorrow," he says. "We'll have a formal hearing."

"Somebody planted it on me, sir," I say. Esposito's rocking on his boots.

"I don't care." Vance turns to the crowd and lifts his voice. "I find that stuff on anybody, I won't tolerate it." The show's over. Vance mutters, "All right, that's it," and walks, waving Roper along with him. Roper stops to grip my shoulder as he goes.

"Goddamn, Jackson," says Esposito, all strut and swagger now that the higher-ups have fuckered-off.

"Fuck you, asshole," I say, and my fingers fly for him, squeezing into a fist just as they reach his face; I feel the smack of his cheekbone, the smudge of his skin. He staggers back, holding his jaw.

"Shit, Jackson."

Hutch catches my arm, dragging me so that my feet stumble. "What the hell, man?"

"It's none of your fucking business, Hutch."

"It's all right, it's all right," says Esposito, checking his palm for blood—there's barely a trickle, the candy-ass motherfucker. I feel the eyes crawling on me and I need to shake them off; the light's dying and the temperature's sunk and I want to get away, and for once I'm glad I'm on first watch.

I grab my stuff and head to the observation tower, high above the dust and the bullshit. In the valley below, a stream worms, and to the east—every time a near-surprise, like the prize in a box of Cracker Jacks—is the South China Sea, hiding beyond the mountains. I crouch down and light a cigarette, watching the sunset rage on the ocean; and I think of the sun blazing orange on the water at the Fleishhacker Pool, diving off the tower with Jeannie and trying to outstare her underwater; coming home, starved and burn-eyed, to Oreos and Tang. Something sour and rotten bloats inside me, and it comes, the puke that's been struggling in my stomach ever since Skid got fried this morning. Old Redneck Corncracker Skid, with his brown teeth and his cold sores and his dreams of pickups and banana pudding. He had the smell of the South all over him—whiskey, hay, dung—was so damn rotten with life, I never marked him to get wasted. And the fog heaves in from the ocean and it's like I'm floating in a cloud; and I know it's only the fog moving, but it feels like the cloud's taking me, lifting me from the watchtower, off Deadman Mountain and over the South China Sea.

———

Here's the thing: Skid didn't die. Skid rode that fat green bird all the way to Danang, morphine rushing through his veins to sluice the pain, the corpsman leaning close, jabbering about how the bleeding had stopped, how Skid was going home to Georgia, how he was never coming back to this dump. Right now, Skid is in the hospital, tucked into cool sheets, watching a foxy nurse wide-eyeing over his wound, drinking orange juice and spooning Jell-O from a glass cup. Soon enough, he'll be back with the peach trees and the Jesus freaks, living his muck-poor, hillbilly life, smearing up the air with his bad smell and disappointing everybody with his slap-jaw, gee-shucks, mother-fucking dumbness, and I'll still be here with Vance and all the other assholes, bored and scared, rotting from the feet up.

At zero six hundred hours I report to the fire direction center, frozen with dew and something else, some dark-faced fury that slunk inside me in the night and didn't leave when dawn came. Vance is bent over a table, fingering maps. Above him a washing line hangs, pinched at three-hundred-millimeter intervals by binder clips that carry charts of coordinates scheduled to be bombed to bejesus. The bunker is dim and smells of farts, and it could be day or night, in any fucking war; except dawn punches through the hatch, and the gasoline reek of napalm rising from the valley reminds me that this is a brave new day of my very own 396-day, catch-me-if-you-can, howitzers-and-ham-and-motherfuckers war.

Everything here is covered in plastic; and as Vance turns, I imagine it being spattered with blood, imagine how it would feel to put my fist in his Ivy League face. He rises up to his full QB height and stares like I'm a stranger.

"Private First Class Jackson, sir," I tell him.

"Private Jackson," he corrects me. "You bring a representative?"

"No, sir."

We stand, and he stares hard at me. He's waiting; there's a question in his face.

"Sir," I say.

"Jackson."

"Sir."

"Well?"

"Sir?"

"You made a decision?"

"It wasn't me, sir."

"I'm not interested."

"It's not right—" My voice gets loud; Vance holds up his palm for me to stop.

"I said, have you made a decision? Do you want me to send you back to your father, or do you want to put on your big-girl panties and make something of yourself here?"

He's standing too close; I can see the pores where his skin breathes.

"Okay, sir."

"Okay what?" Vance slaps at a stinkbug that's crawled onto his shoulder and is gazing at his neck. He's going to make me say it.

"I'll stay. I'll take the punishment, sir." My tongue is all glue and suck and the last word comes out small and swallowed, like I'm some limp-dick punk, like I'm actually afraid of him. Vance thins his eyes, and they gleam with satisfaction, and I know my word mashing confirms everything he thought about me; and all the shit and guts inside me turn hot.

The radio belches static and Vance cocks his head.

"Ghost Actual, this is Yankee 21, adjust fire, over."

"Dismissed," says Vance. He waves his hand and turns back to his table.

Skin burning, I step back into the noise of dawn—trucks snorting, men bitching—and head for my hooch.

Esposito is sitting on my rack, legs look-at-my-big-balls wide; Dopfer and Carter are hunkering on the ground. Esposito stands.

"What happened?"

"Told him to stick his punishment, told him I'd take the court-martial."

"No shit."

"What did he say?"

"Told me he wouldn't do it. Said he needed me up here, with all these VC around."

"Bullshit," says Carter.

"Shut up, Carter," says Esposito, cuffing his shoulder. "C'mon—it's too cramped in here." He muscles me out of the bunker; Dopfer and Carter follow. Dopfer is all meat and no brain—I've never heard him talk except to ask the boom-boom girls in the village how much. Carter's a flesh-lipped, pock-marked kid from Seattle. All that rain must have soaked right through to his soul, because he's one hostile motherfucker; and Somebody Up There seems to know it because Carter's always getting screwed on his Charlie rats—all peanut butter and halved apricots—and he's such a mean son of a bitch, nobody will trade with him.

"I'm sorry about yesterday, man. You got burned," says Esposito, squatting on a sandbag and waving the rest of us to crouch.

"Fuck you, man," I say, standing over him. "It's you that fucking burned me."

Carter smirks, and Dopfer rises to stand, but Esposito holds him down.

"I'm sorry, Jackson, I really am. You're a real man, to take it the way you did. You know I can't mess up my record—it's going to be tough enough for me to get a gig as it is."

Esposito's got a rap sheet as long as the Delaware River, or at least that's what he tells us—it wouldn't surprise me if he'd gone all the way through his law-breaking life pinning his shit on the nearest fucking idiot.

"Come on," he says. "Sit down." I spy Roper watching us from his hooch, Vance approaching him from the FDC.

"All right," I say, crouching down, keeping my eye on Vance, who's talking to Roper and turning his head in our direction.

Esposito hands each of us a cigarette, opens his Zippo, lights mine and Carter's, shuts the Zippo lid, reopens it, and sparks the flame for himself and Dopfer.

Carter shakes his head. "Pussy," he says, cigarette wagging.

"Your funeral, cocksucker," says Esposito.

Esposito likes to punish Carter, keeps him around like a dog he can kick; Carter seems not to mind, but this one landed.

"Superstitious bullshit," he says, spitting a snotball to the ground. It gleams in the sunshine, an inch from Esposito's boot.

Esposito knocks my knee with his fist. "You still getting demoted?"

I nod. Carter's watching me sideways; Dopfer is squatting straight-backed, like he's waiting for orders.

"It doesn't matter," I say.

"I feel bad," says Esposito. A smile spreads over Carter's face. "You lost dollars on this. No pay for a week, lower pay grade." I stare at Esposito, and it comes to me that maybe he means it—he comes from a long line of wops where the worst thing you can do is steal a man's bribe money.

"I'll pay it back," he says. I shake my head. "When I get back to the World," he says. "I'll pay your losses."

Carter tips his chin to study me, his eyes moving across my face like he's reading words there.

"Bullshit," I say.

"I mean it, man," says Esposito, and he's getting all Italian on me, his brown eyes shining and soulful like Sophia fucking Loren's.

"It's not about the money, man," I say.

Esposito has his head low; he's thinking over something heavy. I wait—we all wait—and Dopfer's breath gets thick.

Carter cracks. "Jesus, Dopfer, you kid-simple asshole. Close your damn mouth."

Esposito jerks up his head like whatever's been weighing down his brain has been lifted, and reaches into his back pocket. "Take this," he says, pulling out a photograph. I don't need to look at it—I've seen it before, recognize it from its finger-wearied corners—but Esposito pushes it at my face. A girl, tan and gap-toothed, grinning at the camera, tomato sauce on her cheek. The face is scarred by a fold down the center of the photograph from when he kept it in his wallet back home, and no matter how many empty hours Esposito spends smoothing it with his finger, the damn crease won't heal. Sitting next to the girl, dressed in a vest and a bow tie, is a teddy bear, almost her size. Esposito's baby daughter, died just before he shipped out, choked on an all-American, Land-of-the-Free hot dog.

"Take it," says Esposito. Carter's right, he is a fucking pussy. "As security," he says. "I send you the money, you send me the photograph."

"You men got nowhere to be?" It's Vance, standing behind me, throwing shadow on us. "Jackson, haven't you eaten enough shit for one week?" I turn to squint at him; his boots are flush against my ass. "Esposito, get the hell up. I know all about you."

Esposito scrambles to his feet.

"And the rest of you." Vance bumps me with his boot.

We stand.

"Seeing as you're not busy," says Vance, "I'm sending the four of you out on a listening post tonight. Ground surveillance radar found VC stacked up in the tree line; we think they're planning another probe. Report to Lieutenant Roper at seventeen hundred hours for your orders."

We watch as he strides back toward Roper's hooch.

"Pig lifer," says Carter.

"I hate that motherfucker," says Esposito.

"Yeah," I say, taking the photograph from Esposito and putting it in my pocket.

"Son of a bitch is always marching in our shit," says Esposito.

I think of the way Vance brushed me off in the FDC, like I was another stinkbug, and I feel that fury again, sneaking up through my boots.

"You heard about Delta Company? Did their CO a job," says Carter.

"Bullshit," says Esposito.

"It's true. Son of a bitch was a real hard-charger, kept ordering his men out on suicide patrols and sending Chinooks full of grunts in body bags back to Dong Ha. They sent him a warning—left a Claymore under his bunk with a note saying 'You're shorter than you think.'"

Esposito snuffles a laugh. "That's a good one."

Carter continues. "Next day, the CO told them they were going to take a hill. The ARVN were supposed to take it, but they got chewed up by a .51-caliber and got the hell out of there. That was it—that night someone rigged up a Claymore and a trip wire outside the CO's bunker; and this time it was him riding the chopper in a body bag."

"Shit," I say. "I'm surprised they found anything to put in the bag."

"It's rational. The law of the jungle," says Carter. "Kill them before they kill you, right?"

"Captain Vance could use a frag up his ass," says Esposito.

"Too bad he'd enjoy it," I say, and Esposito laughs, and so does Carter; and Esposito gets to laughing so hard it sounds all hee-hee-hee, just like they write it in the funny pages, and this sets me off too, and that gut-swilling Skid-sickness that I've been humping around eases, and I get an all-of-a-sudden, clear-as-day feeling of certainty—like waking from a dream, or falling into one—that we are brothers-in-arms, and that somehow everything is going to be all right.

At sunset, we get ready to leave for the listening post. I watch Esposito check the rounds in his magazine for the third time, his shoulders hunched, a frown running cracks in his war paint. I wonder if he's got it too, that homesick feeling massing in his stomach: fear, dismay, and lonesomeness, all mixed and stewed together. Lance Corporal Shea is chipper as a Boy Scout, humming the Beatles loud and off-key as he tapes a flare to his flak jacket. The five of us—Shea, Carter, Dopfer, Esposito and me—are readying to go out eight hundred meters beyond the perimeter, in the dark, with no radio.

"Can't run a wire that far," Roper told us hours ago, but we knew the truth, knew that even with a radio, you bleed static for a moment, and those gooks will find you before your mouth has touched the receiver.

"Questions?" says Sergeant Fugate.

"Can you go over our mission again, Sergeant?" I say.

"Your assignment is to listen for the enemy."

"And if we hear them?"

"Track their movements. Watch for a probe."

"And if they're approaching the perimeter?"

"Send up the red flare."

"And engage the enemy—"

"Do not engage the enemy unless necessary." Fugate takes a swig from his canteen. His fingers shake over the lid, and I wonder if he's boozehounding his way through his second tour. "You're a small squad, with no backup. You draw fire, you're dead."

"We send up the flare, we don't have a fucking choice," says Carter.

Fugate rolls his cheeks and spits. "If you need to return before dawn, send up the green flare. So we know you're friendly."

Carter shakes his head, his bottom lip drooping, like my nephew when he's told no ice cream. "There it is," he says.

"Shut up, Carter." Esposito turns away, and I guess he's getting superstitious again, guess he's got that short-timer dread that it will be on that Last-Day-Nearly-Home mission that death will finally track him down.

Carter bitches as he pulls on his asspack. Fugate ignores him. "Lance Corporal Shea, you got the flares?" he says.

"Sergeant."

"All right. Move out."

We patrol down the hill, the sun snitching our eyes, the scrub writhing with beetles and hoppers. The sun is almost gone as we weave into the forest. We walk, boots cracking the undergrowth, rifles aimed at leaves, into the thickness of the bush, until the trees close out the sky. Shea hesitates, then waves his fingers at us.

"Here we fucking go," murmurs Carter. Esposito turns and smacks him in the shoulder; Shea snaps his finger to his lips. We squat together, and wait.

Night falls piece by piece through the trees, the here-and-there scraps of sunset darkening, one by one. There's one lick of light left, running warm down the length of a tree trunk and over the forest floor. In the middle of the puddle of light, a locust squats on a stick, stroking its legs together, catching the last rays. It springs away, into the shadow; the light dies.

The death of the light sets off a commotion: the birds thump and the rats scurry and something—a monkey or a chicken or a lizard—starts cackling. Those dink animals are downright stoked that night's here. But for me, now that the last smear of light has gone, I can feel it, feel its soft, wet fingers on me: Fear—slobbering, bucktoothed, loon-bird Fear. Esposito is crouched down next to me; I hear his throat make a loud *click* and wonder if he feels it too. The bush gets shush-don't-make-a-sound quiet, like all the creatures have reached their positions for a game of hide-and-seek. Sunset has yanked the temperature down low, and I'm cold, the coldest I've been in country, my muscles quivering, my teeth dancing in my mouth. I clench my jaw shut, feel the ridges of my teeth grind and tremble. We wait; and I try to hold still, watching the gloom, the blank shapes of the trees, watching to see if any of them move.

It turns out this jungle-dark's got a playbook, got a whole set of moves laid out to keep a man wired-up scared; and that first sundown dark isn't really dark at all—it's just the murdering of the light; and now that the light's dead, the darkness can start to happen. It shades out the silhouettes of the fat trees that mark the edges of the woods; then it thickens, blotting out the scraggy trees that were four, three, two meters in front of me. As the blackness sets, the distances between me and Esposito and Shea shrink. I hear Shea's breath, Esposito's dry swallow, the *tick* of Shea's knee as he shifts his weight. Now we are elbow-to-elbow, foot-to-foot, leatherneck paper-chain men. Waiting.

I look toward Esposito; but he's gone, obliterated by deep-suck blackness. Shea's gone too. I look for my own body, my boots, knees, hands, but they're snuffed out. I squeeze my fingers, feel them press against my damp palm, stretch my wet toes in their boots, the creak of leather carrying loud. I lean my foot, tilting it to feel the nub of Esposito's boot next to mine. He's there; I think I feel him, feel him maybe press his boot back against mine. And it's starting to freak me, I'm starting to wonder if the dark is inside me or outside of me, if I'm staring into my own brain or gazing out at a darkness that's thick as meat in front of my eyes.

The silence is breathing sick and hot in my ears. I'm blacked up and lush with bullets, but I feel so naked and skinless, I could be wearing my guts outside my body. My heart's banging so hard I can feel it bulging at my chest, like a rat in a bag. And those Fear-fingers grip me; and I remember what my dad told me when I was waiting to bat at a Little League game when we were down five to six in the bottom of the sixth and it was all on me: "It's easy. Just breathe, in and out. Nothing to it." And I breathe. In, out. In, out. In, out. And Fear loosens its grip, just a little, the tips of its fingers cold on my skin.

That's when I hear something, hiding under the silence,

stretching its skin. My ears reach to hear it, my cells huddled and crouched and *Shhhh—*

A soft, prickling noise. Growing louder.

Something moving toward us.

It's getting closer, rolling from a prickle to a crunch: the scrunch, scrunch of twigs and leaves underfoot. A shiver lifts all the way up my spine. My finger stiffens against the trigger of my rifle.

"Hey," somebody whispers, so quiet it's just a breath, like I might not have heard it at all, and I wonder if it came from me.

Sweat rolls into my eyes, carrying the sting of war paint. I blink, and steady my rifle toward the sound.

The sound stops.

I let sweat slide into my eyes, afraid to blink, afraid that the sound of my eyelids slapping together might ricochet across the forest and send bullets flying back.

Scrunch, scrunch. Scrunch, scrunch.

It's getting quieter, moving away. I blink. A snuffling sound rolls across the quiet. *Scrunch-snuffle. Scrunch-snuffle.*

Scrunch-snuffle.

A bear.

We hear them every night in the firebase, hear them sniffing at the perimeter wire, nosing for the beef and gravy they can smell warming over heat tablets.

I hear a blow of breath beside me, and I smile and shake out my trigger-hand, pulling it across my forehead to wipe the sweat. Just a fucking bear. I sit back on my heels and listen. Now my ears are primed I can hear them all, all of God's creatures moving among the trees: the snap-splash-quiet of a monkey; the rustle of a snake; the fuck you of a lizard. And all the while the darkness is getting deeper, richer, and I can see the colors inside it, red and purple.

Something scampers past—a cat, or a mouse—and then, quiet. The animals have stopped noising through the forest and are setting up for another game. We wait, one breath at a time, and we must have been here for hours; but the darkness is still muck thick, and there's no sign of dawn yet. I am mind-tracing the shapes of the others when I hear another noise, this time right in front of me, only meters away.

"Shh."

Scrunch-scrunch. Another moon bear, looking for food.

Scrunch-scrunch.

Scrunch-scrunch.

And then it happens.

A new sound.

Not a bear, a mouse, a squirrel or a bat. A sound I know as well as the bang of my own heart—and when it comes, it floods my cells with a bright white light and there's no fucking doubt I'm alive now because—

Tink.

The sound of hardware: a carbine or a knife or a tin-can grenade. A suck-blow of breath—me, or Shea, or Esposito—whoever it is has picked the wrong fucking moment to get hot and heavy. And here it comes, all of a sudden near and naked—

Tink. Tink.

Esposito's knee swivels against mine like he's looking in the dark, staring for whatever it is that's moving closer, closer. And I feel it more than hear it, the crunch of gook feet on the earth, and Shea's elbow moves against my ribs, and I hear the untacking of electrician's tape and it comes to me in that hot-zone, slow-fast way that the dumb motherfucker's really going to do it, he's really going to light us up. And Esposito gets it too because I feel that inch of knee that's touching mine tense, and he must be reaching to stop Shea, because he falls against me and we thud together on the ground.

"Shi—" whispers somebody, but he doesn't get the curse out before there's a noise so loud it's like the air ripping apart, and the trees turn red and we are lit.

The forest slows, the canopy lit pink like a postcard of a Hawaiian sunset, and in the neon-spoiled shadow I see a gook gazing with stupid wonder at the sky. His chin drops and I point my rifle and his arms move and there we are, eyes laid on eyes, weapons trained, and my finger squeezes and my blood roars and before my rifle punches my shoulder, the gook nods—*vâng, vâng*—and stagger-falls, and the bullet flies from my weapon.

"Got him," says Esposito, and my body is hot and wet like I've been hit or I've pissed myself and my eyes and ears are reaching to see if there is anybody else, but there are no bullets and no bangs and there is nobody.

And then it comes. Looping through the trees, like a swarm of hornets, rounds spiraling down through the canopy. The fucking cavalry. My mind flashes to Captain Vance, standing at the howitzer at the firebase, gripping it like a big metal dick and firing his hot load all over us. We hug the ground and there's a phlunk and Shea jerks, and truth be told that motherfucker deserves it, stupid damn fuck-ass motherfucker. And I hear the rounds bury themselves around me; and Esposito rolls over me and I think he's been hit too, he's lying on me and groping over Shea and I hear a rip and a whoosh and the sky turns green and Esposito screams and the rounds slow and they slow and they slow and they slow and it's stopped, it's stopped and it is quiet and it is dark.

I wait, wait for the pain after the stun, but there isn't any, only the deep, slow ache of crouching in the boonies for hours, and the bone-crush of a musclehead Italian lying on top of me.

Esposito makes a straining noise.

"Jesus," he says. "Got me in the ass."

I pitch him onto the ground. "You okay?"

"I'm okay."

Behind me somebody is gasping, high and tight.

"Carter? Hey!"

And in the gasping there's a note and a sigh and it takes a beat for me to hear that it is laughter.

"Got shot in the butt," manages Carter, broken-voiced.

"Aw, fuck you, dick-breath."

"Shea got hit," I say. I push his body, but he doesn't move. "You all right, Carter?"

Carter sniffs and sighs. "Yeah."

"Dopfer?"

Nothing.

"Jesus, Dopfer, now's the time to fucking talk!"

"Here."

"We've got to get out of here."

"What about Shea?"

"He ain't moving."

"Shea?"

"We got to go."

"Who did that?"

"What?"

"That noise—that Shea?"

"Here." Esposito handles his way over me to Shea. I hear a sound like palms beating a pillow. "Shit, there's blood everywhere."

"Is he all right?"

"I don't know, man."

"Fuck."

"Shea got wasted?"

"I can't hear him breathing."

"Oh, man, this is bad."

"Let's get out of here," says Carter.

"We got to carry him," I say.

Esposito sucks his breath. "I can't do it. Can barely fucking walk myself."

"Marines don't leave their dead," says Carter, and I can't tell if he's being straight or being an asshole.

"I'll take his legs." It's Dopfer, with the most words I've ever heard him say at once. "Jackson and Carter take his arms."

"Which fucking way?" says Carter.

"As long as we go uphill, we'll be okay," I say. I imagine those big, wide-spaced trees at the edge of the forest, try to place them in the darkness.

"Come on," says Dopfer, and there's a dance as he takes the legs and me and Carter take the arms, and I think I hear a tiny sigh puff out of Shea's body; but he's got the drag-limb heaviness of that deer Bobby killed with his car on Highway One.

We are still blind, root-tripping and tree-bumping as we drag Shea through thorns and bushes up the hill. As we stumble, I run my spare hand over the trees, feeling for the thinning of the trunks and bushes, for the stumps and cuts where the grunts hacked back the undergrowth closest to the firebase. And it's only a few hundred meters through the forest, but each meter costs dear, paid in full then-and-there, in sweat and pain and heartbeats. I'm feeling my arm begin to tremble with Shea's weight when the darkness thins and I see a space in the trees. We made it.

We push out of the gap in the trees, and I see the dark shape of the firebase at the top of the hill, when all of a sudden

Shea drops, and there's a scream that crazies the birds from the trees.

I weave for balance and try to keep moving, but there's a dead weight tugging.

"It's Dopfer."

"What the hell?"

A sag and drop as we set down Shea.

Carter crouches to Dopfer. "Shit."

"What?"

"Booby trap."

And Dopfer's scream isn't losing its steam like Skid's did; it's getting harder, and it doesn't sound like a scream anymore —it's a squawk, and it's rising higher and higher above the trees.

"Shut up, Dopfer," says Carter, but the scream keeps going, and I half hear it, like a telephone ringing in another room. And in the moonlit clearing, the sky seems a thousand stories high, and it's crammed with stars, and the trees are moving in the wind. And I'm just thinking that this unhappy country's never been more beautiful when something changes—something unseen—and we freeze because we can all sense it, some big Devil's eye swiveling to find us.

Pop.

Pop-pop.

It found us.

There must be a half-dozen carbines trained on us, because the pops become a crackle.

"Shit," says Esposito. We drop to the ground, inches apart, the noise of bullets slicing my eardrums. Carter's wild-eyed, and I see his mouth move in a yell, but I can't hear a word. I shake my head, and his lips keep working, then he throws his hand forward, and I read the shape of his mouth: *Run.*

"What about them?" I yell, but I can't hear my own voice. I tip my head toward Shea and Dopfer, lying on the ground, one still, one moving.

Carter shrugs. On my other side, Esposito's face is pale, and he's staring at me like he wants an answer. A bullet rips the air between us and I duck my head. When I raise it again, Carter is crouch-running, Esposito limping behind him.

"Fuck," I say.

I scoot backward and try to grab Dopfer, try to hoist him onto my back, but he's struggling, and he's so fucking heavy I fall to the ground, Dopfer writhing off me, bullets digging up the dust ahead of me. I grab Shea's arms and pull him, drag him facedown two, five, ten meters. The rounds are coming thicker, so I huddle to the ground, gathering strength for another stretch. And I do it again, another ten meters; and again, the fibers in my arms ripping; but when I hoist up to pull Shea another stretch, the rounds swarm, and I hear one, two rounds phlunk into flesh, and I don't know if it's me or Shea that got hit, but I know that if I don't beat feet, there's going to be two corpses instead of one, so I drop Shea, and I run.

I run, up the hill, stooping as low as I can, weaving through the brush, elephant grass cutting my hands, rocks rolling my ankles, over the dirt, and the dirt, and the dirt, eyes fixed on the ground a metre ahead of me, breath burning, praying for the coil of wire at the perimeter, for the leveling of the summit under my feet. And my lungs are empty and my heart's punching and my legs are busted but I'm here, I'm at the perimeter, I made it, just behind Esposito, who's shoving through a hole in the wire made by a blacked-up grunt. I push through the wire after him and propel myself forward, alongside Esposito, behind Carter, over the dead land, over the trench, till we are behind the lookout bunkers, and we can stop. As I hard-breathe and taste the sweat on my lips—there's no sweeter taste than the taste that you're still kicking—I see Sergeant Fugate, holding a flashlight.

"What happened?" he says.

"Got caught in enemy fire," I manage, dragging out each word one at a time.

"Right after the fucking friendly fire," says Esposito, bent double, ass-clutching.

"Shit, Esposito, you okay?"

"He got shot in the ass," says Carter.

Fugate lifts his light to inspect Esposito's butt. "Get a corpsman over here! You two all right?"

"Yeah," says Carter. I pat my hands over my body and nod.

"Where are Shea and Dopfer?" says Fugate.

I shake my head. "Shea got hit. At the listening post—" I spit. A tall figure is striding from the FDC, a smaller one scampering at its heels.

"Dopfer?" asks Fugate.

"Booby-trapped, then it got too hot. We had to run," says Carter.

"Shit," says Fugate.

"Private Jackson. Report," calls Vance, lit by the glare of Fugate's flashlight, his face new with rest; Roper, dark-faced at his side.

"Sir." My breath is roaring up and down my throat. I try to swallow it back, but it bursts back through my mouth in a cough. "We heard the enemy approaching and Lance Corporal Shea set off the red flare."

"This was at twenty-three hundred hours?" Vance asks Roper.

"Correct."

There's rocket fuel running through my veins. I glance at Carter, hunched in the shadow, and I wonder if he has it too—that slow-time, bright-light feeling, the electricity of combat still rushing through him.

"And then?"

"We engaged and killed the enemy."

"What was the body count?"

"One, sir."

The shadows on Vance's face move in a frown.

"We sustained friendly fire." I listen to Vance's boots as they creak on the ground, hear every piece of grit crunched under his soles, my senses burned superfine in the forest. "Lance Corporal Shea was hit—more than once. We think he's killed, sir. Esposito's wounded."

"Where's Shea?" says Vance.

"Still out there. I—we—tried to carry him back."

"And the other one?"

"Dopfer. Stepped in a trap. Then we got caught in enemy fire and had to run."

"Leaving Shea and—"

"Dopfer."

"Leaving Shea and Dopfer," Vance says. He pauses, a long, brace-yourself, how-fucking-dare-you pause. He leans in close, his face cut with shadows, and I see his mouth twist in disgust. "You left two fellow Marines behind?" His voice is quiet, but I can hear the revulsion, hear it dripping from his words like fat from a patty.

"You think I would leave you behind? You think Sergeant Fugate would leave you behind?" He's yelling, right into my face; I can smell the meatballs he ate at chowtime.

"No, sir." I think of Shea and Dopfer, bleeding in the dirt, maybe dragged off by those fucking gooks, and shame spreads over me. And I think of the rounds flying and Esposito hurt and those last three hundred meters up the hill and I wonder if I had a choice—if Captain Vance, with his listening post and his howitzer and his *Semper fi* ever gave me a fucking choice. "But, sir—"

"There are no goddamn buts! You never leave a Marine behind. I don't care if he's alive or dead. I don't care if he screwed your mother and murdered your father. I don't care if it's hot as a whorehouse on dollar night. That's what makes us different. You understand?"

"Sir." I step back, away from his big voice and his anger. He steps back too, and shakes his head.

"First drugs, now this—Jesus Christ, Jackson, what made you think you could be a Marine?"

This slaps me so hard my eyes sting, and I drop my head and cough. Fugate must know I've had enough of a bitching, because he grasps Vance's arm and says, "What next, sir?"

"The same goes for the both of you," says Vance to Carter and Esposito. "I don't care if you're hurt or not."

"Sir," says Fugate.

Vance turns to Fugate. "All right, Sergeant, take a patrol and get back out there."

"Sir."

"We got two Marines to pick up, and VC in the tree line. Engage the enemy, and go get the men. You—" He points at Carter, whose face is flared by the match at his cigarette. "You go with Sergeant Fugate." I see the cigarette fall clean out of Carter's mouth. "You—" Vance turns to me. "Show me your hands." I raise them in front of him and Fugate spotlights them with his flashlight. I watch my hands shiver, hear my breath heave through my nostrils, feel my underwear stick wet against my ass. Vance's eyes move over me and he reads something he doesn't like. "Not you," he says. "You're not ready." The flashlight glares my eyes and my heart pounds. Carter mutters something.

"C'mon, sir," I say, raising my voice over the blood that's booming through my brain. "I'm good."

Vance laughs, a short, cold-metal laugh, and murmurs something, but I can't hear it over the noise in my head.

"Sir?" I say.

"I said you're not good, you're a liability." Vance is too loud now, his face half lit and ugly. "You're a danger to yourself and a danger to my men."

"But—"

"That's all," says Vance. He claps his hands, the way my dad did to shut us up when we were kids. I feel a riptide of hatred tug me, the same whip-speed current that used to take me when I was a kid and my dad got fierce. "You—" Vance turns to Esposito, who's got his bare ass out for the corpsman. "You got to sit this one out." If this is a joke, I can't hear a smile. "Flesh wound. Small price for a Purple Heart." He turns and leaves.

"You got to be fucking kidding me," says Carter.

Esposito sucks air as the corpsman checks his buttocks. "Vance just called you a pussy," he calls.

"Fuck you, Esposito."

"A pussy," continues Esposito, "and an idiot—hey! Watch it."

"Sorry." The corpsman raises his white palms to Esposito's offended ass-cheeks. Esposito could use a bit of roughing up—he was getting too smug, with his backlipping and work-dodging—but this Purple Heart graze might make him worse.

"All right, that's enough," says Fugate.

"Well, fuck-a-doodle-doo," says Carter.

"I'll gather the others," says Fugate. "We leave ASAP. Jackson, stay here and tell me what you know. Carter, you'll be walking point. Show us where we're going."

Fugate puts the light on Carter's face; he looks like he's going to faint. "Fuck you, Jackson," he says. "You too, Esposito."

A half hour later, I know I should catch some sleep, but I'm fully charged, gripped by that hate-current like it wants to take me someplace, but I don't know where. When I was back home and that riptide got me, I'd take off on my bike, ride as fast as I could up the highway with the trucks breathing down on me till I skidded off, spent, at Fort Funston, where I'd sit on the cliffs and imagine hurling myself down into the surf. Now I got no place to go, and my feet take me along the perimeter, round the LZ, till I get to Esposito's hooch.

The hooch is lit by a flashlight propped against the wall; and Esposito's awake, lying on his front on his rack, his ass fat with bandages. His face is heavy and doughy, like it gets when he's high.

"Shit, Esposito. What did that corpsman give you?"

"Mamasan gave me a jive pack." He lifts his hand to show me a half-dozen machine-rolled joints. "Pure Cambodian grass."

"That was wild out there," I say.

"Sure was."

"You think Dopfer will be okay?"

"Let's hope that spike bled him to death before those gooks picked him up." Esposito fingers a joint from his pile and sparks it, and I catch a tremble in his fingers. "Fugate won't find nothing." He takes a long drag.

"Shit." I think of Dopfer twisting out of my grip and slapping around in the dirt, like a fat, beached fish. I should have left Shea—stupid kid was dead anyway. I should have tried to yank Dopfer up that hill; he might have been alive enough to haul himself a little of the way. I think of Skid, and Shea and Dopfer, think of the ghosts we're collecting; and that shame comes again, slick in my blood.

Esposito's watching me; he's got a dull, entertained look in his eye. "You think you could have saved him, huh?" He blows his smoke skyward, a smile cupping his mouth.

"We could have tried," I say. "If you and Carter hadn't just run for it."

"Listen to me," says Esposito. He drops his arm so that it hangs over his rack; the joint bleeds smoke. His face has snapped cold and mean. "We didn't run, we'd be dead too." He lifts his arm and takes another pull, and I can hear the judder in his breath as he exhales. "Don't you fucking put this at my door. This is on that asshole Vance. Listening post, my ass."

"It isn't clear how it could have gone our way." My foot is tapping the dust; I try to hold it still.

"No shit."

"You think it was a set up?"

"You don't? We get caught with dope, we get told to pack our bags for a light-'em-up-and-fire adventure. Nice example for the rest of the men. You think it's a coincidence, you're dumber than I thought."

My heart's running. "What about Shea? And Carter and Dopfer?"

"Expendable. Bunch of shitbirds."

Just last week Vance tore Carter and Dopfer a new asshole each for reporting late for maintenance duty.

I shake my head. "I want to get back out there, man. I want to make it right."

"Shame you're such a fucking pussy."

"Screw you, man."

"There it is."

"Captain Vance. Fucking cocksucker. What's his fucking problem?"

"It's not his problem, it's yours."

"Yeah? How the hell do you figure?" I'm glad Esposito's being an asshole about this—it's burning off some of this bright, boom-band energy that's charging through me.

"You keep standing there and taking it from that asshole. It's embarrassing."

"Like you'd do any different."

"He don't mess with me 'cause he knows I ain't weak."

"Tell that to your shot-to-fuck butt-cheeks."

Esposito half-asses a smile. "Carter's pissed."

"Well, stupid motherfuckers. Should have taken me instead."

"Yeah, judging from your lady-shaking hands, that didn't look like a good idea." He's got that wisecracker, Jersey Mafia voice, the one he gets when he's being a real asshole, and real enjoying it.

"Fuck you, Esposito. You don't look so cool yourself."

He ignores this. "Nah," he says, twisting the joint against his rack and flicking it to the ground. "The shit flew, and Vance had to send in the real Marines to clean it up."

I think on Vance, his in-jokes with Roper, his big-man backclaps with Fugate, and wonder if my neck just isn't thick enough, my disposition isn't John Wayne tough enough for the guy; I question what it is he can't stand about me, wonder if it's the same shrimp-muscled ugliness my dad sees in me. Vance, with his tall bones and his square jaw and his self-belief—he's the worst kind of all-American asshole, the kind who's had it real fucking easy and doesn't even know it.

"I've had it with that motherfucker," I say, and I feel my fingers shake, my foot pat the ground.

Esposito looks at me long and slow and hands me one of his special cigarettes. "So do something about it," he says. "Calm down and be a fucking man."

That hot white light that drowned me inside out in the forest—the light that helped me muscle Shea from the ground and chased my cells up that hill with those carbines snapping at my back—it's still burning in my bloodstream, and not even Esposito's wham-bam Mary Jane can douse it. At two o'clock in the morning, Fugate returns. I see Shea and Dopfer being hauled in on stretchers, but something in the loll of their bodies, the whiteness of their faces, stops my relief. Four grunts load them into a Dustoff, and the chopper leaves in a hurry, as if there's something somebody somewhere can do for these kids. I watch that dark bird haul ass away from the strobe lights, foot-tapping and hand-jiggling to get rid of some of the rocket fuel inside me, and I hear somebody vomit over his boots. I go to my hooch and lay down; but the light is pushing my blood and I can't keep still, and I foot-drum and second-count, waiting for dawn. And I think of Vance roostering past me like I didn't exist, striding to meet Fugate as he returned over the perimeter with his spoiled bounty, clapping the men on the back and laughing like he had breath and joy to spare; and those hot white cells snap together in an idea, and I know what happens next.

Zero three hundred hours. The dark time: before dawn bleeds. I creep past the lookout tower. It's heavy in my hand, heavier than I remember. I work my fingers over its shell, finger the pull. A little death fruit.

A body comes. I squat to the ground, hear my breath move the air, feel that white light raging in my fingers, they're fucking glowing with it. I drop my head; my hands are dark, and Sergeant Leatherneck trudges on by. I see the bunker, hiding in the night, think of him, warm and meaty in his cot. And the light blares in my brain, and it's pulling me to the hooch.

There it is: a big mouth ready for the spoon. *Pull.* My finger loops and it's done—pin, clip, lever pulled—easy as opening a Coke. The light's so loud, and I know all I need to do is throw the thing and the light will go with it; and as it leaves my fingers it's like that brick at Old Ted's—my fingers want to suck it back as soon as it leaves. But that slice of air between my skin and the grenade might as well be a fucking world of space, because it's gone, straight inside the hatch, and I feel my dumb ass walking after it to see where it went, and my brain pops and I turn and I run for my life as the grenade explodes in a hot white noise behind me.

Jeannie / May 1968

Jeannie would have known her shape anywhere, even in the struggle of the crowd along the wharf: the blaze of hair, the scoop of her figure, the length of her stride. She was wearing a yellow dress and tall boots, a glossy purse in the crook of her arm. Jeannie's heart quickened; she thought to drag Lee and duck into the gathering of customers at the crab stall, but it was too late—Jeannie could tell by the sharpening of her elbow, the rise of her chin, that Nancy had spotted them.

"Jeannie?"

"Nancy," said Jeannie, hoping Nancy wouldn't hear the falter in her voice. Jeannie shifted her feet to put a little distance between herself and Lee; sensed Lee at her shoulder, her hair catching the wind, her eyes on Nancy. "How are you?" said Jeannie. Nancy's hair was curled into a difficult chignon, her lips painted coral. She looked older, more expensive than she had the last time Jeannie saw her.

"I almost didn't recognize you," said Nancy. "You're such the mother now."

Jeannie heard a small *ha* from Lee, and heat spread up her neck. Nancy's eyes flicked over to the girl before returning, hard and bright, to Jeannie; and Jeannie felt the familiar helplessness in the face of her old friend's spite. She pulled her jacket across her dress. "It's been awhile," she said, then, searching for something else to say, "So . . ."

The wind blew, skidding garbage along the ground and bringing the odor of fish. Nancy's nose crinkled. "How's Billy?" she said.

"Good," said Jeannie, grateful for the question. Lee was fidgeting from one foot to the other, clicking her fingers softly together; Jeannie raised her voice to keep Nancy's attention from the younger girl. “Working all the time. He just passed his board exams. He’s going to—”

“John never talks about him,” said Nancy. “I wondered if he still worked at the hospital.” She lifted her hand to unstick a thread of hair from her lipstick; a pale stone glinted on her ring finger.

Jeannie cleared her throat. “And you?” she said. “Any news?”

Nancy drew her lips into a smile and shrugged. “Not really.”

Lee looped her arm through Jeannie’s and pressed close against her. “We should go,” she whispered.

Nancy turned to face Lee, her eyes taking in the bare face, the flared jeans, the loose hair. Jeannie held her breath. “Hello,” said Nancy. “You are . . . ?”

“Yes, this is—” said Jeannie.

“Lee Walker,” said Lee. She raised her hand in a salute and smirked; embarrassment crawled over Jeannie’s body.

“All right,” said Nancy, raising her eyebrows at Jeannie, a smile—real, this time—touching her mouth. “Don’t let me stop you.”

“Yes, let’s go,” said Jeannie, loosening herself from Lee’s grip. “See you soon.” She went to kiss Nancy on the cheek; Nancy turned her head so that Jeannie’s lips smacked the air.

“I guess so,” said Nancy.

“Who was that?” said Lee as they ducked onto Stockton, past the idling buses and up the hill. “She was a bitch.”

Jeannie felt a flare of irritation. “Someone I knew in high school,” she said.

“Was she your first?”

Jeannie heard the nettle in Lee’s voice and turned. “What are you talking about?”

Lee's eyebrows lifted in innocence; but there was something triumphant about the smile in her mouth. "You were acting strange," she said. "Needy."

"Please," said Jeannie. Lee stopped, and Jeannie wondered if the younger girl wanted to argue; but Lee was peering through the soap-streaked window of a café and making a clicking sound with her mouth.

"Here we are," said Lee. Jeannie felt her blood pulsing. She watched Lee, was relieved to see the command forming in the younger girl's face.

"Let's go," said Lee; and Jeannie let Lee take her by the hand as they pushed through the door.

They waited in the café, among the idlers and sightseers, sinking cream and sugar into their coffees. Jeannie watched the small girl at the next table tear into a jelly donut, her eyes round with delight, and was pinched by the thought of Charlie in Cynthia's apartment back on Noe, trapped with Cynthia's lively, vindictive five-year-old.

"Here," said Lee. "It's got to be."

Jeannie watched as a thin, walnut-faced woman edged across the room, her eyes searching each table until they fell to the daisy fastened at Lee's chest. Jeannie took a breath to steady herself, and smoothed her face into a neutral expression.

"Are you here to see us?" said Lee, half rising in her seat.

The woman nodded, dragged a chair, and sat. Her fingers worked over the buttons on an overcoat that was too heavy for May.

"You found the place okay," said Lee.

"I was expecting a man," said the woman.

"You got us," said Lee.

"Aren't you a little young?"

"Does it matter?"

The woman pressed her lips together and shucked her coat onto the back of her chair.

Lee waved at the waiter. "You want something to drink?"

"Just water," said the woman. The waiter nodded and drifted away; the woman's eyes followed. She fingered the pearls at her neck so that they rattled.

"The man on the telephone." The woman put her elbows on the table and clasped her hands, prayer-like; her fingers were stuffed with rings. "He said you could help me."

"That's why we're here."

"What's your son's name?" ventured Jeannie, emboldened by Lee's brazenness.

The woman didn't look at her, kept her eyes on Lee. "How do I know you won't get me in trouble?"

"That's not the kind of trouble we're into." Lee smiled.

The woman didn't smile back. "Your organization helped my friend. A year or two ago," she said. She watched the waiter place a tumbler of water on the table, and took a long sip. Lee and Jeannie waited. "He's my youngest," the woman explained. "My only boy."

"He got a letter?" asked Jeannie, her voice nearly lost in the noise of the café.

The woman either didn't hear her or decided to ignore her. "I thought it would all be finished by the time he'd be draft age," she said. "I didn't think it would have anything to do with us."

"He's not going to college?" said Lee.

"He's not enrolled. He's never been . . . he found high school challenging. In any case, he wanted to join the family business, right away."

"The family business?" asked Lee.

"You need to know about that too?" The woman gave a tense shrug. "Lingerie. We import it from France."

Jeannie imagined the older woman, under the wrinkles and the tweed, trussed in a red lace bustier, and her nerves loosened. We all wear our secrets, she thought—they're right there, for anybody to find, if they can only get through the layers.

"Last week, we celebrated his birthday," the woman said. "Drove over the bridge to Sausalito, went to the Alta Mira. The whole family. We've been going there every year since he was six years old." She took another sip of water and exhaled. "The next day—the next day!—it came. Sitting in the mailbox, between the electricity bill and the Sears catalog, like it had every right to be there. As soon as I saw the envelope, I knew."

"Did you give the letter to your son?" asked Lee.

"Of course not," said the woman. "You can't trust boys with things like this." She pulled a black purse onto the table and rooted through the contents until she found the letter. "Here," she said. She drew it out, her eyes checking the other tables for unwelcome interest.

Jeannie held out her palm. The woman finally lifted her eyes to Jeannie's and handed it over. Jeannie felt a tweak of success, and removed the letter from the envelope. The name was stamped in capitals: CHARLES HENRY DEWEY. Jeannie touched the name, felt a furtive intimacy; then slid the letter back inside.

"My son is Charles too," she said in a clear voice. "Charlie."

Mrs. Dewey looked at Jeannie for a long time; once again, Jeannie wondered if she'd heard her. "He's always been such a sweet boy," Mrs. Dewey said. "When he was just two years old, I'd wait for him while he climbed down the stairs, and he'd kiss me between every space in the banister." Jeannie felt something sweaty and overfamiliar touch her, like another passenger's body pressing hers in a crowded streetcar. Her mom always called Kip her sweet boy, even when he was thirteen years old and shiny with urges.

"All he ever wanted," Mrs. Dewey was saying, "was to be at home, with me. Even now he's grown—" Wetness touched her eyes, surprising Jeannie, and Mrs. Dewey even more so: the older woman scratched in her purse for a handkerchief; but by the time she found it, the tears had retreated, and she screwed the cloth in her fist. "He's a fine young man—he's not out chasing girls or partying or balling or whatever you young people call it." Lee squeezed Jeannie's knee under the table. "He's—gentle. He's not meant for"—she brushed her dry eyes with her fingertip—"all this."

Jeannie thought of Kip's collection of dime-store soldiers, his scraps in the schoolyard, and his quiet devotion to *Gunsmoke.* Thought of Charlie, his impulses to hit, kick, and climb; his maneuvering of his army men over the kitchen table; his ability to turn anything into a gun—even (with a few well-placed bites) his slice of toast at breakfast. Kip may have once been sweet, but he was never gentle, and neither was Charlie—"spirited" was the word Dorothy used. The thought of Charlie's name thumped onto a draft card sent a shadow to Jeannie's heart, and she felt for the brittle woman who sat before her, scrunching her pearls in her worn fingers. Jeannie slipped the envelope into her purse. "We'll take care of it," she said.

Mrs. Dewey placed a wan look on Jeannie. "Right away?"

"Right away," said Lee.

Spit gathered in Jeannie's mouth; she swallowed.

"He's got to report to the draft board in two weeks," said Mrs. Dewey.

"The next letter in your mailbox with a stamp like that will be an exemption," said Lee.

"Don't worry," said Jeannie; and, rash with sympathy for the older woman, who suddenly looked feeble in her swamping pearls and outsize wing collar, she reached her hand across the table.

"Thank you," said Mrs. Dewey. She took Jeannie's hand, pressing it with cold, strong fingers. "You're doing a good thing." Jeannie squeezed back, her chest flushing warm, and glanced at Lee, who was fixing Mrs. Dewey with an expectant look.

Mrs. Dewey sensed Lee's scrutiny; she let go of Jeannie and patted at the pockets of the coat that hung on the back of her chair. "Here." She drew out a fat, cream-colored envelope. "It's all there."

Lee smiled, took the envelope and stuffed it into the back pocket of her jeans, and turned for the waiter. "Check, please."

The waiter placed the check on the table and stacked their empty cups and tumblers, his dark fingers working to gather the torn sugar packets.

They stood from their chairs, Mrs. Dewey's hands trembling over her coat buttons. Jeannie fastened her purse and looked up to see Mrs. Dewey staring at something behind her, something indecipherable at her lips. She turned to follow the older woman's gaze, and saw the waiter's back retreating into the kitchen.

"Looks like that one's safe," said Mrs. Dewey, her face drawing into an unpleasant smile. "Safe and happy as a clam, bussing tables and taking tips." She hoisted her purse over her shoulder and pushed her way out of the café, disappearing into the traffic on the sidewalk.

"I don't know why he doesn't just tell the draft board he's gay and be done with it," said Lee as they headed for Lombard. They walked fast, Jeannie buzzed on a mix of anxiety and elation, the way she used to feel when she and Nancy skipped out of high school at recess to smoke cigarettes on the beach.

"You think he's a homosexual?"

"Come on, the guy's never had a girlfriend and he wants to work with panties?"

"He's certainly a mommy's boy."

"Rich, white, and dumb. Recipe for a happy life." Lee quickened her pace, like she wanted to keep Jeannie at her heels.

Jeannie half ran to catch her. "What's in the envelope?"

"Money," said Lee, striding.

"How much?"

"A lot." Lee turned her head to give Jeannie a brief smile.

Jeannie caught her arm; Lee slowed. "I thought this was about doing the right thing," said Jeannie. "Not making money."

Lee shrugged. "It's a donation. For the cause."

"It didn't look like a donation. It looked like a fee."

"Who do you think's paying for the buses? And the posters? In any case, we only ask the ones who can afford it. It doesn't mean anything to her. She's a merry-widow millionaire!" They stopped at an intersection; Lee took Jeannie's face in her warm hands. "Trust me," she said.

It was still light when Jeannie returned to Noe. As she walked up the sidewalk, she saw Charlie standing at Cynthia's window, his palm on the glass, watching her approach. He wouldn't speak to her as she carried him back to their apartment, just put his pale face on her shoulder and closed his eyes. That evening, she watched him as he squatted in the bathtub, pudgy and solemn, guiding his boat through the bubbles, and imagined all the things she would do to stop him coming to harm.

"I've had a hell of a day," said Billy, un-nooseing his necktie as Jeannie switched off the television set.

"You want a drink?" said Jeannie. She opened Dorothy's old bar cabinet (still too grand for the room—however much Dorothy insisted, it had never made itself at home) and removed a bottle of Canadian Club.

"Please," he said.

She poured an inch into a dusty tumbler.

Billy paced, touching the photographs on the fireplace. "Well, I didn't get it," he said. He picked up their wedding photograph, rubbed its face with his sleeve, set it down, and turned to Jeannie.

"Didn't get what?" She handed him his drink.

"The fellowship."

"The fellowship?"

"The damn fellowship, Jeannie. You remember? The one I've been slaving for, for months."

"I'm sorry, of course I remember." She'd been so consumed with her own crusades and disobediences, she'd forgotten Billy's struggles.

"Fairchild gave it to Gibb," said Billy. He tipped back the liquor, a wince tightening his face, and Jeannie wondered if he actually liked the stuff.

"Oh, honey." She thought to step toward him; but something in the way he was standing—the tension in his body—stopped her.

"'Not enough clinical experience.'" Billy turned the words out of his mouth like they tasted bad. "Four years living in a hospital, feeling sicker than most of the damn patients, and it's not enough?" He shook his head, his face gripped in an expression of disgust. His suit was creased; he was gray-skinned and bruise-eyed, as though the hospital had left its dirty fingerprints on him.

"Have you talked to your father about it?" She regretted the words as soon as they left her mouth.

Billy clenched his jaw. "What the hell has it got to do with him?" he said. He turned away. "This place is a mess."

Jeannie swallowed the rebuke. "Here," she said, bringing the bottle and pouring him one, two more swigs. He rubbed his chin and swilled the glass, staring as if searching for something under the roll of the liquor.

"I'm working so hard just to stand still," he said. He set his tumbler on the coffee table with a knock, and dropped onto the couch. "My father thinks it's so damn easy—get your fellowship, publish, climb the ladder. In his day you just had to go to Stanford and drink at the Pacific-Union, and soon enough they'd make you chief." He kicked off his shoes; his socks showed sweat at the toes.

"It's hard on you," said Jeannie, sitting beside him and placing a hand on his shoulder. He moved his hand to grip hers, and squeezed.

"At least I have you," he said. He sighed; then, remembering something, he checked his watch. "Damn it. I wanted to catch the news."

"I watched a little," said Jeannie. "They're saying it's the worst month yet for casualties."

"Hmm." Billy leaned for his drink.

"I can't stop thinking about Kip, out there."

"He'll be all right. He's artillery. He's practically in the rear."

"But kids like him are dying. And we're still sending them, more and more of them. Can you imagine? If it were Charlie?"

"Every generation has its war. My grandfather's, it was World War One. My father's, World War Two. Then Korea. This one's ours."

But you missed this one, thought Jeannie. But she said, "You get people coming to you? To get exempted?"

"From the draft? Sometimes."

"And you help them?"

"If they're sick, I'll write that they're sick, yes."

"And if they're not?"

"What kind of a question is that?"

"I heard that—I heard some doctors send letters. To say boys are medically unfit. To save them from the draft."

"Who told you that?"

"I saw it in a newspaper, maybe."

"Well, that's a goddamn stupid thing to do. Not to mention criminal. And unethical and immoral." Billy finished his drink and wiped his mouth on his sleeve.

"But—"

"Look," said Billy. "These boys are being asked to serve their country. They owe it to their country to do it." He pulled off his socks and clenched his soft, white toes. "I tell you, a lot of them are better off going over there than staying here. Take Kip. If he stayed here, Lord knows what trouble he'd be getting into. The Marines will be the making of him. You watch."

Panic climbed over Jeannie; and she realized how idiotic it had been for her to believe she could argue him around. She watched her husband as he sniffed hard and exhaled; and for the first time in weeks—maybe months—she really saw him: the weakening hairline; the wrinkles at his eyes; the baby fold of fat beneath his chin. His collar was missing a button: the kind of detail a wife should have fixed. She put her palm to his cheek and turned his head toward her and, gently, pushed her lips against his. They kissed—like they used to kiss, in his Chevy, pulled up by the park, before they were married. She traveled her hand down his chest; but he held it still, fretting at her nails with a rough finger. He took his lips from hers and sat back against the pillows.

"I don't know what else I can do," he said. His face was strained red. "I try, but I'm not enough." Billy looked straight into her, a sharp candor in his face, like he was seeing her stripped bare, could spy the dress-up clothes crowded at her feet—and here it was, the question she dreaded, forming on his mouth, but when the words came, they weren't what she expected. "Am I enough?"

"What a question," she said, moistening her mouth. "Come here." Jeannie drew his head into her lap and stroked his hair, following the eddy of a cowlick at the back of his head—the same one Charlie had—and felt tender with sympathy for him. "You're enough," she said. Billy breathed, and his body relaxed, and Jeannie saw herself, solid and calm on the couch, the mothering wife, the angel at the hearth. They stayed that way for a little while, listening to the smothered noise of the television set upstairs, the lift and drop of their matched breath. Jeannie, wondering if Billy was asleep, glanced down to see his eyelashes cut a blink. She imagined Mrs. Dewey staring at her son's face, watching his skin-and-tissue vulnerability, his soul made flesh; and feeling safe in their quiet affection, she decided to try again.

"I met up with somebody today," she murmured. "A woman."

Billy shifted in her lap. "Who?"

"I've known her a little while." Here was the opportunity—

with Billy's hours and Dorothy's dinner invites, it wouldn't come around again soon enough. "Her son got called up by the draft board," she said. "She's worried. Real worried."

Billy sat to look at her.

"He's only a kid," said Jeannie. Billy was frowning. "He's—very delicate. Has a delicate heart. Not a medical problem, exactly, but—he won't survive it. I wondered if—"

"If what?"

"If there was anything you could do?"

"What are you talking about?"

"Could you help him? Write a letter for him?"

Disbelief pleated Billy's forehead. "Are you out of your mind?"

Jeannie flushed. "No, I just—" She breathed in, exhaling in a sigh. "You should have seen her, Billy," she said. "She was so—desperate."

Billy dropped his head. "I can't believe I'm hearing this." His voice was a murmur.

"I—"

Billy held up his hand. "I hope to God you didn't tell her I would do this." He was loud now; Jeannie wondered if their neighbors could hear.

"Of course not." Her words had the strange, uneven ring of a lie; she hoped Billy hadn't heard it too.

Billy studied the carpet, then flicked Jeannie a look of contempt. He laughed—a hard, drained laugh—and shook his head. "God."

"What?"

"Is this what this was all about?"

"What do you mean?"

"The drinks, the kiss, the whole good wife act?"

His words, salted with truth, stung. "I don't—"

Billy bent to pull on his socks and shoved his feet into his shoes. "I'm going out," he said.

"Billy."

"Don't wait up for me."

Jeannie heard him stride the hallway and slam the front door. There was a pause—he was buttoning his jacket, or checking for his wallet—then the tap of feet down the steps to the street and a cry as Charlie, moved from his sleep, discovered he was alone in the dark.

Jeannie shushed her son back to sleep, then returned to the living room. She sat, letting tears wet her face, her throat hum with sadness, until the building fell quiet—the television set upstairs switched off, the traffic outside dead. Jeannie heard her own blubbed breaths, and her skin crept with self-dislike.

She waited for hours for Billy to return, switching television networks and searching his backlog of newspapers for articles that would make her afraid—stories of American bases under siege, lost helicopters, burned villages. Billy didn't return. He was probably at the hospital, sleeping in one of the cots they kept for residents; perhaps he was dozing in his car.

As the clock turned one, Jeannie was taken by a thought, and she went to the medical bag that was lying on its belly in the hallway. She parsed through Billy's things—a stethoscope, a pair of medical gloves, several ink-bleeding pens, a half pack of Fruit Stripe gum—until she found what she wanted. She went to her bedroom, pulled her old Smith Corona from under the bed, and carried it to the kitchen table. She sat and hauled up the copy of *Principles of Internal Medicine* that sat, massive and Delphic, in the middle of the table, surrounded by drifts of paper. Even though Billy had passed his boards weeks ago, she still hadn't reclaimed the space; and as she took the book in her hands, helped the cover open and ran her finger over the fine paper, her forehead kinked as she deciphered the type, it was as though she were him, puzzling late into the night over a difficult illness.

She turned to “Diseases of the Organs” and flipped the pages, wavering over the blood and the lungs before settling on the heart. She fed a fresh piece of paper into the typewriter, and rolled it into place. She was rusty—stuck keys, chewed paper—and balled the first two attempts into the pocket of her dress; but the knack returned, and she drummed out the words, carefully pulling the paper from the machine. She pressed her finger to the ink, then slid the paper into a magazine, packed the typewriter into its case, shut off the lights, and headed for bed.

She woke to the sound of the telephone ringing.

“Hello?”

“Jeannie. Did I wake you?”

“It’s all right.” She glanced at the alarm clock—nearly six. “Charlie will be awake soon.”

“I’m sorry I stormed out last night.” Billy breathed into the receiver. “I just—I’m under a lot of pressure at the moment.”

“I know.”

“I came to the hospital,” said Billy. “Not such a bad thing, it turns out. They needed the extra hands.”

“I’m sorry.”

“I know you’re trying to help. But, Jeannie—you have to stay out of things like this. You could get into a lot of trouble.”

“I understand. I’m sorry.”

“Leave the do-gooding to Mrs. Harper Senior, hey?” Jeannie heard the smile in his voice. “I’ve got to go,” he said. “’Bye, honey.”

Jeannie replaced the receiver; then she picked it up again and dialed Mrs. Moon's number.

"Yes?" It was Walter Moon, Mrs. Moon's nephew, with the burned arms and the flat stare; she knew she had woken him, and a part of her was pleased.

"It's Jeannie. Is she there?" Things between Lee and her mother were bad, and more and more often, Lee was crashing at Mrs. Moon's.

"What the hell? What time is it?"

"I need to talk to her."

"At six o'clock in the fucking morning?"

"Can you just get her?"

"She's not here. She'll be here later."

"Tell her to come see me. Today."

"Jesus Christ. Okay." Jeannie set down the receiver and heard the rattle of Charlie's toy rabbit as her son stirred in his bed.

She came later than usual, when darkness had closed in on the street. Charlie was long asleep, and Jeannie was standing in the kitchen, worrying at the casserole on the stove. The knock on the door was slight enough to seem imaginary—but the shadow told Jeannie it was her.

Jeannie opened the door. "It's late."

Lee smiled; her eyes were wide and dark.

"You're high," said Jeannie.

"Are you going to let me in?"

Jeannie stepped aside to let Lee pass, easing the door shut behind them. Lee dropped a light kiss on Jeannie's mouth, then slipped off her sandals and carried her naked feet toward Jeannie's bedroom. She usually came Mondays and Thursdays, when Billy worked late at the hospital; it was Wednesday. Jeannie checked her wristwatch.

"He'll be home soon," she said.

"Has he phoned yet?" Lee called from the bedroom. Billy's habit—romantic, practical, habitual—of telephoning before leaving the hospital.

Jeannie followed her into the bedroom and closed the door. "Not yet," she said, standing with her back against the door.

"There's time," said Lee. She took Jeannie by the hip. Her mouth was warm on Jeannie's neck; her scent of oranges and cigarettes; the sound of her breath. Her lips went to Jeannie's, her tongue light and slow in her mouth; and Jeannie's body filled with heat. She closed her eyes, moved her palm under Lee's blouse, the cotton grainy at her knuckles—over the warmth of her stomach; the ridge of her rib cage; the swell and weight of her breasts. Sweat pooled at the base of Jeannie's back, and she was burning. Lee's fingers went to Jeannie's dress, finding the ease and drag of the zipper; and the air was at Jeannie's throat, her stomach, her thighs—the heft of fabric dropping to the floor. Lee knelt, unclasping and rolling Jeannie's stockings down one leg, then the other; undoing her garter belt, letting it fall; pushing Jeannie's panties down, down to her thighs, to her feet, and now Jeannie was naked, standing in a heap of nylon and cotton, the air clean against her skin.

Jeannie sank into the dusk, her body moving of its own accord as she grasped Lee's hair and strained against her, Lee's mouth cool and wet between Jeannie's legs. And Jeannie felt it first in her skin—the detonation of a thousand tiny charges, then the blaze of fire, the suck of breath; and Jeannie closed her eyes, and let herself disappear.

They lay on the bed, legs tangled, Lee's eyes closed, Jeannie winding Lee's hair around her fingers—until the telephone rang, and the spell was broken. Twenty minutes, maybe a half hour if Billy decided to walk home. Lee shrugged on her blouse, pulled on her skirt, stretched and yawned; smiled blankly as Jeannie struggled to zip her own dress. By the time Jeannie had fixed her face and hair, Lee was already out of the room. Jeannie glanced in on Charlie—he was still sleeping, his fanny pushed into the air, his thumb tucked in his mouth—and went to the kitchen, where she found Lee standing at the stove, her back to Jeannie. Jeannie watched the muscles in Lee's calves stretch as she leaned to taste the casserole that was cauldroning on the stovetop; and she felt a sense of loss, small and sharp as a needle, touch her skin. "I wish you could stay," she said.

"I have to be somewhere," said Lee, dipping the wooden spoon back into the casserole and ducking for another mouthful. "Well, he didn't marry you for your cooking." She turned to Jeannie, that same empty smile on her face, and wiped her mouth with her fingers. "Got to scoot."

"Wait," said Jeannie. "I have something for you." She went to the kitchen table and picked up her copy of *McCall's*.

"Raquel Welch isn't my thing."

"Open it." Jeannie's eyes sought the clock. Ten more minutes.

"'Would he marry you again?' The crap you read!"

"Here." Jeannie opened the magazine. A letter, headed Dr. William Harper, San Francisco General Hospital, 1001 Potrero Avenue, San Francisco; and in typing that didn't quite meet Mrs. Harris's standards, the details: Charles Henry Dewey is not qualified for military service for medical reasons—namely, that he suffers from the congenital heart condition of aortic stenosis.

Lee's eyes widened. "He did it?"

"I did."

Kip / May 1968

"What the fuck is going on?"

"Grenade in the captain's bunker."

"Sir, we've searched the compound—nothing."

"No cuts in the wire."

"Fuck. Was he in there?"

"I'd say he's burned up pretty crispy."

"Shut up, asshole."

"Captain Vance was in the bunker."

"Jesus Christ."

"Sir—Sergeant Gross says he saw someone walking toward the captain's hooch just before the explosion."

"A Marine?"

"Sir."

"You got to be kidding me."

"This shit happens in the Army, not in the fucking Marine Corps."

"Get everybody together."

"This is bad."

"Now."

I was wrong. That dynamite jet-fuel fire that was raging inside me isn't gone, it's just simmered down, low and red and hot, and it's blistering me on the inside. I keep my hands fist-closed, pocketed—if I open them up, they'll fly like birds. The fire smokes and dies, a black smear where the bunker was; sandbags gashed, wood snapped, the stink of firecracker, barbecue, dust. In the half-light of the gasoline lanterns, I watch the corpsmen take Vance's body, and my skin burns raw. I flap-steady my hand from my pocket to touch my face, but it's smooth as a child's: none of that fire touched me, it just stayed inside the bunker and gobbled everything up, and now there isn't anything left. And my blood's running and my heart's dancing and I swear you could be getting lucky or getting fired on or riding a fucking roller coaster and that dumb throbbing piece of chest gristle wouldn't know the difference.

It's Fugate that's herded us together—so much for the chain of command. Roper's scampering in circles, wild-eyed and jumpy as a spooked puppy. If I didn't know better, I'd say it was him that threw the thing.

"Anybody knows anything, speak now," says Fugate, and he's furious, his fingers shaking like he's got a jones for a drink. I feel my own fingers twitch in my pockets, and as I try to still them, those shakes jitterbug down to my knees. I squeeze my toes against my boot soles to stop my feet from dancing in the dirt.

"I saw somebody walking along the LZ around zero three hundred hours, Sergeant." It's Fucking New Guy, fat and clean as a plucked goose. "I was coming off watch."

"Who did you see?"

I watch him, watch for the smallest twitch of his head toward me. A beat, and it swings on its soft neck, and my blood slides from my heart, down my arms and legs, like it's going to run clean out of me. But the head swings back the other way—the kid's just shaking his dumb skull, *I don't know.* My blood gathers in my hands and feet, turning them numb.

"A Marine," says Fucking New Guy. "It was too dark to see his face." My guts are cold and dry. "He was walking pretty fast. Medium height, medium build . . ."

"Real useful, asshole," says a voice—it's Pederson—and there's something in his voice, something I've never heard in him before: the thin-lipped sound of fear. I'm glad I'm not the only one freaked round here, else Roper might sniff me out.

"Anything else?" says Fugate.

I listen for the wet parting of lips, the clearing of a throat, my ears still bat-honed from the forest. My heart's machine-gunning in my chest; but it knocks out two full magazines of heartbeats and I still don't hear a mouth unstick.

Nothing.

"All right," says Fugate. "Anybody who's not due on watch, form a line in front of Lieutenant Roper. You'll be divided into squads and questioned."

"Sergeant—" Somebody's coming, some six-foot black guy built like Woody Strode. I've never seen him before in my life.

Fugate ignores him. "Those who have duties, go to your posts—nobody else can leave, do you understand? There'll be no sleep tonight."

"We found a pull ring, Sergeant," yells the brother.

This gets Fugate's attention. "Where?"

"About five meters from the bunker, toward the LZ."

Fugate turns to Roper. "We're going to need to know about anybody seen near the bunker and the LZ after the incident, sir," he says. Roper nods, dumb quiet, like the explosion sucked out all his words.

The chopper's here—I hear its thump, catch the blare of its landing lights. I imagine them throwing the body bag into its belly, the sag and slosh of the rubber, and that damn vomit surprises me this time, burrows up from my belly fast as a rat and jumps from my mouth. I spit the drag-ends of the puke to my boots and lift my head to check, but nobody noticed—they're too deaf and blind from the Huey, which is lifting away.

And while they watch the Dustoff disappear into the black sky, I see something they don't—Big Brother Strode striding toward Fugate, and handing something over.

I watch Fugate as he burns his flashlight over it—it's small and thin, the size of a playing card. Fugate jerks up his head, like the thing has the damn answer written on it. He stares at the crowd. I can't figure out what he's holding in his hand. Fugate shakes his head and holds the thing up to Roper, who barrels down his flashlight, his mouth moving in a curse.

The base has gone quiet, the noise of the rotor blades fading to a mutter, the engine whine thinned to vanishing. The men turn their heads back to Fugate.

"Nobody move," he says.

He flares his flashlight over us, checking faces, stopping at the edge of the crowd, where I'm standing, my feet gripping the ground like a monkey. The light dazzles my eyes.

"Private Jackson," says Fugate.

"Sergeant," I murmur, close-lipped, afraid to open my mouth, afraid that if I do, my fear will leap out from inside me and sing.

"I ask you a question, you tell me the fucking truth, you understand?"

I nod, mouth clasped shut.

"I said, do you understand?"

"Sergeant." I do it: I retch the word, loud and clear, and close up my lips fast.

"Where is Private First Class Esposito?"

I'm so bowled-over surprised by this question, Fugate might as well have asked me if I know the way to San Jose. My brain clunks and I swallow and I say, "I don't know, Sergeant." And I say it as sure and clear as I can, but it comes out like a question, like I'm guilty or dumb or both.

Heads are turning, looking at me, and I look back through the crowd, but Esposito's nowhere to be seen.

"Search his hooch," says Fugate, holding the card in his

fingers, and Roper's flashlight catches it and I see the long white seam down its center.

Esposito's daughter.

"He was talking about doing a job on the CO," says a voice. It's Carter, standing beside me, and he must have seen that picture too because he's looking right at me, straight in the face, his eyes smart with the truth—that it was me carrying that photograph, not Esposito. A smirk tweaks his mouth.

"Is that right," says Roper, who's found his words again, righteousness in his voice.

The men start jawblocking; I look straight ahead at Fugate. But I still feel them, those dank eyes resting on the side of my face—and I glance back to Carter, who's still gazing at me, his lips curled up nasty.

A grumble and a yell—and we all turn to see him being dragged over: Esposito, stoned out and sore-assed, troubling over his footing like a toddler.

"What the fuck?" he's saying, slurring his words. The light flashes over his face; his eyes are slow with sleep.

"Private First Class Esposito, where were you at zero three hundred hours?" hollers Fugate as Esposito is pulled toward the crowd.

"In my hooch, where else? What is this?" He eyes Vance's blasted bunker. "What the—"

"Any reason you left this by Captain Vance's hooch?" Fugate holds up the photograph; the light flashes off the picture.

"Another probe?" says Esposito; and Pederson, who's pulled him from his rack across the firebase, shakes his head.

Esposito takes his shorn round skull in his hands. "Oh, man," he says. "He was in there?"

"Answer the goddamn question," says Fugate.

"What—" Esposito squints toward the picture, but his mind-cogs are jammed up with the dope, and he's lost.

"Your damn photograph," says Roper.

Carter nudges me—a girl's nudge, light and bony—and I look and he's offering me a cigarette. I shake my head, and he places one in his own mouth; and there's something in the slow way he settles it between his fat lips, the care with which he lights it, that tells me he's going to keep his information to himself.

Esposito's shaking his head—he's so doped up, Roper's words didn't get to his brain, just rolled right back out of his ears.

"Put him in the medical bunker, let him cool off," says Fugate to Pederson. "Make sure he's got no weapons, and watch him. He's a fucking disgrace. They're gonna fry you for this, asshole."

Fugate's holding his flashlight steady over Esposito's face; and I can see Esposito's skin is pulled white, his eyes dim and helpless: this is one bad trip he's riding. I see him search the crowd for a friend, and he clocks me. And I'm thinking that this is just what Raffaele Alberto Esposito had coming—greaseball spent his life passing off his shit to other people—when Esposito's face slackens, mouth upside-downing, eyes screwing; and he's bawling, this big, torn-ass Marine kid blubbing in the dust, his fear and confusion so pungent you can nearly taste it; and it reminds me of my nephew and his wholesale surprise, his soft-limbed weakness when Jeannie took him for spanking, and my mouth drops open and the words fall out: "He gave it to me."

"What did you say, Jackson?" says Fugate.

Carter sucks his smoke too hard, and bursts out coughing. I catch his face in the corner of my eye, sense his dark-eyed, flesh-lipped spite, and I feel the urge to slap him off me, like he's some nasty, jungle-scuttling suckbug. I breathe deep, testing the words in my brain, like I'm running lines for a show.

"He gave me the photograph. Yesterday."

Pederson lets go of Esposito; he staggers.

The base is turned down quiet. Over the mountains, the darkness is getting weak, and dawn is creeping. And my hands and feet get still, like whatever puppet master's been jerking my strings has quit, and that fire inside me dims, and I feel the day fresh and ugly on my face, and I tell the bright, terrible truth.

Jeannie / May 1968

The flag was hanging outside the house; the windows shone clean. Jeannie knocked on the door, and turned to straighten Billy's tie.

"Nobody here," said Charlie.

Jeannie knocked louder; the door swung open and Frank Sinatra, the sound of men laughing, washed over the porch.

"Honey!" Jeannie's dad was wearing a smart suit, pressed and well-fitting. He pulled in for a dry kiss. "You look tired. You okay?"

"She hasn't been sleeping," said Billy, shaking Jeannie's dad by the hand.

"I'm fine," said Jeannie. "My allergies acting up, is all."

"You keep an eye on her, Billy," said her dad, lifting Charlie into his arms and tickling him under the chin. "When she was a kid, only time she couldn't sleep was when she'd done something bad. You better make sure she hasn't been taking your checkbook for a spin in those fancy city stores of yours."

"Daddy," said Jeannie, but the word came out husked. She cleared her throat and glanced at Billy; he was grinning.

"Whatever it takes to keep the old lady happy," he said.

"Too right, too right," said Jeannie's dad. He waved his arm. "Enough hanging around on the doorstep. C'mon in." He tucked Charlie under his arm like a parcel and disappeared into the party. Billy raised his eyebrows; Jeannie took his arm and led him inside.

"I've never seen your father so excited," murmured Billy as they removed their shoes in the hallway, setting them next to the dozen pairs of brogues and loafers that nosed the wall like boats.

"He's always jazzed on Memorial Day," said Jeannie. Feeling a little exposed in her stocking feet, she pushed her pumps back on.

"Hey, you track dirt on that carpet, you're going to clean it up," said Billy.

Jeannie gave him a smile. "He'll hear you," she whispered; then she smoothed down her dress, and stepped into the living room.

Before she left home, Jeannie saw these men together many times, on Memorial Days, Veterans Days, Corps birthdays—each year the group a little sparser, the guts a little fatter, the drinking a little greedier. Today she had expected a small knot of liver-spotted men with thin voices and weak handshakes, and was surprised to find they filled the room with their noise and their shining heads and their softening brawn. Hardly a woman among them—the wives dead, divorced, or excused. As she entered the room, she drew eyes and murmurs, a few nods; then, to her relief, she disappeared again, as anecdotes were resumed and drinks refilled.

"Here she is!" It was Bernie, pushing his way through the group of men that bunched by the record player. He funneled a fistful of potato chips into his mouth and licked grease from each finger before shaking Billy's hand. "You must be the knight in shining armor," he said. Billy grinned. "Happy to meet you."

"You too, sir," said Billy.

"You remember Bernie Garubbo?" said Jeannie. "He was my boss at the diner." She heard the smallness of her own voice.

"Best hamburger I ever had in the city." Billy swabbed his palm on the back of his pant-leg.

"You should come by again."

"I moved across town to SF General, otherwise you wouldn't be able to get rid of me. My father's still at UCSF—I'll send him your way."

"Do, do," said Bernie. The two men nodded at each other in silence. Across the room, Charlie yelped with laughter as Jeannie's dad turned him upside down and ran his fingers over his stomach.

"That your ankle-biter?" said Bernie.

"Sure is," said Billy.

"Lively little fella. Looks just like Kip when he was a kid."

"He's naughty like Kip, that's for sure," said Jeannie.

"A kid's got to have a little mischief. Here, Jeannie—looks like your husband could do with a beer." Bernie drained his Schlitz and shook the bottle. "Another for me too."

Jeannie went to fetch the beers from the kitchen, and she was straight back in the diner, Bernie's Old Spice in her nostrils, her ears burning as she sassed him under her breath. Her heart flared with resentment, and she thought of how wrong he was about her, how she wasn't the shy little good girl anymore, how she was as grown and guilty as the rest of them—guiltier, even. She felt a scuttle of fear. Returning with the beers, her hands sticky on the glass, she told herself that she was safe, that there would be no reason for the draft board to question the letter, that soon Charles Dewey would receive his exemption and it would all be done, forgotten. Billy and Bernie took the beers without looking at her.

"Garubbo." It was Jeannie's dad, grasping Bernie by his stout shoulder and beaming. "What do you think of my baby girl? A doctor's wife now, living in the heart of the city."

"The city's not what it used to be," said Bernie, shaking his head. "Full of faggots and wetbacks." He took a long swallow of beer. "Tell me, how's that boy of yours doing?"

"Still in country. North Central Coast. It's—what?—eighty klicks from Khe Sanh."

Bernie frowned. "It's ugly out there. Kip seeing any action?"

Jeannie's dad nodded. "Wrote me a couple of weeks ago, tells me they're getting a lot of heat—getting probed every few days. They got some big guns up there—155-millimeter howitzers." Bernie whistled. "I tell you, though, those slants don't take no for an answer."

"Those yellow monkeys don't change. Good news is, these days we got better tech-no-lo-gy." Bernie leaned on each syllable of the word as though it might be new to everybody. Billy was nodding.

"Kid's right in the middle of the shitstorm, still manages to crack a few jokes. Here." Jeannie's dad reached inside his jacket and removed an envelope that was soft with handling. He handed it to Bernie and watched his friend as he read the letter, his face twitching in muted reflections of Bernie's expressions—concentration, concern, amusement. Jeannie wished Kip could have seen it.

"Kid's a riot," said Bernie, stuffing the letter back into the envelope and folding it roughly. Jeannie saw something pinch her dad's face; he retrieved the envelope and smoothed it straight before tucking it back against his chest.

"Sure is," he said.

"Still screwing around, even in the goddamn Marine Corps."

Jeannie's dad cleared his throat, his face closing over—and it was gone, the looseness, the bonhomie, and Jeannie knew it would be a few drinks before it came back. She excused herself to pour him another bourbon.

—

An hour later, Jeannie was listening to Bernie loud-voicing about the protesters in Maryland, his shirt showing dabs of sweat at the chest, his neck-folds greasy with perspiration. A series of thud-and-whap noises turned her head, and she was half relieved to see Charlie dragging her dad's American Heritage books from the shelf, one volume at a time. Jeannie excused herself and tidied the spilled books from the carpet.

"Charlie, go play in the backyard. The door's open."

"Mama, come."

"In a minute. Let me check on Grandpa."

Her dad was standing at the television set, a large drink in his hand, his neck craned to bring the numbers on the dial into focus.

"Either those darn numbers are getting smaller or I'm getting older." He smiled at her, a gentle smile, the kind he usually saved for Charlie.

"Let me help you, Daddy."

"Just want to see the headlines."

"Which network?"

"CBS."

Jeannie turned the dial and went outside to find Charlie. He had discovered an old Wiffle ball buried in the prickles; they rolled it to each other across the yard, Charlie squeaking with laughter as it scuttered between his feet. They were bouncing it against the wall when Billy appeared, grim-faced.

"You'd better come."

Jeannie let the ball drop for Charlie and stepped over the threshold. The house was empty, the guests vanished. A soap opera wailed from the television set.

"What's happening?" she asked Billy, a slow fear spreading through her. She heard the sound of glass breaking and ran to the kitchen to find her dad standing at the counter, smashing tumblers into the sink.

"Daddy?"

"Get the hell out!" His thumb was bleeding, dropping crimson spots the size of quarters onto the counter, the floor, the broken glass.

"Sir, you've got to stop." Billy took him by the shoulders, but Jeannie's dad shook him away.

"Get off me."

"Mama?" Charlie was at Jeannie's leg, his eyes round.

"What's going on?" said Jeannie.

Her dad smashed the last tumbler. His hands shook against the countertop, and he breathed hard. When he turned to look at her, his face was putty-colored and slicked with sweat.

"Please," he said.

"You go with Charlie, Jeannie—take him to the beach," said Billy, keeping his eyes close on her dad like he was a loose animal. "Sir, I'm going to stay here, just to make sure you're all right."

"If you have any damn respect, you'll leave," said Jeannie's dad, but the fight had gone out of him, and his shoulders dropped.

Billy sat on a kitchen stool and nodded at Jeannie. She hesitated; *Go,* he mouthed, and, deferring to the doctorly command in his face, she hoisted Charlie into her arms and walked across the kitchen, her heels tapping stupidly on the linoleum.

She stayed in the hallway a little while, listening; but it was quiet, save for the creak of wicker as Billy shifted his weight on his stool. Then she heard a long, shuddering sigh—and, wondering if her dad was crying, thought to turn back into the kitchen, but something held her to the floor.

"Let me check your hand," Billy was saying. "Sir? It's going to be all right."

Jeannie swallowed, opened the front door, and closed it behind her, coming up short against a man sitting on the porch, head in hands. It was Bernie; seeing Jeannie, he staggered to his feet.

"You okay, doll?" He stood too close, staring into her face; she smelled the stench of old swelter under his cologne and took a step back.

"Bernie, what the hell happened?"

"Your father saw something on the news. Something bad." That same unblinking stare—it raised shivers at the nape of Jeannie's neck.

"What?" Jeannie's heart banged. But in all her scenarios of being discovered, this one didn't make sense. "What's going on?"

Before the words left Bernie's mouth, she knew.

"It's Kip."

Pain squeezed her heart, clenching it hard, and harder, until it felt as though the muscle might die.

"There's been an attack. A small Marine base, overrun by Viet Cong. They attacked at night, blew up the ammunition dump. We've re-seized the base, but it was bad. The TV camera showed the sign the Marines had put up on the hill, with their unit written on it. It was Kip's unit."

The grip on her heart tightened, and she opened her mouth, but nothing came out. An aching knot, thick and unrelenting as sinew, climbed her throat.

"It's bad news, Jeannie. Only one infantry platoon survived—they were outside the base when it happened. Nobody else made it."

"So he might be all right," she said, her voice strange in her ears, small and swelling, like the shout of someone falling from a height. "We've got to call somebody." She turned back to the house.

Bernie held her by the wrist. "Only infantry, Jeannie."

She heard his words, but they didn't stick.

"Kip wasn't infantry," said Bernie. "He was artillery."

The squeeze on her heart unclasped, and something cold and excruciating seeped inside her chest.

"They showed pictures," said Bernie. "It's all gone." He shook his head, as though he'd seen a terrible marvel. "There's nothing left."

The story landed on the front pages with a nauseating flourish, elbowing aside the news of trouble in France and speculation over the Democratic nomination. It lingered stubbornly for a few days, growing smaller, more abbreviated with each edition, as though everything that could be said about it, had been; until one day it was blown clean away by the shooting of Bobby Kennedy. A week after Memorial Day, Jeannie found the story dawdling on page five of *The New York Times,* in a small square of newsprint the size of a cracker. Every morning, her dad called the Department of Defense; every day, he was told that Kip's remains would be dispatched as soon as possible —but that, with respect, the Graves Registration was overloaded, and there was a backlog identifying remains. Every night, when the rest of the house was asleep, Jeannie called Mrs. Moon's house, but Lee was never there. Jeannie wondered if she was visiting her apartment, wondered how quickly she had given up coming; and her longing for the younger girl mixed uneasily with her longing for her brother.

There was no question of returning to Noe; an unhappy witchcraft was keeping her in her childhood house until Kip came home. Jeannie slept in her old room, Charlie in a nest of blankets on the floor; some nights Billy would drive over after work and they would spoon together uncomfortably in her childhood bed. Jeannie spent the days sitting in the backyard, shivering and smoking and turning away Aunt Ruth's offers of lemonade and shawls; there was a kind of familiarity in it that was almost reassuring. Jeannie's dad said barely a word, disappearing for long spells before returning white-lipped and panicky, crashing knives and plates as he washed dishes that had already been soaped. "I've never seen him like this," whispered Aunt Ruth; and what her half-dozen ailments didn't do to her, the news about Kip did—something in her demeanor dimmed, her eyelids growing fat and hooded, as though she were perpetually on the brink of sleep. Charlie sat at the picture window for hours at a time, listening to Aunt Ruth's stories and watching visitors come and go, as if he too were waiting for the government vehicle to pull up outside the house, for the officer dressed in a solemn uniform and a poker face to knock at the door.

Ten days after Memorial Day, Jeannie sat on the couch with her eyes shut, imagining Kip was behind the wall in his bedroom, sulking and listening to the Giants game. It was a strange comfort, imagining it was only her mom who was gone. Her grief for her mom had become something solid, perpetual, contained—a familiar and unhappy roommate; but the loss of Kip was ferocious, borderless. She craved these moments of solitude when Charlie was asleep, Billy was at the hospital, and her dad was out roaming. She would call Mrs. Moon's house and leave another message for Lee; then she would switch off the lights, pull the drapes shut, and concentrate on the spell. Sometimes, if she shut her eyes and held still, she could hear the hum of noise from Kip's room, the creak of the floor as he stood to adjust the radio. She could hear it now—could even hear the clenched snarl at a fly out, the low-voiced *yes* at a home run. But another noise intruded—shoes on the porch, the grate of a key at the front door—and the spell was broken. Jeannie opened her eyes to the darkened room, and gathered the blanket that lay across her legs.

"Hi, honey," she said. But it wasn't Billy.

"Jeannie." Her dad stood in the doorway, shadowy in the low light, swaying.

"Daddy?" She was afraid to be alone with him these days. "You all right?"

Her dad switched on the overhead lamp, shocking the room with light. His face was soft with exhaustion.

"You going to bed?" he said.

Jeannie heard the plea in his voice. "No," she said. She guided him to the couch like he was a man much older than his years; he stumbled, his elbow knocking a carton of corn-snacks from the armrest. He watched them spill over the carpet with an expression of defeat.

"Anybody come?" he said.

Jeannie shook her head.

Her dad took a large, noisy breath, as if preparing for a sigh; but it didn't come. "I knew it would end this way," he said. "He wouldn't be told."

"He was always stubborn," said Jeannie.

"He was his mother's boy." The words hurt Jeannie; she bowed her head. "He always listened to you." Her dad took a thick swallow. "I'm sure he talked to you. About enlisting." Jeannie couldn't look at him. "Even you couldn't talk any sense into him."

Jeannie closed her eyes and saw it pressed into the darkness like a weal—the typed name of the boy who had everything, the boy she'd saved. She longed for Lee, perhaps as much as anything because she belonged to a different world, a world away from her dad and Aunt Ruth and death and Toast'ems and the unhappy plaid print on the wallpaper. Jeannie opened her eyes and was surprised to see her dad, only a few inches from her face, looking into her as though for an answer.

"He wouldn't be told," she said.

Days passed, and nobody came. The Department of Defense told them to be patient. Jeannie woke each morning to her house of ghosts. There was a yearning in their waiting, their anticipation of the visit, when they would be given confirmation and condolences; when they would be granted the papers to continue on their journey, to feel the new and foreign country beneath their feet.

One morning, the mailman handed Jeannie an envelope with Kip's writing scratched across the front; she dropped it as though it had burned her.

"Butterfingers today, huh?" said the mailman. Jeannie closed the door on his smiling face and carried the envelope into the house, laid upon her palms like an offering.

"What you got, honey?" said Aunt Ruth. She was pouring coffee from the pot; the steam caught in the air like gauze.

"It's a letter," said Jeannie. Aunt Ruth fumbled the pot, splashing coffee over her hand; she shook it out, her face wincing.

"It's come?" she said. She wiped her fingers on a dish towel.

Jeannie shook her head. "It's from Kip," she said. "He must have mailed it. Before." It always took a couple of weeks to get

Kip's letters, a couple of weeks for him to get theirs—he wrote how screwy it was, getting a response a month after he'd mailed something, like the long wait for the echo when you stood at the edge of the old quarry and yelled.

"Open it, honey," said Aunt Ruth. Her hand showed patches of scald.

"You should put that in water."

"I'm all right."

"It's addressed to Daddy."

"What is it?" Jeannie's dad entered the kitchen, bathrobe parting precariously, showing vein-stenciled white legs.

Jeannie handed him the envelope and watched him balk. He handed it back to her. "Why the hell are you giving me this?"

"It just came, Daddy."

Her dad shook his head and took a step back, his face white. "I can't," he said. "Not now."

At eleven o'clock that night, the telephone rang. Everybody was in bed. Jeannie couldn't sleep, lay wide-eyeing the gloom, listening to the slow drag-and-wash of Charlie's breathing. At the drill of the phone, she struggled from under the bedspread, letting Billy's arm—draped over her waist—drop against the mattress.

"Hello?"

"Jeannie?"

Jeannie felt her heart lift, the warmth of her blood in her body. "Lee."

"I heard about your brother."

Jeannie opened her mouth to speak, but nothing came, only a clicking sound at the back of her throat.

"Jeannie?"

"You did?" managed Jeannie.

"Dorothy told my mom." Lee's voice was cool and dim.

"It's good to hear your voice," said Jeannie, wiping her face with her palm. "Where have you been? Did you get my messages? I was worried you'd think—"

"When are you coming back?" Lee sounded far away.

"I don't know." Jeannie coughed to clear the swelling in her throat. "A while."

"I can't talk. I just wanted to say—" Jeannie could hear music playing in the background—headlong, psychedelic. "Listen. Maybe he didn't die. Maybe he's just—missing."

Frustration prickled Jeannie's neck. "It's not like your brother, Lee."

"They're liars, Jeannie. Don't believe anything they say."

"It was on the TV, Lee. Nobody survived."

"If you hadn't believed it, you wouldn't have seen it."

A sharp pain went to Jeannie's forehead; she rubbed at it with her fingers. "Jesus, Lee. You're stoned."

"Just mellow."

"This is real."

"I got to go."

"Lee—"

"Bye-bye, blackbird."

The line went dead. Jeannie banged down the receiver and leaned against the counter, her head in her hands, her little finger pushing at the blade of pain in her forehead. She stayed that way for a while, her eyes closed, trying to subdue the emotions that Lee had witched out of her—anger, longing, shame, loneliness. When she opened her eyes, she saw Kip's letter, watching her from the counter.

She laid her palm on it, tried to feel its heat, feel the chain of touch with her brother. She took it up, weighed its flimsiness in her hand. She turned over the envelope, eased her finger under the seal, and tugged the letter free. The handwriting ran slant down the page, the jags of the letters pulled high, like stitching yanked tight. The scrawl of someone in a hurry; but Kip had remembered to note the date and place in the top right-hand corner, the way their mom had taught them.

The night still held something of the June sunshine—the darkness was halfhearted—and Jeannie sat on the floor to read the letter, the linoleum warm like skin against her naked legs. She read, starting slowly, then speeding, until she reached the end of the letter; then she read it again, and again, checking and re-checking the date noted at the top of the page.

"Daddy!" she yelled, scrambling from the floor, her feet sliding. She ran to her dad's bedroom, shaking his sheet-cloaked body and shouting into his face. He looked at her with frightened eyes.

"What, what?" He sat up, whipping the sheets to one side—the Marine, ready for anything. He was naked, his skin pulled tight against his bones, his penis flopping grub-like at his groin.

"Kip's alive," she said, and she heard her voice, screamy in the quiet, heard movement in the house. She pushed the letter at her dad; he snatched it and fumbled at the bedside lamp. It fell, throwing its light dementedly up the wall.

"What the hell—"

Billy was at the doorway, eyebrows lifting at the sight of the overturned lamp, his naked father-in-law, Jeannie wild at his side. "What's going on?"

"Kip's okay," said Jeannie, her breath roughing her windpipe. "He wasn't at the base, he was—he was in jail. He's done something bad, real bad."

Jeannie's dad sat up through the night, his pajama pants pulled up skewed, bare-chested, puzzling at the wallpaper of the living room, as though, if he stared long enough, he might unfold the pattern—as though if only he could unknot its corners and smooth its lines, he might discover the answer to a riddle. Jeannie paced, talking and planning; Billy rubbed his eyes, a look of bewilderment stuck on his face.

At dawn, Jeannie packed her things and dressed Charlie, readying to leave with Billy for Noe. While Billy loaded the car, Jeannie scribbled a note and placed it on the coffee table next to her dad, who was curled asleep on the couch, his forehead held in a frown.

They drove alongside the park, the sidewalks clean in the early sunlight, Jeannie leaning forward in her seat and knocking her fingers against the dashboard, until Billy pushed a damp palm over her hand.

"Shush, Jeannie."

"I'll call at nine o'clock," said Jeannie. "I'll find out what's going on."

"They might not be able to tell you a whole lot. Seems like a real mess over there."

"It's some stupid mistake," Jeannie repeated. "Kip wouldn't do that to somebody. Something's wrong." She stuck her thumb between her teeth and bit hard, then sat back and drummed her palms against her knees. "They've arrested the wrong person—or he's gotten mixed up in something. Damn." Jeannie slapped the dashboard; Billy gave her a stern look. "Stupid kid. It's the same damn thing. He gets in with some bad kids, something goes wrong, and they pin it on him. It's Pete Marshall all over again."

"Jeannie," said Billy. "Quit cursing."

Kip / May 1968

I opened my eyes to a knife of light. I was underground, could tell by the damp, the smell of worms, that I was deep in the earth. My lungs panicked, tried to stuff themselves with air; and it took a few moments for my brain to tell my dumb body I wasn't buried, I was bunkered, the sun scoring hot lines around the hatch above me. Pain sizzled my brain. My legs were stiff-sore, and I shifted them to bring the blood back; but the muscles cried, and I stopped. I leaned against the wall of earth and moved my body in tiny, chickenshit experiments. My bones clicked dry. And as the daylight fried blotches into my brain, I had that feeling, the same feeling I had the day after Mom got hit, the day after Bobby smashed his car: that slow-wash feeling of something hazy and evil, some just-vanishing nightmare, curdling into straight, throat-clasping fact.

The previous night came at me in blinks—the hatch wide-mouthing in front of me, the sag of the stretcher, a ripped arm lollygagging over the side. After that, everything was blurred—a movie happening in slow, smeary pieces, with big panicky spaces in between. Hutch's face leering at me like a jack-in-the-box, fist springing for my mouth; me, bunched like a bitch in the dirt, boots slamming my ribs, my back, my ass. Roper yelling.

The blast. I felt the ground shake with it, smelled the punch of cordite, felt the shove of the explosion at my back. It was settled the moment the clip was released, the spoon unlevered; that long saggy moment before the explosion, a moment of no sound, my legs running themselves away as time caught up with itself and the grenade found its mark. It was still all over me—the cookout smell, the dust, the ear-ringing, skin-slapping stun. I felt sick with the fact of it—like that hot bright light was radioactive, leaving every cell shivering and retching in its wake. I wanted it to stop, wanted that clean release, the kind I had when I hurled after Skid died; the sweet-choir deliverance I had felt just hours before, when I opened my mouth and sang the big, brave truth. I tipped myself forward over the earth and tried to force it, opened my mouth and tried to roll the nausea up my throat and over my tongue, heaved my body; but it was no fucking use. Just a dry-heave gagging, the sickness squatting back down in my cells like thousands of tiny rotten toads.

I told myself he would have died anyway, would have kept throwing himself back into this clusterfuck of a war as long as it was still going; and if this war didn't kill him, the next one would, or the one after that. I remembered what Pete told me after Bobby slammed into that tree: "If it's happened, it's past. So it don't fucking exist anymore. You can't sweat something that ain't *real.*" It was how he moved past his dad's beatings, how he blew off the Old Ted business. I closed my eyes and forced the explosion away, focused on the wet silence of the bunker, tried to summon something new, something else to be right-now real.

The hatch blew big with light. My eyes screwed against it. Something bulky slid and landed on the ground.

"Private Jackson."

I opened my eyes. It was the corpsman, the one who'd diapered Esposito's ass, the one who'd helped carry the stretcher from the bunker. He was crouching in front of me, solid in the daylight that poured from overhead.

"I've come to check on you," he said. My eyes eased against the light, and I watched him: his fat-curded muscle bulking his shirt, his round face frowning, his fingers unfastening his bag. And something in his flesh-and-blood presence, in the aliveness thrumming behind his eyes, made me feel ashamed and afraid. All those bones and fibers and nerves and arteries and entrails and brain tissue, all woven and conjured together, adding up to a body, a one-of-a-kind soul. The work of a zillion years; the work of a god. Finished, at the fling of a palm.

"Corpsman," I said, but my voice wasn't ready, had been sunk too long in the dark, and the first part of the word was lost.

He kept his eyes on his bag, flicking through plastic pouches that crinkled at his fingers. He pulled out a small flashlight and aimed it fast and sloppy at my left eye, then my right, then stashed the flashlight away. I watched as he felt the bones of my legs, pressed my belly, my ribs, my collarbone. Pain spread where his fingers went, and I clenched my teeth; but I wanted more—more pain, something that would take everything from me, that would smash everything else out of my brain. He moved his fingers to the bridge of my nose, my cheek—threads of pain, pulling in stings across my face. He was close to me, his nose breath warm and snorty on my skin, and I held my own breath for as long as I could. When I breathed out, his shoulders jumped, his eyes flicking to mine, then away again. And in that instant I saw what he didn't want me to—something shameful in his eyes, something like fear. He moved away, his eyes down.

"Just bruising," he said. "You might have cracked a couple of ribs." His words were quiet and strange-weighted.

"Where am I?" I asked.

"Chopper's coming to take you to Danang," he said. I stared at his large, soft face, willed his eyes to lift to mine again, so I could see what was there. He wouldn't do it.

"The brig," I said.

He fastened his bag and swung it over his shoulder.

"Hey."

"You'll be handed over to CID. They'll explain everything."

"Hey. Look at me." My voice was loud.

The corpsman placed his foot on a snout of rock and hauled himself out of the hatch. The steel door slammed.

Next time I opened my eyes it was to the whump of a chopper closing in on the earth above me. It came again, that free, blank moment before memory lurched in, bringing its cold facts and its charges of murder. I closed my eyes, wanted to sink back into sleep, wanted no part of it, wanted nothing to do with the world and all its fucking history; but metal clanged above me, and the hatch blared open—they wanted me out.

"Move it," came a yell. I eased myself up; my foot gave.

"Jesus fucking Christ," muttered the voice. Then, hollering again, "Hey, you—come help me!"

Hands wriggled down from the light, and I held up my arms. They dragged me out, the sunset smacking me blind. They pulled me across the firebase to the LZ, my ankles rolling, my eyes squinting against snatched faces—Hutch, Pederson, Roper—players in a dream. They pushed me into the Huey, and I slipped on the skids, banging my chin on the metal floor.

"Get the fuck up," somebody yelled, and I heaved myself up to sit, the sun pinching my eyes, the noise of the rotor blades beating through my body, the insecty hum of men shouting. The slow lift, and we were up, the yelling faded out, the air cool and moving. Inside the chopper lay a kid, a blood-wadded bandage around his leg, the slow, patient look of morphine in his eyes, a medic crouching at his side. Next to me slouched the crew chief, a farm-boy type, reading a book. He looked me over and smacked the gum in his mouth.

"Going to Dong Ha," he said, like he was a conductor on a streetcar. "CID will pick you up and fly you to Danang."

I nodded, and put my hand to the sting at my chin. My palm smeared red.

He watched me, gum rolling in his cheeks. He closed his book and tucked it into his jacket pocket. "Why'd you do it, man?"

I turned away and looked out over the canopy, back toward the firebase. I watched it grow smaller, watched belches of smoke rise up from the mountain, flashes of fire.

Jeannie / June 1968

When they arrived back at Noe, Billy telephoned Dorothy to tell her about Kip. Dorothy insisted that Billy, Jeannie, and Charlie stay with her on Spruce for a while. Jeannie bickered—any meeting up with Lee would be impossible under her mother-in-law's roof—but she could find no good argument against it, and moving to neutral ground suited her restlessness.

"We need to draw together at times like this," said Dorothy as she installed Billy and Jeannie in the guest suite at the top of the house and handed Charlie to Fanny, the maid with the cushiony bosom and the hard stare. Jeannie set up at the telephone in the hallway to continue her quest for information through the maze of the Department of Defense telephone exchange. Eventually she connected with a voice named Ettlinger, who told her in chipper tones that Kip had been transported to a secure facility and was awaiting formal charges; that once he'd received these, he'd be assigned legal counsel, who would keep her closely informed; but that until then, she would have to be patient, and wait.

Several days passed. Every morning, Jeannie telephoned Ettlinger, but there was no news. Despite her pestering, Ettlinger remained Labrador-ish in disposition; he was so dependably happy to hear from her that Jeannie began calling more frequently—four, five times a day. Those remaining hours of the day, Jeannie was skittish with anxiety and boredom. One morning over breakfast—always formal, with Charlie expected to sit quietly for up to an hour while Dorothy read *The New York Times* and ate her eggs in small, agonizing bites—Jeannie raised the subject of returning to Noe. Dorothy held up a palm.

"Don't say another word," she said. "You're not imposing one bit."

"But—"

Dorothy leaned across the table and squeezed Jeannie's wrist. "Save your strength for the next few months. You'll need it."

"You're too good to us, Mother," said Billy as he rose from his seat and brushed pastry flakes from his shirt. But Jeannie detected a subdued fury in Dorothy's sugared politeness with Billy, her refusal to look Jeannie in the eye. Dorothy wanted to keep them quarantined—to keep them close, so they couldn't leak their news into the world.

She had proved a diligent warden: Jeannie had not been able to leave the house without her; and every evening, when, dismayed and isolated, she had tried to telephone Lee, Dorothy had appeared like a genie, a question in her face. And so Jeannie would call her dad instead, waiting for the long, lonely ring, each time letting it run a little longer, imagining the receiver shaking on its cradle in the kitchen. Each time, she was relieved he wasn't there. There was something monstrous in his unrealized grief, and it made her afraid.

"Running errands again, is he?" Dorothy would say, strain tightening her beautiful face.

"I guess," Jeannie would murmur; and she wondered where he was running to, which bar he'd chosen to empty his billfold in, before driving home to scrub the house of all its mucky history.

One Saturday morning, Dorothy left the house to play her monthly bridge game, leaving her captives alone for the first time. Billy was at the hospital, and Jeannie was playing doctors with Charlie in the drawing room. Jeannie waited until the noise of Dorothy's car had died, and unhooked herself from the plastic stethoscope.

"Just a minute, Charlie," she said, half running into the hallway. She dialed Mrs. Moon's number. No answer. Noticing Dorothy's address book on the hall table, she picked it up and flicked to *W.* Virginia Walker. She held the page open with her elbow and dialed.

"Walker residence." Lee's mother, Virginia—an ice-cream blonde whose coolness could be felt, even from four miles away.

"Hello." Jeannie cleared her throat. "Is Lee there?"

"Who's speaking?"

"It's—" Jeannie glanced at the address book for a name. "Evelyn. I'm a friend from school."

"Oh." Virginia sounded surprised. "Well, of course. Hold on, dear."

Jeannie's heart rode fast. Her body filled with longing, and for a moment she forgot her spoiled grief and her fear; felt nothing but herself, her body, separate from her dad, her mom, Kip, only hers. She heard movement at the other end of the line, and held her breath.

"Hello?"

Jeannie's heart banged. "Hello."

There was a pause, and Jeannie wondered if Lee had heard her. "Who's this?" said Lee, suspicion in her voice.

"It's me."

"It's you?" Jeannie could hear the slow smile. Lee dropped her voice to a whisper. "Where are you? I've been trying to get ahold of you."

"You were?" Jeannie felt a warm flush of pleasure. "I'm at Dorothy's."

"Sounds like a blast."

"She insisted, after everything that happened."

"Everything that . . . ?"

"With Kip."

"Right." Lee gave a low whistle. "Gee. Like things aren't bad enough, you're shacked up with the Wicked Witch of the West."

The party, the breaking glass, Kip's letter; Jeannie gave a dry swallow.

"You okay?" said Lee.

"You were right," said Jeannie.

"What do you mean?"

"Kip. He's alive." It was Jeannie who was whispering now. She watched the kitchen doorway for a sign of Fanny, listened for footsteps. She heard only Charlie, chattering in the drawing room.

"What?"

"He's—he's all right. He survived."

"No shit," said Lee. There was wonder in her voice, as though her own magic had come true.

"Lee!" came a stern call from the background.

"Sorry, Mom."

Jeannie felt a sting of embarrassment, enough to stay her from asking the question that dragged at her stomach.

Lee said it for her. "I need to see you." Her breath was close.

"I know."

"Today."

Jeannie closed her eyes, saw Lee's heart-shaped face, her sandy skin.

"Meet me at Michel's," said Lee. "It's at California and Mason. Twelve o'clock."

"Can we go someplace private?" said Jeannie.

"Later. Meet me at the restaurant first."

"Why?"

"Let's call it a date," said Lee.

Jeannie watched as Charlie wandered out of the drawing room, clutching a toy syringe, a smile breaking over his face, and was gripped by the need to escape.

"You'll be there?" said Lee.

"Yes," said Jeannie, nodding at Fanny as she stepped from the kitchen, and gesturing for her to take Charlie. "I'm leaving now."

Jeannie knew something was amiss as she climbed the moneyed stretch of California, past the pale-faced cathedral, the leafed hotels, the Frenchified park. She checked the name over the door. The place was too expensive for Lee: an empty French restaurant, grandiose and sad, waiting for its evening life. Nonetheless, Jeannie pushed through the door and stepped inside. The sunlight struggled through the windows, showing every drift of lint on the wooden floor. Jeannie sneezed—an exaggerated *kerchoo* that bounced off the paneled walls. With the beat of heels on wood, a small woman in a dark dress appeared, her face striped with wrinkles.

"I'm sorry," said Jeannie. "I thought I was meeting somebody here, but—"

"In back," said the woman, and gestured for her to follow.

She led Jeannie down a dark corridor. Jeannie heard the murmur of talking, the knock of china. She stepped into a small, electrically lit room hosting a small number of tables, empty but for one. Lee rose from her chair, her face jaundiced by the light.

Seated at the table with her, and turning to look at Jeannie in annoyance, was an enormously fat woman, her face pancaked beige. Next to the woman was a man, his back to Jeannie, his red-raw hand hanging over the edge of the table, dangling a pipe. The man turned his head, and Jeannie took in the beard, the squashed nose, the crawl of hair at the neck of his shirt. Jeannie met Walter's eyes and saw the command, the contempt, forming in his face.

"Who's that?" said the woman, her mouth small between the trembling chunks of her cheeks.

"Hey, come sit," said Lee.

"I don't want anyone else involved," stage-whispered the woman, pitching her bulk over the table toward Lee. Jeannie recognized a certain unsteadiness in the woman's tone—it was the same insulted desperation that Mrs. Dewey had shown in the café on Stockton, just a few weeks ago—and felt uneasy.

Lee was sitting. "She's a friend," she was saying. "She'll help."

They came again, the memories that sutured themselves unhappily together each night as Jeannie lay in bed, awake: Kip in the playground before he enlisted, asking for her to stop him; the night in May, when, soaked in sentiment and self-pity, she'd typed the letter to save someone else's brother; and the punishment—Kip's death, his coming-to-life, his shame. It was happening again—Lee was asking her, persuading her to risk everything for someone else's family.

Jeannie turned and walked. Out of the room, down the corridor, out of the restaurant, letting the door bang behind her; down the sidewalk, her feet brisking with the beat of her heart, avoiding women wearing hats and dragging small dogs, over one, two intersections, pausing at Jones as a bus barreled by—

"Hey!" Jeannie turned to see Lee flying down the street, her hair and beads lifting, her bare thighs shaking with each slap of her sandals against the sidewalk. Jeannie continued across the intersection, listening to the tap-tap of Lee's approach, her self-righteousness gathering.

"What the hell, Jeannie?" Lee grabbed Jeannie's arm and pulled her around.

"You ambushed me, Lee."

"What are you talking about?" Lee's body rose in big breaths, a frown rucking her forehead.

"You tell me how much you need to see me—" Jeannie paused as a gentleman with a large Brylcreemed head walked by, eyeing them vigorously. Lee stared back.

Jeannie lowered her voice. "You say you have to see me here, and now, and it's for this?"

"That's what this is about?"

"These weeks without you . . ." Color spread up Jeannie's neck. Even through the pain and doubt of the past weeks, her desire for Lee had endured, a sickness that wouldn't break.

"I know." Lee smoothed a lick of hair behind Jeannie's ear. "But this is more important. I know you understand that." She brushed her hand down Jeannie's arm, letting their fingers mesh; spines pricked Jeannie's skin.

"I can't worry about the world right now," she said, clasping her fingers with Lee's. "I've got to take care of my own."

Lee frowned, and she tugged her fingers away, pushing her hands into the pockets of her shorts. Jeannie's hand fell awkwardly to her side, and the wind touched her skin. Lee's eyes drew narrow. "'Whoever is not with me is against me, and whoever does not gather with me, scatters.'" Her voice was flat, like she was rehearsing a line; they were the Reverend's words, one of a clutch of hellfire quotes he served up when faced with doubters.

Jeannie gave a half laugh, and, noticing the hard set of Lee's face, said, "You're not serious?"

"You said you were with us."

"I can't do it again. Everything's a mess."

"She's a mother, Jeannie."

"She's a crook." Lee's lips parted in disbelief, and Jeannie felt a tiny squeeze of satisfaction. "This whole thing is crooked." Lee recovered herself, her face wrinkling in impatience as she waved her hand, as if this were a slander she'd heard so often, it couldn't touch her anymore.

"Don't talk shit," she said. "These are lives we're dealing with. Real, flesh-and-blood boys. Slugs and snails and puppy dogs' tails—boys you played Catch-and-Kiss with, boys you were raised with."

"Lee," said Jeannie, reaching her fingers toward the younger girl. "I just can't get involved. You've got to understand that." She touched Lee's arm.

Lee's mouth screwed into a pout. "Unbelievable," she said. "You just—disappear—and now you want out?"

"For Christ's sake," said Jeannie. "Do you have any idea how it's been for us?" Lee shrugged her shoulders, the suggestion of a sneer on her face. Jeannie stepped away to the edge of the sidewalk. "I should never have gotten involved with a damn kid." She felt tears press her eyes; she turned her head to hide them and searched for a cab.

"I might be a kid, but you're selfish as hell," said Lee. "It's the fucking Jeannie Show."

Jeannie turned toward Lee; the distance between them suddenly vast, like they were standing on opposite shores. "You have no idea."

"I get the idea," said Lee. "Kit's okay, so screw everybody else."

"It's *Kip.*" A flush of cold at Jeannie's heart lifted the fine hairs on her skin. "Jesus. I'm an idiot." She saw the yellow of a cab and waved her arm.

"No shit."

"Don't be a brat," said Jeannie. The cab pulled up. Jeannie closed her fingers around the door handle, but Lee stepped forward and prized Jeannie's hand away.

"What are you doing?"

"You can't just leave." Lee moved to block Jeannie's second attempt to open the door, stepping so close their bodies touched. In a crackle of violence and wanting, Jeannie grabbed Lee's arm and yanked her aside.

"You getting in, or what?" yelled the driver.

"She's not," called Lee.

He cursed, and the cab pulled away. Jeannie saw unease reaching across Lee's face.

"You should leave all this behind too, Lee," she said.

The fear disappeared from Lee's face, her features settling into their familiar cocksure expression. "I'm not like you."

They stood in silence, Jeannie turning from Lee to watch for another cab. A long, uncertain moment passed; then Lee spoke.

"What happened?"

"What do you mean?"

"What happened to him? How did he survive?"

"He wasn't there."

"Where was he?"

"He was in jail."

"What?"

Jeannie sighed. "He's accused of—they're saying he blew up his superior. An American. On purpose."

Something faint but electric crossed Lee's face. She placed her hand on Jeannie's wrist; Jeannie didn't move away.

"We only just found out," said Jeannie. "It's a mess, it's a stupid mess."

Lee's face was sharpening into a look of comprehension. "He's one of us," she said. Her fingers closed around Jeannie's wrist.

"What do you mean?" That headache again, pressing her forehead.

"Wow," Lee murmured, shaking her head. "That's something."

"Lee—"

"He's resisting." Lee looked up at Jeannie, glint-eyed. "He's resisting from the inside. There's a movement—the Reverend talked about it. They're dismantling the war from within."

"That's ridiculous." Jeannie pulled her arm free, pain flaring inside her head. Squinting against the sun, she saw another cab loom large, just yards away; she lifted her hand.

"So why did he do it?"

"He didn't do it." The cab drew up; Jeannie opened the door before Lee could stop her. Lee stood, dream-faced.

"Bye, Lee." Jeannie slammed the door and blinked against the needles of light that flashed across her eyes. Lee said nothing, just stared from the sidewalk. As the cab drove away, Jeannie craned her neck to watch Lee recede in the distance. As they reached the end of the block, Jeannie saw Lee lift her arms; it looked as though she was yelling.

Jeannie's headache had eased by the time the cab drew into Spruce. She asked the driver to wait, then rushed inside the house to search for Charlie, finding him asleep in the crib upstairs. She lifted him and ran downstairs, his body bouncing densely in her arms, his face scrunched in confusion. Fanny stood in the hallway, watching resentfully as they descended.

"Back later," called Jeannie, and ducked back into the car, settling Charlie on the seat beside her. He was snug and solid against her. She thought of Lee, the shock of what Jeannie could only see as the end of the affair; the sense of loss imminent but held off, like the blister after a burn. And though Lee's explanation of Kip's situation was cuckoo, it bothered her. Lee, Dorothy, Billy—they assumed that Kip was guilty, that the question wasn't whether he did it, but why.

"The Sunset," she called to the driver. She was going home. He might be angry, drunk, and scared, but her dad was the only one who knew Kip the way she did—the only one who knew that however deluded or misled Kip was, he was the same kid who, every winter at elementary school, would give away his peacoat to the poor Irish kid who lived with his grandmother in the shack near the highway (their mom was too embarrassed to reclaim it), the same kid who spared Jeannie the details of their mom's death. Kip had done his share of lying, stealing, and fighting, but he was a good kid. He was not a murderer.

The drapes were drawn, bottles of milk separating on the doorstep, mail stuffing the mouth of the mailbox. In all his wanderings, her dad had never been gone overnight, had never left for long enough to let the house get shabby. Jeannie knocked on the front door, noticing the twitch of Mrs. Fleish's drapes. She fished the key from her purse and let herself in, hearing Charlie's excited intake of breath: Grandpa's house, where there was a backyard and taffy and his uncle's cowboys and Indians. The house was dim, the suggestion of something unwashed in the air.

"Daddy?" Jeannie called.

Charlie whispered to himself in Jeannie's arms.

She walked into the kitchen, saw scummed plates, a crusted fork lying in the sink, and felt uneasy.

"Daddy? Are you in here?"

She clicked across the linoleum floor, footsteps intruding on the silence, and peered into the living room. It was empty, save for an ugly mess that spilled across the carpet—the drawers of the desk yanked open, dribbling paper, pillows rummaged from the couch, leaves of newspaper strewing the coffee table. A burglary, perhaps—but there was too much order in the derangement of the room: the open-faced books on the floor, the mildewed cups of coffee, the television screen turned toward the wall.

"Mess," said Charlie.

"Daddy?"

Nothing; just the sound of a lawn mower buzzing a few houses away. Jeannie's heart thumped. She remembered the story of her dad's uncle Donald, who was found hanging from a persimmon tree in his backyard right after the Wall Street crash. Jeannie glanced through the back door: the yard was empty, fruit from the tree split and rotting on the ground. A crow clawed at the paving, its beak rooting in the flesh of an orange that was sunken and powdered with mold; sensing her presence, it lifted away.

Jeannie stepped back through the kitchen, Charlie pushing at her encircling arm—"Too tight"—and down the hallway: the door to her bedroom, Kip's bedroom, wide open, mouths to the past, the same Pilgrim wallpaper, the high school trophies and stuffed animals and Snoopy figurines that watched over their childhoods. And here, in the recesses of the house, layers of smell: the deep, innate scent of home, of memory and skin;

the soft reek of incense hovering at Kip's door; the stale breath of cigarettes on the walls; and there it was again, the drift of something overripe, growing stronger as she continued down the hallway toward her dad's bedroom. The door was shut, artificial light seeping from the gap at the floor.

"Hello?" said Jeannie, letting her knuckles brush against the door.

"Where's Grandpa?" asked Charlie.

Jeannie placed a palm against the door and held it there, as though she might be able to feel what lay behind it. The wood was warm against her fingers—it felt strangely distended, as if bulged out by the room within, holding its breath. She closed her eyes and listened. The throb of her blood, the whispered breaths of Charlie, and beyond these, tiny spores of noise—the gurgle of pipes, the fizzle of a fly, and, so quiet as to seem imagined, another, creaking sound.

Jeannie leaned her forehead against the door, feeling the coolness of her skin against the wood, and listened, her ears casting for clues. Nothing; and then, there it was again.

She stood for a long time, listening to the quiet and the creaking, knowing she was on the threshold of something, holding the moment before whatever was waiting behind the door carried her away. And in that long, still moment, she understood that home, as she knew it, might not exist anymore; and all its familiar intimacies—the smells, the give of the floorboards underneath her feet, the ticks and groans of the living building—might be the near-vanishing remnants of something dying. And there it was again—the creaking sound. She opened her eyes, saw Charlie pressing his hand next to hers, a smile on his lips. Then another noise, loud even against the drumming of her blood: *slick-crumple, slick-crumple,* like newspaper pages being turned.

"Pap-Pap," said Charlie; and Jeannie dropped her hand to the doorknob, flinging the door open so hard it bashed the wall.

"Daddy?"

It took a moment for her to see what was in front of her, to unroot the sickening images that had bloomed in her brain as she stood outside the door and to see her dad as he was: unsanitary with life, sitting bony and cross-legged in a circle of light cast by the overhead lamp. He was unshaven, dressed in a set of dirt-seamed pajamas, and surrounded by drifts of paper; he held one piece between a trembling thumb and forefinger, his neck craned to bring its contents into focus.

"Pap-Pap," said Charlie.

Jeannie's dad looked up, then returned to his business, setting the piece of paper on the floor and feeling over the others with his hands. "I can't find it," he murmured.

"You all right, Daddy?" said Jeannie, her heart still hammering in her chest. "You scared me." And hearing the shrillness of her voice, she gathered herself, taking a slow breath and setting Charlie on the carpet. "I was worried," she said. "The house is a mess." She stepped over the papers to open the drapes. A punch of stale sweat and soured liquor hit her as she passed her dad, and Jeannie held her breath. She pulled at the drapes. Sunlight drifted into the room, showing up its dust and disarray: her dad's yellowed sheets, twisted in a sweaty confusion on the bed; a collection of variously full water tumblers arranged in a line on the nightstand, like a high school science experiment; empty liquor bottles rolled under the bed. Dismay weighed down Jeannie's stomach.

"What's been going on, Daddy?"

"No—" said her dad, folding a piece of paper and setting it back on the carpet.

"You've been drinking."

"That's not it . . ."

"When was the last time you took a bath? Have you eaten?"

Her dad's forehead folded in concentration; he closed his eyes and muttered.

"Have Aunt Ruth and Uncle Paulie been by?" Jeannie was half yelling now, an act of near-violence on the quiet. She heard her dad's alarm clock tick, the fly at the windowpane hum in muted reproach.

Her dad opened his eyes and studied her. "Aunt Ruth's in the hospital," he said.

"What? Why didn't you tell me?"

"She's going to be fine. Some stomach thing." He waved his hand to dismiss the subject, then picked up what Jeannie now saw was a letter. He put his face close to it, squinting one eye to bring the handwriting into focus, then flipped the letter with a smack and studied the other side. "Nope," he said.

"What stomach thing?"

Charlie tottered among the paper; he picked up two pieces and threw them, exclaiming in delight.

"Hey," cried Jeannie's dad. "Stop that."

But now it was a game: Charlie bunched another piece of paper in his hand and threw it at his grandfather, rebellion in his face.

"Stop, Charlie." Jeannie crouched and wrested Charlie into her arms. She smoothed the piece of paper; Kip's handwriting stepped in uneven legs down the page.

"These are from Kip?" said Jeannie. Charlie wriggled.

Her dad leaned toward her, releasing a wave of body odor. He shook another letter in his fingers. "I've read them over and over," he said, his breath like spoiled food.

"Daddy, what's going on?" said Jeannie, taking his shoulder, feeling its bone and gristle.

Her dad stared at her, an expression of defeat gathering in his face.

"It doesn't make sense," he said.

Kip / June 1968

You don't know shame till a guy with peach fuzz and pimples has stripped you naked so he can look underneath your balls and up your butthole. He searched everywhere—in my mouth, in my armpits, between my fucking fingers. Didn't find anything but dirt and stink. Then they hosed me down and shaved my head so I was clean and new as a baby rat. I stood in the guard shack, watching a drove of prisoners stringing through the sally port into the brig, heads bowed as they got a frisking and a bitching from the guard. Seated at a makeshift desk in front of me, a fat-gut rear-echelon motherfucker talked at me in a dead-drone voice: rules, regulations, where I'd be assigned.

"Pretrial confinement," he said, digging a booger from his nose and wiping it on the edge of the desk. "Maximum security."

They put me in this box.

A Conex container, two big mouths slit into the front and back to let the box breathe. My cell is the size of my hooch back on the firebase, except there's no cot, just a blanket on the ground and a broken bucket to shit in. Somebody's left a Bible here, but when I open it, it's torn up and smeared with something that sure as hell looks like shit. And the heat—something solid, like the roof pressing down. A bumblebee as big as a thumb drifts in through one of the slits, then knocks itself against the steel wall, over and over, buzzing like crazy; stupid bug got in but can't figure out how to get out again. It's just me and the bumblebee, locked in the furnace—I can make out seven other cells, but they're all empty—and still this place reeks of crotch and ass. I pace, touch the loops and knots of wire that form my cell door, and feel panic getting its hooks in me. Then a yell and a shake of metal, and the light powers in.

"Get in, shit-rat."

A black dude walks past my cell, naked but for boxers and boots, a small beard sprouting on his lower lip. He watches me as he passes, cold freak-eyes taking in every piece of me. I step back toward my shit-bucket, hear the click of a lock. He starts to whistle, a slow, empty sound, with no rounding of a tune.

More inmates, escorted in one at a time, each in their skivvies, sweat greasing their bodies, all black except one, a skinny white guy with a tattoo of a baby covering his back. I count six inmates in all, hear them mumbling in their cells.

"No bullshit," orders the guard.

The guy in the cell next to me starts barking like a dog.

"Shut the hell up!"

But the barking keeps up, and down at the end of the box one inmate starts cock-a-doodle-dooing, another snorting like a pig. The guard strides to the far end of the box and slams something hard against one of the cell doors. The barnyard settles, all except for Freak-Eyes, who's still whistling.

The guard tramps out. Nobody speaks. The door to the Conex is open, and I'm guessing we're all looking out at the sky, feeling the wash of the breeze. Then shadows fall over the light: the last inmate. Freak-Eyes stops whistling. A tree-tall black guy, hunching under the low ceiling, Afro rising from his head. This guy is beefed—his neck sprouting an extra pair of deltoids, his arms swollen with muscles—and I can tell from his slow walk, his tall hair, the hush-down of the others, that this is where the power is: this guy is king of this stinking sweatbox. The Boss. The guard locks him into the cell opposite mine, then walks out of the container, slamming and locking the door behind him. We are in shadow again. My eyes adjust to the murk to see the Boss standing at the front of his cell, gazing at me.

"What you do, Baby-san?" he says.

The others share their theories.

"He caught ass-fucking his hooch mate."

"No, I got it, kid went AWOL, couldn't handle the heat."

"Maybe he gone rape some gook pussy. You fuck a little girl, cracker?"

"Don't look like he got the weapon to do it."

I squat in the back corner of my cell, grateful for the dark, for the chain on my door.

"Nah, that ain't it," says the Boss. He's still watching me, his face pressed against the door of his cell. "What is it, Baby-san?"

"Killed somebody," I say, forcing my voice loud, hoping this will shut the motherfuckers up. But as I say the words, it's like I've breathed ghosts into the cell—they put a shudder on me, put their fingers on my neck; and in my climbing panic, I hear the sound of laughter.

"Ain't that the fucking point, cracker?"

"That's what they send you here for, boy."

"Who you kill?" says the Boss.

I picture his face, the grown-man command in it, the mouth always moving, giving orders; he's so damn real in my head, it feels like a lie when I say, "My CO."

"Your CO? You discharge your weapon or something?"

The palm on the grenade; the noise. "Threw a frag in his hooch."

Silence.

The Boss whistles. "You fucked, Baby-san," he says, voice soft, like he's talking to himself. "Ain't getting out of here for a long fucking time."

I feel a sickness worming in my stomach.

"Crackers greasing crackers. There it is."

"They gonna hang you for that?"

"They gonna *beat* him for that."

"Don't you fall asleep, cracker. Them pigs gonna come, they gonna put that blanket over your head and beat you dead."

I spit a mouthful of vomit juice onto the ground and breathe deep.

"Shut up, brother," says the Boss. "Why you do it, Baby-san?"

I don't answer, just put my hands over my eyes and sit back on my heels, like I'm waiting for a fucking streetcar, like if I dig deep and sit tight, a ride is going to come by and take me out of here, out of all of this, soon.

"Fuck you too," whispers the Boss, and the others raise a murmur, but they hush down fast. The box is pressing the air out of us, and talking costs. It gets quiet, real quiet; and, here, sweating in my own darkness, safe in my cell, I could be anywhere: sitting in my room at home, listening for my dad to leave to go drinking so I can steal some of his liquor; or fishing in the bay with Bobby, soaking up some heat while waiting for a perch to bite; or playing hide-and-seek with Jeannie, squatting behind the trash can with skinned knees and the sun blasting me, wondering if she's given up on the game. There is no fucking ride out of this torture box, might never be a ride; all I got is closing my eyes and letting my brain carry me home.

Time goes, and I feel hot sleep creeping on me, feel my neck sagging under the weight of my head. Then a loud crash; I jerk up and open my eyes. Ahead of me, the Boss is smashing his head against the door of his cell, over and over. Nobody says a word.

Truth is, I did it because of Shea.

Shea was a straight-arrow kid from Cleveland, Ohio, toughed up by nineteen knife-cold winters. He liked to keep quiet and do as he was asked, was told by his dad—who was told by his dad before him—that the best way through life was to keep your head down, your boots clean, and your pecker in your pants.

Shea would have spent a lifetime dodging trouble if Vance hadn't sent him into the forest that night. He would have returned home after a so-so tour with fungus feet, a sun-peeled face, and a crappy service medal that would have gotten his fiancée—a fox named Pamela with bee-stings (he showed everybody her picture, who wouldn't)—hot to trot. (She would have climbed on him in the back of his father's Plymouth and the way she unzipped his zipper and slid right on top of him would've made him wonder if she'd done it before; her all-business smile as she straightened herself out afterward would've made him sure she had.) After a summer of getting fat on hot franks and beer and screwing in the backseat at the drive-in and the lake, Shea would have learned that Pamela was in trouble, and he would have steeled up and asked her to marry him, getting a job at the post office and saving his dollars to rent them a crappy apartment in the city. He would have taken it, taken four decades of a gut-growing wife and bad pay, taken it like a good hardworking American, until, finally, on a dream retirement trip fly-fishing in Montana he would have died quietly, in his wading boots, of a dime-a-dozen, run-of-the-mill heart attack.

Shea didn't get the chance to live out his days, nor did Dopfer or Skid or any of the other suckers that Vance sent on his glory-grubbing, doom-infested gook hunts. What is it the Bible says? Eye for eye, tooth for tooth, hand for hand, foot for foot.

Jeannie / June 1968

Jeannie's dad should never have told Bernie. Bernie told Eugene, who told Kenneth, who told Ray, who told everybody who drank at Flanagan's, which was how his neighbor Mr. Reilly found out; and soon, instead of asking after his dahlias, Jeannie's dad's neighbors were crossing the street to avoid him. At the liquor store, in the post office, at Mae's or Sam's Sports Bar, eyes and whispers followed him. Mr. Jackson, whose son had done something shocking in Southeast Asia. No telephone calls came asking him to join a bowling night or a poker game, or inviting him to make the fourth spot in a round of golf. So he stayed home—couldn't even bear to make the walk from his front door to his car to go to work. Home, where the pressing dirt to clean was Kip's mess, and while he tried to scrub to the bottom of it, the housekeeping could wait.

"What do you know?" he asked Jeannie as he sat on the couch, balancing a plate of saltines on his knee while Jeannie set about tidying the living room.

"Not much," said Jeannie. "I've been calling the DoD several times a day. They keep telling me the same thing—they'll let us know when he's received a formal charge."

"What's taking so long?"

"They said there was a war going on." Jeannie's dad gave a bitter snort. "Daddy, eat."

"I got no stomach for it, honey. Can you fix me a drink?"

"I'll fix you some coffee."

"Just get me a damn drink, will you."

Jeannie went to the kitchen, loaded a glass with ice, and dribbled bourbon so that the ice cracked. Her dad took the drink with a quaking hand. The tips of his fingers were swollen red. He drank in one steady swallow, then gripped the empty glass to his chest.

"He wrote about his commanding officer," he said.

"He did?"

"Just one time. One of his first letters. Here." Her dad reached into the pocket of his pajama pants, pulled out a folded letter, and handed it to Jeannie. She sat on the arm of the couch, and read.

December 30 '67

Dear Dad,

Well, I'm here.

I'm sitting in my hooch on a hill overlooking triple-canopy jungle. We're some 80 or 90 klicks up the coast from Hue, VC hiding all over the forest. Nothing's happened since I landed—shit's been flying, but I missed it. Two days before I got here the base got probed—sappers cut the wire, threw Chicom grenades all over the place. A couple Marines got hurt, but the bad guys came off a hell of a lot worse. I got lucky, Dad—got a CO—name's Vance—he's real salty, gone a couple rounds with this war already and is still standing, had so many near misses he must be bulletproof. As soon as the enemy cut the wire he was ready for them, rallied a dozen gun-bunnies and greased every last dink—before the grunts were even out of their rubber ladies (they're still pissed off about that). The guy's collected. I'm going to be fine.

It's only been a few weeks but it feels like I did my whole thirteen months already. You never told me how damn boring it would be. It won't stop raining—not rain like at home, this rain falls in a damn wall so you can't see squat. And mud everywhere, sucks at you like it's something alive. Most days it feels like we're waiting for something to happen—but if it's going to happen, it'll happen at night. Sleeping's tough.

Truth is, this country's got my feelings on a yo-yo. Yesterday we took a MEDCAP to the local village. Someone's mom sent blow bubbles—the little kids went wild, chased those damn bubbles like they were dollar bills. A bunch of older girls came to watch—these girls are unreal gorgeous, all squaw hair and shy looks, like we're warriors or something. But everybody's your friend here till they cut your throat. Vietnam's the most beautiful place I've seen, and I'll be glad never to see it again.

That's all—the sun's going—

Kip

Jeannie set the letter on her lap, her fingers lingering over the ink.

"He liked him," she said.

"Sure did."

"It doesn't make sense."

"As much sense as a screen door on a submarine."

It was a hick expression of her mom's. Jeannie let a smile touch her lips, but her dad was stone-faced.

"Kip would never do something like this—"

But her dad wasn't listening. "I've been trying to make sense of it," he said, shaking his head. "Why did he go from admiring the guy to blowing him up?"

Jeannie had the slow, unpleasant realization that this wasn't a rhetorical question; this was the puzzle her dad was trying to solve, the enigma that had kept him from his work, his food, his hygiene, his daily obsessions—that had kept him from himself. "You're serious?" she said. "You're really asking why?"

"You know why?" Hope clutched her dad's face.

"But it's the wrong question. You know he didn't do it."

"C'mon, Jeannie." Her dad gave the half note of a laugh, his shoulders lifting and dropping in an exaggerated gesture of defeated amusement. It was like she was a kid again—her naïveté a source of mirth to her parents, and, as she grew older, a source of impatience—and the old heat of injustice flared.

"I don't believe this," she said. Her throat was tight with disappointment. "Of everything you've done to Kip," she said, "this is the worst."

"What do you mean?" Her dad's face made a cartoon expression of surprise, his mouth and eyes forming little matching *O*'s. A spark of anger lit the kindling of resentments Jeannie had put away over weeks and months—the swallowed rebukes to her dad's greedy disapproval, his near dislike of Kip.

"You kept saying he was a disappointment, that he was turning into a bad kid. I didn't think you actually believed it."

"For Christ's sake," said her dad; he swung his glass to his mouth, but only the softening ice slid against his lips. He slammed the glass on the coffee table, his face clenching in annoyance. "You saw that letter. He said it himself: he did it."

"You know how the popular kids can carry him away."

"C'mon, Jeannie. Robbing a liquor store's one thing. But this?"

"He always had a difficult relationship with the truth."

"Yeah, you've never been one for reality either, honey."

"What's that supposed to mean?"

"You want to pretend this isn't happening—like you've been pretending all along, with your too-busy, too-good city life. That's fine. But I don't want to hear it." His voice rose to a shout; his plate tipped from his leg, sliding saltines onto the couch.

"What are you talking about?"

"You come here, with your concern and your half-assed tidying and your saltine meals"—he plucked the crackers from the couch and dropped them back onto the plate one by one, *plink, plink,* disgust in his face—"but it's all too little, too late."

He had hit his stride now, greased by liquor, and he wasn't ready to stop. Jeannie recognized it from when she'd lived at home, the rages that came suddenly, violently—little earthquakes that shook the house, then disappeared, each time leaving something, however small, damaged in their wake. Some strained, tolerant fiber inside her broke.

"I don't need to listen to this anymore."

"We needed you here, Jeannie." She was shocked to see that he was crying—meager tears reeling down his cheeks. "We needed you here a year back when I was working overtime and Kip was losing his way. We needed a woman in the house, somebody to keep a pair of eyes and a pair of hands on things. You were never here." His anger was softening into self-pity, faster than she expected—it surprised her how weakened he was, how uncertain in his moods.

"I have my own family now. That was Mom's job, not mine." A cinch of gratification at the hurt that flashed over her dad's face; but doubt heavied her stomach.

Her dad rooted a handkerchief from his pocket and honked so loudly into it that Charlie—quiet and forgotten, sitting at her feet and rolling a marble over the carpet—giggled. Jeannie heard something in his laugh—hope, entreaty—and pulled him up onto her lap. "It's okay, sweetie," she murmured, kissing his neck.

"You're right. It was your mom's job," said her dad. His face was flushed and tight, but his voice had the reasoned, it-never-happened quality that used to drive Kip crazy. "Truth is, you needed your mom too." Jeannie felt the words like a burn; she turned her head from them.

"We all needed her," said Jeannie. The sulkiness of her tone wasn't lost on either of them. She felt her dad's eyes on her.

"She would have stopped you from being unhappy," he said.

"I'm not unhappy, Daddy." But the words sounded like a lie. "Jesus Christ," she said. She set Charlie on his feet and began gathering her things; then, realizing she had no place to go, dropped into the easy chair and pressed the heels of her wrists to her forehead.

"Remember when you were a kid?" her dad said. "Your mom used to call you her little stargazer." Jeannie had forgotten this. An old yearning flushed warm and empty in her chest. "We never knew where your head was at. You were always that way. You never paid heed to what was going on around you. You were always someplace else, someplace you never invited anybody.

"Kip was a dreamer too," he continued. "But you always knew what he was dreaming about. Buffalo Bill, Al Capone, Audie Murphy. Kip always had too much . . ." He studied the carpet. "Too much of a sense of *history.*" His face loosened. "Too much history, too much nostalgia for things he didn't know squat about. Got him into trouble time and time again. His head was so busy with some hokey idea of the past, he never saw what was going on in front of his nose." Her dad nodded, then stilled, staring into the mid-distance. Jeannie watched as drifts of expression crept back over his face: specters taking up their haunts—regret, dismay, anger. He narrowed his eyes on her; she turned her eyes down.

"But you, Jeannie," her dad said. "You—you've never had

any sense of history at all. No sense of how the world got to the place it is now. Kids like Kip—the world's seen thousands of them. Every damn war they get riled up and sent to some God-awful place to fight, where they'll live, or they'll die, or, sometimes, just sometimes, they'll do something so damn stupid that the life they held on to isn't worth having. Jesus." Her dad sighed, a final sigh. "Maybe that's all there is to say. There's no big mystery. He's just a dumb kid. I thought Kip was smarter than that. I guess I was wrong."

"Kip's not dumb," said Jeannie.

Her dad blew breath from his nostrils, and his mouth tightened.

"Daddy," said Jeannie. "Daddy. We've got to help him."

"He's in the brig, in the middle of a war, and he's blown up his superior. He's deep in a shithole and they're letting him sweat. I can't help him anymore. He's on his own." Her dad put his plate on the coffee table and heaved himself up. He picked up his glass and carried it to the kitchen, pajama pants slipping on his bony hips to show the shocking white of his buttocks. Jeannie heard the unstop-and-slug of bourbon. She watched Charlie pulling her dad's chess set from underneath the coffee table; remembered all the Sundays Kip and her dad had sat for hours, moving pieces over the board, her dad placing his pawns at risk and watching hopefully for Kip to take them, Kip's pride at checking his dad's king.

"Then I'll help him," she said. She stood and gathered the dirty cups, carrying them to the kitchen and splashing out the moldy coffee; then ran the sink full with warm water and squeezed in a quarter bottle of Lux to make a chaos of suds. She dragged a wicker stool to the sink and called for Charlie, then stood him on the stool and handed him a sponge. Letting herself outside, she pulled the mail from the mailbox and—

ignoring the glare of Mr. Kowalski as he dug the weeds from his perennials—brought it inside and slapped it on the countertop.

"Kid's making a damn mess," said her dad.

Jeannie ignored him. She shook out a trash bag and carried it to the living room, stuffing it with armfuls of newspaper, beer bottles, an old pizza box containing curled pieces of pie. Straightened the desk, thumped the couch pillows, dusted, vacuumed—driving a wet Charlie between his Grandpa's feet in fright—and yanked the drapes. Finally, she turned the television to face the room and switched it on.

"Charlie, it's Road Runner. Come sit. I've got to make a phone call."

"Who you calling?" said her dad.

But Jeannie's fingers were already hauling the dial. Three long rings, and just as she was expecting the answering service to kick in—

"Hello?"

"Mr. Ettlinger?"

"Mrs. Harper. Good to hear from you."

"I was going to leave a message. I'm moving back to my apartment and wanted you to have the telephone number. I didn't think you'd be there on a Saturday."

"Saturdays don't seem to count for much these days." His mouth was full of something. Jeannie heard the gluey slap of chewing, imagined the baloney sandwich, the rolled sleeves, the weekend stubble. Ettlinger swallowed. "I've been trying to get ahold of you."

"You have?"

"I have news for you. Are you sitting down?"

Kip / June 1968

Here's the thing: Vance didn't die. He looked dead, arms broke-hanging over the stretcher like a G.I. Joe with its limbs worked loose—it didn't seem like somebody could come out of that bunker any other way—but he was still breathing, grappling onto the world of the living like the dedicated Marine he was. Maybe the sweet-faced corpsman knew it—but even if he felt the flutter of a pulse, the whisper of a breath, he most likely shared the same thought I read in everybody's faces that night: the captain was as good as dead. They flew him to Danang, over the jungle and the war, the bladed air rushing his skin; the man himself must have felt he was dying, lifting into the sky with the dawn, his body burning away. And the medic in the Dustoff would have felt it too—would have wanted him to be comfortable, to disappear quiet and easy—but when they landed at the hospital, he was still fighting. So the surgeons got to work—busywork, keeping their skills sharp, their fingers limber—and after a mess of surgeries, three slugs of morphine, and a night on the fucked-up-and-beyond-repair ward, they were surprised next morning to find him still alive. Flew him to Yokosuka to heal his burns, and finally, when he was strong enough, to the good old U S of A, where he's recovering someplace clean and caring, making plans for the rest of his life.

They put me in this steel box with the killers and the psychos and the rebels. Don't know how long I've been breathing their infected air—after a few days in this shithole, I lost count. I've learned to follow the emptying of a day: the cots confiscated two thousand breaths before dawn, the tongue of light sliding through the mouth of the box, the slow crush of heat, the endless high-noon burn; and then the can peeled open, and we are spilled out into the sun like baked beans, rolling around the yard, greasy with our own juices, blazing in the sun; then back into the can, hotter now though the sun's dying, and everybody is crazed from the air and the space and that giant white sky. They let us settle, wait for the banging and screaming and hollering to stop, then bring us our chow: raw potatoes, bread with bugs baked in, a cup of warm water. The long, gray wait for sundown; and as the slit-mouths darken and disappear, the heat eases from the box, one gasp at a time; and when the sweat stops bleeding at my pores, that's when the guards open the cells and throw us our cots. I lie down, imagine I'm staring at the black open sky, think of home, of baseball and ice cream and Jeannie's chicken casserole, of Charlie and Pete and Bobby.

They treat us like we're human trash: cuss-hurl, power-trip, rough-hand us any chance they get. But the one thing I know is this: I might be a brig-rat, a cracker, and a little bitch; but I am not a murderer.

"Jeannie has news." Billy fumbled his cutlery against his plate. He was always nervous around his father.

"Are you expecting, dear?" asked Dorothy, arranging her mouth in a tasteful smile. "I thought you were looking a little thicker around the middle."

"No, Dorothy," said Jeannie. Billy gave an embarrassed half laugh. "I spoke to the Department of Defense today," Jeannie continued, her voice bright against the muted walls of the room.

"You did?" said Dorothy, carving her meat into neat chunks. "Fanny said you'd been busy."

"It's good news," said Jeannie.

"That's the best kind," said her father-in-law.

"Kip received his charges."

"Yes?" Dorothy's face was held in an expression of patient discomfort.

"His commanding officer didn't die."

"He didn't?" A real smile broke over Dorothy's face.

"Kip's being charged with attempted murder. Which means—"

"Which means they're not going to swing him," said her father-in-law.

Billy choked on his beef; his mother patted his back.

"That's very good news," said Dorothy. "Attempted murder's one thing. But murder's quite another."

"And it means we can start helping him," said Jeannie.

"I don't see how you mean to help him," said Dorothy. Her smile was hardening into the one she used to corral her hennish committees, the one that still reduced Billy to a boy.

"I think Jeannie means we can start thinking about his

future," said Billy. "After all this is . . ." He gave a vague wave of his fork.

"What I mean is, I spoke to Herbert Chapman today," said Jeannie; Billy's cutlery paused over his peas. "Your lawyer friend, Dorothy—the one you introduced me to at your fund-raiser."

"What do you mean, you spoke to him?" said Dorothy.

"I found his telephone number. In your address book." Ettlinger's news had made Jeannie bold; she presented the information without apology, and readied herself.

Billy's face was working in an anxious twitch.

"That's who you were talking to when I came in?" Dorothy was rising in her seat.

"The man at the DoD told me Kip can use a civilian lawyer. Chapman said it was advisable."

"Makes sense," said Jeannie's father-in-law. "I can't see a military lawyer working too hard for your brother, all things considered."

"You spoke to Herb Chapman about what your brother did?" Dorothy was half standing, her voice raised.

"Dolly." Jeannie's father-in-law's face gathered into a shushing expression, and he held his hands out, like he was bringing an orchestra to a pause. Dorothy sat down in her chair; Billy bowed his head.

"I will say my piece, Richard," said Dorothy, shifting in her seat. "It's not Jeannie's place to run around airing her dirty laundry to our friends."

"Mother," said Billy, giving Jeannie an alarmed look. "I'm sure Jeannie's sorry if she—"

"I'm sorry, Dorothy," said Jeannie. "But when you said you'd do anything to help . . ."

"Give you a home? Yes. Care for your child? Yes. But have our name mixed in with a murderer's?"

"Like I said, he's charged with attempted murder." Jeannie heard the sass in her own voice and covered it with a polite smile.

"Jeannie." Billy's hand was in the air, a schoolboy trying to get the teacher's attention.

"You're lucky Chapman is discreet," said Dorothy. "Do you have any idea what this kind of association could do to Richard's reputation?"

"Well, it couldn't get any worse," said Richard. He pressed against Jeannie in a long nudge, giving her a jovial glance; but his mouth was tense, and as he settled back in his chair, Jeannie caught him sending an acid look toward his wife. Dorothy's eyes glittered.

"Now," said Richard through a mouthful of teeth and meat. "Let's hear Jeannie out. What did Chapman suggest?"

"We can fly somebody over to represent him," said Jeannie. "Someone who can get the real truth about what happened, who can help Kip tell his side. Chapman can make someone available."

"And who's going to pay for this?" said Dorothy, voice high-pitched, face taut, as though her strings had been pulled tight.

Jeannie breathed deep. "I wanted to ask if you'd make us a loan."

"Well, I'm not sure that's—" said Billy.

"And how will you pay it back?" said Dorothy. "I'm assuming Muni isn't paying your father handsomely. You're a dependent. And your brother—"

"Enough, Dorothy," said Richard, screwing his napkin and bringing his fist down on the table with a thump. The china trembled. Richard gave a stiff smile of embarrassment.

Jeannie turned to face her father-in-law, Dorothy's eyes sharp on her neck, Billy beet-red and fidgety at the edge of her vision. "I know how generous you and Dorothy are, how you've always helped people who are powerless. I understand it's a lot to ask. But I know Kip's innocent. And whatever happens, doesn't he have a right to a fair trial, to committed representation?"

"I think it's time to change the subject," said Billy.

"But it really is a matter of urgency," Jeannie continued, placing her hand on her father-in-law's arm. Billy bobbed for eye contact; she ignored him.

"You're family, sweetheart," said Richard. "Whatever you need, we'll help."

"Richard, I really think—"

"Shush, shush. It's all right, Dolly. We haven't thrown any money Chapman's way in a while. It's about time we started lining his pockets again. And now that's settled, let's enjoy our dinner. This beef is delicious."

"Thank you," said Jeannie. "I appreciate it."

"Don't say another word," said Richard.

Knives were taken up; the sound of serrations on china. The second hand of the antique wall clock heaved through the seconds. Billy cast sweaty glances at Jeannie, champing on his beef with an indignant vigor, while Richard calmly cleared his plate. Dorothy kept her eyes on Jeannie, following every lift of her fork to her mouth. Jeannie avoided the older woman's gaze, ate her meal quickly and without tasting it, her mind running on what she needed to do next.

"Extraordinary," said her father-in-law, almost to himself, as he placed his knife and fork together on his empty plate.

Dorothy muttered.

"I mean," Richard continued, "that the man survived. A

grenade in his sleeping quarters, is that correct?" Jeannie nodded. "So the force of the explosion is contained inside a bunker. How the hell did he get out alive?"

"Thank God for miracles," Billy said with a forced brightness.

"I have a similar case at the hospital," said Richard. "Officer; got caught in a close-quarters explosion in a terrible battle over there, somehow managed not to die. Terrible thing, multiple wounds—lost a leg and most of a hand, internal injuries, badly burned. We're trying to repair the burns to his face, but"—he shook his head—"he's a damn mess."

"I'm guessing infection's your major problem?" said Billy.

"Yes, well, that and the catastrophic injury to the typical donor sites, the damage to the jawbone, the risk of acute bleeding and hematoma, not to mention graft hypertrophy, contraction and necrosis."

"Of course, of course," said Billy, dropping his head to spoon potato into his mouth, his face darkening.

"Tough kid, though. Knew his father at Stanford. George Vance."

Jeannie's stomach rolled.

"Built like a brick house," continued her father-in-law. "College team quarterback. Hooked the most beautiful girl on campus."

"Your patient," said Jeannie. "He was in the Army, you said?"

"Army? No. Marines. Leatherneck family, all the way back to the Civil War. They flew the poor bastard in from Japan a couple of weeks ago. A lot of blast injuries in this war. They've gotten good at keeping them alive. It's testing this old blade's skills, that's for sure."

"Well, I think that's enough for one night," said Dorothy.

She stood, suddenly frail; Billy rose from his seat and took her arm. "Jeannie, I'll talk with you tomorrow."

Jeannie swallowed. "Charlie and I are heading back to Noe tomorrow morning," she managed. Billy turned to her in surprise.

"Time to return to normalcy, hey?" said Richard.

Jeannie nodded.

"As best you can," said Richard.

"Indeed," said Billy, turning to escort his mother from the room, stiff-shouldered, his ears burning red.

Kip / June 1968

The box has released me, and I'm never going back. They're moving me to medium. A regular cell in a regular block with ordinary, plain-dealing criminals. I'm standing in the guard shack, legs wobbling, while the same rear-echelon motherfucker that checked me into this joint sweats and grunts like a hog in front of me, licking his trotters as he turns the pages in his Big Bad Book.

"You look at it the right way, you were lucky," he says.

"Lucky?"

"At least you're alive."

"Breathing."

"I'll bet your buddies would swap places with you in a heartbeat."

Whatever game this guy is going for, I don't want to play. I ignore him, look out at the yard, where the mediums haul sand into bags and guards circle with their guts puffed, yelling and twirling their batons like fat majorettes.

"Hill 981, right?" says the Hog, hunger gleaming in his little eyes. "FSB Deadwood?"

"What about it?"

"You don't know?"

"Know what?"

"It happened—what?—a couple weeks ago. You must've just missed it. VC cleared those guys out. Killed everybody in the compound. No prisoners taken, everybody dead."

He's fucking with me; just another shit-kicking taunt, and I'm getting tired of it.

"So many bodies the helicopters hauled them away in cargo nets."

"That's some story," I say.

But he's scratching something in his book, his pink head furrowed in a frown. "Bad business," he says. "You were better off out of there, boy." And it dawns on me that this asshole's not joking, that there might not be an ounce of play or wit in his piggish body.

"All over the newspapers," he's saying. "Word is it's got the brass real jumpy, got the commander in chief crawling up their butts."

My breath bellows. I push it down into my chest; it sticks there and I can't shift it and my chest gets tight with it, too tight, like it will burst; and I hear something ringing in the ceiling and the sun switches off and—

"Kid fainted."

"Get him in his cell, give him some water."

"Too much time in that damn Conex."

"He didn't know."

"He didn't know?"

Esposito — Roper — Hutch — Pederson — Carter — Fugate — Baby — McCarthy — Gross — Mayfield — Cheeks — Boyce — Salinas — Womack — Gilligan — Campbell — Tracy — Elvis — Langton — Boston — Krause — Ortiz — Lurch — Hollis — Tucker — Lopey — Corbin — Dammit — Schroeder — Kodak — Montgomery — Dog — Berkowitz — Pussy — Reimey — Boudreaux — Six — Paulsen — Schmidt — Fulgoni — Eightball — Dubois — Skeeter — Tex — Gonzo — Old Dude — Pawlowski — Something-else-ski — Gunny — Chaplain — Carlos — Carlos — Carlos — Communications Guy — Irish — Hillbilly — Fat Kid — Rich Kid — Acne Kid — Jock Kid — Freaked Kid — Mellow Kid — Meathead Kid — Indian Kid — Douche Bag — Power

Brother — Power Brother — Power Brother — Power Brother — Power Brother — Woody Strode — Fucking New Guy — Other New Guy — Corpsman —

We were saved. Vance and me, lifted out of there by angels with blades for wings, before the enemy made its raid. I remember the smoke rising from the firebase as we pulled through the sky; and as the angel bore south, so we turned away from it, from the amazing thing that was happening on that scratch of dirt below, where kids were smearing from life into death, where the battle had arrived that we'd all feared but hoped was just a fantasy. Esposito hiding in his hooch, smoking one of his regulars (scared for good off those Cambodian fuckers); Carter chowing on his beef and gravy; Roper sweating in the FDC; Fugate John-Wayne-ing around the firebase; Elvis singing his songs, still hurting over that girl in Milwaukee; Dog bitching at the bugs; Pussy shit-birding out of patrol; Pawlowski straining in the last of the light to write another goddamn letter; Fucking New Guy still trying to figure out how to fix his pistol belt. And Ortiz, hauling up the observation tower, working a massive wad of gum in his jaws. What did he see? Did he wonder about the shapes moving on the hill? Did he feel it, something invisible and evil, approaching over the scrub? Hear the snip of a wire, the harsh-slop dink-whispers, the click of the charging handle on an SKS?

And I think on it again, that hot white light that ran through my blood, that flew through my fingers and flung that grenade into the darkness; that ripped and hurled Vance, and bore him away someplace safe, where he would live, and keep living; that drove me up into the sky after him, to this place, which might be the scratching asshole of the military justice system, but at least it isn't six feet under. The light took us, and it saved us; the divine plan of a god, of an angel in chief; we two were elected to be redeemed, chosen to be saved.

Beyond the Headlands

Tom / July 1968

He heard the door swing open, the squeak of rubber soles on vinyl. He braced for the pain; it climbed his body, fixing at his cheek. He opened his eye—the other held shut by the padding—and watched for the whip of the curtain.

A half-dozen pairs of eyes were on him. The chief, flanked by rookies. The chief nodded. Tom registered the paunch, the wristwatch, the expensive shirt, and hated him.

"You," said the chief, nodding at a clean-cut kid built like a linebacker. "History, please."

Linebacker stood to attention—military material, should have been humping in country, instead of the shitbird Category Fours they kept sending him. "Yes, sir." He cleared his throat.

"Patient was injured by a fragmentation grenade while serving in Vietnam." Tom imagined Car Wreck and Factory Accident, listening. "When medics reached him at the scene, his right leg was shredded to the thigh. There were multiple pellet puncture wounds over the whole body, and severe injuries to the right hand, fingers amputated at the proximal interphalangeal joints. The patient also sustained second- and third-degree burns to the abdomen, chest, and face."

The other rookies took notes, except for one, the only female, a tall girl who was hard on the eyes, the kind that excelled at field hockey in high school. Her eyes traveled over Tom's dressings. Tom reached for the gripper on his locker; the chief nodded for Linebacker to continue.

"The medic administered morphine and albumin, and the patient was transported to a nearby surgical hospital, where they debrided the wound to the right leg and open-packed it with occlusive dressings, infusing the patient with Ringer's lactate and antibiotics. Surgeons then conducted an exploratory laparotomy, where they removed the right kidney and repaired lacerations to the liver. During the procedure, the patient was administered twenty-five units of blood. The burns to the face and torso were lightly dressed with antibacterial dressings, and the patient was prescribed morphine. In addition to the major traumatic injuries, doctors identified a right upper brachial plexus injury, rupture of the tympanic membranes, and superficial burns to the groin."

Tom squeezed the gripper in his left hand, his arm gristling with the repetition.

"Three days later, the patient was flown to Japan, where the right leg was removed by a right-hip disarticulation and the wounds to the right hand were sutured. During the operation, the patient underwent cardiac arrest, and the surgeons resuscitated him. Post-operation, the patient was ventilated and administered fluids, as well as ephedrine, dopamine, norepinephrine, and antibiotics. The patient was closely monitored and, once stabilized, was flown back to the United States and admitted to the Veterans Affairs Medical Center, before transferring to UCSF. Which brings us here."

It was not how he remembered it. The slam of heat, the force jackhammering his skeleton, splitting him. Then the long wait, watching the fear in other people's eyes, his body light and cold. No sound, but sifts and turns of light and color; his body lifting up and up until the light pulled to a grain of black; and the thought, that death was a small thing after all.

But then, the pain. Like something alive, murdering him from the inside. There was no soul, there was only the body: piss and blood and shit, bagged and separated by layers of cells thinner than newspaper. A series of rooms, unsure if he was awake or asleep, his body a site for dredging, excavation, extraction. His recall of those days confused; the first clear moment when he woke from the surgery, the hard prank of feeling the agony in his right leg but seeing nothing there.

Tom's arm cramped.

"Thank you—?"

"Bremmer."

"Thank you, Bremmer." The chief approached the bed. "The patient has responded positively to treatment," he said. "The wounds to the leg and hand are healing well. The tympanic membranes are repaired, without identifiable hearing loss. And the burns to the genitalia have healed almost completely." The chief paused, a nice, fat period, to make sure everybody on the ward heard. Tom's eyes went to Girl Medic, scared and excited as a cherry. She caught his gaze and looked away, and he wanted to smack the blush off her face.

"The partial-thickness burns to the abdomen have healed, but with scarring. And we have successfully performed skin grafts to the second-degree burns to the chest," continued the chief. "There is significant neuropathy as a result of the brachial plexus injury, and we're working to improve this with physical therapy." Tom tried to jerk his right arm, tried to ambush it into remembering what to do; but it lay gimpy at his side. "But our area of principal concern now is the burn damage to the face."

The chief's hand closed in. In spite of himself, Tom shut his eyes. The dressing lifted, but the pressure still bore down on his face like a vise.

"As you can see," said the chief, "this livid coloring tends to white, then brown as the burn extends through the entire dermis above the jaw. Note the leathery texture of the skin, the spots of charring. No sensation here, but plenty here where the burn only reaches the papillary dermis." A judder of pain

("That's good; it's good it hurts," murmured the chief); Tom squeezed the gripper hard. The chief lifted his fingers away. "This area, extending above the right jaw, requires a skin graft.

"Because of the damage to the patient's face, we'll harvest the graft from the supraclavicular skin on the left clavicle. We've attempted the surgery twice so far but have had to postpone due to signs of infection at the graft site. The patient completed a course of antibiotics yesterday, and the surgery has been rescheduled for tomorrow. Swabs of the area are being taken and plated daily to ensure we're clear to go ahead." The chief replaced the dressing. Tom opened his eyes.

"Gentlemen," said the chief. Girl Medic's face didn't move. "The patient came here because we're the best plastic surgery center on the West Coast." He put his hands on his hips. "Let's not let him down."

Wash time.

"How are you today, Captain?"

Donna helped him to sit, her body his crutch as he lowered himself into the wheelchair: a girl handling a six-foot-four Marine.

"They taking care of you today?" she said, her sweet, serious face close to his as she released the brake of the chair.

"Let's just say I'm happy you're here."

Her nose wrinkled in a smile. "Good to see you too, sir." She straightened and placed a palm on his shoulder. "There. All set?"

He nodded. She pushed him along the ward, past Burned Feet and Firecracker Kid. As they neared the swing doors, a noise escaped Tom's mouth, but she was already slowing, stopping at the window that looked over the bay, and finding herself some busywork at the desk. It was a fine day, and the bridge drew the light. A tugboat sailed in the bay, its horn sounding gorgeously, like a bugle. Tom remembered his commissioning ceremony, the feel of the gloves on his hands, the sound of the brass band, pride building like pressure in his chest. He sensed Donna standing behind him, and kept still, wanting to stretch the moment.

"Sir," she whispered.

"Okay."

She wheeled him through the swing doors; along the corridor, past the curious and the uninterested; through another set of doors, and into the wet heat of the shower room. Tom exhaled, tried to empty himself of sensation.

She spoke softly, crouching in front of him. Eased off his hospital gown, lifted his dressings, her face level with his crotch, his stump lifting at his thigh. He kept his eyes blind, ignored her reassurances, her careful hands; tried to unsee the traumas and genitals of the men being washed in the other stalls. She wheeled him into their stall. Squeezed soap over his arms, his shoulders, his chest and stomach, over his crotch, his stump, down his leg. Unhooked the showerhead, turned on the faucet, and rinsed his skin, up, down, careful to avoid his face, sweating under the dressing.

She shut off the water. It was almost over. He closed his eyes, and felt himself being wheeled out. Heard her shake open the towel—the approach like an embrace, like a mother taking an infant—and humiliation locked his throat. He felt the pat of cotton, and lifted his left arm and swatted her away, hard. She brought her face to his and gave him a warning look.

"Don't fight me," she said.

She pressed him with the towel and handled him back into the gown, then pushed him out of the room and back along the corridor. The gown gripped his skin. He listened to the squeak of the rear left wheel, the squelch of the soles of her shoes. She was moving faster than normal. He wanted her to slow down.

"I hear they're operating tomorrow, sir," she said as they reached the swing doors. Her voice had the sealed-up quality she used with the others.

"That's right. Tomorrow morning."

She propped the door open with her hip and wheeled him in with one hand. "That's something, huh?"

"It is."

They traveled the ward, past Car Wreck and Factory Accident. He saw his bed, straightened and turned over, ready to ingest him for another day, and jerked his hand. She slowed.

"When they're done, I'll be the handsomest guy here," he said.

She crouched to engage the brake.

"Is that right?" She smelled clean and unused—she belonged out there, with the fresh air and uncomplicated views. She helped him to stand. He lingered over the sensation of towering over her.

"You better snap me up while you have the chance."

She let him have a smile, and eased him backward, supporting his weight as he lay. She called to the nurse, "Patient needs new dressings."

The nurse approached and set about bandaging and taping him with cold fingers. Donna walked away.

A brunette was staring through the glass of the swing doors. She had a clear, clever face—a real beauty. Her eyes roamed the ward, looking for somebody. She was a social worker, or a shrink; a physical therapist; maybe the chief's secretary. He watched, thought he caught her eye; but a nurse busied past him, and when he had his line of sight again, she was gone.

"No physical therapy today."

"The doctor said every day."

"You have your surgery tomorrow."

"I'm aware of that."

"You need to rest."

"I've been resting for weeks. My muscles are deteriorating to shit."

"There's no need to curse."

"Jesus Christ."

"One day won't make a difference."

"It's about discipline. Discipline and consistency, being systematic."

"With respect, sir, this isn't the Army—"

"The Army doesn't know the first damn thing about discipline—"

"This is a Hospital . . . be *sensible* . . . Duty . . . by the *protocols* . . . *very* serious . . . Respect . . . aggressive . . . follow *orders* . . . the *rules* . . . *Lay* down and *Rest*."

He crawled from sleep to find a shadow standing over him. A shock of hardware on the left breast, four glimmers on each shoulder, and a face with the fierceness of a battle-tested leader. God was a general in the United States Marine Corps.

"Good views up here, Captain."

"General?" Tom tried to hoist himself to sit, but his head reeled.

"At ease," said the general. He held up his hand. "Stay right there. How are you doing, Captain?"

"Recovering well, General."

"Good. Good." The general's face loomed, his hair glowing white. "I know your father. Instructed him at Quantico."

"General?"

"He's darn proud of you, Captain."

"General."

The general's body wavered. "Talks about you a great deal. About your service. Says he wasn't half the Marine you are, and, Lord, he was a hell of a Marine."

"Thank you, General."

"Seems civilian life's treating him well," said the general. "Getting fat on it."

Tom tried to rig a smile.

"He come by much?" The general was hardening into focus, the lapels and pockets of his service uniform making perfect angles, green on green.

"Some." Tom's voice broke adolescently over the word.

The general eyed him. "It's been a while, huh, Captain?"

Tom didn't trust himself to speak.

"He's an old-fashioned man. This will be difficult for him, Captain."

A cynical noise escaped Tom's mouth. The general talked over it. "My nephew was hurt in Chu Lai, back in '66. Stepped on an MD-82."

"I'm sorry to hear that, General."

"You have to remain disciplined," said the general. "Keep hold of your courage."

"Yes, General. I will, General."

The general nodded and straightened himself, as though he'd completed his business. "Well," he said. "I didn't just come here to make conversation, Captain."

"No, General."

The general took something from his pocket. He leaned

over Tom, his badges swinging. "In the name of the president of the United States of America, I proudly present you with the Purple Heart." He pressed a box into Tom's left hand.

Tom tried to speak, but his words came out mauled.

"What is it, Captain?" Tom heard the beginnings of impatience.

"Why, General?"

"Why? I would say that's obvious, Captain."

Tom lowered his voice. "But it wasn't the enemy, General."

"You were wounded in action," said the general, refusing to drop his voice in line with Tom's. "You were an excellent Marine. This"—he waved his hand—"is less than you deserve. Courage is courage, wherever it's found."

"I don't deserve a Purple Heart, General."

"I'm ordering you to take it," said the general. His hands made fists at his sides.

Tom swallowed. He covered the box with his palm. "Yes, General," he said.

"Good," said the general. "Captain." Tom watched him disappear through the swing doors. He put the box on top of his locker and turned his face into the pillow.

Tom / 1965

He leans against the FDC, watching the men play softball. Feels a moment of breeze, then the heat again, close and heavy. The light's going, and the game scatters. He wipes the sweat from his face and walks to his tent.

"All squared away, Lieutenant?" says Captain Roach as he strides to his hooch.

"Sir," he says, standing to attention.

The captain waves him on. "Get some rest," he says. "Looks quiet out there. Recon patrol just came back; they think the enemy's moved on."

"Sir."

He pulls off his boots and lies on his rack, listens to the bugs, the distant boom of guns. Sleep comes like a punch to the head.

An explosion of gunfire, and the ground shakes. He scrambles up, hears the tent rip, feels a bullet *fwit* by. Yanks on his flak jacket, can't find his helmet. Scrabbles under his rack for it, alarm climbing; and there it is, solid in his fingers, thank Christ. Jams it on his head, shells tearing canvas. Pulls his pistol belt around his waist, his fingers clumsy. Shoves his feet into his boots, grabs his rifle, and ducks out of the tent.

Head down, knees crouched. The air rips past him—noise like rocks falling. The moon throws down gray; he drives his legs faster, watching for trips, holes. Along the LZ, past Lieutenant Colbert's hooch—torn, smoking—a pull like elastic at his back, slowing him. But the sounds close in—M16s thudding, carbines popping, someone yelling (Sergeant Bryce?)—and he continues on, ears straining for clues, and underneath the mass of noise, he hears the unmistakable *chukk* of an RPG.

He drops to the ground. The air slaps out of his body. Flames strike up eighty, one hundred meters away. He checks for landmarks. They got the aid station. He tries to drag himself to his feet, but fear has climbed onto his back. He raises his head, heavy on his neck, and peers into the dark.

They're close, along the northeast perimeter: small groups of shadows, spaced along the inside of the wire. And, strewn across the space between, the half-curled bodies of Marines. Panic lights him up. He breathes hard, clenches his fists to screw up the courage they taught in Basics. The M16s are easing, and the sappers hear it too: they scatter into the firebase, strings of shadows, two groups heading east, one southeast, one south.

The artillery batteries—the fire direction center—the command post.

A moment of indecision. A mortar bursts fifty meters away, throwing dust. The guns or the radio. He sets his rifle to automatic, pulls the butt tight to his chest, stretches the barrel forward, like he's trying to pull the thing apart, lines his finger along the barrel, tracks the target, and fires.

The sapper leading the team south startles and folds. Tom keeps his finger tight on the trigger, follows the line, takes the next sapper. Tom squints. A shape rises from the ground; a pause, and it shakes on his gunfire. A mortar trembles the earth. Tom watches the dark, hears his breath, loud and fast. He scrabbles to his feet.

A snap of gunfire, stinging his legs. He runs till he sees it, the command post, thirty meters away. A figure steps from the shadows. Time slows, and Tom knows what's going to happen, knows he's the audience as the sapper turns and raises his arm.

Flash, *crack*.

Tom lifts his head. The sapper has vanished, the command post is blown, and paper glides through the air.

Someone is screaming.

Tom sprints, through smoke and dust, over burned ground, and he's inside the torn bunker. Fire crackles. He sees Captain Roach, legs turned wrong, chest shiny with blood; and the thought scrolls loud and dumb in his head: He's dead. A white arm lies on the ground and, three meters away, burrowing his body into the earth, Sergeant Louie, screaming.

Tom turns from Louie, finds the radio. Pushes the sergeant's cries down low, twists the dials. Nothing. His blood thumps. Heat presses his cheek, and the flames grow loud. He bangs the radio with his fist; it bleeds static.

"LZ Bear, this is FSB Lilley, over."

Silence. Tom counts Louie's screams. One, two, three.

A wet, clicking sound, and Tom's body hums.

"LZ Bear, receiving, over."

"We are under ground attack, repeat, we are under ground attack. Estimate thirty VC inside the firebase. We are also taking incoming at this time, over."

"Can we get a direction on the incoming, over."

Tom peers through the rip in the bunker, sees only smoke. "I can't get a position. Request artillery fire sixty meters out, three hundred and sixty degrees around our position, over."

"Roger that."

"Also request illumination and gunships, over."

"Any casualties, over?"

"Affirmative. Will require medical evacuation, over."

"Copy. Stand by."

The flames make a wall. He turns his face away, hears the zip of ammunition exploding in the fire.

"Likely to lose radio contact, over."

The zips come faster, bullets flying red. Louie buries his mouth in the rubble. Tom drags the sergeant over his shoulder, and runs.

Dawn comes, and they count the bodies. Twenty-one dead VC, but there had been more: there are smears of blood where the enemy dragged the bodies away. He takes his camera and clicks a picture, then another; he wants to use up the film so he can send it to his father. Firman and Webb lift the bodies of the dead Marines to a waiting cargo truck, and he stows the camera in his pocket. Six Americans, Captain Roach and Lieutenant Colbert among them. He crosses himself, and walks away. He sits on a sandbag, watches the medevac sink to collect the last wounded. Lieutenant Moore squats before him, palms his shoulders. "You'll get a Silver Star for this," he says.

That night, fear is lying with him. He's on his rack, flak jacket zipped, helmet strapped, boots laced. The moon's big enough that he can count the rips in his tent. Seventy-six. He thinks of Captain Roach, who seemed unbeatable, like all his superiors, and his stomach bleeds with fear. A gun fires in the distance, and his body startles.

It's him and fear.

Tom / July 1968

The brunette walked by and peered through the glass. Tom watched the doors, but she didn't return. Just the Italian orderly, leaning against the door until it gave way to his bulk and his bucket and mop. Tom closed his eyes.

Visiting hours. His mother came, bringing Girl Scout cookies.

"I've got Peanut Butter," she said.

"No, thanks."

"You're not hungry?"

"I can't eat."

She put the box on his locker. "You never could before a big day," she said. "What time's the surgery?"

"Eleven hundred hours."

"It's going to happen this time, honey. I can feel it." She leaned over to squeeze his hand, throwing a drift of maternal incense across his bed.

"The chief said it might not look half bad," he said. "When it's done."

"You're always handsome to me."

His throat tightened. "You're not listening," he said. "He thinks he might be able to cover the worst of the damage. I might look half normal."

"Yes, honey," said his mother. He heard the appeasement in her voice, recognized the forced optimism from the dozen disappointments they'd endured along his recovery.

"Forget it," he said. He banged the rail of the bed with his palm.

"I'm listening, Tom," said his mother. "I'm on your side."

He stared at the ceiling, heard her pour a cup of water.

"What's this?" she said. The box was in her hand.

"Mom," he said, but she was already opening it.

"They gave you a medal?"

"It's nothing, Mom. Give it to me."

"Of course it's not nothing."

His voice rose. "Give it to me." She handed it over. He pushed the box under his sheet.

He felt her soft scrutiny. "You can have the cookies after your surgery," she said. "When you've got your appetite back." She straightened the things on his locker. "I wanted to bring the Chocolate Mints too, but your father ate the whole boxful."

"He didn't come."

"No, honey." His mother fell silent, an old deflection strategy. Tom faced her, and waited. She gazed back, her eyes dumb and gentle as a cow's.

"You said he'd come," said Tom.

"I know, honey."

"It's been two weeks."

"It's busy at the bank right now. He's barely out of the office."

"We both know that's not the reason."

"Tom—"

"I just had a four-star general in here, saying how proud my father is of me. But the guy can't bring himself to come look at me."

"This is new for him, honey. He doesn't know how to deal with it. Give him time."

"If I'd been blown up by the enemy instead of by one of my own damn men, he'd be dealing with it fine."

"You don't know that."

"We both know that."

At first, his father came often. He sat and watched Tom for what seemed like days at a time. "He didn't think you'd make it," his mother told him later; but as Tom labored on, his father grew impatient, pacing the ward and sniping at the nurses. When the chief told his parents their son had done "most of the job of healing," Tom saw the distaste stiffen his father's features. His son—the college athlete, the decorated Marine—was a victim, a cripple; not at the hands of the enemy, but at the doing of some shitbrain American punk. His father's visits dwindled. Soon it was only his mother and aunts coming by. His father had abandoned him to the women.

"Don't get yourself upset," said his mother. "Keep your strength for tomorrow. You look tired."

"I can't sleep."

"This is a much smaller surgery, honey," she said. "You're stronger now."

She thought he was afraid of dying; but he'd learned to control that fear a long time ago. The trick was to persist for another minute, and another minute. Once he discovered the trick, it was straightforward. But now it wasn't the dying to be mastered, it was the carrying on. Each night he pictured that grain of black, hauling him in, and tried to disappear into it. Each morning, he woke to his face and his body. He wasn't afraid he wouldn't survive the surgery; he was afraid it wouldn't work, and he'd have to carry on.

"I need to get the hell out of here," he said.

He woke hours before dawn. Watched the shadows, knew from the uneven breaths that he wasn't the only one awake. By the time the chief arrived at zero nine hundred hours, Tom was taut with anticipation. He clocked the chief's slow walk, and dismay spiked his throat.

"I'm sorry," said the chief.

"Just tell me."

"Your plates showed signs of infection."

Tom waited. Frustration flashed across the older man's face.

"So, we can't operate," he said.

"I'm fine," said Tom.

"It's not worth the risk."

"I'll risk it."

"We'll place you on antibiotics and test again in a week or so."

"If you don't do the graft, it'll get infected anyway."

"You have to trust us."

"This is the third time."

"We'll get there."

"Please," said Tom. He heard the beg in his voice and felt a sting of self-contempt.

"We'll get you through this." The chief gripped his shoulder. "You have to be patient."

The curtains were pulled open, a dozen hopefuls on display. He watched the Italian couple head for Car Wreck, the woman with the toddler for Factory Accident. The curtains were closed, one set after another. Tom heard low voices, care packages being unwrapped, and, somewhere, the plunk of a liquor stopper. He eyed his neighbor, who'd been wheeled in this morning from God knows where—some medical close-quarters combat where they yanked the kid away from dying decently. The kid was in a bad way, his whole face covered with a thick dressing, pits cut for the eyes and mouth. Pus seeped through the gauze on his arms.

The doors opened, and a teenybopper entered. She stopped to speak with the desk nurse. She was toothy and tan, dressed for shopping in the city. The nurse pointed. There was something stuck-up in the way the girl clicked down the ward, like she was bracing for a wolf whistle or a holler. She was here for the New Kid—he could tell by the slowing at ten paces, the show on her face: uncertainty, disbelief, revulsion.

He'd seen it before—in his own mother, his aunts—the female reflex to seeing a burned body, the disgust that registered before all the other responses that came trooping in the rear: fear, pity, tenderness. He didn't know which was worse, the revulsion or the crying. And here it came—he saw the teenybopper's chin give, the roll of tears, and felt a lurch of ferocity—he wanted to hit her or fuck her, make her scream or shut up, anything to stop the weeping.

"Danny," she whispered, dragging her wrist across her nose. She crept to the bed and touched the mattress.

"Danny." Her eyes moved over the dressings, the pus. She leaned in, enough to get a noseful of it, the smell of the dying. She stepped back, nausea rolling up her neck. The Kid moaned.

A nurse walked by. "You okay, sweetheart?"

The teenybopper nodded, her mouth clamped.

"Go grab yourself a chair," said the nurse. "You've got plenty of time."

"Thanks," the teenybopper managed; but she kept standing. The Kid moaned again. The teenybopper took another step back, and, glancing to check that the nurse had gone, turned to leave.

"Miss?" said Tom. She startled. "Miss?" She looked over her shoulder for someone who could answer for her, but there was nobody. "Could you get me a cup of water?" He smiled. The doubt in her face eased as she took in his good side.

"Sure," she said.

He watched her. She kept her eyes down, filled the cup to the brim, and returned the pitcher to the locker, knocking over his clock. She hurried to set it straight, and turned to go.

Tom grabbed her wrist.

"Come here."

She gasped, wriggled her arm. He gripped harder, yanking her inward.

"Hey—"

"Want to see under these bandages?"

"You're hurting me."

"Come closer." He pulled so her face was an inch from his. Her cheeks were covered in blond down.

"Why were you leaving?"

Her breath smelled of cinnamon. Tom remembered Sharon Gust under the bleachers at senior prom, her damp panties and her Hot Tamales breath, and felt the tug of a hard-on.

"Please, let go of me," said the teenybopper.

"Answer me."

"Let go." Her voice shook.

"Tell me why."

"Nurse!" she called, craning her neck. Tom could see the nurse standing outside the ward, talking to a doctor.

Tom twisted the teenybopper's wrist; her head swung back to face him, her eyes widening.

"Go sit with your boyfriend until they throw your bony ass out of here." She sobbed. "I don't care if you never come back. Right now, you stay." He let go; she stumbled, her face crumpling. She rubbed her wrist and backed away.

"You all right, sweetheart?" called the nurse, walking back down the ward. "You're still standing? Here." The nurse dragged a chair beside the Kid's bed and took the teenybopper's arm, steered her to sit, and patted her shoulder. "You call if you need anything." The nurse shut the curtains. Quiet; then the sound of crying. The Kid groaned. Tom listened to the snuffling and keening until the sun leveled with the window and baked the air out of the ward. A shift nurse came by to syringe morphine into his mouth. Tom's throat furred, his eyes grew heavy, and he slept.

When he woke, the Kid's curtains were open. The teeny-bopper had disappeared, and the Kid's bed was empty. A young nurse was tucking new sheets over the mattress, her hands shaking.

Kip / July 1968

The piggies are getting roasted.

The more men they cram in these cages, the more the cages are getting rattled. You can see fear sweating on the piggies' faces as they pace the cellblocks. A few weeks back, you swear or spit at a Brig Pig, they would throw you in the Box, and mess you up on the way. But now it's a rite of passage for the new brothers, a blood game, and the piggies don't want to play. Besides, the Box is stuffed full. Sometimes on sandbag duty I think I see a pair of eyes blinking through that slit cut into the Conex; and sometimes when the heat has got its thick breath all over me, I wonder if that pair of eyes is me.

The truth is, this place will crack you faster than any combat zone. When you're baking your ass on a hill in gook country, waiting for Victor Charlie to light you up, you know the exact number of days you have left before you get home, provided you don't get the bejesus blown out of you first. But I've been in this shithole for so many weeks I can't even count them, and still I got no word on What's Next, or even if there is a fucking Next. It's not just me—there are rats who've been waiting months longer than me for their court-martial, waiting for the Big Men with their good, easy lives to decide their destiny.

Whether it's Mr. Marshall, Mr. Huffacker, Justice Choate, Vance, the brig L-C, Westmoreland, McNamara, or President LBJ, there's fleshy, loaded white men stacked up all the way on top of me, sitting their saggy old-man balls on my face and making me smell their power. They don't wish us life, liberty, or happiness, they just want to get rid of us, and they have all kinds of ways, from pushing us through courts, to burying us in cells, to throwing us into war. At least with psychos like

Mr. Marshall and LBJ you can see the meanness in their eyes; they know that you know they want to hurt you, and there's an honesty in it. But Captain Vance and all those other Marine-in-Chiefs are the worst kind of torturers, the kind who think they're doing you a favor by hounding you and ripping you and sending your torn-up ass out into the woods to bait gooks. You treat a man like an animal, you take away his pride and his comforts and make him live in the dirt, he'll grow claws.

Captain Vance pushed me too far, shamed me, punished me, nearly got me wasted, then shamed me again. It broke me down, unhooked my wires and scrambled my signals, so I had no control. He did wrong, and he got corrected—that white light in my hands was made up of thousands of tiny vengeances, mine and Esposito's and those of every single enlisted man he bitched and shafted and slid into the heat of a hot combat zone.

And I can feel another correction coming. There's violence in these cells, and it's about to break loose.

"Not today," he told the nurse, a heavy Asian woman with a pockmarked face.

She laughed. "The sun rise in the west today."

"What do you mean?"

"Every time, you can't wait for physical therapy. I come, you already sitting up with leg over side of bed, ready to get in that chair."

"It's not a good day."

"You go, sir. You got to get strong."

"I say I'm not going, I'm not going, you understand?" He spoke loudly, as though across a language barrier. Offense creased her forehead.

"I not stupid, sir. You come." She gripped his crippled arm, the flesh swinging at her upper arms. She was strong, had real muscles beneath the fat.

"Get your hand off me. You're out of line."

"I don't care about your line or any other stuff about you," she said, trying to pull him to sit. "You go for him." She jerked her head toward Factory Accident, who was sitting in his wheelchair by the doors, waiting. "He got a baby and another one coming," said the Asian woman. "He need to get strong to help his wife. You get tough, sir."

"It's nothing to do with me," said Tom.

Factory Accident was a wimpish guy his age with a permanent expression of terror on his face. Tom assumed that until he was caught up in the explosion at the paint factory, the guy really didn't have anything to be scared of: homely wife, standard-issue kid, steady job, nothing too beautiful or terrible to get worked up about. The first time they met in PT, Tom asked him if he was okay. "Yeah, don't worry at all. My face was made this way. They called me Bambi in high school." Tom couldn't remember his real name and sure as hell wasn't going to call him Bambi. But the guy's panicked expression, even in the most tame situations, amused Tom; and he was the closest thing Tom had to a comrade on the ward. Ever since that first session, Factory Accident had shadowed him at PT, selecting the same weights and asking Tom which machines to use. He caught Tom's eye and waved. Tom sighed and pulled himself up to sit.

"You not so much asshole after all," said the Asian woman.

They rolled down the corridor. As they rounded the corner, Tom was run straight into a pair of stockinged legs, knocking their owner into his lap. The pain sucked his breath.

"Oh, God." She found her feet, using his armrest to push herself up. It was the brunette. She was even finer up close—full lips, big breasts. She looked down at him. "You're Captain Thomas Vance," she said in a hurry.

He winced.

"I'm sorry." The brunette crouched. "Are you all right?"

"He fine," said the Asian woman.

"I'm fine," he said. The pain along his right side was burning away, leaving a long glow of agony. The brunette stood. "You were looking for me?" he said.

"I . . . ?"

"I've seen you outside the ward. Ward 4-B."

"Right. Yes," she said, but she was distracted, taking in his stump, his hand, his face, her expression factual, professional.

"You Veterans Affairs?" asked Tom. "They promised me somebody weeks ago, when I left the VA hospital. We're only six kilometers away, but you'd think I'd left the country. My mother's been calling but can't get any damn sense out of them." The brunette stared. That's all he needed, a birdbrain looking after his affairs.

"This your first day on the job or something, ma'am?" said Factory Accident. "My friend asked you a question, but you can't quit staring."

The brunette blinked, then smiled. She might as well have held a sword at Factory Accident's neck, for the way it set him back in his chair. "I'm new, sir. But, yes. I'm with Veterans Affairs." She cleared her throat. "There's a few things I need to discuss with you, Captain Vance. Privately." The Asian woman clucked her cheek. The brunette flushed. "When's a good time?"

She came the next day, after his meds. The morphine was warm, softening his pain and loosening his anger. He felt the strange weight and lightness of the drug, the heaviness in his eyes, the emptiness in his chest. Now he understood why people got high. Except it was more a feeling of sinking, into the dark, and as much as it saved him, he feared sliding away.

He didn't hear her approach. She slipped through the curtains, head bowed, like a thief. Tom dragged himself up to sit, drawing spit into his dry mouth.

"Captain Vance," she said.

"You didn't tell me your name," he said.

"It's Genevieve."

"French name."

She nodded. "Francophile mother." Her features sharpened with some tremendous focus. She was nervous. Irritation chewed him. That the VA would send him not only a chick but a green one—however easy on the eyes—was an insult.

"Well, let's get to it," he said.

"Right," she said. "How are you doing?"

"Listen, honey," he said, leaning forward; and as he did so, he felt a small reaching movement in his right arm. He paused, moved his elbow, saw his forearm move across the sheet. "Jesus Christ." He shifted it again. It was recovering; his right arm was finding itself, and even in this twitch, a different kind of future showed itself—one where he could use both arms, where maybe his face would heal too. A smile flopped over his mouth. He looked up to see her gazing at him, and his smile stiffened; but the electricity of the movement had lit his imagination, and new possibilities crowded his brain.

"Are you all right?" she said.

"Yes, yes—"

"Can I get you something?"

He reached his right arm once more, felt it come to life.

"Look at that," he murmured.

"Sir?" She was looking at his mangled hand, her eyes tender with pity.

"Hey," he said, clicking his good fingers until her eyes met his.

She frowned. "Yes, sir?"

He moved his arm again, felt it travel further this time.

"Captain Vance?"

"My disability compensation hasn't come through. I need you to help me get ahold of it."

She hesitated.

"There's a problem?"

"No, sir, it's just—"

"Insurance too. I'll be out of here soon, and nothing's ready."

She looked afraid.

"Sweetheart," he said, frustration gathering. "If you can't handle it, you need to get someone who can. I've waited weeks for someone in your department to show up. All kinds of other people have come that I didn't want to see"—the American Legion men with their goddamn optimism, the crippled vets with the DAV—"but you're the ones I need, and now you have to help." Her eyes sought the ground. He stared at her until she made eye contact. "I'm getting better, and as soon as my face is healed up, I'll be out of here. I want to know when my money's coming. And I need you to help me find a job."

"A job?"

"A job."

"But what kind of—" She stretched out her hand, her fingers splayed.

"They gave you a job, didn't they?" He shook his head, tasted bitterness. "All right, let's call it quits, shall we? You run on." He waved his good hand. "Go get your boss to send someone who knows what he's doing."

He was ready for it—the tears, the running from the room. But she stood still and dry-eyed, taking a breath that swelled her breasts under her dress.

"I need to ask you something," she said. And whether it was the morphine or his arm or this small show of courage from one of the few fuckable girls he'd seen in weeks, he waited.

"What makes you think you can work again?"

The words were a woman's slap, sharp and spiteful. He looked into her face for ridicule but saw only a surprised earnestness, as though she were taken aback by her own bluntness. He heard the sound of his own laughter.

A nurse poked her head through the curtain. "Is everything all right?" Tom nodded, his laughter coming in small bursts. "Ma'am, visiting hours are from two to four."

"She's not a visitor," said Tom. "She's from Veterans Affairs." The brunette smiled.

———

He'd graduated from Stanford magna cum laude, majoring in mechanical engineering and leading the Indians to victory in his final year in the big game against Cal. By the time he left campus, he had job offers from California Gas & Electric and the Pacific Railroad; and his uncle had gotten him an interview with one of the banks downtown. He was engaged to a Whitson heiress who lived off saltines and vodka stingers and had the sexual energy of an athlete. Life was turning out fat and rosy. But watching Jack Kennedy talk about military service on the Whitsons' new TV set seemed to leach its colors. When Tom signed up for the Corps later that year, his father shook his hand hard, and he hadn't missed the flash of triumph on his mother's face when he told her he'd broken off his engagement to Kathryn.

Tom gave the bare bones of his résumé to the brunette—Stanford, Officer Candidate School, Amphibious Warfare School—but she didn't write anything down, just nodded and wrung her hands and, when he'd exhausted himself, said, "My brother's in the Marine Corps." Then Donna came.

"Sir," she said. "It's time."

Tom raised his hand to stop Donna pulling back the sheets; he didn't want the girl to see the amputation, or the gown that barely covered his crotch. The brunette must have noticed his discomfort because she exited through the curtains, as quietly as she'd come.

"Who was that?" said Donna. "She was pretty."

"Just another girl, hanging around," he said.

The next day he watched for her, surveilled the doors for her face among the trail of staff and visitors. When the Asian woman came to take him away for PT, he stalled, and she smacked her tongue in her mouth. The day bled out, with only his mother for a visitor. Night came, and Tom fell into a strange, light-filled sleep.

A week passed. His surgery had been rescheduled for Thursday. With each day, the ward grew hotter, and his body grew tighter with impatience. He asked a volunteer to wheel him down to the courtyard, a square of grass at the base of his building. It was eighty degrees out, but the courtyard was shaded. Tom waited until the volunteer had gone, then tested his right arm, squeezing his hand around the wheel and pushing it down. The chair nosed forward. He was getting stronger: his hourly exercises with the gripper were paying off. He pushed the wheel down again, and again, until his chair was skewed and his arm was tired. He righted himself so he could look across the courtyard. He watched a blackbird parade across the grass, picking for worms. Here, outside, there was a different quiet to the silence of the ward, which was a thing of absence; here, the quiet was a secrecy of sounds, layered, inaudible—the push of the wind, the grind of insects, the movement of the trees.

He felt it before he heard it: the approach of somebody along one of the paths between the buildings. It was her. She was dressed for the dog days of summer, wearing a dress patterned like picnic cloth. He took in the slimness of her waist, the roundness of her ass. She stopped outside his building and bent over her purse, straightening to light a cigarette. Turned, and saw him.

She stubbed out her cigarette against the wall and walked toward him.

"Captain Vance."

"About time."

She blushed. Ripe and bright and flushed—he could imagine how she'd look after getting fucked.

"What have you got for me?" he said.

The sun rolled from a cloud and blazed at her back, putting her body into shadow. Her hair moved in the breeze.

"I'm not sure I have what you want," she said. The sun rolled away again, and he saw her swallow, the hollow of her throat rising and dipping.

"You're going to tell me to be patient," he said. He pushed his right hand down on the wheel again, moved the chair further this time. He was learning about patience, how it was courage, not cowardice.

"I don't have anything to give you," she said. He was struck again by her mix of nerves and sass. He used to get this all the time—the chicks hovering to speak with him, pink and tongue-tied. But this was something different. She glanced over her shoulder as if to leave.

"Your brother's a Marine?" he said, words coming in a hurry.

"He is, sir. In the Quang Tri province."

"That right? I was out there too. He's infantry? Artillery?"

"Artillery."

"Which battalion?"

"I'm not sure, sir."

"Know which base?"

"No, sir."

Tom nodded. "Officer or enlisted?"

"Enlisted."

"Right." Tom had had enough of enlisted men to last a lifetime.

The blackbird dragged a worm from the ground and gulped it whole.

"What's it like over there?" she said.

"Hot," he said. "Hot, humid. Beautiful country."

"It's dangerous?"

"A little dicey now and then. But, no, he's artillery, he'll be on a firebase or some such for the most part. Not a lot of direct engagement with the enemy. You shouldn't worry."

"He says he's seen a lot of combat."

"That's unusual. You might catch a little heat on patrol. And you'll get some rounds coming into the base. Attacks happen." Deadwood. He pushed the thought away. "But they're rare. Bigger problem's boredom."

"That's hard to believe."

Tom shrugged. "Harder to lead men through boredom than it is through battle. When the bullets fly, a Marine will rally. But it's the months when nothing happens that men get wild."

"Wild?"

"They look for a release. Booze. Marijuana." She shifted her feet. "Black kids, hand-shaking, hanging out, brawling—especially after Reverend King. The kind of thing my father never had to deal with." They made wars differently then: front lines, clear enemies, a patient, sacrificing public. Glory was easier come by, sooner recognized—his father wasn't braver than he was; he was luckier.

Sweat showed on her forehead. She wiped her mouth with her fingers. He'd been too honest.

"Look, most Marines are disciplined and focused, like I'm sure your brother is. But in a war like this, where they're lowering standards to get the numbers up, you'll get a couple bad ones in the yield."

"You ever had any bad ones?"

"How do you think I got like this?" He regretted the words as he spoke them.

"What happened?"

"It doesn't matter."

"It matters to me."

"It has nothing to do with you." The courtyard clouded. From the recesses of the hospital, yelling.

"Maybe it does," she said.

Misgiving crept over his skin. "Who are you?" he said.

"I . . ."

"Who are you with?" It would explain it—her incompetence, her nerves, her damn persistence.

"I came alone."

"For Christ's sake—who do you write for?"

The girl paused, her skirt parachuting in the wind. He watched her playing dumb, stalling, and violence gathered in his blood. "Who do you write for?"

"I don't write for anybody," she said. She flinched. His chair was on her feet, its wheels squashing her toes; he must have driven it forward. He pushed back on his wheels, freeing inches of space between them.

"I'm not a journalist," she said. Her eyes smarted.

"So why all the goddamn questions?"

She said nothing, slipped a foot from its shoe and rubbed it against the back of her calf.

"What did you want to find out?" he said. "You digging for something? Or just damn nosy?"

"I wanted to know what it was like out there," she said, her voice plain, bare—honest. He studied her keen face. "What it was like for you."

If she was a journalist, she was a bad one—no notes, a shaky cover story. She folded her leg like a dancer to rub her naked foot.

"There are a lot of journalists running around in this war," he said.

She shook her head. "I don't know about that." She pushed her foot back into her shoe. Her toenails were lacquered red.

Tom remembered Donna in the shower, telling him she wasn't the enemy; remembered twisting the skin on that kid's wrist when she came to visit her burned-to-death boyfriend. "I'm sorry," he said.

"It doesn't matter," she said.

"My mother says I act like I'm still at war."

She lifted her eyes to his. "It's okay."

Tom felt the shade, cold on his skin. "I'm not stupid, you know," he said. Electricity traveled across the girl's face. "I know you can't do a lot for me. Maybe an office job with the DoD, maybe clerking with the VA." The electricity was gone, the girl's face smoothed to stone. "But I know you'll do your job."

"Sir—"

"Come back, so we can talk some more about it. Whatever happened today. You'll come back."

Jeannie / July 1968

Jeannie ducked her head as the cab drove down Parnassus, her heart thumping. As they turned onto Stanyan, the pounding softened, but her body still crawled with swelter. When the cab pulled up outside Chapman & Macht, the lining of her dress was greased with sweat. She pulled herself onto the sidewalk, smoothed her skirt, and stepped through the gilded door.

The woman at the desk greeted her and gestured for her to pass. The building was quiet, sound falling dead against the carpets and drapes, the atmosphere of strained concentration nearly touchable. Jeannie found the door, and knocked.

"Mrs. Harper." Albert Macht stood at his desk, his fingertips touching his papers, as though unwilling to let go. He gave a tidy smile and nodded for her to sit. "How are things?"

Jeannie's mouth was dry. "I just came from the hospital."

"Ah." Macht tugged the fabric at the knees of his pants and placed himself in his chair. "How did it go?" His face collected into an expression of concern.

"I didn't get far."

"But you asked him?"

She shook her head. "He doesn't know who I am."

"You spoke to him?"

"He thinks I'm with Veterans Affairs."

"Is that what you told him?"

"I don't know." Jeannie couldn't remember lying outright; remembered a half-dozen spaces in their conversations when the truth had stuck in her mouth.

"I see." Macht pressed his lips together. "Well, Mrs. Harper, I'm afraid that's not going to get us anywhere at all."

Jeannie prickled with irritation. "I'm aware of that, Mr. Macht."

He nodded as she spoke; he wasn't listening at all. "The good thing is, you have access," he said.

Access wasn't difficult—the hospital was busy and the staff overwhelmed; nobody had the time or the inclination to question a respectable-looking woman walking the wards. Avoiding her father-in-law was harder. Jeannie thought of her close questioning of Richard, her curiosity about his schedule, the time she ducked into an empty office as he strode the corridor toward her.

"The captain," she said, wrinkling her toes inside her pumps. "He's a difficult man."

"Mmm." Macht gave a slow shrug. "It was never going to be easy."

"He's very . . . he's badly wounded."

"I can imagine." Jeannie wondered if he could, if his expensive existence ever touched against a sick human body.

"I tried to prepare myself. But he's . . ." Jeannie shook her head. She'd known about the captain's injuries, had been casually asking after her father-in-law's patient for weeks. But she hadn't accounted for the size of him, the height and heft of him that made the space where his leg should have been look so strange, like a lie or a joke; she hadn't accounted for the winces of pain that pulled his face taut, or for his smell—even outside, and at a couple of paces—of sweat and antiseptic.

"How could you prepare?" said Macht. "A girl from the Outside Lands coming up against the human cost of a war being fought nearly eight thousand miles away."

The Outside Lands. It was a strange expression, but one he'd used before, a reminder of his seniority and education, of her quaintness, her irrelevance. Her scattered energies found a focus in resentment.

"I'm not an idiot, Mr. Macht," she said.

"I'm not suggesting . . ." Macht's eyebrows fell into a frown, and his cheeks blotched. He coughed and rearranged his expression into one of calm control; Jeannie wondered if he was remembering her father-in-law's larded account with the firm. "I have only respect for you, Mrs. Harper."

A growl, and a spaniel scuffled from underneath the desk. Relief loosened Macht's face; he opened his drawer, removed a bone-shaped biscuit, and slipped it onto the dog's tongue. It cracked the treat between its teeth.

"Anthony Dwight Jones," said Macht. "Twenty years' hard labor. Miguel Perea. Four years' imprisonment. Both sentenced in the last six months, both convicted of the same crime: attempted murder of an officer." He picked up his pen, made a dot on his notepad, and set the pen down. He was master of his domain once more. "There's no standard for sentencing in these matters. It comes down to the judge, to the court members, to counsel, to the damn weather. But most of all, it comes down to mitigating circumstances. Was the accused misled, immature, mentally impaired, addicted to drugs? Does he have a troubled family history? Is he of good character? Does he possess a good service record? In the absence of any witnesses to this crime or the prior circumstances"—Jeannie's mind went to the newspaper pictures of the smoking firebase, helicopters hovering, the grim-faced general—"we've got nobody to shore up Kip's case."

"Which is?" asked Jeannie.

"We're finalizing the details," said Macht. "He'll continue to plead guilty—"

Jeannie shook her head.

"Whether you believe he did it or not, Mrs. Harper, he's already confessed. Pleading guilty will lessen his sentence. Now it's up to us to show that there were extenuating factors:

that he was a good Marine, but that he was vulnerable, that he was corrupted by somebody or something."

"Has your attorney gotten any sense out of him?"

"I spoke with Dellinger yesterday. It seems your brother's still coming to terms with his situation. The kid's story is—let's say it's still a little jumbled." The spaniel grunted. Macht held out his hand, and the dog licked his fingers.

"I wish I was there," said Jeannie. Corresponding with Kip by mail was like calling down a well—it took an age to get anything back, and none of it made sense. The few letters she had received veered between indecipherable rants and lists of homesick questions; Jeannie couldn't pick the truth from them.

"You can help him by concentrating your efforts this side of the Pacific."

Jeannie sighed. "There's nothing else we can do?"

"It's the only avenue we have to pursue, Mrs. Harper. We need to do our damnedest to get something we can use out of Captain Vance. An account of good service, a character reference, an acknowledgment of surprise that your brother would attack him in that way. Now, I'm happy to talk to him for you." Macht's mouth puckered as though he'd tasted something disgusting. He shuffled his papers into a pile: her time was up. "But in my experience, the personal approach gets you further with victims. Lets them put a human face to the accused."

Macht stood, and Jeannie followed suit. She thought of Kip, small and scared in his cell thousands of miles away; thought of Captain Vance, the pleasure in his face when he noticed her in the courtyard, his entreaty that she return, and knew that there was power in this, however small or fraudulent. "I'll try again," she said; but Macht was already sitting, his face bending over a thick book.

Jeannie walked home, the sun close and harsh on her face, her mind turning. She walked up Noe, and saw a figure sitting on the steps to the house. The figure stood, its hair falling long and disheveled, its shadow kinking up the steps.

Jeannie felt the smile in her mouth, round and unyielding as a jawbreaker candy. Lee had telephoned once since their argument on California; and Jeannie, still bruised by the girl's lack of heart, had set down the receiver right away, then waited, sweaty-handed, for it to ring again. But it didn't, and Lee didn't call back; and through all the strange and fearful adventures of the last weeks, Jeannie's lingering desire for Lee was stitched through the days like a brilliant-colored thread, a drop of blood on the cotton.

"Lee," said Jeannie; but Lee's face was expressionless.

"I need you," said Lee. In all Jeannie's imaginings of the moment, she hadn't heard the words like this—brisk, sunken. In the falling light, Jeannie could see that Lee's skin was sheened with sweat.

"Are you all right?"

"No," said Lee, shaking her head. "I'm not all right."

"Are you sick? Come inside. I'll get you a glass of water." Jeannie tried to take Lee's arm, but Lee jerked away.

"I need more letters," she said.

Jeannie felt the disappointment like something hard in her throat—like she'd swallowed the solid, round smile that was in her mouth a moment ago and it had gotten stuck. But there was something panicky in Lee's eyes; and Jeannie tried to ignore her own dismay. She touched the younger girl's hand. "What's happened?"

Lee shook her off. "Cut it out, Jeannie. Either get me some letters or give me the fucking letterhead and Billy's signature and I'll do it myself."

"You know I can't do that." Jeannie's body grew tight.

"You don't have a choice. There's no way out now."

"What are you talking about?"

"The Reverend placed an ad. In the *Daily News*. Some dumb poem Walter came up with, and a bunch of people took the bait."

Jeannie heard the strangeness of this last turn of phrase; remembered the bill-stuffed envelope in Lee's back pocket.

"Jesus, Lee."

"We got people calling every day. We can't keep up." Lee gnawed her thumb.

"But if you have that many people, it could draw attention—"

"I told him that, but he won't listen. He's a fucking nut."

"So tell him no. Get out."

"I can't."

"Of course you can."

Lee was shaking her head.

"What is it, Lee?"

"He's got photographs of me. We were so fucking high. Me and Silver . . ." Lee raised her eyes to Jeannie, shame raw and slick on her face. Something oily stirred in Jeannie's stomach. Lee watched her. "It was before us," she murmured.

Jeannie blinked, saw Lee's mouth at Silver's small breasts, Lee's hand between Silver's pale legs, and felt nauseated.

"If I don't get the letters, he'll send the pictures to my parents."

Jeannie swallowed her queasiness and studied Lee's face. There was fear in it, and something else—something shrewd and assured, like power.

"I won't do it," said Jeannie.

Lee's eyes rounded. "Please."

"No."

"Please." Lee gripped Jeannie's stiff hands. "My mother—you have no idea. She'll put me away, have me locked up in some asylum somewhere with a bunch of freaks—somewhere I can't embarrass her anymore."

Jeannie saw the drama lighting Lee's face and felt a surge of frustration. "It's all bullshit, Lee," she said. She thought of Tom, his jail of a body; of Kip and his crippled life; saw the performance in Lee's imploring stance. "The protests, the Reverend, running away from home, even you and me—you love a show."

Lee's face drew into an expression of incredulity, but Jeannie didn't miss the blush spreading at her jaw.

"Something real's happening," said Jeannie. "And there's no room for . . ." She shook her head. "For you. And all this."

Lee's face darkened. She let go of Jeannie's fingers, moved her hands to Jeannie's shoulders, and placed a slow kiss on her collarbone. "Please," she whispered. The husk of her voice was like old comfort, and Jeannie felt needles at her skin. Lee tipped her face up to Jeannie's and gave a cattish smile. Jeannie saw the drab look in the younger girl's eyes, and the needles at her skin sharpened.

"You're on your own, Lee," she said. She turned, strode up the steps to the house, and pushed the door shut behind her, then leaned against the wall, readying herself for the sense of loss that had touched her throat like a blade ever since that day on California. It came, pressed her neck; but the blade was dulled, and a new feeling came, warm and vigorous as fresh blood: relief.

Billy returned from the hospital early, just as Jeannie was browning the chicken for dinner. He dropped his bag in the hallway and came to the kitchen—his face still imprinted with the struggle of the day—and leaned to kiss Jeannie's cheek; she turned, knocking his spectacles askew, and their kisses fell wrong, smearing an ear, a nose. But there was something safe in her husband's nearness, his careworn solidity, and Jeannie had the urge to press herself into his arms, to feel his comfortable heaviness. She put her arms around his soft waist; he bent to her, spreading his fingers lightly at her back, cautiously, as though she might detonate.

"I saw Albert Macht today," she murmured into Billy's shoulder.

"Mmm," he said. He straightened, his fingers loosening at her back.

"Kip's case is a mess."

"Jeannie," said Billy, taking her by her forearms and easing her away. "I've had a long day."

"He's still saying he's guilty."

"You need to let this go, Jeannie. You can't save him."

"But—"

"I can't talk with you about this, Jeannie. You know this whole business has put me in an impossible position."

"Your mother's let it go."

"My mother never lets anything go." Billy rubbed his face. "The sooner all this is over with, the sooner we can all get back to normal."

The next day, Jeannie left Charlie with Cynthia and took the bus, then the streetcar, to the hospital. Jeannie peered into the ward; his head was turned away. A tired-looking woman with a girl Charlie's age pushed the door, and held it open for Jeannie, giving a flat, empathetic smile. Jeannie breathed out hard, forcing down her rib cage to subdue the nervous pounding of her heart, and stepped into the ward.

He was asleep, his body unevenly bulking the sheets, half his face and neck crusted in its thick bandage. The bare part of his face was clean and freckled, his chest slow in rising and falling; he looked still and lovely as a sleeping child.

The ward was noisy with visitors. She stepped toward his bed and drew the curtains, creating a small, ceilingless room. The smell of sleep and exertion reeked from his sheets.

He opened his eye, and closed it again. Jeannie's heart thumped.

She watched him, waited for him to wake fully, but his eyelid remained shut, his eyeball moving under the skin, following the last unspooling of a dream.

"Sir," she whispered.

He emptied out a long breath. She waited for him to breathe in again, but he was still, his chest hollowed.

"Sir."

The eye jerked open.

Tom / July 1968

The smell of jasmine, hair lifting in the wind.

The girl, whispering.

Sunlight ribboning, dream weaving, the girl, the girl.

The Girl.

Tom woke, slipping in the borrowed moment before the pain came, and there she stood. A blister of pain ran along his right side. He tried to sit, but his body hadn't found its weight and strength.

"Sir," she whispered. She wore white, her hands folded against her skirt like a bride's. He wondered if he was dreaming; but she spoke again, and the sound of his name was hard and real on his ear.

"Captain Vance."

"Genevieve," he said. His sense of time was strangely assembled, his recollection of recent hours and days all mixed up. Then he remembered his news, and smiled. The smile echoed across the girl's face.

"You can call me Jeannie," she said.

"Jeannie." He shifted so he was upright against the pillow. "I prefer it to Genevieve."

"I always hated Genevieve."

"Call me Tom." He saw hesitation in her face, and hurried past it. "About yesterday—"

"It doesn't matter."

A pause.

"My last surgery's tomorrow," he said. That morning he'd braced himself for the infected plates visit from the chief; but only Girl Medic came, to tell him the surgery would go ahead as planned.

"What's the surgery?" Jeannie asked.

"Skin graft. Heal up this part." He raised his right arm to the bandages at his face, felt a boyish pride as he showed off his improved movement. She didn't register the significance of the gesture. "Of all the damage the explosion caused, I didn't think this would take the longest to heal. I'll be able to take off this damn dressing, look like a human being again."

She gave an awkward nod. "When will you be out of here?"

"Could be two or three weeks. I'm recovering well. The chief says I can do most of the healing outside of the hospital. Got a cousin who's going to rent me his two-bed in the Marina. It's pretty flat around there, first-floor apartment, no stairs." Discomfort touched her face. "We don't need to talk about that now. It'll be a while before I can think about work. I've got money saved." But she still looked uneasy. After two tours in Vietnam, Tom was used to the hesitation on the faces of rookies who were scared shitless, but wanted to suggest competence. But he wondered at how she kept coming back, each time as clueless as the last, ready to take on what even he had to admit was no cakewalk of a case. Pity might have been some of it, but it wasn't all of it—the girl seemed somehow unsentimental. He wondered if she was lonely; there was something strangely depleted about her. The excruciating idea that she already knew him fired his brain.

"We've met before? Before all this?" One of his wrecked lays between tours, or one of the girls whose letters he fell in love with in Quang Tri.

"We've not met."

Relief. A spasm of laughter came from across the ward; they turned their heads. As she returned to face him, he saw she was at a loss for words.

Time to build a new fence! somebody cried; more laughter.

He searched for something to say. He wanted to keep her at his side but didn't want to ask her any of the questions that were becoming increasingly pressing—about his compensation, insurance, employment. If he pushed too hard, she might seize up, or leave. "Thirteen," he said.

"I'm sorry?"

"Number thirteen. My thirteenth surgery." He tried to whistle, but it came as a blow.

"Tell me," she said. "Tell me all of it."

Midway through his story, Jeannie left the curtained cubicle to find herself a chair. The heat and the smell were making her swoony. She sat, and listened; and as the words dried up his mouth, she leaned to pour him another cup of water from the pitcher that stood on the locker beside his bed. She wanted to keep him talking, to keep the connection between them burning long enough for her to find the nerve to change the subject to Kip, to the attack. But as Tom spoke, careful with the dates and locations of his surgeries, going fast-slow over the medical details, she understood that that was what they were talking about, after all.

In spite of his bedbound state, he was something of a performer. It was in his expectation that his audience would hush up and listen, in the attentiveness of his eye contact. He would have been a commanding leader; and Jeannie could see how Kip, who had always loved a show, could have found something to admire in somebody so different.

The more he told her about his recovery, the more she saw his grotesqueness; and, like a child watching a horror show on TV, she couldn't unhook from the words or draw her eyes away. And there it was, at first remote and scattered, the scuttle of disquiet that scurried nearer, until it was spidering over her skin. That Kip—the naïve, sensitive kid who loved comics till he was way too old for them, who organized Aunt Ruth's pills each week and who helped Mr. Nowak box away his dead son's things—that he could have anything to do with this catastrophe, that he could even lie about inflicting this kind of pain on another person, was horrifying and impossible; and as she realized the contradiction in this thought, she saw that Tom was slowing, his lips parched.

She lifted the pitcher; he shook his head, and his eyelids dipped with fatigue. How do you continue? she thought, and heard the words fall from her mouth.

"What's the alternative?" He wriggled to reposition himself. She stood and adjusted his pillow behind his back. As she touched his shoulder for him to lie down, he put his hand on hers. The warmth and muscle of his hand surprised her.

"What's happened is done," he said. "And the guy who did it is paying for it." Jeannie tried to pull her fingers away, but he pressed his hand over hers and held it fast. Her fingertips grew damp. "What I mean is, I have to look forward."

That's all, folks, a nurse called; and Jeannie heard chairs scraping the floor, curtains whisking along rails. She tugged her hand from beneath his; it hung wetly at her side. "I should go," she said.

Jeannie sat at the kitchen table, rubbing at the bones in her face until the light left the room and Cynthia was buzzing at her door, a wide-eyed Charlie in her arms. He was tired and fractious, and it took over an hour to settle him to sleep; but Jeannie was grateful for the work. For the first time in weeks, she felt lost. Through the attorney updates and the visits to the hospital, she had been ruddered, setting course to save Kip. But now it felt as though he were already gone, as though he had died along the way sometime that summer—as though their grief for him had somehow killed him. She tried to imagine him, waiting in his cell; but her memory of him was slipping. She went to the living room, pulled the wide leather wedding album from the shelf, switched on the overhead lamp, and moved her finger over the pictures to find her brother's small, dark face. He seemed like someone from another time. But Tom—he'd never seemed so real as when he pressed her hand in that hot, stinking cubicle. She could still feel his fingers, feel their heat and strength.

She thought of calling her dad, but her hand stopped over the dial. She'd held him at a distance, telephoning every week or so and visiting with Charlie once or twice a month, giving him plenty of warning so he had a chance to straighten himself out. Charlie had a way of taking her dad out of himself, and sometimes on those warm, windy afternoons at the beach, with Charlie licking ice cream from his fingers and her dad digging for sea glass, it felt as though things were normal. But the time would come for them to leave; and the look of desperation on her dad's face would keep Jeannie away from the Sunset for weeks at a time. And all through those telephone calls and afternoons she'd been sparing with the details of her efforts for Kip, and her dad had neglected to ask. She was waiting to bring home the prize.

Her mind turned to her mom. Even now, years after her death, Jeannie felt herself grasp for her mother when she was adrift, a native, infant instinct she couldn't uncouple from. Her mom would never have met Kip's misfortune with her dad's passivity, would never have allowed Kip to enlist (that afternoon in the playground, how Jeannie had turned away from her own brother—she closed her eyes to squeeze the recollection away). If her mom had been alive, Kip would never have wanted to leave; he'd still be the star of his own movie, the golden boy, and there would be enough glory in his universe to stop him from seeking it in a war halfway around the world. It all started with that wet day in November; and when her mom, happy, dreamy, perhaps a little buzzed, had stepped in front of the cable car, it was as though she'd dragged Kip with her, under the steel car.

Jeannie heard a buzz at the door. Billy again, forgetting his key. He'd been more scattered lately, fatter, pastier, his shirts rumpled, his collars bent, regardless of her laundering.

She dragged herself to her feet and opened the front door.

Lee stood leaning against the doorjamb. Her hair was ganged together in a braid that reached her waist. In the weak fluorescence of the streetlight, her skin was the color of lavender. She wore shorts printed with flowers, and a thin shirt that clung. Her arrival was like a seltzer tablet dropped in water, a moment of effervescence that hushed Jeannie's thoughts.

"You okay?" said Lee. Her foot tapped the threshold.

"What are you doing here?"

"You going to let me in?"

"You need to go home," said Jeannie, closing the door; Lee nosed her foot over the threshold and pushed the door back open. She walked past Jeannie and took off her sandals.

"Billy's on his way."

"Relax," called Lee. "I'm not here to jump your bones."

Jeannie's face grew warm in the gloom. She watched Lee move down the shadowed hallway and disappear into the living room. Jeannie followed and flipped the light switch. Lee stood at the record player, flicking through Billy's Roy Orbison records. "No decent fucking music," said Lee, dragging her fingers over the shelves and collapsing onto the couch. She folded her legs beneath her, leaned over the coffee table, and riffled through a pile of medical journals. Frustration prickled the back of Jeannie's neck.

"If you're asking for help, you're wasting your time," said Jeannie. She lifted the journals away, placing them high on the bookshelf, the way she'd move something breakable out of Charlie's reach. As she turned back to the couch, she saw Lee's strange smile.

"What do you want?"

Lee's pupils were wide as pennies. Her smile hardened. "Walter's in jail."

"What?"

"They arrested him yesterday."

"What for?"

"Selling falsified documents. For the purpose of draft evasion." Jeannie's nerve endings lit bright with fear. "It was a sting. He went to see a couple about fixing a 4-F deferment and the guy pulled out a badge and handcuffs. Like I said, that ad was a dumb fucking idea."

"Oh, my God." Panic gripped Jeannie, and she paced to loosen it from her body, but her heart only flickered faster.

"They set bail at five thousand dollars. The Reverend said he'd pay, but this morning Mrs. Moon found his room was empty. He's gone, taken everything with him, all the money."

Jeannie sat, put her palms to her forehead, the sweat oily at her fingers. She felt the couch jiggle under the bounce of Lee's leg.

"The guy was a fucking crook."

"Jesus," whispered Jeannie.

Lee leaned toward her, her breath warm on Jeannie's face. "I don't think he's really a priest." She drew back, and Jeannie caught the slant of her smile, the wheedle in her eyes, and felt a cold blanch of horror. Lee thought this was a game.

"Mrs. Moon is freaking out. In that big, nasty house, all by herself, saying how Walter's all she's got left."

"Lee."

"It's a felony charge. She's talking about selling the place, just to pay for a lawyer."

"Lee."

"When I went by, Silver was there, crying. I think the Reverend was fucking her. He was fucking June too." Lee shook her head back and forth, fingers fidgeting at the folds of her braid. "I'm just glad the son of a bitch is gone. Now he can't hurt me." She slid a sly glance at Jeannie. "Not that you give a damn."

Jeannie gripped Lee's face, forcing her chin up so their eyes met. Lee gave a strange roll of her jaw; her teeth ground together. Beads of sweat showed on her upper lip. "You think you're safe now the Reverend's disappeared?" said Jeannie. "What about the police? What about me?"

Lee's eyes twitched over Jeannie's. Jeannie squeezed Lee's chin, brought it higher. "For Christ's sake, Lee."

"Walter won't give anybody up," said Lee. She pulled away and touched her hand to her jaw. "He might be an asshole, but he's an asshole with a sense of duty. He won't hurt the cause."

"Jesus, Lee. You're so naïve."

"I'm not naïve."

"And you're high." Jeannie shook her head in disgust; stood, and walked to the cloaked window. Lee's arms were folded, her face earnest.

"You don't know Walter," she said.

"People surprise you when they want to save themselves." Jeannie paced.

"Not Walter. He lost two cousins in Vietnam. He served most of last year in jail for breaking into an induction center. He's pissed off he's too old to get drafted. He'd gladly serve time as a CO. He's the genuine article."

"You thought that about the Reverend."

Lee shrugged. "I'm telling you what I know," she said. "The guy's dying for a cause to die for." The same grating of her teeth; she unfolded her arms and put her hands to her waist. Her body rocked, her eyebrows lifting in screwball arches. "I guess we'll know soon enough."

Jeannie slapped the wall. "For Christ's sake, Lee, this isn't a joke." Her palm stung; she closed it and pressed her fist against her thigh. "What about Billy? I have a child, Jesus, what about Charlie?" Jeannie felt sick; she leaned against the wall and closed her eyes.

"Everything will work out."

The front door slammed. Jeannie startled—she hadn't heard the ratchet of the key. They listened to his footsteps: Billy, large and pallid in his fatigue-grimed shirt, his spectacles smudged with grease.

"Lee Walker," he said, his face rounding with pleasure. "What are you doing here?"

"Billy." Jeannie stepped toward her husband.

Lee stood and moved between them. "I was in the neighborhood," she said. "I thought I'd stop by and say hello to Jeannie."

"It's good to see you." Billy held Lee by her upper arms and looked her over. "It's been awhile," he said. "You look like quite the hippie."

Lee grinned. "And you the square."

Billy laughed, bashfulness reddening his cheeks—Jeannie had forgotten that Lee and Billy had their own intimacy. "Still a brat, I see," he said good-naturedly; and Jeannie felt a tenderness for him that mixed unhappily with her fear. She stood, her hands dangling at her sides, aware of every joint and hang of her body, like a convict, waiting for the floor to drop. Billy looked from Lee to Jeannie, a delighted smile stretching over his cheeks.

"I didn't know you two had gotten to be friends," he said.

Lee's foot was dancing on the rug. "Sisters-in-arms against Dorothy and Virginia."

"Now, now." Billy wagged his finger.

Jeannie swallowed. "You'll have a drink, Billy?"

"Canadian Club, please." He planted a kiss on the side of Jeannie's face. "You okay, honey? You feel a little warm."

"Just a headache," said Jeannie. "I'm going to turn in. Lee was just leaving."

Disappointment flashed across Lee's face. "Yes, I'll go." She pushed her hands into her pockets. "Oh."

"Everything all right?" Billy's mouth winced over his drink.

"I don't have my key," she said, patting her shorts. "My parents are out of town, and I've gone and locked myself out."

"Shoot," said Billy.

"They're back tomorrow." Lee shook her head. "It doesn't matter. I'll go see if I can stay with my friend."

"Baloney," said Billy. "You'll stay with us."

Jeannie lay awake until dawn thinned the shadows, listening to Billy's comfortable breaths and Charlie's coughs as he turned in his blankets. Lee was in the living room, a prowler in the dark. Jeannie thought of Walter Moon, crawling with hair and anger, lying on his prison rack, full of poison; Kip, someplace she couldn't imagine, waiting for the spill of light at his door; Tom, damaged, yet somehow alive in his sleep-worn bed: all the men in buried places. The sparrows sang, and sleep pressed down on her. She woke to the push of a body at her back, frantic buzzing at the front door.

Lee was in bed beside her, her hand resting on Jeannie's stomach. Jeannie sat upright.

"What the hell—"

Lee sat too. She was naked. Whoever was at the front door had given up buzzing and was thumping on the wood. Jeannie checked the clock—9 A.M.: Billy would be long gone. Fear rinsed her. She roughed the bedspread aside and swung her feet to the floor.

"Hey," said Lee.

Jeannie hurried on a robe. "Get dressed, for Christ's sake," she said, and yanked the bedroom door shut behind her, slapping straight into Charlie, who craned his neck to look at her, his face breaking into a scream.

"Shush," said Jeannie, scooping him into her arms and barefooting down the hallway. She paused at the door, her heart hammering. The door shook with another knock. Jeannie gathered her courage, and opened it.

"Billy told me you were unwell." Dorothy leaned to set down her purse in the hallway. Jeannie felt loose with relief; she should have known it was her mother-in-law, who never met a door that wouldn't open, should have expected the news of her headache to have already reached Dorothy via the long, invisible umbilical cord that ran between her and Billy.

Dorothy must have seen the thought in Jeannie's face: she made a *tut* sound as she untied the belt of her raincoat. "He telephoned because he was worried about you," she said. "I said I'd come and help with Charlie." She stepped into the hallway and stretched her arms for her grandson; he launched himself forward, taking Dorothy's locket in his fist.

Jeannie's heart was slowing fatly in her chest. "That's kind of you, Dorothy, but I'm doing a lot better." She spoke loudly so that Lee might hear, tilting her body so she blocked Dorothy's way.

"You can't get rid of me that easily," said Dorothy. She kissed Charlie's nose, leaving a pink smudge. "I want to see my best boy."

The release of a door handle sounded from down the hallway. Jeannie's shoulders locked.

"Who's that?" Dorothy peered past Jeannie.

Jeannie turned and saw Lee, muss-haired and barefoot, her shorts seemingly even shorter than the night before, her shirt misbuttoned. A guilty sweat fingered Jeannie's skin.

"Hullo, Mrs. Harper," said Lee.

Jeannie watched Dorothy's face, saw all its parts in fine definition—the waxy gathering of lipstick at the corners of her mouth, the Carole Lombard eyebrows, the powder silted in the creases of her nose—but her mother-in-law's expression remained smooth.

"Leonora," said Dorothy.

"My mother locked me out," said Lee. She found her sandals in the hallway, pushed her feet into them, and smiled. Her face was still tender with sleep.

"Lee was nearby," said Jeannie, "we—"

Dorothy held up her hand. "If you're in trouble again, I don't want to hear it," she said. "Go home, and clean up before your mother gets back."

Dorothy and Jeannie stood aside as Lee brushed by in a sweep of bed-warm scent. She turned on the doorstep to face them. "So long," she said, and blew a kiss.

Jeannie closed the door, pausing to gather her composure before turning back to Dorothy.

"What on earth was she doing in your bedroom?" Dorothy's eyes were acid bright.

"Oh," said Jeannie, forcing herself to hold Dorothy's gaze. "She wanted to fix her hair, use my makeup."

Dorothy stared into Jeannie's face; Jeannie felt heat rising in her skin. "So." She clapped her hands together. "Coffee?"

"Cream and two sugars," said Dorothy, her lips pulling into

a distracted smile as Charlie palmed her face. Jeannie stepped past her down the hallway, and was surprised by the older woman catching her hand. "You're not to see that girl, do you hear me?" she said. She brought her mouth close to Jeannie's ear, whispered, her breath on Jeannie's neck. "She's rotten, all the way through."

Tom / August 1968

He lay in the dark, listened to the sounds of footsteps and talking outside. Sometimes the sounds hesitated at his door, then started up again and moved away. At first the solitude of the private room was welcome—between the LZs, the firebases, and the hospitals, he hadn't slept alone in a long time. Even between tours, there were the girls, the tan, gutsy Virginia babes who rode the back of his motorcycle and sneaked past the sentries onto the base (Bonnie, Ruth, Lucy, Gloria—oh, Gloria). But after three days on his own, he felt as though he was disappearing. Some moments he imagined that all that was left was the patch of skin that itched and burned on his face, floating in the dark.

He wanted to touch that part of his face, feel its newness, check that it was him. But the chief had warned against it, and Tom imagined the new skin coming away in his fingers. He had to be patient.

A tap at the door, and light washed the room.

Jeannie / August 1968

There was an unexpected comfort in his familiar bulking of the sheets.

"You were hard to find," she said.

"They moved me after my surgery."

"How was it?"

"Pull the blinds. Take a look."

He sounded different, his voice harder, brighter. She raised the blind in three long pulls. The window was muzzled with fog.

"Tell me," he said.

Jeannie turned toward the bed, and focused on removing all expression from her face. The dressings on his face were gone, but what was beneath looked raw as a fresh wound. Part of his cheek was hollowed away, a plum-colored, wet patch of skin covering the pit that sunk at his cheekbone. Pink, shiny skin pulled in ridges from his cheek, down to his neck and up to his hairline; and Jeannie thought of Dubble Bubble gum, the way it used to look when Nancy stretched it from her teeth in long strings. Part of his lower eyelid was pulled away, and his milky eyeball bulged from its socket. A white scum gathered at the place where his nose met his cheek. And against all this, the good part of his face—the strong bones, the smooth skin, the dusty freckles—seemed to disappear. Jeannie tried to recalibrate her view of him, but he was as half stuffed and lopsided as something half made; and when he spoke, she didn't know where to look.

"How does it look? Nobody will give me a straight answer."

Jeannie kept her gaze fixed on his good eye. "I . . ."

"They won't give me a mirror. Do you have one?"

Jeannie remembered the powder compact in her purse.

"No," she said. She saw his disappointment, his dependency, and pity made her correct herself. "Hold on." She opened her purse and pushed through it; saw the compact sitting next to her coin purse, and kept digging through her things—handkerchief, lipstick, compact, coin purse, compact—while she decided what to do.

"Two tours in Vietnam, and all this"—he waved his hand over his body—"and they think I'm afraid of my own reflection? How bad is it?"

"I don't think it's . . ."

"C'mon. I've never met a woman who doesn't carry a mirror."

"All right," said Jeannie. She drew the compact from her purse and handed it to him. She wanted to prepare him without hurting him. She forced her eyes over his grafted cheek while she searched for the words. "It looks painful," she said.

Tom / August 1968

It was everything he'd feared, and more.

The mirror was small, and it showed the graft in small, hideous pieces—the hollow cheek, the thick scars, the rot on his nose, the horror-show eyeball. Distress rose in a hard knot up his throat. He swallowed, but the knot wouldn't subside.

"Jesus," he said. The word came out strangled. After they took his leg, he made a quiet deal with God: that if they could repair his face, that would be enough; he would take the rest —the amputated leg, the scars covering his body, the chronic pain, even the goddamn gimpy arm. When his arm found its movement again, it felt like a divine show of willingness, a sign that there were greater gifts to come, that he just needed to be patient, and his face would heal. But this was it: the last surgery—there were no other magic tricks up the chief's sleeve, God's sleeve—and it was a fucking swindle. "Jesus Christ."

She brought her face close to his. He closed his eyes; he didn't want her to see their wetness. "It looks bad because it's healing," she said. "You can see there's blood coming into the graft—that's what's making this piece of skin purple. That's good. And the patches by the nose—they look strange because they're scabbing over. The side of your face is getting pulled by the new skin—I think that's why your eyeball's prominent. That should calm down as the graft takes." He made a humming sound. Her palm was on his chest.

"Look at me," she said.

He opened his eyes and willed them dry. Her face was gentle.

"I can see the shape of your face underneath," she said. "I can see you." She took the mirror from his hand and opened it. It caught the light and blazed. "Look," she said, holding it up to his face. "Look again. You'll see it too."

She sat by his side—his bad side—as he forced himself to make a study of his face. However long he gazed at it, its ugliness didn't diminish. But when she looked at him, her face showed no horror or judgment. She sat with him until his eyes grew tired and his cheek grew hot. "Drop the blinds," he said; and they sat in the dark together, and for all his disappointment, he was grateful for this: a beautiful girl, sitting beside him. Sleep heavied his eyes, and when he woke, parched, confused, the sun making a red line under the blinds, she was still there.

Two days later, she returned. The blinds were drawn; she crossed the room to open them.

"No light."

"I can't see you."

"It's for the graft," he said. "It's okay."

She sat at his side. Even in the dark, he could sense her unhappiness—she carried it like a knife strapped to her thigh.

"Apparently, it's healing up okay," he said. "I'm still planning to leave this place in a week or two." He tried to animate his voice, but it came out flat.

"That's good," she said. There was a forced brightness there, too.

"I got word from my cousin," he said. "The apartment comes free in twelve days." His whole life he'd been counting time: days to graduation, to deployment, to returning home.

"Twelve days." She seemed close, her mouth at his ear.

"I'll get myself settled, then I'll find something." He didn't ask how she could help him; he knew she wouldn't have an answer, and whatever it was that was bringing her to him, with her secrets and her strange beauty, he didn't want to stop her. "A family friend offered to have me work for him in Connecticut. Help run his farm, keep the books."

"You'll go?"

"I'm a California boy. The world is here—ocean, mountains, desert. Couldn't settle anywhere else."

He paused; she didn't fill the silence.

"Got to keep working on this arm, so I can go back fishing on Lake Shasta."

"My dad took my brother to climb Mount Shasta. Wanted to cure him of his overconfidence."

"And did it?"

"My brother bitched the whole time." He heard the smile in her voice. "But he came home saying he was going to climb Mount Whitney next."

"And did he?"

"He went to Vietnam."

"Another cure for overconfidence."

"Except my dad thought it might just kill him over there. He was a Marine too, and his father before him. He didn't want my brother to enlist. Wanted me to dissuade him."

"He wouldn't hear it, huh?"

"I didn't try." She sat at his side, gray, still.

"It wasn't your place," he said.

He heard footsteps running outside the room, then fading to quiet. They were alone in his cave.

"I saved someone else's brother instead," she said. "I broke the law. To stop somebody getting drafted."

She clasped her hands in her lap. Her scent floated into him.

"Why?" He heard his own abruptness, wished he'd softened it.

She inhaled, her breath reedy in her nostrils, and sighed. "I don't know."

Her silhouette seemed hazy at the edges, as if she were losing her shape. He squinted, tried to harden her outline. Lifted his hand, wanted to touch her shadow, but his fingers stopped at the rails of his bed.

"You asked me what happened. When we were in the garden."

He felt her quiet eyes on him.

"Some kid in my company walks over to my bunker in the middle of the night and tosses in a grenade." He said it fast, to shake the memories that stuck to the words. "This is an ordinary kid. Young. Young for his age." He was through the facts of the attack, and slowed. "Came into my company fresh off the plane, green as they come. As soon as I laid eyes on him, I knew he'd be headed back before his tour was up—fungus foot, malaria, worse. Had an unlucky look about him. Unloved—like a damn stray dog."

She was leaning close. He saw the shadows of her face, her eyes shining like coins.

"He started out okay. No major problems. But months go by, and it's too damn quiet on the base—the enemy hasn't closed in on us yet. And that's when the rot starts, and it starts with the bad, the weak. The scared." His spit was briny in his throat. "There's drugs. Marijuana. Opium. Other things I don't even know the damn names of. Some of my men are getting sloppy, and this kid is one of them, but he's the runt of the litter, you know, the puppy the mean dogs keep around to bite on.

"That night—" He kept his eyes wide; behind his eyelids was where the fire was—heat, smoke. "That night this kid got his first real taste of it, his first taste of war. They're in the trees, take some rounds, and one of them gets himself killed. And the excitement—it cracked him. Broke him open, and everything violent and polluted inside of him flew out." Drool was gathering bitter and copious in his mouth; he nudged his shoulder forward and spit wetly into his hospital gown.

"The kid should never have been in Vietnam. Didn't have a scrap of military material in him—a maggot, a child, the kind of delinquent bullshitter that gets sent home in a body bag. I wish to hell he had been." Her eyes blazed on him. "If we lose this war, it won't be because of the Chinese or the hippies or the liberals or the media. It will be because the government is pumping the military full of kids that haven't got the moxie to handle the sheer thrill of war."

"So." He stretched his arm toward her, his stump fingers reaching in the dark. "For the kid you got exempted, you had your reasons. War's not for everybody."

She took his hand in hers. Her hand was warm and damp, a tremble in the fingers.

Jeannie / August 1968

Jeannie stood on the sidewalk, watching for the streetcar. And as she stood, dazzled in the concrete heat of the afternoon, she felt it sharpening like a knife in her stomach, the knowledge that had made its first cut the day Kip shipped out—that she was the only one who could have saved him, and she was too late.

Jeannie sat at the bay window overlooking Noe, waiting for Billy's approach. She felt the apartment like a cave behind her, full of shadows. She kept her eyes on the street outside, the bloodying sunlight; saw a man on crutches limping up the hill, and had the strange sensation that it was Tom, and he was coming to save her. But it was just a stranger; he labored by, his eyes moving over her dispassionately as he passed the window. Jeannie woke in the dark to the sound of Billy at the doorway of the living room, telling her it was late, and he was tired, and she should come to bed.

The next day, Tom was sitting in his bed, the blinds low. She pulled a chair to his side and sat. He rolled his head toward her, then back again, his ear nuzzling dementedly against the pillow.

"Are you . . ." She half stood, looking toward the door, peering for a nurse.

"It's just my face. It's tight as a drum and itchy as hell."

Jeannie straightened to stand. "I'll get somebody—"

"No, no. Don't. A nurse will come in a while. Just needs lotion, all day long." He waved his hand toward the large plastic bottle that stood on his locker.

Jeannie sat. The silence grew dense. She opened her mouth,

but found nothing to say. She heard his unsteady breathing, felt the tension rising off his body, wondered if this discomfort was a torture too far, the tick that crazed the bear.

She stood, went to the sink that stood in the corner of the room, and washed her hands. She walked back to the bed, took the bottle from the locker, and squeezed lotion onto her palm. It was as thick and pale as mayonnaise. She dipped her fore-finger into it, felt its puddingy coolness, leaned against the rails of his bed, and lowered her hand to his face.

"Here?"

He made a soft, mangled noise.

Jeannie touched the lotion to the dark strip on his cheek, and made brushstrokes with her finger to spread it over the graft. The skin was smooth and glossy to the touch, bordered by hard striated scars whose dead, fibrous feel tested Jeannie's stomach. She worked the lotion into the graft and the edges until it vanished, then squeezed some more into her palm, massaging it into his cheek until her fingers slicked over the grease. He let out a hot sigh, and she smelled the hunger on his breath. She placed her whole palm against his cheek and moved it in slow sweeps.

He caught his breath in a hiss. "Your ring."

"I'm sorry." She pulled her hand away and drew up straight. "Did I hurt you?"

A pause. "You're married?"

She wiped her palms together; she felt a childish urge to smear the ointment on her dress, and gave into it, rubbing her hands against the cotton until there was only a sticky film covering her palms.

"I have a husband."

His breath maintained a slow tempo.

"He loves you?"

"He does."

"You love him."

"Yes. He's a good man." She went to the sink, held her hands under the cold water until they were numb. "I'm not a good wife," she murmured.

"You're not?" he said, and she felt a prick of surprise that he'd heard her. She turned off the faucet and took a paper towel, drying her palms, the backs of her hands, between her fingers, the ridges of her nails, the nubs of her wrists, before balling the paper and letting it drop into the trash can. He was silent; she wondered if the moment had passed. She was turning back toward him when he said, "How so?"

The room was dark, and they were silhouettes. Jeannie felt the truth like a bird in her mouth. She opened it, let the words beat free, let them join the shadow, with its secrets and its shame. "There's been somebody." Her jaw felt loose and dark; some small, tight place inside her breathed.

He was still, his face sharpening in the gloom. It was finding its weight and focus, and her eyes were learning where to look, learning to bring his unharmed side to the foreground, and to reduce the damaged side to a blur. There was something new in his expression, and she couldn't read it.

"We got married pretty fast," she said, heard how this sounded like an excuse; her fingers found the lip of the sink behind her and gripped. "He was the first guy who really saw me."

Tom was silent. An unnamed, muscular emotion palpitated the air.

"I don't know if he still sees me. I don't see him." Shame seeped warm and unpleasant beneath her skin, alongside something light and cool—something like release. "Sometimes he comes through the door at night and he looks like he's aged five years, and I've missed it." Jeannie watched Tom's face; his eyes were bright.

"My father told me marriage is like war," he said. His hand was squeezing the rail of his bed. "It's about endurance. And both parties need to deploy all the resources they can in order to endure. But," he said, his voice thinning with fatigue, "my father thinks everything is like war."

Tom / August 1968

She came every afternoon, stood close in the dark and confessed.

"It was my husband's signature," she said, rubbing lotion into his face, her palms against his skin.

"What do you mean?"

"He's a doctor. I forged his signature. On the exemption letter."

He struggled for something to say. "That's some risk." Her palms stopped on his face.

"It was stupid," she said.

"You had your reasons," he said. Her thumbs made circles at his jaw.

"They arrested someone," she told him.

"What do you mean?"

"The contact guy—the man who found the families, or they found him. They got him for selling fake exemptions."

"Jesus Christ."

"He's a man of principle," she said. Tom snorted. "I mean that it's a form of protest for him, so he'll stay quiet." She bowed her head and pressed her palms together; it looked like she was praying.

"Who is it?" He'd waited until she was turned from him, filling the pitcher at the sink. Her back tensed. "You said there was somebody."

She turned, walked to the bed, and put the pitcher on the locker. The water rocked inside it.

"Was it the guy they arrested?" he said.

Surprise lifted her face. "No." She bent to rearrange his

pillow, her mouth close to his ear. "Worse," she said. "It was worse."

She said nothing more about betraying her husband, his attempts to delve it from her like a shovel hitting rock, and he suspected that her sins were all connected. But in the moments between sleep and waking, he imagined the somebody was him. And in the long, bare mornings, he began to stretch the dream, to imagine her face lowering to his, her breasts pressing against his chest, her clever face as she waited for him outside the hospital, her smile as they drove to where the city met the ocean, and the bridge—magnificent as a thousand howitzers—that guarded the gateway to the world.

The doctor told him his face could bear the light. The Mexican orderly pulled the blinds and moved his bed so he could see the bay. But when she came, she hardly spoke; she sat squinting in the sunlight, avoiding him. It wasn't his face: her eyes, her hands, knew that part of him, accepted it. He wondered if she was afraid of him seeing her in too much brightness, if she could only show herself to him in the dark, like a virgin. After that, he told the kid who cleared his lunch every day to shut the blinds. In the shadow of those afternoons, she nursed him, touched him; turned him from bedsores; pressed flannels to his chest; cut his nails; told him secrets.

Jeannie / August 1968

She told him about the accident. About how her aunt Ruth never forgave Jeannie's mom for her beauty, not even after her mom's death; how Aunt Ruth threw out her mom's things because she said they were growing mold in her garage. About those months after the accident, when her brother wanted Jeannie for a mother, how it made her want to run; how she ran to Nancy, the sweet torture of their friendship; how the feeling that rode sharp and clear over the others as Jeannie left the church with her new husband was satisfaction at the stunned look on Nancy's face; how Nancy vanishing, exquisite and untouchable as a damselfly into the garden, an older man trailing after her, felt like revenge. About how Jeannie watched her brother pack for training, how narrow his shoulders seemed, his face asking for help, his pride preventing him. About the time she saw her dad shove her mother against the bedroom closet, cracking the mirror in the closet door; how, when Jeannie and Billy fought, she needled him, tried to get him to do the same, to push her, grip her arm too hard, so she could feel unhappy, and right.

She told him about her brother taking off that afternoon in the playground, bound for the ocean, the world, a wobble in his bike as he found his weight on the pedals, his body growing lonely in the distance. Told him about the feeling she had—like falling, or dying—when a stranger kissed her in the dark at a party, her husband, innocent and shiny-faced, searching for her in the crowd; about the woman in the café and her expensive love for her son, how she prized and fretted over him like she did the yellowed pearls that clacked between her fingers; about Charlie, how her love for him was frightening but finite; how if she broke the law for someone else's child, she might believe she'd be able to risk everything for her own son, when the day came. About Walter Moon, how the moment he laid eyes on Jeannie he seemed to hate her; about how she was afraid.

He listened in the darkness, asked her questions. She sensed him getting stronger, sensed the toughening of his body—his movements becoming more resolute. When she massaged the lotion into his face, the scars felt taut as cables, the scabs crumb-like under her fingers. When she was done, he would push his hand into hers and squeeze, his fingers finding her wedding band and twisting it on her greased finger. Every morning, Jeannie woke with a burden as heavy as a boulder sitting on her chest, and in those hours until she could visit the hospital she hauled it with her, clammy and patient, until she could sit in the warm shadows with him, hear his steady breath, and lay her burden down.

Tom / August 1968

Their faces gathered before him:

Roper, Fugate, Schmidt.

Krause, Ortiz.

Gunny.

Schroeder, Berkowitz.

They drew up into their lines before folding to the ground. Not human heads after all, but playing cards, facedown, dealt. He pulled from sleep to find her face over his, her hand in his hair.

"A dream," she said.

"I could have saved them." Correa. Hollis.

"Only a dream."

"I stopped it from happening before."

"Shh." Fingers pushing against his scalp. He closed his eyes.

His men.

"The damage he did. It goes on."

"Mrs. Harper."

"Mr. Macht? Is everything all right?"

"Any progress with the captain? Mrs. Harper? Are you there?"

"I'm working on it."

"Well, you need to work harder. The brig's commanding officer is expediting all legal process following the riot. Dellinger says they're moving to court-martial next week."

"There's no way—"

"We need to find a way. Come by my office Friday. If we haven't got anything by then—"

"I understand, Mr. Macht. Good-bye."

Kip / August 1968

Nothing like a riot to fry off the violence that sits on the skins of idle men.

It was movie night, and some King Rat inmate threw blows on a brig guard who eyeballed him all wrong. Soon it was rats on pigs, and the rats took the cage. The guards were on the wrong side of the gates, and it was wild time. A pack of inmates ripped the place apart with their bare fingers. These are no ordinary rats—these are blood stripe Marine rats. Locks cracked, gates ripped, a whole fucking cellblock blazed down. Me and a long, streaky kid from North Carolina broke open the contraband locker, found enough reefers to mellow a churchful of virgins. We sat and smoked and passed out the joints, staying out of the sights and hands of the brothers that were striding the walls and meting out some justice of their own. And in the end, it passed, just like we all knew it would, and the brass took control, put the bad guys in dog cages and screwed things tight again. But all of that smashing and brawling seems to have hurried those JAG motherfuckers along: cases are moving through the system like hot shit through a stinker, and mine is ready to drop.

They hauled me out this morning for another talk with my attorney. Douglas Dellinger, with his snap-white shirts that don't last three cigarettes in the Danang heat. Can't be more than a half hour we chew the fat, but he wilts in front of my eyes, his shirt yellowing against his chest, a drag-down tired look on his face. And whatever kind of night I've had in the brig, whatever kind of bug-scuttling or home-dreaming I've had to stomach, I get a lift seeing this expensive dork brought down after a few minutes on my strip.

Today it starts off the same as always. I watch him tic and

snit, see the frustration he's got throttled down under that Ivy League hood of his. He's already sucking on a Marlboro; this time he doesn't offer me one, just holds the pack in his smooth fingers and taps it on the table, like it's the prize.

"Private Jackson." His eyes go to the wristwatch he's laid on the table: he's already counting the minutes till he can get back to his hotel, switch on the air-con, take off his shoes, and drink a cold Coke. Before he opens his mouth, I know what he's going to ask.

"The court-martial is scheduled for next week. We need to bring a lucid account"—he corrects himself—"a clear story to the judge, explaining your actions."

He wants to know why. Was I loony? Was I high? Was I freaked out, messed up, wigged out, psycho, dumb, sad, juked, fooled, abused? Was I all of it, mixed up and fried together? They've all come by—the shrink, the priest, the Marine counsel, and now this joker—with the same damn questions, the same doubt paining their sweaty faces.

I'll tell you why.

They sent us here with our howitzers and M16s, our Hueys and M60s and Gatlings, to blow pieces out of those commies, those red guys and gals, to rip the jungle from its roots and noise up the sky with our big blind birds. Sent boys from the cities and the farms, the swamps and the deserts, the prairies and the mountains—white boys, black boys, brown boys, black boys—to help out Uncle Sam, on the promise of honor, uncommon valor, and the Greatest Show on Earth. To a raggedy, skid-row country that switches between mud slick and dust bowl, where the ghosts that spook us in the dark have jack shit to do with the quiet villagers that work the green sunlit land. This place had nothing to do with us until we soaked our guts into the ground. Like that boxer said, I got no quarrel with these slopes.

But the higher-ups keep on with their listening posts and their patrols and their baits and traps, throwing good blood after bad; like they haven't heard the war is over, that the good folks back home aren't hungry for it anymore. And he was the worst—Captain Vance, Mister America himself—greedy for the mission, for the glory, for the fucking lie. I am Private Kipling Jackson, and I protest this war. Write it on my helmet, pin it on my chest—all hands off Vietnam.

Jeannie / August 1968

Charlie wriggled in Cynthia's arms and began to cry.

"I'll be back soon, honey."

"He's got a temperature," said Cynthia, holding the back of her hand to Charlie's forehead. He yanked her fingers away, ribbons of spit between his lips.

"Billy will take a look at him when he's back from work."

"Jeannie—"

"Thanks, Cynthia." Jeannie tapped down the steps, head down, saw the bare legs waiting for her on the sidewalk.

"Lee—" Jeannie turned her head to see Cynthia standing at the top of the steps, her arms closed around a tearful Charlie, her easy face gathering into a frown as she closed the front door on them.

Lee's face was bright with excitement, her chest rising and falling with large breaths, as though she'd been running.

"Something happened," she said, her voice light and rough; and, registering Lee's elation, Jeannie's heart lightened. "Is it Walter? They let him go?"

"They arrested the Reverend," said Lee. "They found him in some motel in Los Angeles. Silver told me. They got him on all kinds of charges: not just selling falsified documents but mail fraud, obstructing justice, criminal battery, possession of controlled substances, and—get this—statutory rape. They're going to sink his fucking ship."

Jeannie's blood grayed. She heard Cynthia's door open, Charlie's cries turned up loud, the smack of Cynthia's Mary Janes on the steps.

"You know what, you take him." Cynthia loaded Charlie into Jeannie's arms.

"Cynthia—just today. Please."

"He spends more time with me than he does with you."

"Just one more afternoon. Please, Cynthia."

"Why? So you can go hang out with your hippie friends?" Cynthia looked Lee up and down, took in the bruises on her shins, the thrift-store dress, the leather bands fraying at her wrists. Lee smiled back. "I'd sure like to know what you're up to all these hours while I'm looking after your kid."

Jeannie felt the hard inquiry of Lee's eyes. "I'm visiting a friend. In the hospital. I have to go, and I can't take Charlie with me."

"Then she can take him," said Cynthia, waving her fingers. "Now, excuse me while I go see to my own child." She turned, her thin freckled legs taking two steps at a time, and slammed the door behind her.

"I'll take him," said Lee.

Tom / August 1968

A nurse came to lotion his face and jack up the blinds. "So gloomy in here," she said. Tom took in the sad, flat sun. She was late.

The meds trolley had come and gone by the time her footsteps closed in on his room. They were faster than usual. She opened the door. She crossed the room to lower the blinds, leaving a narrow stripe of light at the bottom.

"More light," he said. She widened the stripe. She didn't sit. Her hair spilled from its pins, and her cheeks were pink.

"Pass me that shirt," he said.

She handed him the button-down that was folded on the locker; he sat and showed what he'd been practicing—the push of each arm through the holes, the two-handed buttoning of the front, propping his good fingers against the severed ones to push the buttons through the holes. Once he'd buttoned it all the way to the collar of his hospital gown, he unbuttoned it again, flipping the buttons as fast as he could from their slits. "The chief said he'll discharge me tomorrow."

"They got someone else."

He looked up; she stood, jiggling her heel. "They arrested the man who ran the whole thing. The Reverend." A cynical sound escaped Tom's mouth. Her heel stopped mid-bounce. "They're drawing in the nets," she said.

"Jeannie . . . " He heard the sticky undulation in her throat as she swallowed. She looked as though she was going to cry.

"You need a lawyer," he said.

She stared at him, empty-eyed.

"I'm always trying to save the wrong people," she said.

The door opened.

"Passing through the building, thought I'd stop by," said

the chief. “How are—” He stopped and gazed at Jeannie, a stunned look on his face. Tom guessed what the old man was thinking—who was the lovely girl, and why was she with the cripple?

“Excuse me,” said the chief. “I—”

She was already gone.

Jeannie / August 1968

Jeannie ducked out of the room, head bowed, shoes brisk on the vinyl, out of the building, through the courtyard, along the dark pathways that expelled her at the main entrance. The sunlight exploded on her. She shouldered through the lingerers on the sidewalk, down Parnassus, onto Stanyan, along the park, past women pushing babies, children chasing birds, lovers walking, the heels of her pumps growing rickety on the sidewalk as she hurried into a half run, like she was being followed, devils at her back; onto Oak, along the din of traffic, across the street, turning into the park at Clayton, through the trees and across the grass, her breath quickening.

She scanned the playground, sweat spreading under her arms. Saw Lee's black hair rising in the wind, called out. Lee turned. Her face was strange; she ran toward Jeannie. Jeannie looked for Charlie, and couldn't see him.

"Where is he?"

"He's gone."

Alarm swung at Jeannie; her feet faltered.

"I was talking to somebody and he disappeared. I looked all over. I can't find him."

The sun dropped, raising black midges into the air.

"He just vanished."

Kip / August 1968

He got what was coming to him.

My mom used to say that heaven and hell were lies, that God made his justice happen right here on earth. One way or another, you get yours—all your goods and bads and uglies paid back in full by the big bean-counting Universe. Vance didn't die—but that grenade would've done its work, would have torn great strips off him, wrecked that movie-star jaw of his, ruined him. All this talk of justice, of charges and courts-martial and punishments, but Vance got his too. Shea was just one of us he murdered—if it hadn't been for his gung-ho bullshit, those VC never would have come for us that day. They never would have cut the wire, wriggled their bellies over the dirt, and killed all those American boys. Seventy-four good American boys.

When all's said and done, he got his.

Jeannie / August 1968

Jeannie ran among the eucalyptus trees, checked under benches and picnic tables, behind trash cans, hollered until her voice scratched. Soon a gang of mothers gathered behind her, spreading the search, clutching their own infants to their chests. The sun blared her eyes as it sank, and she felt the slow seep of despair. She ran back to the playground, her lungs raw, and checked every piece of equipment for the fourth time: the playhouse, jungle gym, swing set, sandbox. Schoolkids covered the asphalt; Jeannie craned her neck over the crowd, elbowed through their stubborn bodies.

No Charlie.

She stood in the corner of the playground, shielded her eyes, and scanned the crowded space. At the far edge of the play area, pushing its fronds through the chain-link fence, was a juniper bush, dark and overgrown, its berries fat as grapes. Memories of Charlie last summer, dirty with elderberries in her dad's backyard. She ran, called out; heard a noise. As she neared the bush, she heard crying.

"Charlie?"

She scissored her legs over the chain and squatted, pushing her arms through the branches.

"Charlie?"

Crouched in the shadows of the bush, limbs tangled in untidy branches, dark scrapes on his bare legs, sat Charlie, his face a mess of tears.

He saw her, and his face split.

She scrabbled through the brush, branches scratching her skin, and pulled him out. He held fast to her, his whole body palpitating with the beat of his heart; she felt his heat and sweat, and pushed her mouth to his wet hair.

Her eyes rose to the playground, saw the soft acknowledgment in the other mothers' faces before they turned away. Only Lee approached, arms outstretched. The sound of thunder.

The rain thickened, driving mothers under trees and tempting good shoes into puddles. Soon Jeannie's dress was pulled wet against her skin. Charlie burrowed into her shoulder, his legs cold and sodden.

"I have to get him home," called Jeannie. Lee's hair was slicked like eels over her shoulders, the dark circles of her nipples pressing through her pale dress.

Lee nodded, and followed. Jeannie shook her head. "Go home," she said. She quickened her stride, Charlie solid in her arms, the rain hissing on the path. She turned her head to see Lee following like a stray, and spurred her feet out of the park. Thunder exploded; she looked up to see a sky of hot silver, clouds rolling like smoke.

The rain misted the sidewalk. Jeannie paused at Clayton and Fell and scanned for the warm light of a cab; but lights were dimmed, and windows were dark with bodies.

Lee was at her side. "I'm sorry," she said.

Jeannie looked into Lee's face and felt empty of feeling—the heat of desire and anger now cooled to ash. She was just a girl; all the threads that had tied them together slackened and split. "It's all right," she said, gripping Charlie tighter and continuing up Clayton, her eyes searching for a cab. She walked, fatigued with relief, looking for a street that would deliver her a ride home, until she found herself all the way up on Geary. Lee trailed behind, hangdog in the rain. The sky darkened.

Jeannie felt Charlie shivering against her shoulder. She realized she was only a few hundred yards from shelter. She found the turning, and walked.

Fanny opened the door and called out in surprise. Dorothy appeared, concern and offense already mingling in her face. She reached for Charlie and pulled his soaking body against her linen suit, then turned to Fanny and ordered her to fetch some towels.

"My boy," said Dorothy, pushing her face into Charlie's neck. "Quick, quick." She beckoned Jeannie, who ducked her head under the threshold, water dripping warm down the back of her neck. Dorothy looked beyond Jeannie to see Lee, near-stripped by the rain, knees shivering. Something like sadness touched the older woman's face. As she edged back under the porch, she caught Jeannie watching her, and her face closed over.

"Leonora Walker," said the older woman, her voice soft against the rain. "Get inside."

Lee obeyed, her sandals sucking against the soles of her feet and leaving dreggy smears on the tiles. She bowed her head and allowed Fanny to swallow her in a large monogrammed towel. Dorothy gave Jeannie a look of such naked accusation that she wondered if her father-in-law had already reported her presence at the hospital. She dropped her eyes to the floor.

"What happened?" said Dorothy.

"We got caught out," said Jeannie.

Lee found Jeannie in the guest room, buttoning herself into an old day dress of Dorothy's. Lee looked like an unhappy

Deanna Durbin, all gussied up in a smocked gown with puffed sleeves. "I'm sorry I lost him," she said.

"It's okay. He's safe. It's fine." Jeannie fixed her eyes on the cloth button at her cuff that rolled stubbornly at her fingers.

"Where were you?" said Lee.

Jeannie couldn't answer, couldn't find the place where the story began. Lee stood, her hips rolled forward, her hands awkward on her hips. She looked younger than her years. "Please, Jeannie," she said. Her eyes were as hard and pretty as beads.

"It's over, Lee." Jeannie heard a creak along the hallway, glanced at the open doorway, saw nothing.

"I'm going away, anyways. Heading south." Lee's hand was pulling Jeannie's cuff tight. Jeannie drew her wrist away; Lee's hand went to Jeannie's chin, tipping it so that Jeannie would see the invitation in her face.

"You're running away," said Jeannie, contempt slipping into her voice. Lee heard it; she edged backward, sliding her hand from Jeannie's chin so that it rested where her shoulder met her neck.

"I'm moving on," said Lee; and there was something about the casualness of her hand at Jeannie's neck, the strangeness and possessiveness, that ran Jeannie's blood warm and cool, an odd mix of pity and alienation. "I can't be around her anymore," said Lee. Jeannie thought of Virginia, with her milky beauty and her steel; how strange it must be for her to have a daughter like Lee.

"This isn't about your mom," said Jeannie. "You're afraid."

Lee raised her other hand, placed it on the other side of Jeannie's neck, her fingers loose, her face tilted up to Jeannie's. "Afraid of what?"

"Afraid of—" Jeannie's eyes went to the door, and she

shrugged herself from Lee's embrace, hushed her voice. "Of Walter, the Reverend. Of getting caught."

Lee gave a lazy smile. "I won't get caught." Her breath smelled of burned leaves. "They don't know who I am," she said. "They called me Lyla."

"And what about me?"

"They don't know who you are either. I didn't tell them."

"Then Mrs. Dewey. Walter just needs to give her name to the police and they'll find Billy's name on the medical letter."

"She never gave Walter her name. Why would she? He just gave her a time and place to meet us. He doesn't know anything."

Jeannie thought of the cold control in Walter's eyes, the way he weighed and measured her at each encounter. "He knows everything," she said.

"Walter? He thinks he does."

"So why didn't you tell me this before?"

"I was going to," said Lee. She gave an exaggerated shrug.

She wanted a reason to come back, thought Jeannie. She studied Lee's face. "I don't know if I can trust you."

"I've not lied to you, Jeannie," said Lee; and Jeannie struggled to thumb down whether this was true. She remembered what her mom used to tell Kip—if you're going to lie, tell someone who wants to believe you; she wondered if she was falling for Lee's bullshit all over again.

Jeannie took a breath and closed her eyes, tried to find where she was, to place her sense of danger. The darkness behind her eyes blotched with light, and Lee's lips were on hers, her tongue pushing soft and bitter into her mouth, her hand pressing the nape of her neck, the taste of ash; and she felt the death of the kiss even as it was on her mouth, Lee's lips always on the point of falling away: a last kiss.

Jeannie stepped back, felt Lee's body drop away, opened her eyes.

Saw someone, moving from the doorway.

A car sounded its horn outside.

"That's my cue," said Lee, disappearing before Jeannie could say anything. Jeannie wiped her mouth with the back of her hand. She listened to the thud, then the pat, of Lee's footsteps; heard murmurs, the slam of the front door. Jeannie went to the window. The glass was warped with age, and the street below shimmered. Rain drew in long strokes over the sky. Jeannie watched Lee run to the waiting cab, her dark hair slapping against her dress, which billowed pale and showy in the wind—like a heroine in a black-and-white movie. At the last moment, Lee turned and lifted her face to Jeannie's window, raised her palm, mouthing something unreadable, then folded into the cab, which shined its weak lights into the afternoon and drew away.

Jeannie sat on the bed, her body rimpling the silk beneath her, her heart scurrying. She listened to the sounds of the house: Fanny crashing pans in the kitchen; Charlie hurtling down the hallway; Dorothy's low murmurs—a story, maybe a game; the opening and closing of the front door; the whistle of the kettle; a bang, a cry—Charlie; Dorothy shushing; the bawl rising, lifting in the house—*Mommy.*

Jeannie stood. She walked slowly down the stairs, saw Charlie in Dorothy's arms, his face angled up to Jeannie, his arms outstretched. Dorothy had her back to Jeannie, and Jeannie noticed a small bald place at the top of Dorothy's head, the scalp showing soft and pink beneath her silvered hair. Dorothy's back stooped against Charlie's weight, her knees moving stiffly to bounce him; and Jeannie was surprised by a feeling of tenderness for her, the mighty, declining matriarch—until Dorothy turned to look at her, and Jeannie saw the truth in her face.

"Dorothy, we should go," said Jeannie, taking Charlie into her arms; but the words were feeble in her mouth.

"Fanny's set a tray with tea and English muffins," said Dorothy. "Let's go sit."

They sat in the dining room, Charlie on Jeannie's lap, sniffing and chewing, snowing fat crumbs over the parquet floor. Dorothy ate greedily, talking in bright tones about her fund-raiser for Nixon. She seemed excited. Unease climbed Jeannie's body as she sipped her tea. After pushing two muffin halves into his mouth, Charlie slid off Jeannie's lap to make his escape. The tightness in Dorothy's body stopped Jeannie from taking him to the bathroom to clean up, and both women watched as he careened, greasy-fingered and dirty with bread crumbs, out of the room, yelling for his toy car.

Dorothy took another muffin from the tray. "And you?" she said.

"I'm sorry?"

Dorothy smeared the muffin with grape jelly. "You're coming to the fund-raiser?"

"Yes," said Jeannie. "We'll be there. I'll bring a meatloaf."

Dorothy stared. A sticky sweat filmed Jeannie's upper lip. Dorothy raised the muffin to her mouth and took a bite, chewed, then touched her mouth with her napkin. "I don't think that's necessary," she said.

They listened to the snip of the wall clock, to Charlie spinning his car across the hallway. Dorothy dragged her eyes over Jeannie—the wet hair, the makeup-smirched eyes, the unbuttoned cuff resting on the table—until she drew blood to

Jeannie's face. A smile toughened the older woman's mouth. She folded her napkin and pushed her plate aside, the knife slithering off the china and landing jammily on the eyelet tablecloth.

"Your generation," she said. "You think you're the first to taste the world. But we saw it all—saw all the life and death of it. Your mother shielded you, raised you in a nice house with a backyard and barbecues and milk and cookies. And now you're out into real life, and you act like you discovered it."

In the time they had known each other, Dorothy had never mentioned Jeannie's mom, never asked a question about her—not through unkindness, it seemed, but through a kind of brisk respect. Jeannie had been grateful for this, perhaps more than anything because she knew her mom would have liked Dorothy, admired her, even. They had their beauty in common, their love of men and style. Dorothy's allusion to Jeannie's mom stung, and Jeannie recognized it as an opening shot.

"Genevieve," said Dorothy; and Jeannie felt a small grasp of hope that this was about Tom, about something she could explain. "I asked you not to see Leonora Walker."

Jeannie nodded. She smelled the sweetness of the jelly, heard the saliva in Dorothy's throat. "She was just minding Charlie for me," she said, stale-mouthed. She took a sip of tea, felt the tannin film her palate.

Dorothy's smile tightened. "When Leonora was born," she said, "her mother cried for a year. I couldn't understand it. Babies are so—enchanting; and Leonora was a good baby—quiet, watchful. Just like Charlie was." Dorothy gave Jeannie a look that was thick with significance. "It's been that way ever since. The tears Virginia has shed over that girl. And after everything with her brother." Dorothy shook her head. "She's a vicious thing."

Jeannie cleared her throat. She still hoped this was all this was: a lecture about the company she kept; she hoped the figure at the doorway had seen nothing, that it hadn't been Dorothy but Fanny, that she'd been returning towels to the bathroom to dry and hadn't paused to look in the room. "Lee's just a little lost," she said, holding her voice steady.

"She is." Dorothy nodded, rocking back and forth. "She wanted to be lost." The older woman stilled, her body pitched forward over the table; she studied Jeannie, her face a show of calm—but there was a tremble in her little finger as she placed her palms on the tablecloth. "So did you."

Jeannie's heart clambered. "So did I?"

"You wanted to get lost." Dorothy leaned across the table, slid her palms toward Jeannie, as though to touch her hands; but her fingers stopped inches short, her nails blanching against the linen. "When William told me about you, of course I was worried. I didn't want him to chain his life to an accident." Jeannie heard the insult, but Dorothy's tone was neutral. "But you were sweet, and he couldn't take his eyes off you, and the day you got married was so—happy."

That day pushed into Jeannie's mind—the hot, stiff dress, Kip's clinginess, the wetness of Billy's hands as they exchanged vows.

"Of all the things I feared for him," said Dorothy, "that he'd be bored, or tied down, or unfulfilled—I never thought you could hurt him like this."

"Dorothy, listen—"

"It's disgusting." Dorothy picked over each syllable of the word, her beautiful face sucking sour. "You're disgusting." She drew her hands into fists and straightened in her chair. "She's a child, for Christ's sake."

"It's not what you think."

"You could go to jail."

Fanny appeared at the doorway. Jeannie and Dorothy turned their heads toward her; Fanny, reading the look on Dorothy's face, murmured and disappeared.

Jeannie's hand went to her throat. The neck of her dress was too tight. "Dorothy, this is silly."

"They'll take Charlie away from you." The words struck Jeannie like a blade. Dorothy's mouth curled. "They'll give him to me. And if you think that silly, selfish girl will protect you, you're more naïve than I thought."

The heat left Jeannie's body. Dorothy's lips drew back, the threat held in her teeth. Jeannie's fear sharpened, and she found her fight. She leaned to put her hands over Dorothy's, felt their loose skin. "Be careful, Dorothy," she said.

Dorothy's hands twitched. "All he's done is care for you," she said. "Provide for you, love you. You could live a dozen lifetimes and not deserve him."

"I didn't say I deserved him."

"You got the prize, Jeannie," said Dorothy, taking her hands from under Jeannie's, spit showing on her lips. "What else was waiting for you? A little job, an unremarkable husband, a sad little house? A girl like you." It was Dorothy's turn to blush, her cheeks mottling under the powder. "You took the brass ring, and you're not happy? Is marriage too difficult for you?" Dorothy's voice rose; Jeannie realized that Charlie had fallen silent in the hallway. "It's not supposed to be easy. It's about tenacity. It's about grit. Women used to have that, but you girls . . ." She fidgeted in her seat. She had lost control of the conversation; and she touched her hair to correct herself. Jeannie breathed slow to tamp her adrenaline.

"I'm telling William," said Dorothy.

"He won't believe you," said Jeannie; but as she said it, she realized this wasn't true. Billy would believe it, he would believe that Jeannie had betrayed him; because, like a cheap lining to good fabric, Jeannie's love for him had never matched his for her, and they both knew it. In the small intimacies and sacrifices of married life, Jeannie's reluctance with her husband had been as stubborn and discountable as grit on an eyeball. "It would hurt him," she said.

"He would survive it," said Dorothy.

"He won't leave me," said Jeannie; but she saw the triumph in Dorothy's face, and doubt moved. She imagined it—Billy with a straining suitcase, his body stiff with hurt and anger, Dorothy waiting outside in the car—and mixed with the sadness and disgrace there was something else, a strange, dead feeling, as though the scene belonged to someone else's story, as though it were a loss that, after it was all played out, could be put away, and survived. Dorothy was watching her, a hard, expectant look on her face, and Jeannie realized she was waiting.

"What do you want, Dorothy?"

Dorothy smiled, a real smile. "I want you to stop helping your brother. I want you to terminate Chapman and Macht's involvement in his case."

"But Kip's court-martial is next week."

"Then he'll have to make other arrangements."

"This is his chance, Dorothy."

"Herb Chapman told me they're not making a lot of progress, anyhow."

"A good defense could make the difference of fifteen years in his sentence."

"The whole thing is nasty and degrading."

"Chapman's firm has been handling the case for weeks. What difference can it make to you now?"

Dorothy spread her fingers on the table, as though showing a hand of cards. Spite lit her face. This wasn't about ethics, or reputation, or money—it was about punishment.

"It's up to you, Jeannie."

The phrase seized Jeannie, like a hand grabbing her on a busy street. She thought of the choices she'd made, who to save, who to lose. Thought of Kip, the star of his own stupid movie, emptying his life away in a jail cell, giving his lawyers the runaround while he pretended the ax that was about to fall wasn't real. Thought of Tom, the bulk and strength of him, confined to his bed, his defaced, amputated body; his strange charisma, which mixed power and yearning; his loneliness. Kip had done it; she'd come to understand that in those dark, vivid hours at Tom's bedside. As Tom had come into focus, Kip had blurred and then re-formed, rendered in small, cold relief. He had done it, not because he was bad or crazy but because, as Tom told her and her dad before that, he was so damn stupid. His punishment would be to live with it; and it was Tom's punishment too—needless, undeserved—that he would have to go on. Jeannie felt a sharp pain in her chest, as fine and conclusive as a skewer. She couldn't save Kip from what was coming next; and her feet had continued to carry her to Tom's bedside long after this realization made its first incision. Kip would have to tell his own story.

She took in Dorothy, pulled-together and hungry for the show. "It's not difficult," said Dorothy, licking her lower lip. "You give up on a lost cause, or you lose your nice, comfortable life with my son."

The walls of the Noe apartment were narrow, and the rooms grew dark after noon. Jeannie thought of Billy, drab-faced and soft-bellied, coming through the door like he'd been in a war; long, gray Sundays sitting in the living room, rolling die-cast toy cars around Charlie's toes. Dorothy's lips parted, showing the thick, creamy edges of her teeth; she was waiting for Jeannie to submit.

Jeannie stood and brushed the crumbs from her dress. "Fire the lawyers, tell your son, do what you want," she said. Dorothy's eyes widened; and in the momentary nakedness of her mother-in-law's bewilderment, Jeannie saw the imprint of Billy's astonished face, and her gratification smeared with unease. She dropped her napkin on her plate and stepped from the table.

"Where the hell are you going?" said Dorothy, her chair scraping, her voice rising to a holler.

But Jeannie was already out of the room. "Let's go, Charlie," she said, pulling him from the floor, his body lengthening reluctantly like a cat's as she lifted him. She closed the door behind them, and turned away from the house, down Spruce, Charlie's hand in hers, their shadows alone and bright on the dim, wet sidewalk.

Tom / August 1968

She returned when the hospital was handing over to night: pills dispensed, lights turned low. She switched on the overhead light. There was a kid in her arms. When it turned its face to him, he felt a sense of uncanniness and reprieve—the features were Jeannie's, no other face forcing its presence there.

"Are you all right?" he said.

She walked to his bed, the kid hanging like a primate, watching. She touched the raw part of his face. "It's getting better," she said.

"I'm leaving in the morning," he said. Her face was blank. "For the apartment." She smiled; but there was something off in it, some stowaway emotion. "What happened?"

She placed her keen eyes on him. In the dead light, he saw the early lines in her face, the tautness of her skin over her skull. She was skin and flesh and bone: he could see her heat, her muscle and frailty. There was death and life in every shadow and swell of her; and as he looked at her, he felt once again, with the force of the obvious, that here was the truth of things—not in the sad bodies filling the beds around him, not in the scale and brilliance of combat, but here: a beautiful girl in his room. For all his damage, she was here for him; and alongside everything else that was waiting for him beyond his bed, alongside the shame and the struggle and the disability payments, there might be this.

He felt the question in his mouth, as hard and slippery as a marble.

"Come with me," he said.

He sat, gripping the rails of his bed. She imagined his heart muscling inside his body; sensed his mind beating, like a bird; felt her own blood thrum. She felt Tom's loneliness as her own, imagined the two of them, consigned to their separate lives in their separate, muted apartments, and something inside her went dark.

"Yes," she said.

The next morning, he dressed himself, enlisting the Mexican orderly to help with the pants, knotting the leg at the stump. Buttoned his shirt, and smoothed it over his chest. Put a comb to his hair—too long in back; he would get it cut. Heaved himself into his wheelchair, and wheeled himself into the corridor, out of the building, across the courtyard, and into the main building, taking the wide corridors until he was in the main lobby. He saw the sunlight smoke through the entrance, felt the sun's hot stripe over the floor, the bad breath of the hospital at his back. He pushed himself out, into the city, its smell of heat, asphalt, the ocean.

He was relieved to see her sitting on the curb outside the apartment. She was sitting next to her son, and they were playing a clapping game. When she saw the cab draw up, her hands dropped. She watched as the cabdriver helped him out, into his chair, as if he were a stranger. But when the cab drew away, she stood and picked up the large bag at her feet, an uncertainty in her face that he hoped was anticipation. The keys jangled in his hand, and the three of them said nothing as he let them into the lobby, and into Apartment 1. The place smelled of dust and newspaper. The living room overlooked the street through half-opened drapes, and was sparsely furnished: a table, four chairs, a couch. A few bits of old wood were scattered under the table; the kid crawled between the chairs and stacked the pieces.

"Come," said Tom, dropping the keys on the table and pushing the chair through the apartment: a galley kitchen, a bathroom, a storage room with a pullout bed, a master bedroom overlooking a backyard. He rolled the chair to the bed in the master bedroom, hoisted himself to sit on the mattress, and watched her. She stood in the center of the room, turning her body as she took in the scratched closet, the dated wallpaper, the silvered mirror, the muscles in her calves undulating as she turned. He felt his heart beating in his throat, and held out his arm to her. "Here," he said. He heard the kid's tower fall.

Her heels echoed off the wood. She crouched in front of him and closed her eyes. Her lips opened, showing her teeth, her pink tongue. His cock felt warm and heavy in his lap.

She sighed, a soft, full sigh. Her breath was damp on his face. His own breath emptied out. "Jeannie," he said.

She leaned in and kissed him.

Jeannie / August 1968

Jeannie tasted the cool wetness of his mouth, smelled the lotion on his face. She swallowed down her spit, and gripped the edge of the bed as he pushed against her, her footing unsteady. She sat back on her heels, and he moved with her, leaning forward, his hand locking the back of her head. She could feel the press of his severed fingers in her hair, the knot of fabric at his thigh. She stood, her hand palming his face, easing him away.

"Jeannie," he said, rough-voiced; and she gave a smile that felt phony on her mouth.

"Charlie—" she said, and went to peer around the doorframe. Charlie was kneeling, the back of his head still with concentration. She shut the door.

"Here," he said.

She steeled herself, and turned. He was sitting on the bed, his body pitched forward, desire smearing his face. She sat on the bed beside him, felt his heat, felt the stiff reluctance of her own body. He put his face into the crook of her neck; she felt the smoothness of his burns, the uneven bristle on his jaw. She knew that this was what she'd promised him, that this was part of their unspoken exchange, for his confidence, his refuge. She thought of Billy, how it had been an act of will with him, too; but whether it was the rawness of Tom's need, the awkward abbreviations of his body, or the noise of Charlie playing in the next room, this was more difficult. She took a breath—breathed in Tom's sick, musky smell—and knew that if she couldn't save Kip, she could do his penance.

Her tongue was soft and light. She tasted of peppermint. He felt the ridge of her teeth against his tongue, the hard roof of her mouth. He pushed his hand into her hair, heard his sigh come in a long hum. He felt her swallow, felt her fingers, warm on his face. His hands went to her breasts, felt their round denseness; he found the zipper at the back of her dress, and eased it down. He pushed her dress to her waist, took in her slim white stomach. She pulled away, her eyes squeezed shut; hooked her leg so that she was straddling him, her cunt pressing against his cock. She was arched over him, her hair falling against his face, her eyes still closed, her face solemn as a Madonna's. He encircled her with his arm, released the fastening at her back, and her breasts spilled free. He pushed his face to them, felt their cool weight, let one fill his mouth. She made a strange, heavy noise.

He looked up at her; her teeth pressed her lower lip. He leaned back, strutted himself on his elbow, and, with his good hand, loosened his zipper. Freed his cock, felt the warmth of her cunt against it, the cotton of her panties; put his hand to the small of her back and pressed her to him. She moved her hips, and—

"No." She slipped from his lap onto the mattress, her legs folded, her dress shambled, the air cold on her skin. She saw the surprise in his face, the scald of humiliation at his jaw. She didn't look at his groin; fixed her eyes on the crawl of a house spider across the mattress.

"I'm an idiot," he said, and hurried to fasten his pants, his hands fumbling with the task, his shoulder angling to stop her seeing his nakedness.

She covered herself with her dress. "You're not. I just—"

"It was wrong of me. I'm sorry."

"I want to," she said. She wanted to bring him close. And she could do it—she could close her eyes and her mind, and give him what he wanted. But it would be a cheap intimacy, a betrayal too far. He turned to look at her, his face open and unsure. She couldn't give herself to him if he didn't know who she was. She watched the spider clamber over the edge of the mattress, heard the subdued knock of wood in the other room.

"There's something I need to tell you."

She licked her lips, her tongue pink and plump. His cock twitched damply. She put her hands in her lap and bowed her head, like a scolded child, and even in the torture of the moment, this was charming. He waited, his tongue large in his mouth; he didn't want to imagine what was coming next.

"My brother," she said. His fear loosened—whatever this was, it didn't sound like a reason for her to walk away. She closed her eyes. "He was one of yours."

He waited for more, but she was silent, her eyes shut. He tried to make the connection, patched through the men who'd been killed, whose family might have unfinished business with him—thought of Lance Corporal Shea, who shouldn't have died that night, who deserved better; of Private Henderson, who'd drowned while on R&R in Nha Trang; of Sergeant McKellen, who'd disappeared in Dalat two years ago.

"I don't . . ." he said, shaking his head.

Her eyes opened. There was something naked and spoiled in her face—something like guilt—and he realized that it was she that was doing the confessing.

The light dipped.

The watchfulness, the high color; with a pitch of alarm, he saw it.

"Kip Jackson," she said.

As she raised her head to him, observing the intimacy of her own violence, she understood that there was little solace or freedom to be had, after all, in the telling of truths; and that perhaps Kip, with his dreams and stories, was at least right on this.

He sat hunched, clutching the edge of the mattress, his mind thumping.

"It doesn't matter," he said. "It doesn't have to matter."

She saw his knuckles whiten. His face turned to hers. She touched his shoulder, brought her lips to his, pressed for a kiss; but his mouth was slack, and when she flicked open her eyes, she saw that he was watching her as she kissed him. She kissed him again, with the insistence of a nurse reviving a patient—tried to somehow undo the harm she'd done—but he sat as dull-lipped and open-eyed as a doll. He drew away, his face gathering in a question.

"I wanted you to help him." As she said it out loud, she heard how absurd it sounded. "There was nobody else." Her throat closed around the words. "But it was wrong, and it's done."

His eyes picked over her face. He nodded; gently, then emphatically. He straightened, the muscles in his upper body tight with resolve, his mouth running in a determined line. "He's not your brother," he said.

"Tom—"

"He won't be in our lives."

Jeannie heard Charlie calling from the other room, the run of his feet on the floorboards, heard the bright, practical sounds of the world outside the apartment—cars, a siren, a woman laughing. The spell was breaking; and it cracked through her, as gray as dawn, that whatever contract she and Tom had, Kip underwrote it. She took in the quiet sanctuary of the room: the thin saltiness of the air that belonged to the ocean, to her childhood; the meager furniture arranged carefully, like the first pieces of a life; Tom, seeing her, wanting her anyway. As she grasped it all, she felt the loss of it, knew that what the room offered was impossible: that she couldn't give Tom what he wanted—a new life together, with no ties to the past, a life that wasn't founded on penance or fear or pity but was shared freely, willingly—and that whatever reparation she was making for her past negligence, with Kip's life, with her own, it was too late, and too foolish, and it would fail.

She took his hand, brought her face close to his, paused to find the words that would have no room for confusion, and spoke slowly and clearly.

"You can't have me," she said. "I can't give you what you want."

He felt Jackson's soft stuntedness in her fingers, her gentleness. Anger seeped like concrete in his chest, expanding and hardening till it had nowhere to go—the pressure tightening his throat, driving pain into his head.

"It won't work," she said. "I want to make things right, but I can't." Tears streaked her face, wetting his knuckles. He pulled his hand from hers, pressed his fist against his skull till he felt his forehead blanch, the reverberation down his forearm somehow bleeding the pressure from his head.

"I'm sorry," she said, speaking the words by rote, the same way he'd heard them a hundred different times from a dozen different mouths.

"Fuck." His voice jumped off the walls.

"Tom."

He heard the tremble in her voice, saw the ugliness and beauty in her: the coward jaw, the plump mouth. She was close enough that he could squeeze the breath out of her. He thumped the bed with his fist. She drew away, her pulse twittering in her slim neck.

"I'm sorry."

He saw the fear in her face; tried to muscle down his anger.

"You have to go," he said, trying to keep his voice low.

She sat still. "You deserved the truth," she said, quiet, uncertain. "It could never have worked." Her face was all hollow places. She drew her hand across her mouth, smudging lipstick over her cheek.

He saw the room in all its poverty; saw her sitting before him, half naked and begging as a slut. The distance between this and what he'd imagined—a home, a life—was so great it took his breath.

"I'm so damn stupid."

"You're not stupid."

"To believe I could have . . . this."

"It wasn't all a lie."

"It was a damn lie." But the distress in her face told him he wasn't right on this, and he felt a small, unhappy hope.

"I can love you—" she said.

"Then love me."

"But like a sister." She winced at her own choice of words, and he shut his eyes. "Not a wife."

He tested himself against this—imagined them living together, sexless, castrated; he the sad-sack uncle, she the matron—and his heart went dark. It would be easy in ways—comfortable, better than whatever else was waiting for him out there, whatever small compromise of a life he would have to make for himself alone. But those words he'd learned to live by—*honor, courage, commitment*—what could they mean in that kind of a life? A life of restrictions, celibacy, charity: the life of a dependent. He couldn't do it.

"Then leave. You and your kid, you need to leave." She didn't move. The pain in his head thickened, pushing blood against the backs of his eyeballs. The room was stifling; he couldn't be in it any longer, with or without her. He reached for his chair, yanked it toward him, hauled himself in. Took the wheels, pushed them so his chair took the room.

"Where are you going?"

He pulled open the door; the kid stood outside the bedroom, smiling shyly, holding the keys to the apartment in his hand.

"Poor fucking kid," he said.

"Tom—"

He plunged the wheels down, out of the building, onto the street, away from the apartment, from the place he'd dreamed of all those long, blind hours in the hospital, imagining a life that was never real. He would leave that cripple, that fantasist, that half a man—the sap to be sponged, dressed, handled, manipulated—leave his husk in that dim, quiet bedroom, with the unhappy girl and her chickenshit brother and the kid that had nothing to do with him.

He wheeled himself onto Scott, down toward Lombard, loss sinking its teeth into his gut. He drove the wheels until his arms burned and his shirt was stuck with sweat. He stopped on Lombard and let the sun blaze his face, watched the passing cars, their mirrors catching fire in the light. He played over the scene in the bedroom (his easy heart—her breast in his mouth—how she slipped from his lap—) and felt greasy with shame. All he could imagine, sitting on that mattress, his skin crawling over his face, his cock damp-heaped in his crotch and humiliation covering his face like a muzzle, was escape—to feel the ground slide beneath him, to make his own way.

A truck screamed by, Nevada-plated, dirty with dust. He thought of the Mojave, of trips with his father when he was a kid, camping in the desert: a place where, in a landscape that hadn't changed in a thousand years, a boy and everything he was made of—fears, hopes, struggles, shortcomings—was nothing but grit. Large skies, cruel rock, heat that crushed introspection, where in the need to survive the day, everything else was obliterated. However hot it got in the desert, the death of the day brought coolness.

Rain nipped his face. He hadn't felt rain since he was in country. The rain in Vietnam washed away sight and sound; it was everywhere and everything. This was California rain: pissy, apologetic. He would get distance from her, from all of it, would leave it all to be washed away in that hot, weeping city.

He skewed his chair to face the oncoming traffic, brushed the wetness from his face, and raised his arm.

Jeannie / August 1968

Jeannie let herself into the apartment on Noe, placed the carpetbag in the hallway, and watched it settle against the floorboards. She nudged off her pumps, letting them fall untidily, and bent to untie Charlie's shoes. The apartment was neat and ready, full of quiet expectancy, as though it had always assumed she would return. She sat in the living room, listening to the stillness, while Charlie tinkered with his train set, discreet, self-possessed, as though he was intuitively aware of her inability to play. Jeannie sat on the couch, watching the sunlight lengthen over the wall, playing the scene in the apartment over and over to see if it could have ended differently, each time arriving in the same, unhappy place, the two of them half naked, alone, ashamed. When the sunlight began to darken, Charlie climbed into her lap, and they slept. She woke to the sound of the telephone ringing, her head thick, her body soggy with sweat; she eased herself from under Charlie, and answered.

"It's done." It was Dorothy, breathy and loud through the receiver.

Jeannie tried to orient herself. "What's done?"

"I called Chapman and Macht. They're discontinuing the case."

It came to her as though from another life—Lee coming in from the rain, Dorothy's ultimatum, Kip. She thought of Tom, laboring out of the apartment, his speechlessness, his taste in her mouth, and felt hot with shame. She wondered where he'd gone, what he'd gone looking for in the city, if he had already returned to his empty apartment, which she had left unlocked, the key to the building hidden beneath the plant pot outside.

"Richard told me he saw you at the hospital," said Dorothy. "It's time to put all this to bed."

A couple of days later, Jeannie returned to the Marina apartment. She planned on walking by with Charlie, head bent, brisk-footed on the other side of the street, sliding a sidelong glance to check that there was life behind the windows, that he was safe. But the drapes in the front window were still awkwardly half pulled, the glass murky. Jeannie crossed the street. She tipped the plant-pot and found the keys hiding. She let herself in at the front entrance and knocked on the door to the apartment. Listened to the silence, then turned the handle.

There was nobody there. The apartment was still filled with the uninhabited scent of dust and the ocean, the blocks of wood scattered as Charlie had left them; and the hopeful emptiness of the place resonated with some dark, open place in Jeannie's heart. She felt her stomach grip against something dense and impossible, and she recognized it as loss. Her hands hurried through her purse; she found an old streetcar ticket and penned her telephone number on it in shaky digits. She knew he wouldn't return—that he would try to force himself a different life, someplace he could free himself from what had happened between them. But she placed the stub in the center of the table anyway, her fingers clumsy: left the bread crumb for him to trace her by, though the birds might have it.

Kip / August 1968

Tomorrow is Judgment Day.

That snout-faced Brig Hog laid it on me this morning when I was taking a shit in the craphouse, yelled it through the corrugated metal door just as I was hanging a rat. I could hear the fat smile in his voice, and all of a sudden the stench of all that piss and shit—mine and everybody else's—made my stomach heave; and there I was, puke and crap tunneling from my gut all at once, like my insides were spooling free. I sat, empty and sweating, letting drool gather in my mouth and spitting the sourness away, till my stomach stilled and my legs stopped trembling and I could stand.

The Hog was waiting when I pushed open the door. "Christ, Jackson," he said, his pinwheel eyes fired and glistering, "your fee-cees stinks like death." He took me to the bright, boiling shack where I meet my attorney. I sat, and waited. Dellinger was late. I thought of him taking a peaceful dump in a porcelain bowl, spinning TP around his fingers to make a lavish shit-mitten, soaping his hands under hot water, then stepping into the shower to clean up and jerk off. The asshole was making me wait.

The room was empty but for a table and four chairs, all bolted down so my felon hands couldn't make any trouble. I could see the Hog in his guard shack just five meters away, watching me through the wire-mesh windows. A plaque was screwed into the wall of the room; I stood and went to it, read the small lettering—IN MEMORY OF SOMEBODY—and caught the shine of the metal. And for the first time in weeks—since that morning Skid got blown up—I saw my face. I saw my face, and it was still me. Whatever that grenade did, whatever it ripped up and destroyed, it didn't leave a mark on my face—

you couldn't look at me and know. And I remembered that morning before my trial back home, how my dad fussed over the sheen on my shoes, how Huffacker spun his sad yarn for that freak Choate, how they let me go free. Dellinger was an asshole, but he was an Honor Roll, Big Swinging Dick kind of asshole, and if it would get me out of this dump, get me home somehow to Jeannie and Charlie and hamburgers and TV, I'd do what I was told.

I waited till the sun had lost its high-noon burn and the afternoon rain was tick-tacking on the steel roof. Some change of plan—I imagined Dellinger under one of those green library lamps, scribbling on a legal pad, underlining the answer, the answer that could catch me a break. I felt the Hog's eyes on me in his guard shack, and looked away; then he was in the room with me, and that smile of his had thinned.

"Back to the yard," he said, his voice tired, his shoulders drooping with the long heat of the day.

"My attorney—" I said.

"Ain't coming, son."

I shrugged. "Guess I'll see him tomorrow."

And I could see it—that smile of his fattening again, like there was a delicious secret under his lips; but there was something careful in his eyes, and I could tell that whatever blow he was about to serve up, his heart wasn't in it. "He quit," he said.

"What?"

"Quit. Fired. Either way, off the case. You'll have to make do with one of ours."

"But the court-martial's tomorrow. There's no time . . ." No time to get the story right, I thought, and a chill was seeping in my chest, pressing cold sweat through my skin.

It was his turn to shrug. "Then it's up to you," he said.

"C'mon." He waved for me to get up, his face folding in a frown.

I sat, staring at the room. On the wall opposite there were great finger-shaped patches of damp, like some giant, sodden thing had smeared a palm print there before dying back to the earth. The corners where the room pinched itself together were sharp and dark, and rust chawed at the edges of the table. Through the window, the sky was milky with clouds, and everything was panting with the heat—the huts wavered and the wire lines sagged, and the inmates walked like they carried their sins on their backs. The smell of dung pushed sick-sweet in my nostrils and I could hear the faint noise of helicopter blades biting the sky. Seven thousand five hundred miles from home, and I felt every single damn one of them. I thought of my dad, of Jeannie, wondered how the hell they let this happen, tried to picture them carrying on with their easy-street lives, with their coffee and their newspapers and their clean clothes—but their faces smeared, like they were standing behind waved glass.

"C'mon," repeated the Hog, and his hand was on me. He lifted me by the neck of my shirt, snuffled his face close to my neck. "Listen, son," he said. "You got to give them a reason. A reason they can pity you. Because right now"—he pushed me through the door, out into the yard—"you're twenty-four hours away from someone throwing away the key." He shoved me, letting go of the scruff of my shirt; my feet stumbled in the dust. "Now fuck off, you nasty little skidmark. Back to fucking work."

I'm at the edge of the yard, by the Box, filling my nineteenth sandbag. The light's beginning to darken and the heat's loosening its grip. The nearest guard is twenty meters away; I sit on my sandbag to watch the sinking of the sun. And as the last fingers of light draw back from the earth, as shadow swallows the yard, I feel Fear reaching for me from the darkness, hear it whisper in my ear.

"You."

There are ghosts around me—Skid and Shea and Dopfer and Bobby and Mom and even him, even Captain Vance, who died and lived that day; he is here too.

"Baby-san."

I turn. Through the slit of the Box, a pair of eyes, watching.

I did it because I was scared, because this shit-burning war wasn't what they said it was, because there weren't any bad guys to kill or girls to fuck, because I wanted the damn thrill, because my crotch was rotting and my feet were peeling, because I wanted to go home, because I smelled Shea's shit when he dropped, because that Cambodian dope was fucked, because none of it was real, it was all a fucking movie, because I was bored, because I was dumb, because I got a dead mom and a deadbeat dad; because he was fucking there.

Jeannie / August 1968

At one o'clock in the morning, the telephone rang.

Jeannie put down the receiver and woke Billy. They laid Charlie in the backseat of the car, her mom's quilt laid over him, his eyes bright in the dark. Jeannie sat in front, watched the car swallow the road, and felt afraid.

Her dad was awake, standing at the picture window, waiting. The headlights flared over his face, and he screwed his eyes shut. He didn't open them until Jeannie slammed the car door.

He opened the front door. He was clean-shaven, his hair trimmed, his bathrobe tied neatly around his body. Jeannie held out her hand; he took it, and Jeannie felt the steel in his fingers. She stepped inside; Billy hung back. "Charlie," he murmured, and Jeannie nodded, and eased the door closed.

In the kitchen, her dad waved her to sit. He stood, his hands resting on the top of a wicker chair. His face was fuller, the old keenness in his eyes. "Tell me," he said.

"Twenty years," said Jeannie. "They sentenced him to twenty years."

The following Wednesday, Billy came home early from work. Jeannie was sitting on the living room floor, doing a world map puzzle with Charlie, listening to a speech by Hubert Humphrey on the radio. Jeannie heard shoes take the steps outside two at a time, heard the push of Billy's key in the lock, saw Billy's face appear, shining with excitement.

"Get in the car," he said. "You too, bud."

Charlie scrammed to find his shoes; Jeannie stood.

"You eat anything today, honey?" said Billy. "You look beat."

"What's going on?" she said.

"Get your purse. We're going for a ride."

They drove over the Golden Gate Bridge. Jeannie craned her neck to gaze at the city, wondered if it was hiding Tom, if he'd found a place between its close, pale buildings; imagined he felt the weight of her eyes.

"Beautiful day," said Billy. The September sun had burned off the fog, and the ocean chopped blue-black beneath them. The bridge slipped under the wheels. Jeannie rolled down the window, felt the air slice into the car, felt the reflex of freedom she always felt crossing the bay; thought of Kip, and her breath caught.

Billy placed a hand on hers. "I've got something to show you," he said.

They drove through Sausalito, through Mill Valley, past signs for San Quentin. It was the first time Jeannie had driven beyond the headlands. It was beachy and bleak, scrubgrass showing bald patches of sand, communities gathering in clumped strings, then trailing away. It smelled like the Sunset—grass and dust and salt. They reached a small town, ropes of white bungalows stringing from a cutesy center with a church, an elementary school, and a general store called Monroe's. Billy pulled up outside a large tan house with a bare front yard and dim windows.

"Here we are," he said, looking up at the house, admiration in his face.

"What, Daddy?" said Charlie.

Billy pushed open his door and stepped out of the car, waving his hand for Jeannie to do the same. He lifted Charlie from the backseat, raised him in one arm, and pointed to the house.

"This is our new home," he said.

"What do you mean?" said Jeannie, climbing out of the car.

"I made an offer on it," said Billy, pushing open the front gate. He set Charlie down in the yard; Charlie ran to the old swing, lay his belly on it, and swung.

"But how . . . ?"

"My folks lent me the money," said Billy. "My mother and I thought it would be good for you to get out of the city. Get a fresh start. After the shock with Kip."

Jeannie looked up at the house, with its smooth walls and its dark glass. She heard the noise of a car door closing down the street, saw a heavy middle-aged woman wearing loose plaid pants and a tennis visor carrying bags of groceries into a near-identical house. Across the street, an old man with an anxious face mowed the lawn. A fat tabby cat stretched on the sidewalk, and at the end of the street, a homely freckled girl rode circles on her bicycle. It was the kind of place that you didn't need to move from—plenty of space, safe neighborhood, commutable to the city. Room to grow, to grow old.

"It's fifteen hundred square feet. There's a big backyard. We could have a couple more ankle-biters."

Charlie was at her knee. "Mommy, there's a swing." She placed her hand on his sun-warmed hair.

"There is," she said.

Billy pushed his glasses up his nose and blinked. "What do you think, honey?"

Jeannie thought of Kip, of Walter, locked in jails an ocean apart; thought of Lee, hiding from her mother at Mrs. Moon's; of her dad, stuck in a house she couldn't spend another minute in. Thought of Tom, trapped in his own body, cutting a life for himself, somewhere she couldn't know. And this was where her life would slow and narrow and stop: a family home in a quiet suburban street across the bridge, sheltered from the assaults of the city, the Pacific, from the marvels and inducements of the world.

"I think," she said, accepting his hand in hers and swallowing the breath that thickened in her throat, "this is it."

Jeannie / 1969

The room took Jeannie back to the cafeteria at Liberty High—the kids hunched in their chairs, the attendants hovering, the slow shuffle through the door, eyes craning for a place to sit.

"Physical contact is prohibited. Please do not touch or hold hands—"

Jeannie scanned the room, hurrying over strange faces. A meat-faced inmate with stitches running over his shaved scalp caught her glance; he pressed his fingers in a *V* against his mouth and moused a fat, wet tongue between them. Jeannie looked away. She felt eyes on her, saw a figure rising from a chair in the corner. "Jackson, *sit.*"

Kip. He raised his hand in a slow salute, mouthed *Hi,* as though across a noisy street.

She crossed the room, her heels sounding bright above scraping chairs and low voices. He was sitting straight and square in his seat, his forearms laid flat on the table—the way a soldier might sit, and the thought made her afraid. He had grown muscled and mustached, and had an awkward, unfinished tattoo of a cross inked on his forearm. She placed her hand on the chair opposite him, saw the closed look on his face, and her mouth grew sticky.

"Kip," she managed. She sat herself in the chair, her heart chasing, her arms uncertain where to place themselves. And then he grinned: that shit-eating, annoying, kid-brother grin.

"You're getting fat," he said. He slid a hand across the table, as though to touch her.

"You're getting . . . I don't know." She covered her awkwardness with a smile, put her hands in her lap.

He was watching her with sharp, steady eyes. Jeannie remembered how it was growing up, how in the everyday acting-out and dressing-up of family life, it was Kip who really saw her.

"Where's Dad?" he said.

"Waiting outside. He'll visit tomorrow," she said, recalling the look on her dad's face outside as he looked up at the immense, crenellated structure, its windows full of darkness; how like a child he was in his naked trepidation. Kip was bobbing his head in a nod—too fast, and for too long—and Jeannie felt the sting of his disappointment.

"How's Charlie?" he said.

"Good. Naughty. He's starting kindergarten next year."

Kip whistled. "Big boy. He'll be a man by the time I'm out." Jeannie was silent. Nineteen eighty-eight. Perhaps sooner, with clemency and parole. Kip seemed to trace the thought in her face. "The nineteen-eighties," he said. "I've been reading about it. We'll get electricity from the sun and people will be able to vacation on the moon. And everything will be covered in plastic—carpet and walls and stuff—and when shit gets dirty, you'll just hose it down."

A smile pricked Jeannie's face. Here was Kip, full of zip and bullshit.

He caught her smile, his eyes wide. "I'm serious. We'll get our food from these little green pills, and cars will be able to fly, like rockets. War will be dead, the commies will surrender, and blacks and whites will live in peace." Kip's voice sailed the room; a colored inmate sitting three tables away turned his head and stared. "Dad might even be able to see me by then." This in a murmur, his mouth curled in a smile, but Jeannie heard the roughness in his voice, saw the purpling skin beneath his eyes, the eczema that chapped his cheeks. She wondered how it had been for him, over there, over here.

"I'm sorry," she said.

He leaned back in his chair, linked his fingers, and pushed his arms in a long stretch. He was eyeing something beyond her shoulder; Jeannie glanced behind her, and saw a pale guard, lingering.

"About the lawyer . . ."

He cracked his neck: one side, then the other. "Doesn't matter anyway." He watched the guard walk by. "Wouldn't have changed anything. It was done." He turned his head away, his face pinching at the white light that streaked the window.

Jeannie thought of the drab water surrounding the prison, wondered if, when glimpsed through bars, that cold, muscular river might seem somehow gorgeous, benevolent. "How is it?" she said. Kip kept his face to the window, tapped his palm on the table. The tips of his fingers were chewed sore. Jeannie leaned toward him. "Kip. In here—how is it?"

He faced her. "Better than sitting in that dick-licking, horror-show, motherfucking war." He ran his voice loud, drew eyes. A flicker of gratification crossed his face.

Jeannie swallowed. "I shouldn't have let you go," she said, setting her voice low.

He studied her, something clear and even in his expression. "You wanted me gone."

"That's not true," she said, but she heard the lie in it. Her throat was tight and gluey. "It was hard. After Mom died."

He was gone again, her kid brother—his face cowled, all pallor and shadowed places. The silence dragged between them, heavied with all the things unsaid since it happened, the fears and longings and resentments that words couldn't find. Until—

"He was wrong, you know," said Kip.

"What do you mean?"

"Dad was wrong. She did feel it." Jeannie felt the fever of that day return to her skin, raising heat beneath her dress. "She didn't die right away." A forcefulness loomed in Kip's face, and she knew he was going to hurt her. Tom pressed into her mind, a body floating to the surface of the water. "She was lying there . . . her legs under the car . . . and she was blinking, all slow and dumbfounded. Like she was trying to figure out what had just happened." Jeannie shut her eyes. "And even before it hit her . . . I was yelling, and she turned, and froze. Just for that moment, before it hit—there was the start of a smile on her face, like it was some kind of joke."

Jeannie's face stung; she put her palms to her eyes.

"I didn't want you to replace her," said Kip. Jeannie heard the strange labor in the words, his difficulty in saying them; she remembered his searching face, the grip of his hand in hers at the funeral.

She sighed. "I couldn't replace her," she said, dragging her palms to wipe her cheeks. She burrowed a handkerchief from the wrist of her dress and pushed it to her nose; it smelled of home.

"You couldn't," said Kip, and Jeannie was surprised to see the thuggishness still pressing in his face.

"We've all had to grow up," said Jeannie.

Kip blew a sharp, "*Ha.*"

"I mean," she said, moving to place her hands on his and, remembering herself, pulling them back to grip the edge of the table, "I'm trying to do what's right now. I'm trying to take care of my family." She felt it move inside her, an elbow pushing at her stomach, the roll of a shoulder.

"I never saw you as a housewife," said Kip, and Jeannie looked for the contempt in his face, but his features had softened.

“I never saw you here,” said Jeannie. Tom again, bobbing at the surface of her thoughts, nudging circles in the water. “What happened, Kip?”

He sighed, a long, emptying sigh, one that implied that everything that needed to be said had been, and in it, Jeannie recognized the weariness and impatience of their father. “There was murder everywhere,” said Kip. “It was in me, but it was all around me, too.” He pushed back his chair, as though readying to leave. “You’ll know about it one day, sis. Something dark in you catches something out there, and it carries you off. Even you. Even in fucking Marin County.”

“Visitation is over. Inmates are to stay seated. Visitors are to exit slowly and in an orderly manner through the far door.”

“I better go,” said Jeannie, standing; and suddenly, Kip looked as lonely and daunted as a schoolboy.

“Hand your passes over at the door; collect any personal items in the waiting area. Exit slowly and quietly. No touching, ma’am.”

“I’ll come again soon,” she said, and he dropped his head in a nod. As she walked through the door, she turned, saw Kip’s face, dark with secrets, the narrow hunch of his shoulders, the smallness of his frame against the pale hard vastness of the room.

Jeannie / 1975

She watched Saigon fall on television, Charlie and Michael sitting on the floor, dirty-kneed and too close to the set, Joe sitting frog-legged in her lap, a bottle lolling at his lips.

"Did Uncle Kip kill bad guys in Vietnam?" said Michael.

"I don't know, honey. He was only there a little while."

"I'm going to write him and ask," said Charlie. He turned to face his mother. "Can Grandpa take my drawing too?"

"Sure, honey. You give it to him tomorrow."

Charlie gave a large, contented sigh. They watched helicopters drag and fall into the ocean, their blades churning spray like smoke, their tadpole heads sinking in the water.

"Cool," said Michael.

Since Kip had been moved from Portsmouth to Fort Leavenworth, their dad had visited every month, making the thirty-five-hour drive to Kansas, sleeping in his car at the side of the highway. But it had been almost a year since Jeannie had seen her brother. In the long spaces between her visits, she boxed him away, tried not to think of him, writing short, factual letters about the boys and briskly scanning his letters before stuffing them in the trash. Each visit, she felt a kind of powerful surprise that he was still alive, that he was still Kip; those days after a visit, the pain of his absence was so sharp it made her chest hurt, and it was weeks before she could bury him again. And though she hadn't visited him in Kansas—she was too busy caring for Joe—each trip her dad made (the preparations, the gathering of authorized gifts, the meticulous debriefs) skewered her as though she'd made the trip herself.

And now the war was over; and the sight of the crammed helicopters lifting into the sky, the Vietnamese women staring, the scrawny children playing on the roof of the embassy, brought up the other bodies from that hot, violent summer.

It had been a long time since she'd thought of Lee, years since she'd visited her in the San Jose mental institution her mother had placed her in after Lee had some kind of breakdown. It had been a warm November day, the sun pushing through the windows in thick, orange fingers. Jeannie had been directed to a long room with a dirty tiled floor. It was the day before Thanksgiving, and two inmates—an old woman with long, lank hair and a middle-aged woman with a large fat flap for a stomach—were fixing what looked like arts and crafts creations to the wall with tape: a wreath made of dead leaves, a painting of a turkey (a footprint for the body, handprints for the feathers), pinecones hanging on threads. Lee was sitting in the corner, blank and slow with barbiturates, hair cropped short to reveal ears like small pink cups. Jeannie pulled up a chair to speak to her; but Lee stared emptily and didn't move, even when a fly landed on her cheek and crawled over her lower lip. When Jeannie leaned in to brush the fly away, she let her fingers touch the girl's mouth; it was sticky, as though she'd eaten something sweet. Jeannie held the younger girl's hand and watched as her head dipped and she fell into a gawk-necked sleep. When the nurse came to take Lee away for shock therapy, Jeannie was relieved, and ran back to the waiting cab, shutting her eyes until Lee's face dimmed—*it's not my fault, it's not my fault*—opening them onto the gray slide of the highway and letting the words murmur from her lips: "It's not my fault."

And Tom—swallowed by the city that warm, sick August day, vanished. She had buried him too; whenever her mind strayed too close, she turned it away, like a face turning from a low sun. But sometimes, when the house was dark, the boys were asleep, and there was a drink in her stomach, she would picture him sitting in the shadows and run a silent conversation with him, whispering the secret tests and triumphs of her life—Billy's disappointments; the long, quiet evenings; Joe's easy smile—until the lights came on, and Billy was home, and dinner was waiting.

Harry Reasoner wound up his broadcast, and Charlie stood to switch networks. "Let's look at CBS," he said. Walter Cronkite shimmered onto the screen. "That's enough," said Jeannie. She heaved herself up, propping Joe at her shoulder, and switched off the TV set, the picture contracting to a small white circle. The world disappeared, fuzzed to a distant crush of sound and energy, like closing a window overlooking a busy street.

"Homework," she said, waving the older boys to the table and pouring glasses of milk. She carried Joe to the nursery, changed his diaper, dressed him in his footed pajamas, folded him in her arms, and rocked him till he sank asleep. Lowered him into his crib—careful not to startle him—and crept from the room. Filled the bathtub, watching Mrs. Bundy struggle through her calisthenics in her backyard and savoring her own solitude before returning to the kitchen, where she spelled *b-r-i-d-g-e* for Michael and untangled Charlie's math. Supervised bathing, brushing, peeing; read a chapter of *Where the Red Fern Grows;* switched off the lights. Warmed the casserole, mixed a blue cheese dressing for the lettuce wedges, set the table. Billy returned, white-faced from his commute; he swiped the *Examiner* from the countertop and retired to the bathroom, emerging twenty minutes later to inquire after dinner and the baby. After their casserole, after Billy had smoked a Dutch and Jeannie had done the dishes, they dressed for bed and climbed under the bedspread. Jeannie sank into a blind sleep before waking two hours later, soaked in anxiety and swelter, Joe pleading from his crib. Outside, the moon slept, a sliver of light curving against the dark, a parted eyelid, dreaming blind.

Acknowledgments

A special thank you to Jonathan Myerson for his guidance, tutelage, and support.

Thank you to Joshua Ferris and Lucy Caldwell for their challenge and mentorship. Thanks to my fellow writers at City University, London, for their constructive criticism and their camaraderie—Giles Hazelgrove, Helen Donohoe, Harkiran Dhindsa, Josh Du Sautoy, Kirsten Disley and Caroline Dean. Thanks to Mike Wozniak for being my first reader.

A big thank you to David Godwin, Heather Godwin, and the rest of the wonderful team at DGA—Amy Mitchell, Lisette Verhagen, and Philippa Sitters—for believing in the book and finding it a home.

Thank you to my brilliant editors, Ravi Mirchandani and George Witte, to their assistants, Ansa Khan Khattak and Sara Thwaite, and to the rest of the fantastic staff at Picador and St. Martin's Press.

Thank you to Lt. Col. Ron Coulter, USMC (Ret.), and Dr. Rik Thomas for being so generous with their time in helping me with my research; any inaccuracies are mine alone.

I am also indebted to the following authors and books: Robert Peter Thompson, *Everything Happened In Vietnam: The Year of the Rat;* Ron Kovic, *Born on the Fourth of July;* George Lepre, *Fragging: Why U.S. Soldiers Assaulted Their Officers in Vietnam;* Cecil Barr Currey, *Long Binh Jail: An Oral History of Vietnam's Notorious U.S. Military Prison;* Michael Herr, *Dispatches;* Lieutenant Colonel Gary D. Solis, *Marines and Military Law in Vietnam: Trial By Fire;* Randy E. M. Foster and Peter Dennis, *Vietnam Firebases 1965–73: American and Australian Forces;* Ronald J. Glasser, M.D., *365 Days;* and *Dear America: Letters Home From Vietnam,* ed. Bernard Edelman.

A huge thank you to my parents, Judith and Ted Wozniak, for coming every week without fail to look after my two small children while I disappeared to write. Thanks to Lucy Wozniak, Ed Fidoe, Anandi Peiris, Yaso Walker, Alice Moss and Darren Janger for cheering me on.

And thank you to my husband, Phil Kohler, for his unflagging encouragement and enthusiasm, and for giving me the space and time to pursue a dream.